DISTURBANCE ON BERRY HILL
A NIGHT RUN

Two Novels by
Elizabeth Fenwick

Introduction by Curtis Evans

Stark House Press • Eureka California

DISTURBANCE ON BERRY HILL / A NIGHT RUN

Published by Stark House Press
1315 H Street
Eureka, CA 95501, USA
griffinskye3@sbcglobal.net
www.starkhousepress.com

DISTURBANCE ON BERRY HILL
Originally published by Atheneum Publishers, New York, 1967; and Gollancz, London, 1968; and copyright © 1967 by Elizabeth Fenwick. Reprinted in paperback by Dell Books, New York, 1969.

A NIGHT RUN
Originally published by Victor Gollancz, London, 1961; and copyright © 1961 by Elizabeth Fenwick.

Reprinted by permission of the Elizabeth Fenwick estate. All rights reserved under International and Pan-American Copyright Conventions.

"Unpeaceable Kingdom: Elizabeth Fenwick's Connecticut Crime Scenes"
© 2024 by Curtis Evans

ISBN: 979-8-88601-089-3

Text design by Mark Shepard, shepgraphics.com
Cover design by Jeff Vorzimmer, ¡caliente!design, Austin, Texas
Cover art by Tom Lovell
Proofreading by Bill Kelly

PUBLISHER'S NOTE:
This is a work of fiction. Names, characters, places and incidents are either the products of the author's imagination or used fictionally, and any resemblance to actual persons, living or dead, events or locales, is entirely coincidental.
Without limiting the rights under copyright reserved above, no part of this publication may be reproduced, stored, or introduced into a retrieval system or transmitted in any form or by any means (electronic, mechanical, photocopying, recording or otherwise) without the prior written permission of both the copyright owner and the above publisher of the book.

First Stark House Press Edition: August 2024

Elizabeth Fenwick Bibliography (1916-1996)

Mysteries:

The Inconvenient Corpse (1943; as E. P. Fenwick)
Murder in Haste (1944; as E. P. Fenwick)
Two Names For Death (1945; as E. P. Fenwick)
Poor Harriet (1957)
A Long Way Down (1959)
A Night Run (1961)
A Friend of Mary Rose (1961)
The Silent Cousin (1962)
The Make-Believe Man (1963)
The Passenger (1967)
Disturbance on Berry Hill (1968)
Goodbye, Aunt Elva (1968)
Impeccable People (1971)
The Last of Lysandra (1973)

Mainstream Novels:

The Long Wing (1947)
Afterwards (1950)
Days of Plenty (1956)

Children's:

Cockleberry Castle (1963)

DISTURBANCE ON BERRY HILL

Berry Hill is an older, well-to-do neighborhood. Most of the seven houses here are occupied by residents who have lived on the hill for many years. Maggie and Sam love it. There is a communal feeling, with everyone dropping by at all hours of the day, no need to lock doors. Then one day while in the bath, Maggie hears someone walking into her bedroom. The person doesn't answer, just walks around touching things, finally breaking a picture frame before leaving. Maggie soon finds that there are other neighbors who have experienced similar intrusions—one person grabbed from behind, a cake pushed off the counter. It's unsettling, but the men don't take it seriously. Until one day a neighbor is found murdered…

A NIGHT RUN

When Waldon hears that the police have arrested Buffy Oliver as a suspect in Mrs. Kavanaugh's brutal slaying, he knows he should do something. Hadn't he seen her running that night? She couldn't possibly have committed the murder—she wasn't there. Even though Martha Mary had reported the news to Mother, the local papers don't mention a thing. Still, the townspeople are talking about it, and Waldon slowly begins to fill with rage. He tries to assure Buffy that he'll tell everyone he saw her on a run that night. But Buffy contradicts him— she hadn't been running. And now Mother is acting peculiar. Is the world going mad? After all, Buffy couldn't have done it… this is one thing that Waldon knows for sure.

7
Unpeaceable Kingdom
Elizabeth Fenwick's
Connecticut Crime Scenes
By Curtis Evans

15
Disturbance on Berry Hill
By Elizabeth Fenwick

113
A Night Run
By Elizabeth Fenwick

Unpeaceable Kingdom
Elizabeth Fenwick's Connecticut Crime Scenes

By Curtis Evans

I. Life is real, life is enervating

In 1951 thirty-five-year-old author Elizabeth Fenwick—married since the previous year to David Jacques Way, a tall, bespectacled, fiery-haired and fiery-tempered partner in a small publishing and printing firm—moved some 140 miles with her husband and their infant daughter Deborah from an apartment in Greenwich Village to a house in the small town of Stonington in far eastern Connecticut. Fenwick was seeking a healthier environment for little Deborah, having quickly tired every day of seeing her daughter's "aired-out" baby carriage getting systematically covered over in soot from the apartment complex's incinerator. The small family's home in Stonington on 110 Water Street was an elegant Federal style structure directly accessing the town dock in the back, allowing David, who took a long commute to work in New York and stayed at the old apartment Mondays through Fridays, to keep a little sailboat for his weekend diversion.

In Stonington, Elizabeth, who had published her second well-praised but low-selling mainstream novel, *Afterward*, in 1950, could afford little of her own precious time for writing, what with caring for her growing daughter, renovating the huge old home and managing a small book and games shop across a narrow alleyway. She made some friends in Stonington, most notably native English artist Catherine Church and her husband, author Anthony West, son of Rebecca West and H. G. Wells. (Fenwick had a knack for kindling acquaintanceships with famous writers, having previously befriended Tennessee Williams and Flannery O'Connor, the latter of whom became the dearest of friends until her untimely death from lupus.) Yet she later confided that she felt "isolated and miserable" in Stonington, frequently oppressed by nighttime loneliness in vast, silent, nineteenth-century rooms, punctuated only by the melancholy suspiration of the wind and sea and the weekend outbursts of her towering rageful husband, who sometimes in his vicious, recriminating furies so dishonored himself as to treat her with actual physical violence.

After only two years Elizabeth and David returned in 1953 to the city, where on East 77th Street they took individual apartments separated by two floors, Elizabeth living above David with Deborah and her beloved pet dachshund, Ranny, and seeing her husband only at family dinners. For a time, Tony, David's son from his second marriage (Fenwick was his third wife) came to live with them and both Elizabeth and Deborah felt great fondness for the kindly if troubled teenage boy. This arrangement lasted for three years, ending in 1956 when Elizabeth and David moved with Deborah to Mamaroneck, an affluent New York bedroom community, in a final hopeful attempt to live together as a family. For a full decade Elizabeth raised Deborah and relaunched herself as a crime writer in 1957 with the suspenser *Poor Harriet*, yet she still was unhappy living with David, who never changed his errant ways, as it were; and her crime writing, while lauded by critics in the United States and United Kingdom, did not make her financially independent of her mercurial spouse, who maddeningly would deliberately stop bringing home money whenever Elizabeth herself was actually making it.

In 1966 the whole tense and unhappy state of affairs finally was brought to an abrupt end when David, who for years had resisted assenting to a divorce, now asked his fifty-year-old wife for one, having fallen in love with a woman graphic designer in his office who at twenty-three was proverbially and literally young enough to be his daughter. This woman would become David's fourth and final wife, remaining with him until his death, while Elizabeth finally would bid adieu to life in the North Atlantic states and move to California, where Deborah, who graduated from high school in 1967, had enrolled in college. Yet it was affluent communities in Connecticut that continued to provide Fenwick with settings for her five remaining crime novels, in which she obsessively explored the dysfunctions and dissatisfactions of middle-class white people like herself, whose outwardly happy appearances concealed what in fact were deeply troubled, frequently psychotic, states of personal misery.

II. Crazy in Connecticut

Occasionally crime in an affluent white Connecticut community will make national news headlines, the media finding the incongruity between the shocking murder (or more likely murders) and the privileged setting too hard to resist. Obviously, the horrible Sandy Hook school shooting in Newtown Connecticut, with its twenty-six fatalities produced by a psychotic twenty-year-old, was natural media fodder, illustrating as it did America's ongoing crisis of mass gun violence, but there was also, for example, the ghastly 2007 Cheshire, Connecticut, home invasion murders, where a suburban wife and her two teenage daughters were brutally assaulted and slain by a pair of bestial, seemingly utterly conscienceless ex-cons. Elizabeth Fenwick looks at the impact of psychosis in such communities as well, altogether more subtly, to be sure, but still providing her readers, whether today or over half a century ago, with a formidable frisson of fear and unease.

The author's eleven-novel crime writing career breaks down into two temporal phases. Phase one extended over a half-dozen years from 1957 to 1963, encompassing the six novels *Poor Harriet* (1957), *A Long Way Down* (1959), *A Night Run* (1961), *A Friend of Mary Rose* (1961), *The Silent Cousin* (1962) and *The Make-Believe Man* (1963); while phase two extended another half-dozen years, from 1967 to 1973, encompassing another five additional novels: *The Passenger* (1967), *Disturbance at Berry Hill* (1968), *Goodbye, Aunt Elva* (1968), *Impeccable People* (1971) and *The Last Of Lysandra* (1973). *A Night Run*, then, was actually the author's third crime tale (discounting three detective novels written back in the 1940s under the androgynous handle E. P. Fenwick), although the book was only published in England, having been rejected, evidently, by Fenwick's American publisher, Harper & Row. Harper & Row's mystery section was then run by influential and highly opinionated editor Joan Kahn, who never hesitated to say no to an author when she did not like a book. (Kahn would also turn down Fenwick's *The Silent Cousin*, which would not see publication in the US until 1966.)

Possibly Kahn's beef with *A Night Run* was that the book—which is set in the snooty, old money enclave of Beecham, Connecticut (recalling the then recently-deceased conductor Sir Thomas Beecham)—was too much like a mainstream novel, more a sober study of psychopathy than a jump-scare crime thriller. Crime there is in the novel to be sure, a horrific murder, but the author's focus throughout the tale is on the progressively accelerating mental disintegration of the novel's protagonist: twenty-nine-year-old Waldron Coutts, son of one of the prominent couples of the town, an attorney and his (unsuccessful) concert pianist wife. When the story opens Waldron is much vexed to learn that his platonic lady friend—twenty-one-year-old dachshund breeder Buffy Oliver, granddaughter of the town's austere patrician bigwig, composer Dr. Boes Oliver—has been taken in for questioning by the local police in the matter of the savage murder of Rose Kavanaugh, a single, middle-aged woman brutally beaten to death late at night at her home, the millhouse. (In more restful, bygone days, this could have been a pleasant detective novel entitled *Murder at the Millhouse*.)

Waldron is much vexed over Buffy's possible fate at the ungentle hands of the police, yet as the novel progresses it becomes clear that the lilies in his own backyard are foully festered, smelling something rather less than sweet. Living at home with his parents as he nears his thirtieth birthday (his largely absentee, withdrawn father commutes to work in New York Mondays through Fridays), Waldron fecklessly employs himself, as he preciously puts it, at "grounds planning and care" of his Beecham neighbors' lawns. ("I can't bear 'landscape' for a word, can you?") But he is always forgetting things and failing to follow through, like with his customers' plantings or when he volunteers to walk Buffy's beloved dachshunds in her absence. He demonstrates an utter inability to see other people's points of view and gets impatient, even violently angry, when others fail to view things his way. (He knows what is best for them.) Although he professes great confidence in his own wisdom, his mother still dresses him like an early grade schooler, choosing his clothes for the day and handing him clean underwear through the bathroom door.

The character of Waldron Coutts at a number of points seems to me to draw on the author's own husband, David Jacques Way, both in physical details (both have mustaches) and in mental ones. By his wife's own account (corroborated by their daughter), David was a very difficult person to live with, demanding, hectoring, mansplaining, impatient and frequently angry—sometimes violently so (with her, if not his daughter). Waldron's fascination with lawn and domestic machinery recalls David's own love of cameras and other gadgetry. (He later became a noted harpsichord maker, something for which he is still remembered today.) Once in the Fifties David began ragefully yelling in a public park for his wife and daughter to keep still while he tried to photograph them with a new camera. The resulting photo survives today, showing Elizabeth tightly holding Deborah, both mother and daughter with outraged, scared, admonishing expressions on their faces. Only a man deeply in mental denial could have been satisfied with the result which his fury had wrought. For good reason, David started seeing a psychiatrist, who all too soon, according to Elizabeth, became afraid of him as well.

It is hard not to see in Waldron Coutts something of a portrait of Fenwick's husband, with his faults admittedly deepened and darkened. Deborah recently recalled to me of her mother's writing:

> My mom used to say that writers write because they have to, and she desperately wanted any other profession for me. I think what she meant was that writers have so much stuff that they have to get out of their head and on to the page, to try to take the pain out of it. Wrestle it out onto the page to finally make sense of it and get rid of it. You wouldn't want that kind of life for someone you love.... I think my mom felt trapped with someone [David] she saw as a malignant force, hidden behind the pleasant facade of suburban life. That's the tension I felt when I tried to read one of her books—I couldn't enter into that claustrophobic world with her.

Or, as Waldron himself puts it with unrealized irony in *A Night Run*: "How awful people could be really—even the most harmless seeming ones."

Aspects of the author herself can be seen both in Waldron's long-suffering doting mother—a talented concert pianist reduced to micromanaging a perpetual adolescent son and holding local "musicales" obligatorily attended by the neighbors while consoling herself with the runic musings of philosopher P. D. Ouspensky (Fenwick's mother found solace in Christian Science)—and in young Buffy Oliver, who finds relief from her repressed life with her grandfather and great-aunt in her elemental nightly runs—which some town scolds claim she makes scandalously in the nude. *A Night Run* by no means makes easy or consoling reading, but it does offer a compelling portrait of neuroticism and uncomprehending madness, reminiscent of books likes Patricia Highsmith's *This Sweet Sickness* (1960) and Ruth Rendell's *The Face of Trespass* (1974). The former novel preceded Fenwick's into print by but a single year—was there an influence? Both Highsmith and Fenwick had been guests at the celebrated Yaddo artists' colony in upstate New York a dozen years earlier in 1948 (though apparently their time there just missed overlapping) and both women shared the ministrations of Joan Kahn as editor at Harper & Row. "Christ, what a little dictator she was!" recalled Highsmith hatefully of Kahn.

A Night Run received admiring notices from the organs of the British empire, where the novel was loyally published by Victor Gollancz, like all of the others which Fenwick wrote. In *The Guardian* Francis Iles called it "an eerie study of madness seen through the distorted vision of the sufferer [that is] uncomfortably good of its kind." The reviewer for the *Glasgow Herald* pronounced the novel "[r]elentless, frightening, progressively chilling," adding weightily: "After Simenon most samples of crime fiction are apt to seem patently contrived and unreal: but not this one, on any account." At the *Sunday Times* Julian Symons, a critic much jaded with by-the-book detective fiction, declared that *A Night Run* was "[w]ritten with real skill, subtlety, sympathy." All true—and, it might be added, a great deal of sadness, drawn from a real life that was all too much afflicted with that state of mind.

□ □ □

Published in 1968, seven years after *A Night Run*, *Disturbance at Berry Hill* takes place in yet another privileged suburban Connecticut commuter enclave, this time the highly desirable, heavily wooded neighborhood of Berry Hill, which consists of seven households, composed primarily of middle-aged couples: Sam and Maggie Leavis (daughter Dolly in college); Geoffrey and Lou Morgan; Carl and Clare Hoffman (son Mark idling away a year off from college); Bob and Dee Halley (a lone young couple with two little, frequently unsupervised children); genteel, old Mrs. Ross and her middle-aged, career woman daughter Georgia; Ralph and Inez Webb (with housekeeper Mrs. Hempel); and Jack and Susan Squires (with a couple of teenaged daughters, Tina and Janie). In Berry Hill the individuals seemingly lead such placid, ordered existences, that the little community might almost be a village out of classic English detective fiction. Included in both the American and English editions of the book there is, as a frontispiece, a map of the seven houses. *The Body on Berry Hill*, it might have been titled back in the 1930s. (It was this map which persuaded me, back in my English detective novel days, to buy the American hardcover edition of *Berry Hill* at a used bookshop around a quarter of a century ago.)

During a slushy February at Berry Hill, a series of off-kilter "disturbances" occurs. At first they are easy enough for most of the Berry Hillers (who do not even make a habit of locking their doors) to dismiss as the work of a rough, adolescent prankster: Lou is shoved from behind while struggling outside with a load of garbage; Susan is shut in her garage in darkness when someone from outside pulls down the door; a cake which Dee made for her father's birthday is overturned in the kitchen; Maggie while soaking in her tub hears an intruder prowling about her bedroom, a poltergeist-like unknown who breaks a framed picture of Dolly but leaves a substantial sum of money untouched in the kitchen.

This situation quickly escalates, however. Left alone by Georgia, who frequently stays overnight in the city with her hot shot attorney boss (though that is not quite how she tells it to her mother), imperious old Mrs. Ross glimpses a red-clad trespasser by her barn and, startled and outraged, falls down the cellar steps, resulting in her hospitalization with a fractured hip. And something worse yet soon follows, when a woman is discovered with her neck broken down by the creek that winds around Berry Hill....

Disturbance at Berry Hill is a superbly suspenseful tale of unease, lent force in its day by a decade rent by perceptions of increasing social chaos and disorder. (Come to think of it, this seems pretty timely.) In between the apparently endless cups of coffee quaffed by Berry Hillers, they listen to their televisions "inexorably" imparting each day's seemingly inevitable "bad news," barely taking it in anymore as it all just becomes more background noise attuned to a particularly malignant frequency. "I've always locked up, wherever I am," wise Mrs. Hempel tells Maggie over, naturally, coffee. "In fact, it surprised me when I came here and found that most of you didn't. The world's not the way it was, Mrs. Leavis."

Clare Hoffman, well-steeped in fashionable theories of psychology and sociology, professes authoritatively to have all the answers (young Dee Halley finds her fascinating), yet her explanations always seem to arrive after the fact and she has not yet solved the problem of her own wayward adult son, Mark, who is still hanging around Berry Hill with idle time on his hands. Young Bob Halley, along with Dee, new to Berry Hill, contemptuously dismisses the prestigious enclave as just "a bunch of middle-aged eggheads" living in denial of unpleasant facts. Can the eggheads put their noggins together and determine just who—or what—is the source of the now murderous malefic presence on Berry Hill?

In *Disturbance at Berry Hill* Elizabeth Fenwick teases her threads of suspense with the all the ancient skill of an Ariadne, inerrantly guiding events to a climax of sharp, sudden and surprising violence. Critics in the US and UK were again impressed. Avowed "E. K." in the *Montreal Gazette*: "Elizabeth Fenwick has the knack of writing about [murder] in the most ordinary way. It is understated and simple, yet suspense is maintained in an extraordinary fashion. A subtle art." *Chicago Tribune* reviewer Alice Cromie asserted that *Berry Hill* "sustains the already formidable reputation of the author who deals with the ever so slightly awry situation which builds invariably to infinite peril." "At first it seems almost as if a poltergeist has come to stay," grimly observed Maurice Richardson at the *London Observer*, "but then the strangling starts. Plenty of grip and not easy to guess." *San Francisco Examiner* reviewer and crime writer Lenore Glen Offord chose *Berry Hill* as one of favorite mysteries of 1968.

Disturbance at Berry Hill saw Elizabeth Fenwick's triumphant return, after a few wavering years since the publication of the Edgar-nominated *The Make-Believe Man* in 1963, as one of the nation's premier authors of domestic suspense, a classic American criminous art. She would follow it later in 1968 with *Goodbye, Aunt Elva*, a book which bid fair, for a time, to become her most famous novel. But that is a story for discussion in a later Elizabeth Fenwick volume. In the meantime, you have set before you, for your delectation, a pair of most *disturbing* novels indeed.

—May 2024

Curtis Evans received a PhD in American history in 1998. He is the author of *Masters of the "Humdrum" Mystery: Cecil John Charles Street, Freeman Wills Crofts, Alfred Walter Stewart and British Detective Fiction, 1920-1961* (2012), *Clues and Corpses: The Detective Fiction and Mystery Criticism of Todd Downing* (2013), *The Spectrum of English Murder: The Detective Fiction of Henry Lancelot Aubrey-Fletcher and G. D. H. and Margaret Cole* (2015) and editor of the Edgar nominated *Murder in the Closet: Essays on Queer Clues in Crime Fiction Before Stonewall* (2017). He writes about vintage crime fiction at his blog The Passing Tramp and at Crimereads.

DISTURBANCE ON BERRY HILL
Elizabeth Fenwick

CHAPTER ONE

Sam Leavis found himself locked out of his house when he arrived home one winter evening. Since this was a thing that had never happened before, it did not occur to him that the door was locked. He spent several cold, patient moments working at the latch before his wife came to let him in.

"I'm sorry, Sam," she said, pulling the door inward. His numb hand was still attached to it. He got out of his glove, and then freed the glove.

"All right, dear.... Sill sank again, I suppose?"

"No, it's locked."

He received this news, and her kiss faintly fragrant of gin, in thoughtful silence.

"Take off your rubbers," she said. "Come on out and get warm."

She meant, in the kitchen; and with this return to the familiar they parted briefly—he to get out of his melancholy wrappings and place them in the cavern of the big closet, she to the warmth. When the dark months of winter closed in (and they were in February) the Leavises made no pretense of inhabiting their entire high-ceilinged 1870's house. The kitchen, the bed, the new bathroom which they had presented to themselves when their last child left for college comprised their winter quarters. Sometimes Sam built a great fire in the living room and kept it going, on weekends or when they had company. Otherwise they hibernated, and rather enjoyed it.

The kitchen was a pleasant room at any time of the year, but in winter it added the attractions of a refuge. Large enough to move round in, not too large to stay warm, it kept its iron stove, which had been fitted with gas, its woodbox turned into a water-boiler. Effortless, kindly heat emanated from this black presence at any hour, and small portions of sleeping cat showed beneath. At this hour the dinner cooked on top, while across the room the television inexorably told Maggie the day's bad news.

When Sam came in she was perched on the big table, not listening, sipping the last of a large gin. She looked at him rather blankly.

"Well," he said. "I see you're one up on me."

"Two up. You want one?"

"Nope. Just hungry. Everything all right?"

"No, I don't think so."

He sat down at his place, with an absent glance for the riot scene being televised to him, and watched his wife begin rapidly to dish up their dinner.

"You all right?"

"Shook," she replied briefly. Maggie liked to attend to one thing at a time. He waited until everything was on the table and she in place, with a background of distant shots and shouts. Then he began to eat.

"Well, I took the car over today," she began. "It's the choke, and we won't get it back till tomorrow. They'll change the oil, too."

He nodded. She wasn't eating.

"They were busy, and I would have to wait for a ride back—fifteen or twenty minutes, that was all right—but I took a notion to walk."

"Good Lord."

It was over three miles from the town to their house, most of it country road.

"Well, it just seemed a pleasant idea. No wind, and everything sort of grey and still. And it wasn't icy. Besides," she said frankly, "somebody usually picks you up."

He nodded again. In their mechanized, inbred community you had to take a dog with you if you really wanted a walk. They no longer had a dog.

"But this time nobody came along. I didn't see a soul on the road. Wrong time of day, I guess—it was just after lunch. Anyway, I didn't mind, it was nice. But by the time I got here I was really chilled—I thought I'd have a hot soak, maybe a nap."

Whatever it was hadn't happened on the road, then. His attention deepened slightly; he would have liked to reach out and turn down the news a bit, but that would only have distracted her.

"I shut the bathroom door, of course. To steam it up good. And I didn't have the light on. I was just lying there drowsing, in the gloom. Getting warm and sleepy."

His own mind tuned out the television at this point.

Picture and sound both. All he was aware of was Maggie trying to tell him what had frightened her.

Because something had.

"A person came in our house," she said then, with care, and stopped.

"A *person?*"

"Well, somebody. No, I know—wait," she said, forestalling interruption. "I thought the same thing when I first heard—somebody borrowing a potato. Only it wasn't, Sam."

"What did he do?" said Sam, ominous.

"Calm down, I didn't get raped." She suddenly grinned at him, all her long teeth still there—a little longer, perhaps. "They weren't that hard up." She gave him a minute to resent this; and when he did, went on more naturally: "I could have missed a boo-hoo—maybe I wouldn't even have heard somebody go out and borrow the kitchen. But you can't miss those stairs, you know that."

"He came upstairs?"

"Certainly did. Just like he lived here. That was the first I heard, and it didn't scare me—just surprised me no end, I wondered which one of you it was. I was half asleep, not thinking. Then all of a sudden I knew it was … somebody else."

She stopped again. This time he reached out and turned off the television; she didn't notice.

"I think I began to get annoyed, then," she resumed slowly. "Coming upstairs is a little much. I wouldn't do it, even at Lou's."

"No. What happened?"

"He came in our room. The … person. Just stood there. Then I got scared, it seemed as if he was standing there looking at the bathroom door, as if he knew I was in here—or I felt as if he did. I almost didn't breathe!"

Dogged, Sam said again: "What happened?"

"Nothing, Sam. He ruffled through things a bit—drawers, and the desk, I think. And he knocked Dolly's picture on the floor. Then after a while he left. Went downstairs and out. The back way," she said. "I was all ears by then."

"Car?"

"No. Not within hearing distance."

He started to push back his chair.

"There's nothing to see," she said. "Finish your dinner, dear. The glass cracked, on Dolly, but that's absolutely all."

"No money up there…. What about your jewelry?"

"My jewelry," she said, with a shadow of her grin, "is still there. Maybe it's been stirred a little more, I don't know."

He was still half-risen, undecided. She put out a hand to persuade him back into his chair.

"Honestly, Sam—there's nothing to see. You can believe I prowled around that room a long time, trying to figure out what in the world … If only I wasn't so messy," she said, exasperated. "I can't tell what he looked through and what he didn't. But one thing I do know—my bag was lying on the kitchen table, in plain sight. He must have seen it on the way out, and there's nearly sixty dollars in the wallet. He wasn't interested."

"It's a pity you didn't make it to a window in time to see him come out," he muttered presently. He had sat down again, but in glum conference only; the food might as well have disappeared. He was extremely upset.

She picked up her own fork, saying with compunction: "Please eat, dear—don't let it get cold."

He didn't hear her.

"You think he knew all the time you were there? In the bathroom?"

"Well, no. It's hard to tell, I certainly knew I was there, and that makes you think the other person must, too. But I doubt it. The point is, if anybody was watching, I had gone out in the car and the car wasn't back yet. And I came home the back way. Sam, I'm going to feed you myself in a minute."

She leaned and turned the television on again as she spoke, adding: "Just let me hear the weather."

Soon after that instructive voice reentered the room Sam found himself at his dinner—which made him feel like Pavlov's dog. But he was glad of the respite. After all, Maggie had had some hours to consider this puzzle, he could use a few minutes.

"How long did he stay?" he asked presently. But the weatherman was with them now, and she raised a cautionary hand. She seemed, in fact, back to normal now that she had handed her fright over to him. He allowed her the rest.

But while she was clearing for dessert he went upstairs. Went up the narrow, not-silent stairs as both agent and listener, calculating echo. Went along the hall and considered, as an unknown might, the obviously untenanted rooms that had been the children's—still were, on their infrequent returns. Even the old bathroom had an impossibly tidy and cleared look. No, it was plain which room still held life ... and whatever else their intruder had come to find.

He went in there, seeing again what he no longer saw objectively: the room he and Maggie had shared for years. A big, pleasant room at the back of the house, a bit too full of things: with all the room in the world now, she still liked to cram everything in here. Beside the fine old highboy stood a painted chest, for overflow. The chaise longue they had fallen over in the dining room till it was banished had its corner here. Maggie's desk, which he had himself rooted out of the kitchen, overflowed onto the windowsill.

His eyes traveled on, to the bathroom door. It stood open now; but closed it would perhaps seem another closet, which in fact it had been, and before that a child's room perhaps. He shut the door, went back and considered. The other closet door stood open as it always did, you could tell by the look of it that it always stood open.

Then why had he not opened that one closed door—the only closed door up here, except for the one to the attic? Did he know it was simply a bathroom?

Did he know Maggie was there, and helpless?

A new uneasy wonder struck Sam, at the thought of all Maggie's lonely days here in this house. He had never before thought of her as alone during his absence—possibly because she did not think of herself that way. In fact, they both still felt themselves to be part of an active and peopled life; but when you came down to it, there was just Maggie and himself. Or just Maggie.

He went back downstairs and sat at the table, quiet.

She said sympathetically, "Baffling, isn't it? But never mind. There's no harm done, and it'll be a warning for us to lock up after this. Most people do, nowadays—I suppose we're behind the times."

"Did you report this to the police?"

"No—what could I report? Nothing was taken."

"It should still be reported, Maggie. I'll do it."

She said, "No, Sam!" with an earnestness that checked him.

"Why not?"

"Because," she said. But she had to do better than that to satisfy him, and he saw her trying.

"Because it makes me look so silly," she said. "Sitting there in the bathtub scared to death, and nothing even happened! They'll think I imagined it. Middle-aged woman hearing people creep around her house—and my purse lying right out there all the time! It's too silly, I don't want to explain to strangers about it."

He was a little surprised at her shyness—for it was that—yet he accepted it. She had been a shy and gawky big girl when he married her, and perhaps he alone remembered that girl. It was touching to glimpse her again in the matter-of-fact woman her life had made of her. He yielded, at least for the time, and took his paper over to the basket chair by the stove; but his thoughts remained diffused.

One thing was certain: he would have to check and oil all the locks and bolts on the door. God knew where the keys were.

Well, the world was changing. He didn't need the six-o'clock news to tell him that every day. Perhaps they were lucky to have got off with a warning.

CHAPTER TWO

Maggie acknowledged to herself that it had been rather mean to dump her story on Sam and then refuse to brood over it with him all evening. But she couldn't bring herself to talk of it anymore. Instead, she condemned them to a long discussion, on television, of juvenile delinquency. Sam silently withdrew, and she heard him at intervals prowling the cellar or opening and shutting doors. He was repairing their defenses. Her heart went out to him; but she sat on, through an old BBC play she had seen before.

In the morning he said only, "Where's your key?"—and waited until she found it, in a catch-all bowl in the pantry. He took it from her, tried it, and brought it back. She said humbly, "I will use it, Sam"; and he left without further injunction.

This was Clare Hoffmann's week to drive the men to the station—those who took the 8:15 to New York. Maggie watched while, in grey light, the car filled. Carl Hoffmann sat beside his wife, with Jack Squires sprawled over the back seat. He moved to let Sam climb in beside him as Geoffrey Morgan appeared from the house next door. Leisurely as always, he seemed mainly occupied in pulling his gloves on without dropping his briefcase; he gave the front door only a casual pull behind him. But if the spring lock were on, that would suffice.

It had been on, yesterday morning, for the first time in daylight that Maggie could remember. At the time it had passed for some oversight. But if that lock functioned again today, Maggie meant to know why.

The Hoffmann car, complete, pulled away and vanished down their narrow road. This began at the main road some half-mile away and ended here on Berry Hill. Around their scatter of seven houses, most of them visible from Maggie's windows, the land was private back to a small, encircling creek. Beyond the creek lay the town's Nature Preserve, which allowed no picnicking and was closed at sundown. They were buffered from the road by land which old Mrs. Ross refused to sell. So the families of Berry Hill were fortunate in their privacy—or had been fortunate. The difference between privacy and isolation, Maggie supposed, could be a state of mind.

Considering, she stood a while longer at her front window, giving her friend Lou Morgan a chance to tidy up a bit. There couldn't be much tidying to do, with their one child off at Pembroke and Lou emptying ashtrays before they went to bed; but her standards were higher than Maggie's. So Maggie gave her a long fifteen minutes. Then she slung on a coat and started out the back door.

It was bolted.

She made a chastened retreat, picking up her forgotten key as she went. This was going to end in her being locked out more than once before she became trained. She had better leave a spare key with Lou.

Lou was locked up again. It had been no oversight. Glum, Maggie rang and waited to be let in. Her expression seemed to surprise her friend.

Lou said at once, "What's the matter?"

Maggie relaxed her face.

"Nothing. Just thinking."

"Thinking! Hexing, I'd say."

They went without hesitation through the immaculate house to the modern kitchen, also tidy except for dishes in the sink which Lou was in the process of sterilizing. Maggie could not tell if the back door were locked or not. This was a 1950's house, with less primitive arrangements than her own.

"Maggie, what *is* it?"

Maggie took a hand from the doorknob, where it furtively had moved, and turned away.

"Just looking out. The gardens seem so dead, don't they?"

"You just noticed?"

"Oh, come and sit down," said Maggie. "I can't tell you creepy stories while you're rattling dishes. Isn't there any coffee?"

Lou abandoned the sink without a word, put on the kettle, and measured coffee into the pot. Then she came and sat down.

"All right; tell."

After her practice on Sam, Maggie felt that she made a better, more concise tale of it this time. Anyway, she wasn't after the same reaction. She had had her comforting. Now she wanted to think; and Lou had a way of clarifying whatever you tried to tell her.

Small and quiet, she sat and listened to Maggie without interruption, without exclamation or question. The effect was not at all—as Clare Hoffmann obtusely said—like dropping data into a computer. Rather it seemed to Maggie a way of sorting out experience, without heat and fluster, and finding out what you really made of it.

She was interested to find, now, that she had made more than she had thought of her strange visitor.

"Of course I looked all around, afterwards," she said. "But I didn't expect to find anything taken, Lou. It wasn't a thief, I knew it before I looked. Thieves don't come upstairs that way, and—stand around. I think I would have been relieved if he had taken something!"

Lou stirred. "Then what was the point, do you suppose?"

"I have no idea. It certainly wasn't a friendly visit—that was no accident about Dolly's picture. If it had been knocked to the floor, other things would have gone with it. He must have picked it out of the clutter and deliberately dropped it. And I still can't decide whether he knew I was there or not."

"You go on saying 'he.' Do you mean it?"

"No. They. It. I never felt any certainty about what was out there—man or woman. Boy or girl. Not a child, though. No child moves and breathes that way."

"No," said Lou, looking away. "Not a child. It would be hard to be sure it was even a human being, except that I can't think of anything non-human that would behave so strangely."

Maggie said promptly, "You sound as if you'd met"; and Lou looked back at her.

"Yes. It jumped me. Night before last, when I was taking out the garbage."

"Oh, *Lou*."

"Well, that's dramatizing. Caught hold of me, say. From behind—a sort of bear-hug. Only for a moment. I had my hands full, and lost my balance and fell across the containers. Or perhaps he gave me a push, I don't really know," she said, ending it. "It was confusing, and brief ... and I didn't register well. But it was quite deliberate, not any sort of accidental encounter. Besides, who would accidentally be out there at nine-thirty at night?"

"Didn't you hear where he came from, or went to?"

"He didn't come from anywhere—he just seemed to be there behind me. Perhaps in the arbor vitae, I don't know. And I have no idea where he got to, by the time I got sorted out. I ran back inside. What I remember best," she said, producing a half-smile, "is sitting here in the kitchen afterwards, trying to calm down so I wouldn't upset Geoffrey. Don't mention it to him, by the way—I haven't. There's nothing he can do about it except worry."

This was probably true; but although Maggie admired Geoffrey's handsome, pipe-smoking calm as much as any of them, she did think there were times when it might be ruffled. Also, as a lawyer—even a corporation lawyer—Geoffrey might have had some practical suggestions.

"Sam wanted to report it to the police," Maggie said. "Then he went around and fixed all our locks and bolts. Castle keep, we are."

"Well, I think it's time we began using our locks," Lou replied, with returning composure. "Geoffrey's been saying so for a long time, he's rather pleased I've finally converted. I take it you didn't want to report your visitor to the police. Why not?"

"Oh, I don't know. Nothing was taken—the house wasn't even broken into. It seems such a ridiculous thing to explain to a policeman. Why didn't you report it?" she demanded.

"How could I, without telling Geoffrey? Besides, as you say, there was no real damage to report. I was just frightened, and made to look foolish for a while. I'd feel even more foolish reporting something like that officially."

"We're probably wrong," Maggie said gloomily. "It may sound like a silly prank, but it didn't feel like one."

"No." Lou considered her friend, and then asked: "Has anyone else taken to locking up, Maggie?"

"I don't know. I wasn't even sure you had, you could have forgotten to take off the night latch...."

"Nonsense. That's not why you were trying the back door. Haven't you tried any others?"

"No. Why don't I, though? Warn the rest of them, if they're not locking up. Or even if they are! After all, not many of the gents take out the garbage. Or not very often."

"Well ... we don't want to throw anybody into a panic," said Lou. "Susan, for instance. Or Dee. You know, this would all be much simpler if someone *had* taken that money of yours, Maggie."

Maggie agreed.

"Absolutely. A dear little sneak thief, instead of this—creature. Well, all right," she decided. "I'll tone it down somehow. And I'll say I'm coming round about the road surfacing, I should have done that last week anyway."

Lou thought this a good idea. She did not offer to help. It was the sort of errand that Maggie enjoyed and Lou did not; they both understood this. Lou's function would be to help Maggie sort out the results, if any.

Her bathtub experience had lost most of its distress by the time Maggie set out. Between Lou and Sam she had got it—as Clare would say—"objectified," and she was curious about the negotiating that lay ahead. Still ... Lou's lock clicked sharply in place behind her when she left. That was a new and unpleasant sound, on Berry Hill.

CHAPTER THREE

The seven households on the Hill inherited the tradition of being a family group, since all the land had originally belonged to one family. Old Mrs. Ross, in the Farmhouse, was the last survivor. But she was not even a descendant of the original family, being the widow of a nephew who did not even carry the family name. Still, the first three houses had been for the old family, and a later two for family connections; and the fiction of some sort of connectedness persisted even today, although any of them could sell his house as he chose, if he chose.

Few did. The houses were hard to come by, and no more would be allowed to be built during Mrs. Ross's lifetime—nor probably by her daughter, Georgia, although one could speculate about this. It was Georgia who had persuaded her mother to sell land to Geoffrey and Lou Morgan, the last to build; there had been a little uneasiness about this at the time. The addition had been a success, yet Georgia had never offered to repeat it. True, there was really no more room unless the buffer strips were eaten into. One day, no doubt, they would be.

Meanwhile, no Berry Hiller would think of selling without thought for the replacement he would leave behind him. Georgia had brought Geoffrey and Lou out for several visits before suggesting they might come there to live. Yet accidents could happen. Like the death of Mrs. Kroll. (Even widows stayed on at Berry Hill, in houses too large for them, rather than go and be comfortable amid strangers.) Mrs. Kroll's son, far away and indifferent, had turned the house over to an agent. Luckily they had got a nice young couple, the Halleys, who didn't mind being junior to all their neighbors and spent eye-popping amounts of money in fixing up the old Kroll house. It was true that they begot, an activity long past for most of their neighbors, and that Dee Halley was not very careful about letting the children wander. But she was also amiable about retrieving them, and Bob Halley was punctilious about repairing the damage they caused—so much so that Ralph Webb had started one of his jokes about it. He said he would like to know how old they had to be before he could provide them with little hatchets to work on that mangy old apple tree he had. But he didn't want another apple tree to replace it, he said. What he had in mind was a corkbark euonymus. Well grown, of course. Bob had laughed heartily, and then suggested a business connection of his father-in-law with whom Ralph could probably work out a good deal about those trees. Ralph said he would rather wait and buy the hatchets, thanks.

In such ways, Berry Hill homogeneity staggered on, incorporating Bob and Dee Halley. Some of the relationships were a little wary, and there had been one sharp exchange between Clare Hoffmann and Ralph Webb because of a joke Ralph had made on the touchy subject of the Hoffmann boy, who was going through a period of adjustment. But Clare and Ralph still came to the same parties, and Ralph continued to needle, and Clare to explain his motives to him pretty plainly.

There was no house on Berry Hill into which Maggie could not go and be welcome—pushing the door open and calling, as most of them did to save each other steps. But the tacitly accepted rule was to come just inside, calling brightly, and wait there until answered. If no answer came the neighbor was not home, or not "at home," and the caller went away again—except, in cases of desperation, for a brief foray into the kitchen. Dee Halley had had a little trouble grasping this, and had been discovered curled up reading a magazine one day in Clare's house, waiting for her. Fortunately Clare was used to working with adolescents, and she frankly considered Dee to be in this category. They had a good, tactful talk, over coffee, and evidently it had been successful. Dee not only mended her ways, but apparently conceived the greatest admiration for Clare.

Since Clare was likely to have the most time-consuming views on resurfacing their road—which was technically a town road, but could rot away entirely before the town would mend it—Maggie tackled her first. She had then the excuse of having all the others to call on. In fact, Clare was not home. She seemed to have gone on somewhere else after taking the men to the station; Maggie rather wondered where, at eight on a February morning? The missing car informed her plainly of Clare's absence, but she trudged up their drive and tried the door. Unlocked.

A sharp hail from the house stopped her, going away. She turned to find the Hoffmann boy, Mark, peering out the door. He was a well-grown nineteen, and taking some time at home to reorient himself after a year at college; Maggie had forgotten he was there. He had gone through a troublesome phase the summer before, and everyone was carefully cordial to him now to show that bygones were bygones.

Maggie mustered a wave and a smile.

"You want Ma? She's not here," he called out.

"All right—ask her to call me, would you, Mark?" she called back.

He shut the door. Probably he had nodded, or said something inaudible. Or possibly he had done neither. Anyway, who would bother to lock up, with Mark at home all day? Who would come prowling, for that matter? Cross Clare off the list.

The logical next call from Hoffmanns' was Mrs. Ross at the Farmhouse. Unless Georgia were still at home, having one of her late mornings, the call would be formal and not comfortable. There was no way to tell about Georgia; her little Volkswagen was always tucked neatly into the barn and the barn door kept shut whether empty or occupied. Maggie went up and tried the door. Locked.

The wait was a long one, and ended in the audible removal of a chain, the turning of a key. Mrs. Ross became narrowly visible, peering out.

Maggie gave up all idea of confidences here and said frankly: "It's only me. You're all locked up, aren't you?"

Years of grievance had given Mrs. Ross her dignity.

She replied only, "Good morning, Maggie. Come in."

They went decorously into a cold sitting room, and Maggie was asked to sit down.

"I'm afraid you've missed Georgia by about twenty minutes," said her mother. "Or did you want me?"

Maggie weakly mentioned the proposed road surfacing, and met the prompt and cold surprise she had expected. Surely the road was a town responsibility, it simply set a bad precedent for them to keep resurfacing it themselves, not to mention the expense which some of them could not afford. (She meant herself.) It seemed to her that all that was needed was a strong stand with the town authorities. (She meant, by one of the men. Or all of them.)

"Well, Clare's been after them, but it doesn't seem to do much good," said Maggie. "And meanwhile we're getting in worse shape every day."

"Then the town should be made to realize that," Mrs. Ross replied. "And perhaps by someone else. Clare is an admirable woman, but she is dealing with a type of official who is apt to resent her forcefulness. As well as her being a woman."

This was perfectly true, and perfectly unanswerable. It was also true that none of the men wanted any more to do with the local city hall. Maggie prepared to leave.

Mrs. Ross then offered her some coffee cake. Since this would be from the supermarket's Reduced Goods counter and accompanied by weak powdered coffee Maggie refused with thanks.

At the door she made one more try.

"Sam is locking up our doors now," she said. "It's awfully hard to get used to. Don't you find it a bother?"

"I go out so seldom, it really hardly matters."

"But you have to remember to lock up after Georgia, and let her in, and so on."

This was a little too persistent, and Mrs. Ross's cold blue eyes said as much.

But she replied: "Georgia uses the side door. She is a good, careful girl. I think Sam is quite right, Maggie."

The key turned, the chain went up again behind Maggie. It had been so long since she had last come unexpectedly to visit Mrs. Ross that this might be nothing new; the chaining and latching might have been going on for years. Georgia, who would have to be reached privately, would adore Maggie's story and gladly reciprocate if she could. Not to mention subscribing to the road surfacing without a murmur.

She walked on, beginning to enjoy her morning outing. It was going to be another mild day, once the night's chill was lifted. If this went on they would see the last of the tiresome old snow that stuck, hardened, to crevices and hollows. They might even achieve a little moist, spring-like mud before the next storm hit.

The Halley children, a girl of five and a boy of four, were playing down by the creek behind their house. Maggie could see the brave reds of their snowsuits bobbing around, a little closer to the creek's edge than was comfortable. Dee was presumably keeping an eye on them out the window—at least, one always hoped so.

The front door was not only unlatched but gaping slightly. Maggie shut it behind her and halloo'd, waiting. No one answered. Warm and quiet air soon swallowed the small disturbance of her arrival. There seemed to be no one else in the house.

But there were the children; Dee must be here. Maggie walked through to Dee's famous utility room, where pastel washer, dryer, freezer, ironer—God knew what—supposedly took the place of a Mrs. Hempel. She called again; and an unmistakable thump sounded overhead, of bare feet swinging out of bed and hitting the floor.

Maggie stood still, caught.

"Who's there?" Dee's sleepy voice called down the stairs.

"Maggie. Never mind, Dee—it's nothing important."

"No, wait—I was just coming down."

Some time went by. Maggie spent it at the kitchen window, watching the red snowsuits. Dee's backless slippers were heard on the stairs and then she came in, still tying a cherry-red robe round her tall, sturdy body. Her face glowed as if she had just scrubbed it, and her short, fair curls kept some dampness. Otherwise she hadn't done a thing to herself. She didn't need to.

"I didn't feel too well," she said, a little defensively. "Sit down—let's have some coffee."

She shuffled over to the stove, without a glance for the window. Maggie left it too, and sat down. The children had only fallen in once, luckily in summer, and Mrs. Hempel had got them out right away.

"It's only about the road, Dee. Shame to get you up."

"Oh, if you didn't the kids would. You don't mind reheated, do you? Bob always makes plenty. I hope he left some of that pecan ring...."

Dee found it and ate hungrily. Maggie suppressed an impulse to offer to make her some additional breakfast, which she could obviously have eaten. When Dee had first come among them, as a young wife, then a young mother, a tradition had grown up of helping Dee out. Maggie admitted it had got out of hand. There was nothing to prevent Dee from doing things herself; it was only that she somehow did not. But until Clare pointed out to them that Dee would never develop any "caretaker incentive" unless they left her alone, the women of Berry Hill had gone on "daughtering" her in a kind of bewildered habit. Then they stopped. Mrs. Hempel had been detached from her anxious baby-watching. Clare, who had wisely never pampered, still found it necessary to cut down, as kindly as possible, on the little talks that Dee found so fascinating. They had, in short, conspired to wean her—but it seemed that all they had done was to wean themselves from responsibility. Dee appeared to go on as usual without them, her caretaker incentive failing to develop.

But they all survived, and seemed healthy and reasonably content. Dee herself seemed hardly to notice the abstention program; she was not much of a talker at any time, although she liked to listen. But her television sets upstairs and down kept her company, and she did not look for more. She turned the television on now, returning to the stove for more coffee, and let a cheerful torrent of morning talk run between Maggie and herself.

Nervous she was not. Maggie could not see any use in making her so. She did mention that the front door had been open. Dee said she would tell Bob.

"I don't think it closes too good when the kids go in and out. If he doesn't fix it, it'll make the heating bill go up," Dee said sagely.

She said she would tell Bob about the road surfacing. He would go along with whatever the rest of them wanted.

The children were coming around the corner of the house as Maggie left. The little boy's cap and mittens were gone; he did not seem to understand Maggie's question about them. Both children stood still and looked at her, with no expression that she could define.

A little guiltily, Maggie called them over to see how the door latch worked when the door was really shut. They came quite readily, and became interested in opening and shutting the door themselves. She had at last to put an end to it and shoo them in.

But as she reached the road, she heard them resuming their lesson, with scuffles and cries. She hesitated; then went on, knowing how easy it was to fall back into old bad habits.

CHAPTER FOUR

The Webbs' house was next closest, but Inez was a late riser—as she could afford to be, with the only live-in help on the Hill. Maggie was tempted to go in and talk to Mrs. Hempel, the housekeeper; but what if she only succeeded in alarming her? Mrs. Hempel was a jewel; better keep hands off and try for Inez later.

So she walked past the Webbs'—enjoying and rather envying, as usual, their well-planted and tended grounds. An oasis of professional calm, on this island of Try-and-do-it-yourself.

The Squires had the only hidden house on the Hill, their driveway going off from the end of the road, winding back almost to the edge of the creek. That driveway, in fact, was another road in itself; and Jack would argue about its inclusion in the general resurfacing, which would be a bargain for him. Maggie didn't mean to get into the argument. She would leave some message with Susan, try the door, and leave.

Their door was locked.

This was definitely not usual. Frowning a little, Maggie rang and looked round her. The car stood by the house; but it might be one of the days when Susan had gone off on her bicycle. Maggie hoped it was. Whatever had happened, if anything had, would somehow turn out to be Jack's fault; and would reopen the question of how long such a marriage should be endured for the sake of the children?

It was all very well for Clare to say, Ignore it. They might well be in perfect sado-masochistic balance, Jack and Susan, with neither of them really desiring any change. But it was hard to have to listen to the details and yet remember, as Clare advised, that the kindest response was to refuse to participate. Listening was in itself a participation; and how could you help it?

Only by keeping away. Maggie waited, fiddling with her glove, and at last turned to go. Then she turned back and gave one more ring. As she did so, the door opened.

Susan stood there, looking dully out. She said in a flat voice, "Come in, Maggie."

An incongruous wailing from upstairs turned out to be music, of a young kind. Susan seemed unaware of it, or of Maggie's hesitation.

"Somebody sick?"

"Tina's home with a cold. It's all right."

Maggie came in.

"I just dropped in for a minute," she said idiotically.

"All right."

"Are you all right?"

"I haven't got the cold," said Susan, after a pause.

Awkwardness made Maggie say, without preamble, "Why are you all locked up this morning?"

Susan looked at her steadily. Then she reached out and turned back the latch, fastening it in place.

"That's a mistake," she said. "A stupid mistake."

She turned and walked away. Maggie followed, in growing wonder, to the large and light dining room where Susan kept most of her daytime concerns. Her sewing machine was open, and she sat down to it as if returning to work. But her hands lay still.

"Susan dear, what is it?" Maggie asked, standing behind her. "Do you want me to go away again? It isn't anything important."

Susan shook her head. She gripped a skirt lying on the table and thrust it under the machine foot. Then she said, "Sit down. I'll make you some coffee in a minute." She still did not sew.

Maggie pulled up a chair and sat beside her. She said, making up her mind: "I don't want any—I'm floating in it. I'll just tell you what a silly errand I'm on and then beat it unless you want me to stay. As a matter of fact, I only wanted to see if your door was locked. Mine is; so's Lou's. Because we've both had an unpleasant kind of prowler, and we wondered if anybody else had. That's all."

Had she really said all this? Susan's downbent head, in the quiet room, was that of a person in contemplation. She showed no consciousness of having been spoken to.

"Susan?"

Susan's head turned, her tragic eyes looked into Maggie's. Then she said, "Oh ... thank God"; and her eyes closed.

Maggie got to her just before she swayed off her chair. Just got to her, catching an awkward weight at an awkward angle, and shoring it up as best she could. Against her waist, Susan was moaning:

"I thought I was losing my mind.... I thought it had finally happened...."

"Susie dear—what nonsense."

"No. No. It really was—" She pushed herself free of Maggie, still keeping a tight grip, and said with new vigor: "But it wasn't like a prowler! It wasn't like anything ... except a nightmare!"

"Then that's our boy," Maggie encouraged her. "That sounds like him."

"And then when Jack said I just imagined it—and he got so angry— I thought—" She said urgently, "Tell me what happened to you, Maggie. And to Lou!"

Maggie at once gave her a brisk report of Lou among the garbage cans and the arbor vitae; herself surprised in the bathtub by someone who searched her room, broke Dolly's picture glass, and went away again, taking nothing.

"It was just mischief," she said. "But such queer mischief! It really shook us."

"Yes. Yes. That's exactly it. Queer mischief!"

Life was coming back to Susan, like an eagerness. "Mine was in the garage," she said rapidly. "Last week—the night we were supposed to have the storm. I went out and ran the car in, after I heard the weather."

"Well?" said Maggie, as Susan stopped.

"I want to be sure I'm telling it right," Susan said, doubtful again. "The door was up—you know it's a rolldown, but it was *up*. I drove the car in, and turned off the motor and lights. Then the door rolled down behind me." She said, with increasing doubt: "Sometimes it does roll down, if you don't push it up far enough. But if it's up far enough for the car to go in, Maggie, it stays!"

"Yes, of course."

"Well, it did startle me. It never happened before. But I got out of the car, and went over to pull it up again. It wouldn't pull."

"Locked?"

"No," Susan said, with care. "There's a handle you can turn, and a bar holds the door shut. After a while I realized the bar was in place. All I had to do was turn the handle on my side, and the bar went back, and I could pull the door up. That was all that happened," she said, her voice wavering. "I suppose I did get rather hysterical about it."

"Now wait a minute—if something did make the door fall shut by itself, could that fall have jarred the handle into turning?"

"No. At least, we went out and tried, and it didn't turn. But I *could* have turned it myself, Maggie, trying to get out—and been too upset to remember. I could have done that."

"Do you think you might have?"

"No," said Susan, with renewed firmness. "I didn't. I know I didn't."

"Then someone must have done it, Susan. Waited till you were in and slammed the door down and turned the handle. There's no light in your garage, is there?"

"No. I could have gone back and turned on the car lights—I should have. But I just kept pulling on the door, and even—even hitting it. I didn't—I didn't use my head."

"Well, welcome to the group, love," Maggie said grimly. "We all behaved like perfect asses. This creature is a big success—you know that? He must be awfully pleased with himself."

"Maggie, he didn't go away. All the time I was trying to pull the door up and—getting more upset every minute, he was out there. He didn't go away till I turned the handle and found out the bar was in place. I knew he was out there, and I thought he was holding the door down...."

She began to cry, but in a relaxed, almost absent manner that Maggie saw no reason to interfere with.

She said, "Well, I think he's had enough fun, Susan. I'm going to tell Sam about this tonight, and Lou's going to have to tell Geoffrey. They'll think of something. Meanwhile, you go on locking up—we are."

"Lou hasn't told Geoffrey?"

"She thought it would worry him."

Susan stared at her.

"Worry Geoffrey? But didn't he notice—? No," she said, sadly, "Lou sat down and pulled herself together. I know. Oh, I wish I had, Maggie! I know I looked awful, rushing in all dirty and crying, and even talking about someone holding the door down.... But he didn't have to fly into such a rage, did he? And take me out there and prove how I imagined the whole thing! I didn't turn that handle, I *didn't!*" She said with sudden fierceness, "Can I tell him about you and Lou?"

"Yes, of course. What do you think I'm doing all this canvassing for? Keeping it secret makes it more frightening."

"Yes, it does—you don't know how frightened I've been, I really had begun to think I was getting queer. How could Jack be so *brutal* to me, Maggie? And now he's going to be absolutely furious, you know. As if I were saying 'I told you so'—making a fool of him in public because he wouldn't believe me.... Oh, I don't know," she said, despairing. "Maybe I'll just leave it alone. Let him think he's right. At least I know I didn't imagine it—and you can't imagine how much difference that makes, Maggie. Maybe I'd better just leave it at that. What do you think?"

It was time to not-participate. Maggie prepared to leave.

"Whatever you think, I expect Sam will be talking to him anyway."

"Oh, do you think so? Oh, well then perhaps I'd better warn him first. That it isn't just his own crazy wife, I mean." She gave a small, bitter laugh, broken off as Maggie got up. "But don't go—let's have some coffee. Or a drink, or something! Oh, I do feel so much better—I'm so glad you came, don't go?"

At the door she pointedly released the catch on her lock.

"There! And it stays on."

"Good. And cheer up, Susie. Hope Tina feels better."

"It's just a cold.... You don't suppose this could be Mark Hoffmann again, do you? He's home, you know."

"I'm not going to start supposing anything," Maggie told her earnestly, "and I hope you won't, Susan. That won't help."

"No, no—I wouldn't say it to anybody but you. And I do hope not, because Carl takes it so hard. But you know that's the first thing Jack's going to think of!"

"Then I hope he thinks to himself," said Maggie—and escaped, non-participant to the end, she hoped.

But she shared none of Susan's new cheer. The story was depressing, in every way; and she did rather mind having her bathing scene retailed to Jack, who still took a furtive interest in such details. Although he was a biochemist, and Maggie kept an almost superstitious respect for scientific authority, Jack's brilliant side did not shine on Berry Hill. Maggie simply thought of him as two persons—one whom she knew and one whom she accepted on good authority. It was a compromise she would not have liked Clare to discover.

Dee's children were playing on Maggie's lawn when she returned, digging holes with remarkable competence. Perhaps they had enjoyed the game with their front door and were waiting for her to come back and resume it. They came willingly across the road with her, for whatever reason, and Maggie made sure their own house would admit them. The television played audibly in the kitchen. They wandered away toward that sound, and Maggie shut them in. It would have been simple and rather pleasant to fix them a little lunch, with herself, but those days were over; and no one would thank Maggie for starting them again.

CHAPTER FIVE

"'The wish to wound,'" Geoffrey Morgan said thoughtfully, "'without the will to strike.'"

This was obviously a quotation; and Ralph Webb murmured automatically: "Shakespeare; period."

They were gathered at the Leavises' house, late on Sunday afternoon. Sam had decided on a Berry Hill meeting, to share and discuss this new problem of a prowler, so that whatever action they decided upon might be joint.

Everyone had come except Mrs. Ross, who came only to holiday gatherings, and Georgia, who had to be in New York. Inez Webb was engaged elsewhere, as usual, but Ralph had wandered over. He said she would try to drop in later. No one expected her to; they were supposedly here to settle the road surfacing.

Maggie had issued the telephone invitations. She later excused herself to Sam for not mentioning his first order of business, her prowler.

"They'll hear about it when they come. I'm sick of talking about it."

He accepted this as reasonable, and was perfectly willing to do the talking. She thought he had done it very well. He had simply told them, as a preliminary, that three of the girls had had disagreeable experiences lately. Then he told what they were.

Murmurs and exclamations accompanied the telling, which Sam kept quite simple. But when he had finished, no one seemed to know what to say. Geoffrey had been the first to speak, after a long and almost wary pause, but his quotation hadn't much practical value.

It seemed to irritate Jack Squires.

"So who was wounded?" he demanded. "What's the point, Jeff?"

"No one. That's the point."

"I don't get it."

"Causing fear is a kind of wounding," Lou said suddenly. She spoke to her own hands, and looked very small in her dark woolen dress. No one argued with her. Even Jack turned his discontent on Sam.

"Well, I don't know why you didn't report it to the police, Sam. I mean, Lou's garbage can kid—that's nothing much, and I still say old Susie locked herself in the garage. But breaking and entering is serious business. Maggie was just damn lucky he beat it when he spotted her, instead of cutting up rough. You should have called the police right then and there."

"He didn't spot me, Jack," Maggie said. "There wasn't the slightest sign that he did. Whoever it was just rummaged around till he had enough, and then left. And passed up sixty dollars on the kitchen table! What kind of thief is that?"

"Oh, come on—he knew you were there. You glupped around a little, and he heard you and cut out. Fast. You didn't sit there all that time and not even shift your fanny, come on."

Maggie was too annoyed to answer; but Susan Squires, across the room from her husband, spoke up clearly.

"I did not lock myself in the garage, Jack. I don't want to hear you say that again."

"Well, and this garbage can business," Carl Hoffmann said quickly. "That doesn't really sound like a youngster's prank to me. I mean, turning cans over, or tossing lids around when nobody's there, that's one thing. Regrettable, but not unheard of," he said, with his peacemaker's light smile. "But this was actual physical assault, as I understand you, Lou. Even though it wasn't followed up. Isn't that right?"

Her husband removed his pipe and answered for her.

"Doesn't sound particularly childlike; no. Nor even normally adolescent."

"I absolutely agree." Clare Hoffmann's clear voice moved center stage, with the committee woman's long authority. "This is quite different from the hostility that normal young people express. It would take years of repression to develop this sort of furtive violence, years. I would almost guarantee that this person is an adult—and a seriously disturbed one who needs the help he didn't get years ago."

"Help, help," Ralph Webb murmured.

Clare gave him a clear glance, ready for battle; but Sam moved in.

"Well, then, what about it?" he asked. "What do we want to do about this poltergeist we seem to have around here? Shall we take our own precautions—try to cope with it ourselves—or turn it over to the town police?"

Someone groaned, but did not follow up this gloomy comment. No one, in fact, seemed to find an immediate answer. A wary pause extended itself.

Maggie thought. We should have done the road surfacing first and had a good fight. That would have loosened them up. But it was too late.

Once again, Geoffrey Morgan's calm voice broke the pause.

"That's an interesting use of the word, Sam. I don't believe I've ever heard of a neighborhood poltergeist. Aren't they usually housebound creatures?"

"Perhaps we've got the first," Ralph Webb said pleasantly. "Beat the Russians again." He pushed himself up—a dapper, rather bored little man. "Anybody's drink want freshening? You stay put, Sam—lead the band, man. Lead the band."

But the band wasn't following. Maggie had never seen them so unaroused in meeting. Whatever they were, Berry Hillers were not inarticulate; almost anything would serve to start a long discussion among them—which might spin out in wrangling, true, or dissipate in hilarity, but at least went somewhere. But they did not seem to know, or want to know, how even to approach this subject—except with vague defensiveness. (Or, in Clare's case, not in the least vague.) It crossed Maggie's mind that poltergeists were usually associated with adolescents—a guilty thought which pushed her at once into speech.

"I suppose we'd better just report it to the police and be done with it, then," she said flatly. "I will if you will, Lou. Susan."

"Certainly I will," said Susan. Her husband threw up his hands, but she did not look at him.

Lou glanced at Geoffrey, who shrugged.

"I don't think either of us really likes the idea," he said, "but we don't oppose it."

"Why don't you like it, Geoffrey?" Clare asked.

"I don't know. Seems rather ridiculous, doesn't it?"

"No, I don't think so. Not in the least. I don't like the police idea either, but for quite different reasons."

"Tell us, darling," Ralph murmured, passing her. She closed her mouth; then resolutely opened it again.

"I don't like to report anyone to the police who is asking for help—and I think that's what this person is doing. Rather desperately, too. We've offended someone," she explained. "Someone who isn't capable of expressing himself as an adult, and who had regressed to telling us about it like the child he is, inside."

"That's just lovely, Clare," Dee Halley said earnestly. "Isn't it, hon?"

Bob said, "That certainly is one way of looking at it, Clare"—which appeared to satisfy his wife, though Clare seemed slightly annoyed by the interruption.

Her husband then added to Clare's diagnosis.

"As a matter of fact," he said, "we had a slightly similar experience once with a fellow who was doing odd jobs for us. Quite a few years ago, I might add. He wasn't much good at anything, but we hoped he might regain a little self-respect by working more or less steadily around our place. He couldn't quite make it, though—and the interesting part is, he built up quite a resentment against us because of it. Transferring his resentment you see. Couldn't face the fact of his own inadequacy."

"What happened?" Maggie asked. She was trying hard to think who this could have been.

But Clare broke in, with controlled impatience. "Nothing important. Actually, I don't think it's really a good example, Carl—that was a definite relationship, and this seems diffused. Among Maggie and Lou and Susan, I mean. And it is rather interesting that they're all women, by the way, isn't it?"

"Sex at last," said Ralph. "Good for you, Clare-oh."

"As a matter of fact, all these town people that come out here to work hate our guts," Jack Squires said, grinning. "Just about the way we hate theirs. But I can't see any of them brooding about it, any more than we do. As long as we've got the cash, they'll come—and we'll put up with it, to spare our flabby muscles."

"Oh, *Jack!*"

"Jack, what a rotten thing to say! And you with dear old Mrs. Polotti—"

"Dear old Mrs. P. thinks we're a bunch of lazy heretics, and she comes out to pick us to the bone," he replied calmly. "She's got Susie so buffaloed she hands over stuff we're still using, hot off our backs. And with good reason, too—if she wants to keep dear old Mrs. P. Which she apparently does."

There was a small pause; then Clare said, smiling: "All right, Jack dear—we're all furious at you now, so relax, and let's get back to this unhappy person."

He gave a shout of laughter, and got up to cross the room—leaned to give Clare a savage kiss, which Carl smilingly watched.

"By God, I could get somewhere with a bitch like you," he said cheerfully. "Okay—have fun. I still say Maggie had a sneak thief and Susie had the willies. But live it up."

"Jack! Where are you going?"

His wife roused herself from the resigned inattention she kept for his public performances. He replied, to the room at large: "We happen to have a sick kid at home, and old Mrs. Polluted didn't show. Don't let me disturb you—Susie will carry the banner."

"But Tina's perfectly all right—and Janie's there.... I didn't even *call* Mrs. Polotti!"

He was already going out, bareheaded and coat-less as he had arrived, with an expansive wave. Maggie thought he could hardly have found a better way to quash his wife's rebellion—and the whole intruder discussion with it.

CHAPTER SIX

"Oh, I wish he wouldn't—he'll just upset them, they're perfectly all right, and Tina just has a cold—"

Susan's faint cries were met by the usual murmurs, except for Clare, who kept prudently silent. Dee was apparently half asleep against her husband's arm. None of the men proposed to comment on a scene like that.

Bob Halley offered a change of subject.

He said to his drowsing wife, "How about that cake of yours, honey?"

"Oh, God ... Don't remind me."

"Dee made this cake, for her old man's birthday," he explained for her. "We were going to take it over that evening—a week ago Wednesday, it was. And when I went out to the kitchen to get it, the damn thing was upside down in the middle of the floor. A real mess."

"Oh, what a shame," Susan cried. Into leaden silence.

"It really was one mess, I can tell you."

"But what did you think had happened? I mean, cat? dog? kids?"

"It wasn't the kids, we were sure of that," Bob said quickly. "Mrs. Rich was sitting with them, and she came early so we could dress in peace. They hadn't even been downstairs since Dee put the cake out. And we don't let Dukie in any more, he doesn't seem to get the bathroom idea too well. Don't have a cat," he added, scrupulous.

"Well, that just leaves you, boy," Ralph remarked.

"Where were you when Daddy's cake hit the deck?" This wasn't a happy joke, since Dee's father was Bob's boss, and was known to have given them their house as a wedding present. But Bob took it cheerfully.

"Hell, I don't fool around with cakes, Ralph. I just beat up on Dee."

"You think he's kidding," she drawled, complacent.

None of them knew what to say. Susan alone persisted: "But you must have had some idea about what happened—it couldn't have jumped off!"

"God knows," said Dee. "It sure was a mess, though."

She sounded bored; and in fact this small, dull anecdote seemed to conclude what Jack Squires had begun: the total burying of the topic.

Bob himself seemed aware of this, and turned to Sam.

"Look, if you people don't want to make an official complaint to the police, why don't I sort of ask around? See if they've had any other prowler reports recently. I do know some of the guys, being in business more or less locally, and we could keep it informal."

"It would be one way," Sam agreed. "Any comments?"

Maggie had to object.

"I think we ought to keep Bob for the road surfacing, if we're going to try at all. There isn't anyone else left that they're likely to listen to. If you're willing to try, Bob."

"Ouch," he said. "That's a tough one, Maggie. Don't overrate my nodding acquaintance down there."

Listlessness now vanished from the room. The familiar road surfacing arguments began to crowd one another out: "... not as if we were asking for anything we're not entitled to ..." "... afraid we've already set a precedent by resurfacing ourselves, last time ..." "... simply deduct the pro-rata cost from our town taxes, and ..." When Ralph Webb rose to make a modest proposal, that they should blow a large hole in the main road and then commandeer the equipment sent to repair it,

Maggie excused herself and went out to the kitchen.

It was her own fault. She had brought up the damned road surfacing herself. That didn't make her any more pleased with the result.

Lou came after her. "Can I help?"

"Not unless you want to stamp your foot and spit. That's all I'm doing."

Lou smiled. "We didn't get far with our female trouble, did we?"

"They couldn't care less."

"Oh, I don't think it's that. We've embarrassed them—especially the men. And the—the people with adolescents."

"Their name is Hoffmann," Maggie said coldly. "And the day we succeed in embarrassing Clare, I'll eat her. Besides, why should they be embarrassed? We're the ones somebody doesn't like."

"Yes, it would seem so."

Maggie considered her awhile, with growing irritation. Then she burst out: "I simply don't understand you, Lou. Are you perfectly satisfied with this great big bust, or didn't you expect anything else? And if you didn't, what's the point of getting everybody together to talk about it? You look as if you knew it was going to fall flat, all the time!"

"I didn't know it would. Maybe it hasn't."

"Oh, yes it has. Nobody's going to mention this poltergeist of ours again, you wait and see. I'm certainly not! Are you?"

"No."

"Well, then," said Maggie. She glanced at her friend and began to feel some compunction. Whatever Lou's reason for agreeing to the public discussion of their incidents, she hadn't enjoyed it.

Automatically, Maggie handed her a sliver of the ham she was slicing.

"Then what did you have in mind, Lou? Just making it public? You think that will help?"

"I don't know. I hope so. At least, if it happens to anyone else, she won't feel quite so isolated. And this might just possibly end it, Maggie. It seemed worth a try."

"Not unless it's one of us," Maggie replied.

Her careless words met silence and returned to her, thus enforced. She stopped slicing and looked up in surprise. Lou was taking down a platter for the ham; she began arranging the slices from the board. Maggie watched this process briefly, and discovered she had pursued the subject as far as she cared to. They were working together quietly when Sam put his head into the room.

"Maggie ..."

"What?"

"That was Jack ..."

"What was?"

She had tuned the others out. He recognized this and began over.

"Jack came by and said there's a police car in front of the Rosses'. You don't know where Georgia is, do you?"

She came toward him at once, wiping her hands.

"Why—in the city, I suppose. A police car? Oh, lord—I hope Mrs. Ross hasn't had some kind of attack! Is it still there?"

They went out to the dining room bay, where there was a view of the Rosses' house. Clare was already there.

She said crisply, "It's a State car—a trooper just came out of the house and got in, I think he's using the transmitter. Carl, would you go over and see if we can help?"

"I'll come with you," said Sam.

They went to put on their coats—deliberate, middle-aged men with serious faces, seriously watched by the others as they prepared to go out.

Clare put her husband's scarf around his neck. "Ask if they're in touch with Georgia, or if they'd like us to try and reach her."

"All right, dear."

They went out, and could be heard crunching down the sanded steps in heavy unison; then the night absorbed them. Clare said thoughtfully, "She's got very high blood pressure, I know that, and I suspect her heart may be affected. She really should not be there alone so much. It's not Georgia's fault, of course—it's quite natural, but she's hardly ever there. We really must get after Mrs. Ross to have someone there with her. She can perfectly well afford it."

No one disagreed. They were united now only in waiting. The brief flurry of liveliness over the road mending, the police car, died away completely. Susan was huddled up with her worries, Dee Halley frankly drowsed against Bob's shoulder. Lou came in and sat down by her husband, who was thoughtfully attending to his pipe. Ralph Webb got up to make himself another drink, forgetting this time his role of barman. Maggie saw him yawn as he poured—the frank yawn of a man alone—and sympathized with him. They had somehow become, all at once, a collection of separates. Fallen apart from a whole, like the pieces of a chocolate apple that has been tapped.

And not one of them was going to wonder aloud if this was more prowler trouble.

CHAPTER SEVEN

Sam was shaken to learn that Georgia herself had called the State Police, when her mother failed to answer the telephone for over an hour.

It was no time to criticize; but he did say gravely:

"You could have called us, Georgia. You knew we'd be here."

"No, I couldn't, Sam. By that time I knew something was wrong and every minute counted. Like the lady says, friends are dandy but cops are quicker."

This effort at resilience did not in the least disguise her exhaustion after half a night at the hospital and hours of bitter self-reproach. Mrs. Ross had lain for over an hour at the foot of the cellar steps with, it turned out, a fractured hip. Being Mrs. Ross, she was still conscious when they found her, although taciturn with pain and rage.

At the hospital she had said to Georgia only: "Why didn't you call me back?"—and turned her head away. Since she had been hypo'd out soon after, this grim question had lain in Georgia's mind all night and still remained. Sam had brought her home, crying, at three in the morning, and she had stayed with them. But she had been up at seven, telephoning, and was roaming the downstairs when Maggie and Sam staggered down later.

She was dressed and made up; she apologized briskly for "messing up" Sam's day and offered to drive him to the station; she confessed total incompetence in the kitchen and begged for coffee. But her liveliness, her trimness, gave off an echo-like quality this morning. She was, in fact, a woman well into her forties—too old to be still the errant daughter, the clever personal assistant to her boss, a prominent criminal lawyer known to Berry Hill as "Himself." Too real to be imprisoned in this young woman impersonation. With Mrs. Ross gone, who had seemed so immovable, the impersonation lost its plausibility. Georgia seemed to feel this, too.

Or perhaps they were simply worn out. Maggie did not know what to do but begin making a large breakfast.

Sam was still brooding about the police.

"We could at least have let them in without their having to rip up the door frame like that. Don't you still keep that side door key in the barn?"

"All right—I lost my head. Don't beat me with it anymore, Sammy. But I felt so guilty, ducking her calls all afternoon—and then when I finally did call back, no answer! And no answer, and no answer. You know the worst of it? I thought she might be doing it on purpose. Not speaking. So I'd come rushing home. Isn't that a creepy thing to think? But it did happen once...."

Maggie and Sam exchanged a glance, but refrained from comment. Sam said doggedly, "All the more reason for calling us, I should think. But never mind."

"Yes. You're right. Oh, lord, I hope I didn't call the police to be *mean!* I can just hear Clare—"

"Then don't listen," said Sam; and Maggie added: "I'm sure that wasn't it, Georgia, and so are you."

"Well, I really don't think it's true. I did feel so strongly—all at once!—that something was wrong. And, I know quite a few of those State boys, they're darling—I love them. If I'd wanted to be mean I'd have called town police," she argued, working it out. "Wouldn't I? Imagine how grumpy and slow they'd be—and then it would all be in the local paper... Yes, I'm sure I'd have done that. Except that I wouldn't, ever."

"Of course not."

"I'm going to stop lying to her," Georgia said suddenly. "Of course I wasn't at the office—except for just a minute. And I did call the answering service, I have to on account of Himself. It's stupid and unkind to keep telling her lies, no wonder she keeps trying to catch me at it! And I'm going to start smoking at home, too."

The Leavises did not smile. Georgia was expressing real penitence, of a kind. Being Georgia, though, she cut it short.

"All right, enough of that. Now tell me what I missed last night."

"Nothing," said Maggie. "Road surfacing ..."

"Everybody come?"

"Except you, and Inez. Very dull. We didn't even settle anything except that Bob Halley may make a try at the town."

"He really is the sweetest guy," Georgia said wistfully. "Sometimes I envy that pretty little feeb of his. Suppose if I played dumber I could get one too?"

"Honey, you can get whatever you want, when you decide you want it," Sam told her; and she glowed with pleasure. Then shook her head.

"No ... I don't know, Sam. There always seem to be complications ... I suppose it would be a big weight off Mother's mind, though, wouldn't it?"

Since the present complication was twenty-six and a struggling freelance photographer, it was hard to see him as mental uplift for Mrs. Ross. Georgia herself grinned into their silence, and then got up.

"I'm going to run home and change. Then I'll whisk you down to your train—just think, you'll get the bankers' special this morning!"

She left almost her entire breakfast. Maggie shook her head, then abstracted the bacon to divide between Sam and herself. The egg went to the cats.

He said, "Why didn't you tell her about your prowler? That may be what the old lady was trying to call her about."

"That's just why. No use worrying Georgia any more till we have to. Mrs. Ross could very well have just fallen down those steps, the police don't think there was anything strange about it—do they?"

"How do I know? You don't suppose I asked them, do you?"

"Well, why didn't you?"

He didn't bother to answer, she didn't expect him to. At the moment they were equally weary of the subject of those incidents, equally wary of bringing them up again. Their first attempt had been discouraging enough. If this was how their neighbors reacted, what could they expect from the police? Warning had been given; they were not required to pound it home. Meanwhile their house stayed locked up and Maggie now wore her key on a string round her neck.

She tried not to remember that Mrs. Ross's house had been locked up too.

That afternoon she took a neat little floral arrangement over to the hospital. She did not expect to be allowed to see Mrs. Ross; Georgia was her objective. Who came down at once, to Maggie's relayed suggestion, and seemed glad to come.

"I thought I'd take you back for supper and a rest," said Maggie. "Don't you think you've been here long enough without any sleep?"

"Oh, I doze. Mother mostly sleeps, so I do too."

"Well, then, come back tomorrow when she'll be more awake. You won't really know how things are until tomorrow anyway, will you?"

Mrs. Ross's hip had been set that morning, apparently with success.

"We won't know for ages, I suppose," Georgia said. "I just have it in my mind about the first twenty-four hours after an operation, I don't know why."

"What about them?"

"Well, if you survive."

"Oh," said Maggie. "Who told you that?"

"I don't know. I just have it in my mind."

"I don't think it applies to things like hip fractures," Maggie said doubtfully. But Georgia only shrugged. She had it in her mind; she wasn't going to leave. Perhaps it was more penance.

Maggie then gave up any idea of asking Georgia what her mother had said about her fall, if anything.

They sat on rather glumly together in the coffee shop, Georgia greedily inhaling cigarettes.

"Really spectacular flowers from Inez and Ralph," Georgia said presently. "I hope Mother won't hate it."

"What—orchids?"

"I don't know what it is. And you know I've sent out some pretty snazzy things for Himself."

They grinned together; and as if this small rise in spirits had lifted her courage too, Georgia looked directly at Maggie and said: "She says she was upset. That was why she fell."

"Upset about what?"

"She says somebody was prowling around in the barn. That was why she kept trying to call me."

Caution like a cold hand touched at Maggie. She asked presently, "Well, why call you? Why not the police?"

Georgia looked vaguely surprised. It was long understood that Mrs. Ross never called anyone but Georgia, no matter what happened. (Ralph did a very funny telephone monologue of Mrs. Ross discovering the house to be on fire.)

"Oh, she wouldn't do that, Maggie. I gather it was somebody local."

"In the barn? She recognized them?"

A small pulse had begun to beat in Maggie's throat; she could feel it.

"I'm not sure, you know she isn't really all that awake, she just mumbles at me a bit now and then. But she was more angry about it than frightened, I think. Says she won't tolerate it, and stuff like that. Lord, I hope it's not Mark Hoffmann starting up again. Carl takes it so hard."

"Oh, I don't think so. Mark never actually did anything but borrow those cars. And grump around a bit."

"Well, he really banged up the Halleys' car, though. He was just lucky he picked that one, Bob's so patient. And Dee doesn't give a damn."

"She was probably the one who left the keys in." The prowler topic now lay behind them, where Maggie thought it should stay until Georgia was home and calm again. But Georgia wouldn't leave it there.

"I'm really dreading the idea of tackling Clare. If it was Mark."

"Perhaps it was just Dee's children."

"No. Mother calls up about the children herself. Oh, damn ..."

"Why don't you try to find out who she thinks it was, next time she comes round?" Maggie asked casually. "Why did she go down cellar, anyway?"

"I don't know, probably checking all the doors. Sometimes I forget," said Georgia sadly.

"Well, find out who it was when you get a chance. At least you'll know what you do or don't have to cope with," Maggie said. "It may be something simple, like a tramp, that you can report and forget about."

She left a key with Georgia, in case she felt like coming to them during the night, and drove home, feeling devious enough for two people. Conning Georgia, however considerately, was only part of it; she was herself in two minds about what Mrs. Ross might have to say.

For Maggie was suddenly not sure she wanted to know who their prowler was. She was not, it would seem, any more courageous than the rest of them ... and began to feel some empathy with the blank-faced and silent others at their Sunday meeting. If it really should be one of them behaving this oddly, was she so eager to know which one?

She had never believed it to be Mark out there in her bedroom. If the money had vanished, she could privately admit that she might have wondered about him. But not simply to prowl and destructively explore. He was not that interested in the adults who were his parents' friends. Nor, frankly, did she think it would amuse him to frighten Lou, or shut Susan in her dark garage. He was too bored with them all to bother.

As usual, she found herself in reluctant agreement with Clare: they had become unpleasantly attractive to a peer. An apparent peer, a seeming grown-up ... but that was a most dismal line to explore. Once you began questioning everyone's grown-upness, where would you end? With secret wonder for adolescent Jack, even for Clare herself—like a severe little girl who knew her lessons perfectly, if you wanted to put it like that. And how about Mrs. Maggie Leavis, growing all those seedlings in cut-down milk cartons, like a ten-year-old?

Perhaps there were some things it was easier to live through in ignorance. Lock the doors and wait for it to pass, which seemed to be Lou's answer. But how grown-up was that?

Increasingly appalled, Maggie reached home—and locked herself in and went out in the kitchen to drink gin and wait for Sam. Grown-up Sam.

CHAPTER EIGHT

That night, Inez Webb's body was found down by the creek behind her house.

Dee's children had discovered her lying there in the early evening, but either they had not told their mother or she had not understood them. Bob, later, patiently untangling inquiries about the "hurt lady," had taken a flashlight and gone with the children on what he supposed was a journey of reassurance so that they might sleep in peace.

What he found was Inez.

With the serious, vindicated children at his heels, he had come up to the Webbs' back door and asked for Ralph. Mrs. Hempel said that what stuck in her mind most, somehow, was those poor tinies with their big eyes—the little girl repeating earnestly, "She was real, wasn't she, Daddy?"

Mrs. Hempel kept the children with her while the two men went out together. Very soon Mr. Halley came back alone and called the State Police on her kitchen telephone. Then, apologizing for leaving her alone—imagine!—he took his children and went away.

The invasion that happened to them afterward was unbelievable. Even the Squires, in their seclusion, heard the series of sirens turning off the main road and coming toward them. The two girls, Tina and Janie, ran up to discover that there were two police cars by Mr. Webb's house—and another one arriving! Intimidated, they ran back home and told their father, who angrily forbade any more prying. Susan, however, put on her coat and head scarf and went across the field to the Morgans', nearest to her and directly across from the Webbs'. Jack, trying to stop her, had torn the shoulder seam of her coat; later she sat indifferently sewing this while they waited.

The three cars quickly increased to five. Everything happened so quickly, in fact, that there was no chance of finding out what was wrong. To approach a single police car and an ambulance drawn up in front of an elderly neighbor's house was entirely permissible. But no one considered bursting into a mass of official cars, some of them still whining and flashing roof lights.

Carl Hoffmann did telephone the Webbs' when the invasion began, but he got a trooper who told him Mr. Webb was not available and asked for his name and message. It had then occurred to Carl (or to Clare) that he might call the Halleys', next door to Ralph. He got no answer there at all.

The explanation for that arrived soon after, in the form of all four Halleys themselves: Bob had been trying to drive Dee and the children to her parents' house for the night, but there was a block across their road and they were not allowed to leave.

Dee was limp with fright. She refused to go home. Bob wondered if she could stay the night with the Hoffmanns? He would take the children home and stay with them; it was only Dee who could not bear the idea of staying in their house just then.

Clare had insisted on keeping them all. They did not seem to be in bad shape, except for Dee, who was listless with terror. In Clare's opinion, they needed to meet the emergency as a family group, wherever they met it, in order to check Dee's tendency to regress in emergencies.

She did allow Dee to retire right away—it would have been difficult to keep her with them, since she put her hands over her ears and began to cry if Inez was mentioned. Clare turned the children over to Mark, who was wonderful with them, left Dee in bed with the light on and the door open, and rejoined the men in the kitchen.

Downstairs, Bob had explained to Carl as much as he knew about the trouble. He was pretty shaken himself, now that he might show it, but Clare gave him another large Scotch and took him slowly through the facts once more. Not only to clear his mind of the uncertainties and emotions of the past few hours, but in order that they might all understand as quickly as possible what they had to face.

Then she called the Leavises'.

"Sam," she said firmly. "It's Clare. I'm afraid I have sad news for you. Inez is dead."

"Good lord," said Sam. He let the receiver droop and looked helplessly toward the kitchen and Maggie—losing, in this way, several long sentences being delivered into his ear. He said into the middle of another: "*Inez?* But what happened to her? What are all those cars for?"

There was a pause—probably this was what Clare had been telling him. But she started over, in exemplary patience, and told him of the Halleys' arrival and Bob's news.

"So all we really can be sure of is that Bob found her down back, by the creek, about an hour ago. Ralph was home, and he knows. I don't think there's anything we can do yet except to call and leave a message—perhaps with Mrs. Hempel—that we want to help in any way we can. I can do that for all of us, if you like."

"But—what happened to her? What was she doing down by the creek?"

"I don't know, Sam. But I think we should all stay up and dressed, in case we can be of any use. Besides, I expect the police will want to talk to us."

"Yes. Yes, of course."

"Are the Morgans with you? Is Georgia?"

"No. Georgia's coming later, I guess. Why? Is there—"

"Perhaps you wouldn't mind telling them? And Jack and Susan. I'll get on to Mrs. Hempel, or perhaps Ralph himself. I believe that's all we can do now."

He mumbled, "Good lord," again—adding a late "Well—thanks, Clare," which she probably did not hear. Then he wandered out to the kitchen.

Susan was with Maggie now; and when they had all pulled themselves together sufficiently, the telephoning began.

Susan went first, to call her husband. Then she came back.

"Sam, you do it. He'll take it better from you. After all, he didn't want me to come...."

Sam got up again without a word.

But when Maggie asked, "Well, are you here or not?" Susan put out a hand to stop him.

"Wait—I'd better ... No," she said, firm. "I'm here. And I'd like to stay awhile, if you don't mind. All right; forget it. I'll call him."

She went to do so.

Afterward, Sam called the Morgans'. A listener who asked no questions, Geoffrey said finally:

"Well, this is tragic news indeed, Sam. And very hard to understand. What can Inez have been doing down in that mucky wilderness? She was the last person in the world for country walks."

"I don't know," said Sam.

"One can't help wondering if this has some connection with this—unpleasantness we've been having. Do we bring up our incidents if the police come round, I wonder?"

"I suppose so. Who knows what's relevant to a thing like this?"

"Very true. Well, all right. I wish there were something we could do."

It was a common wish—more than a wish, a common uneasiness, which grew. In all their years as a tiny community, or compound, or whatever they were, the folk of Berry Hill had not yet had the experience of being shut out of an emergency. Any illness, the death of a relative, a fire or a temporarily defunct furnace, trouble of any sort had been the signal for instant, kindly invasion. Ralph himself had said once (when they were talking of noble last words) that you would need a bullhorn by your deathbed on Berry Hill to be heard over your loving friends. An uncomfortable joke to remember now.

Still, what kept them away from Ralph tonight was the practical fact that he was not alone, that he was in fact already invaded by the police. Probably by all sorts of dismal technicians as well; and almost certainly there were reporters there. Susan definitely recognized a dirty white sports car as belonging to a reporter on their local paper. But what disturbed them most was the fact that an ambulance was not sent for Inez, but the limousine from the funeral home.

This happened quite late, when they were worn with waiting, and watching, and wondering. Listless telephoning occurred now and then between the houses. Jack called twice, ordering his wife to return home; after a last, defiant cigarette, Susan left. Carl Hoffmann checked periodically to see if any of the others had been visited by police; none had. Sam began to think they were behaving absurdly, sitting around on Clare's instructions, waiting for people who had other things to do. The mortuary limousine finished him; he went gloomily up to bed and advised Maggie to do the same.

She meant to follow. She went round and turned off lights (except for Georgia's beacon), but then sat down in darkness by the front window. Curiosity was dead in her by now, or buried alive beneath the baffled sadness that had become her present mood. Her present watch was curiously like waiting for one of the children: an unwanted vigil, which she would furtively end as soon as a car drew up before the house. Except that what she waited for now she could not have said—unless it was to see Ralph's house darken at last, and know that he had been allowed to go up to rest.

His front door opened, as she sat there, and Lou Morgan came out. Ralph was behind her. He laid his arm round her shoulders and drew her against him, kissing her cheek—Lou put a hand up to his face as he did so. Then, small and quick, she went down the walk without looking back and crossed the road to her own house. Ralph waited motionless in his doorway until she was home.

This was apparently what Maggie had waited for. When Ralph disappeared, she went quietly up to bed.

CHAPTER NINE

The saddest aspect of Inez's death was that it brought so little sense of loss to any of them. This was not really anyone's fault. Inez had been a lively and popular woman among her own friends, and Berry Hill had accepted the fact that these friends lay elsewhere. Habit had separated them, more than any incompatibility, helped by the fact that Inez had shown a smiling and total lack of guilt at refusing to change her ways.

When they had bought their house twelve years ago, the Webbs were newlyweds—but in a mature and matter-of-fact way which discouraged interest. Inez brought with her two half-grown sons from another marriage, and Ralph's first wife was understood to be living in California. The Webbs settled at once into the comfortable and amiable-seeming life they had lived ever since, Inez continuing the active social life of her first marriage, in the richer and livelier shore community she had belonged to, and Ralph commuting to New York, from which he had come, and where he prosperously managed real estate. The two boys, apparently well provided for, were hardly ever seen: between school-and-camp, and then college-and-travel, they grew up almost entirely away from Berry Hill. One of them had taken Dolly Leavis out rather steadily in a long-ago summer, but Maggie was relieved when this ended. The parties they went to were late ones, and involved a surprising amount of distance driving. Once, in desperation, she had called Inez to find out where in the world they were. Inez had seemed surprised, but cordial. She didn't know.

Once a year, in the dark days after the holidays, Inez had given a magnificent buffet supper to her neighbors. It was a social high point of their year, and even Mrs. Ross came. It was understood that this expressed Inez's regret for all the meetings, cookouts, and other haphazard gatherings she was obliged to miss during the year, and also repaid Ralph's obligations, since he usually came to Berry Hill affairs. They were not a month past the last party, a great success as always. There was no doubt that Ralph enjoyed them himself, and seemed proud of his wife's talent for entertaining.

In his wry, self-contained way he had seemed generally content with her. She was certainly a charming woman, carefully dressed and tended, lively and frank. He went dutifully with her to the parties where his presence was required, and seemed quite happy to be excused from the others. He was alone a lot—though well cared for by Mrs. Hempel—but, oddly, the men of Berry Hill found this more disturbing than the women.

"You can't tell me she isn't playing around," said Jack Squires. "She's right at the age for it, too."

As usual, no one argued with him. Clearly Inez was playing—at the game she most enjoyed, social activity. Clare assured them that Inez showed no signs of the gnawing insecurity that led to sexual disasters.

"If she has a liaison now and then, I imagine she simply enjoys it and forgets it," she said calmly. "And I for one am perfectly prepared to believe there's no such thing. They seem very well matched."

The only really odd thing about them was why they had chosen to buy in Berry Hill. It was far homelier than Inez's former surroundings, where private beaches and pools and tennis courts were usual; and Ralph was a lifelong New Yorker. Perhaps Ralph had jibbed at living on the fringes of Inez's former life and Inez had been unwilling to move clear away from it. If Berry Hill had been a compromise, it was seeming a happy one. Inez "commuted" easily to her friends in Greens Farms and Greenwich, and Ralph placidly rode the train and played bridge. He had also developed what Geoffrey called a "detached attachment" to the small group in which he found himself, and usually wandered over to their gatherings—and stayed.

Yet none of them knew with any certainty, now, how to approach him. (Except Lou; and only Maggie and she knew of that brief visit.) He had no need of the women, of the comforts and attentions they might bring into his house. Mrs. Hempel continued to provide these. Besides, he always seemed somewhat easier with the men. Yet even these masculine relationships, comfortable but casual, depended on Ralph's following his usual routine; and of course he was absent from it now.

The morning car left for the station without him. There was no sign of activity around the Webbs' house at all—not at that hour. Then Bob Halley walked down the road with his children, going from the Hoffmanns' house to his own. No sign of Dee. He put the children in his car after a time and drove off—taking them to Dee's parents while she remained with Clare? It seemed a strange compromise.

Maggie, alone in the house except for a sleeping Georgia—whose hours were more irregular than usual, with her mother in the hospital—found herself haunting the front windows. What she waited for, or expected, she did not know. Someone to tell her what had happened to Inez; someone whom she could ask what had happened to them all.

She longed for Lou; but the secret and touching encounter between Ralph and her friend somehow put a visit to Lou out of bounds. It would seem like prying, to go to Lou now. And Lou did not come to her.

At last Maggie went up and woke Georgia.

"Almost nine," she murmured, apologetic. "Is that okay?"

"Oh, lord—no—"

And Georgia rolled out, staggered round collecting things, made for the bathroom. She looked appealing, like a girl, in her rumpled sleepiness—perhaps because she was little and thin and had a mop of blond hair that wasn't allowed to show grey. And partly because she was a girl, still, at heart. Maggie went down to get her breakfast.

That was when the police came.

They weren't in uniform, and she didn't recognize either of them, but she had no doubt who they were even before they introduced themselves, showed identification. She scarcely saw this, didn't catch any part of, their names, got them into the house and seated without (it seemed to her) uttering one coherent sound. All the shyness of her most awkward youth clamped round her again; inside she remained amazed and helpless.

They didn't seem to notice. They only wanted to know if Maggie had seen Mrs. Webb at any time yesterday—talked to her? It happened that she had not. Her mind bubbled with imploring questions; she could hardly croak.

Mr. Webb had mentioned that there had been some sort of prowler in Mrs. Leavis's house the previous week—could she tell them about that?

"Oh, yes," said Maggie. "Yes, there was. That's true."

They waited.

"I was in the bathtub," she said firmly. Then she changed her mind. "The point is, you see, I'd left the car in the village and walked home. So it probably looked as if I hadn't come back. And I'm afraid the house wasn't locked."

"That's never wise, Mrs. Leavis."

"Yes, we decided that too. It's locked all the time now." And she fished for her key on the string round her neck—a doubly idiotic idea, since it wasn't there. Perhaps they thought she had a broken strap. Or fleas. She said, "Oh, dear," without explanation, and floundered on with the rest of the story.

They listened, they helped; they asked none of the by now familiar questions: why hadn't she called out, why hadn't she tried to see who left the house. Not even, why hadn't she called the police. Instead they rebuilt her tale with a pleasant precision, getting a closer estimate of time and sequence than Maggie would have thought possible.

Encouragement rose in her, so that she felt she might ask: "Could you tell me—are you allowed to say what happened to Mrs. Webb? Was it an accident?"

"It would seem so. We don't have a definite report yet, ourselves, but it seems safe to say that it wasn't a natural death."

"Not heart failure, or something like that?"

"Well, it's always heart failure," the older man replied agreeably. "What they have to tell us is what made the heart stop. I understand you have Miss Ross here with you, Mrs. Leavis?"

Georgia was coming downstairs, they could all hear her. Maggie got up.

"I'm afraid I have to get her breakfast—she's late already. Could you—I'd be very glad to get some for you, too?"

They had had breakfast, but would appreciate some coffee. And they had no objection to moving out to the kitchen. Maggie led them through the house, with the beginning of hostess-like pleasure, and they came on Georgia struggling with a garter in the kitchen. She was a slow waker, but the sight of the men roused her like coffee. She gave a little scream, and then grinned helplessly.

"Oh—no fair ..."

By some alchemy, Maggie now perceived that the younger of the two men was nice-looking and even the older one attractive in a rugged sort of way. Georgia put this sort of spotlight on men; they seemed to enjoy it. So did she.

The three of them got acquainted—Maggie almost thought, "made friends"—without any help needed. Maggie could cook and listen, which she preferred, while Georgia's hoarse voice rattled on.

"Then you're Dick Appleby? Of course—Barney Rogowski told me, before he was transferred, the most wonderful man was coming in. Well, I feel better about losing Barney, now—I always felt so *safe* when—"

And on. Without even any coffee. Maggie got it to her as soon as she could. The men seemed glad of theirs as well. What they wanted of Georgia was to hear of her mother's experience with the person in the barn. She was quite firm about sending them over to the hospital.

"Mother's perfectly able to see you, and I think it would do her worlds of good to make a real, official complaint. Don't pay any attention if she balks a bit, just make her tell you. Especially about him banging on the tin, or whatever."

"What banging?" Maggie asked, startled.

Georgia's hands went out.

"You see? I'll forget bits. But just to get Mother started," she said, business-like, "so she'll see you already know—here's the bones of it. She caught a glimpse of somebody through the barn window, from the house. I'm supposed to keep the place locked, but usually I just fox the padlock so it looks locked, you know? It's a sad old drag trying to fiddle that combination every time, I can tell you. Well, she bundled up and went out, and the padlock was open, and so was the door—a bit. This is the big door," she explained. "The one I drive in and out of. So she stood by it and said, very army-style—you'll meet her, you'll see—'I want you out of there in two minutes, or I'll call the police.' And then she turned round to start back to the house, so the kid could get out, or whoever, and before she could take a *step* the person inside absolutely whanged on the old washtub with something like iron, so it made a horrible crashing, and scared her to death. Like answering back with a cannon, you know? Poor love."

Her thin little face forgot its audience, for the moment.

The older man (the Dick Appleby one) said kindly, "Yes, that must have been frightening. But she didn't call the police?"

"No. No, she kept trying to call me."

"Why, Miss Ross?"

"Well, if you find out," said Georgia, with a rueful smile, "you tell me."

She glanced at her watch, then, and prepared to abandon another nourishing breakfast. She said she was late; she advised the men to get all the timing and details from her mother; she really had to dash.

"Just be firm," she said, pulling on some very smart boots. "She has this idea about not discussing your private affairs—but this isn't a private affair any more, is it?"

They agreed it wasn't. They thanked Maggie for their coffee, and left. Georgia was now snatching up her various belongings, en route to the door. There, she kissed Maggie hastily.

"I may stay down," she said. "We're awfully behind, and Himself may keep me too late. But it's all right—he puts me up very comfortably."

"Oh, Georgia ... I'm not your mother."

Georgia fell into a sudden dead pause.

"No, but it's *true*," she stammered then; and looked at Maggie with a child's distress.

"All right, love."

Georgia turned and slipped out, like an escapee, leaving Maggie regretful of her impatience. Perhaps it was true. In any case, what did it matter?

She looked after her hurrying friend, wishing the moment back. Georgia did not hop into her little red Volkswagen. Late or no, she was hurrying across to the Webbs' house, ringing the bell. Mrs. Hempel let her in.

Scrupulously, Maggie moved away so that she would have no idea when the little red car finally left. An increasing wonder filled her that she could not bring herself to this simple action of going to Ralph. If only he needed something! But his meals were cooked, his rooms tidied, his clothes cared for ... and to admit it, she was rather shy of him, simply to go and talk.

In mid-morning, when she had forgotten the whole thing and was upstairs, her doorbell rang. She paused, waiting for whoever it was to come in and call. Then she remembered; and belatedly clattered downstairs.

Ralph Webb was going away, down the walk.

CHAPTER TEN

The awful lock stuck again.

Ralph heard her efforts and turned, however. Came back.

She was dismayed by a difference in him. Yet what made it? He was as meticulously dressed as always, neither pale nor hollow-eyed; and when she could finally let him in he remarked that he was sorry to make her put down her drawbridge. He did seem very small, beside her almost-six-feet. And far too tidy to embrace.

In confusion, she led him back to the kitchen. He was not a kitchen sort of man—in fact, looked round him once as if he had heard of kitchens and was interested to see one ... though not very. But she gave him coffee, and sat down with him, and somehow got past what had to be said.

Then he came to the point.

"I've never buried anyone, Maggie. Lou says you went through this last year, with your mother. I thought you might help me. I'd like it to be well done," he said.

"Ralph, I'd be so glad ... I mean, glad to help in some way, I've been trying all morning to think of some way to be of use to you...."

"This would be very useful indeed, Maggie. A real kindness. I don't even like to ask you, I dread the idea so much myself. But it's got to be done."

She was touched almost beyond words.

"The worst of it is, your—your arranging will have to depend in some way on the police. They have taken charge of her," he said. "I don't even know where she is."

An autopsy.

"An autopsy," he said, so immediate to her thought that she started. "They still aren't sure what caused her death—though I can't see what difference the details make. It was obviously violence. You couldn't see her lying there and not know that. I suppose they have their reasons for wanting to know precisely what—damage—was done to her, but I should think ..." He said with cold anger: "I should think the important thing to find out is who did such a thing. And *why*. She was the least violent person in the world, herself—you know that, Maggie. These stupid questions about her life ..."

"I suppose they have a certain routine, Ralph. They have to follow it."

"Yes," he said, unyielding. "Well, the real blame I think must be on those of us who heard you out, last Sunday, and wouldn't listen. What we obviously should have done was to hire a private guard, right away. Inez thought so herself."

"Inez did? You told her about it?"

"Yes, that night. When she came home we sometimes had a nightcap and a chat." He said without expression, "I thought it might amuse her. To hear about you in the bathtub, and Susan in the garage, and Lou among the garbage cans."

He was hurting himself, and had forgotten or did not care that Maggie might feel offense. She felt none—only increasing anxiety for him as he went on: "She wasn't in the least amused, of course. She wanted to ring up first thing Monday morning—it seems there's a kind of service—and have a man stationed here at once. I asked her if she was prepared for us to foot the bill ourselves and upset all our neighbors into the bargain. I reminded her that this wasn't, for instance, Greens Farms."

To stop this painful self-wounding, Maggie spoke out as bluntly as if he were Sam, or Lou.

"Well, you would have had to, you know. Pay for him yourself. And you would probably have run into an awful lot of hard feeling besides. This isn't Greens Farms, Ralph. I don't know that I would have liked the idea of a private guard around here myself. Besides, not one of us believed that—that a thing like this could happen. I didn't. Neither did you."

"Lou did," he said.

Maggie felt one of her rare moments of exasperation with her friend. What a time to say so! "Hindsight," she said shortly.

"No, she didn't say anything. But Sunday night she was the only one of you who was really frightened. Still frightened, I mean—for the future. Susan wasn't, or she wouldn't have left her girls at home alone. And you were no more than irritated, by the time we got around to talking. Isn't that right?"

Maggie supposed it was. She said absently, "I suppose the difference was that no one actually touched Susan or me. The way he did Lou."

And Inez. Too late, she groped for an escape from this idea. The best she could find was: "If we could only think of some reason for her to go down back, by the creek. Could she possibly have been taking a walk, Ralph?"

"No. She didn't walk there. She was taken."

"Taken? But why would she go—without even calling out?"

"They don't think she was conscious. Perhaps she wasn't alive." He went on, talking to the tabletop: "What they think is that someone met her near the house when she came home. She'd been to a bridge game, in Greenwich. The car was still sitting outside the garage—perhaps she meant to go out again for some reason, though I don't know why she would."

"What time?" Maggie asked.

"Mrs. Hempel heard the car drive in around six—just before. Then, when Inez didn't come in the house, she supposed that she had stopped in at one of the neighbors'. It wasn't a usual thing for her to do, as you know," he said dully. "But I suppose Mrs. Hempel explained things to herself the only reasonable way she could. As we all do. I might have thought the same."

He said after a moment, "Or I might have gone out to see if she was having some trouble with the car, or the garage. If I'd been home."

He was back to desolation again, bleak and contained. Anything was better than to leave him there.

"Well, it was good and dark by then, Ralph," she said. "And Inez was on her guard. Whatever happened must have been very quick. Even if you'd been home, it would have taken you a while to wonder what she was doing and go out to see."

He made no reply.

She added, "You don't even know that it was Inez driving the car."

That interested him. He raised his head.

"I don't believe anyone's thought of that, Maggie."

She was glad to have found something new for him to think about. When he rose, with an absent murmur, she followed him in silence to the door.

"As a matter of fact," he said there, "the keys were in the dash. That wasn't usual, for Inez. I wonder what they've done about fingerprints...."

With his coat on, he remembered her again.

"Well, I'm more grateful than I can say, Maggie. I'll tell Mrs. Hempel you're handling things, I'm sure she'll help."

He reached up and gave her a firm kiss.

"Now lock up behind me, my dear. Someone around here doesn't like women."

It could almost have been one of his jokes. If he hadn't been dead serious. If it hadn't happened to be true.

Maggie locked up.

CHAPTER ELEVEN

By noon, Berry Hill's long illusion of privacy had been shattered. Their potholed road was still monitored by the police, but an awful lot of people seemed to be passed in. When Maggie drove in, around noon, she could not even get her car past some enormous congregation of peculiar trucks, many more cars, and an absolute mob of people—very few of whom looked like any kind of police.

She sat gaping at this display until she realized—seeing a boom-like object being solicitously adjusted—that television crews were among them. A most unholy thrill, half panic, half fascination, made her pull aside without attempting to go farther and take refuge in the Hoffmanns' house.

The door was still unlocked. Mark was alone downstairs, reading on the couch. He looked unpleasantly startled by her call.

"Oh—Mark, I didn't see you. Is—?"

"Upstairs," he replied briefly.

"Have you seen all those television things? Out on the road?"

"Yes," he said, reading again.

She went upstairs. Halfway she began to hear Clare's voice, issuing from the open door of her bedroom.

"... just nonsense," she was saying. "You know quite well your father would have been much more pleased to build you a new house. Now why should you want to—"

"Clare?" said Maggie, before these revelations could go on, whatever they were. Clare's voice barely paused, did not change.

"Yes, Maggie. In here."

She came in to find Clare lying on one of the beds, propped with pillows, and Dee Halley sprawled across the foot of the other. Clare was fully dressed, Dee was in her soiled cherry-colored robe, her fair hair tumbled, her face flushed. She stared at Maggie as if she could not at once place her.

"You ill, Clare?"

"No, no—just this knee acting up a bit. I keep off it for a day or so, and it's all right. Have you been out?"

This meant, out of the compound.

Maggie nodded. "We seem to be invaded. I lost my head and ducked in here. Have you seen all those television trucks, and things?"

"Carl told me—he's staying home today. Take off your coat, Maggie, you probably won't be able to get to your house in peace for a while. Carl's fixing us lunch, why don't you stay?"

"All right. I'll go help him."

She began to unbutton her coat and found that her hands trembled slightly. Although this was probably not noticeable to the others, she excused herself.

"This is so awful ... and I've just come from the funeral home."

"Mr. Packer's?" said Dee, showing faint interest. "Is that where she is?"

"No, not yet," Maggie replied carefully, as she might have done to a child. This disconcerted her. She turned back to Clare. "He knew all about it, it's been on the radio. I hope Ralph isn't— They aren't allowed to come right in his house, are they?"

"The television people? Oh, I shouldn't think so. He sent you down to Packer's, Maggie?"

"Well, he asked me if I'd mind doing it. Of course I don't."

"We thought of offering, this morning, but it seemed to me that he would probably prefer to turn to Lou. I'm surprised he didn't."

"Lou suggested me," Maggie said, swallowing astonishment. She herself would not—until that glimpse of Lou's visit—have supposed that there was any particular rapport between her friend and Ralph. Sometimes Clare intimidated her. "On account of Mother," she added.

"Yes, of course. Very sensible. Dee, you'd better go get dressed now, you've got lots to do this afternoon."

"I'm *not* going, Clare. I can't."

"Of course you can, you'll see. Mark can go with you, if you like."

There was no way to tell from her expression whether Dee considered this a threat or a promise. She got off the bed and trailed away.

"Come downstairs when you're ready—I'm going down too," Clare said after her.

"Where are you sending her?" Maggie asked in a low voice.

"I'm not sending her anywhere," Clare replied, entirely audibly. "The children are going to stay with her parents until things calm down here, and Dee wants to take some things to them."

Well, obviously she didn't; but there was no point in pursuing it. Maggie handed Clare her cane and gave her some unnecessary help in getting off the bed. The trouble was an old one, a torn cartilage which still gave a little trouble now and then. They were all familiar with each other's weaknesses, and Clare and her cane caused little comment—she did not welcome comment. Maggie could not even remember how Clare had come to have a Football Knee; all she recalled was an unusually acid joke of Ralph's, that Clare had probably got it kicking Carl out of her bed.

What a thing to remember, after so long, and at this moment! As though the turmoil around them had caused an answering displacement within herself, stirring her mind to yield up all sorts of irrelevancies. She reminded herself to watch it, and be relevant. Also, for good measure, non-participant. Then she went to help Carl.

In slacks and sweater, he was absorbed in laying out his work. He seemed glad to see her, and told her precisely what she might do to help; Maggie knew better than to depart from his instructions. A senior editor in one of the large textbook houses, Carl was easygoing about everything except the job in hand; then he became meticulous.

Clare called placidly from the dining room: "Napkins, dear. And the ladle." Maggie was deputed to bring them in. Clare went on, to her son in the other room, "Brush up a bit, Mark. We're nearly ready."

"I'm not hungry. I had a sandwich a little while ago."

"Well, come to the table anyway, please."

He did not move. Maggie retreated to the kitchen. An unobtrusive radio which had been keeping Carl company seemed suddenly to catch his attention, and he turned up the volume.

A man's rapid voice was saying: "... in the death of society matron Inez Webb. Police said today that Mrs. Webb, found yesterday evening in the woods behind her Connecticut home, may have died of a fractured larynx. Authorities are investigating reports of a prowler said to have entered several homes in the isolated community. A trailer truck which overturned this morning on the Connecticut Thruway ..."

Carl turned it off. Maggie's hand had gone to her own throat. Carl shook his head at her, gravely.

"Awful. Awful."

"But—that's a broken neck, isn't it, Carl?"

"I suppose so. Although I think they usually mean one of the cervical vertebrae when they say that.... This is pretty awful for Ralph, Maggie. Pretty awful."

She went back into the dining room.

"Clare, did you hear that?"

"No," said Clare. Her color was a little fresher than usual; Mark had vanished from the couch. "What?"

Maggie told her. She sat in silence, compressing her lips. Then Carl came in with a large platter of cold meats. Subdued but persistent, he said: "Where are the others? We're ready."

Clare looked at him.

"Mugging," she said.

"What?"

"That's what happens when people are mugged. Someone puts an arm around the throat, from behind, and jerks the head back. Inez was mugged."

Carl uneasily moved a chair, but did not sit down. Clare went on, "I'm beginning to think that this is something quite separate from those other annoyances. This sounds professional. And Inez was the sort of target a professional would pick. She did come and go at all hours, and she wore some very fine jewelry. And I'll be surprised if she didn't carry a lot of money to those bridge games."

Carl cleared his throat. "Well—we don't know that anything was taken."

"Please sit down, both of you," she said then. "We won't wait for the— the children. I really am not going to have Dee holing up here any longer," she added, when they complied. "There's no reason why she can't stay in her house like the rest of us—she has a husband. What she does with her children is her own affair."

Unfortunately, Dee appeared in the archway as Clare was speaking.

She stopped; said: "What?"

Clare looked up at her.

"Where's Mark?" she demanded.

"Mark? I don't know." Doubtfully, she asked; "Should I—do you want me to go see?"

"No, of course not. He's not a child. Sit down, Dee."

Dee, with uncertain looks at the others, complied. Clare went on, as if they had not left the subject of Inez.

"Even if nothing was taken, it only means he was interrupted. Or perhaps he lost his head when he realized that Inez was dead, and wasted time dragging her down back, that way. And then he may have run into the children...."

She stopped, perhaps remembering whose children these were; but Dee said only:

"Who are you talking about?"

"Inez, Dee," Carl said kindly.

"I know, but who—?"

He then explained to her what they had heard on the radio, and Clare's opinion that a professional mugger was involved.

"Although I must say I don't really understand your conclusion, dear," he added. "I don't believe it takes any particular expertise to—I mean; it isn't as if it had been a karate blow, is it? Couldn't it have been an unlucky, um, grasp, by almost anyone?"

"But it isn't a *normal* grasp, Carl—surely you see that? I mean, the ordinary person doesn't wrap an arm around the throat—he either ..."

Maggie then lost the rest of the exchange, in a sudden, sharp struggle not to be sick. Eventually successful—amazed at herself, and shaken—she found herself under inspection by Dee's round eyes.

"What's the matter?" Dee asked.

"Nothing. Just had a little turn."

Dee looked at Maggie's untouched soup. Then, with a rictus of woe, she pushed her own empty plate away. "It's awful, talking like this. Everything's awful—I wish I were a thousand miles away from here."

"Dee." It was Clare's voice, perfectly quiet. "That doesn't help. Not you, nor anybody."

"Well, it's true. And I'm not going to stay with my parents, I won't!"

"I hope you won't," Clare agreed. "You have your own home now, and a husband who needs you. Like the rest of us."

"Carl's home," Dee muttered. "Bob wouldn't stay."

"Of course not, he can't. And Carl is only home today because he has some work to do. He'll be gone tomorrow, like the rest of the men. Your position is no different from that of the *other women* here, my dear."

Clare said this with a slow, almost hypnotic emphasis to which Dee seemed to respond—but only for a moment.

"But you're not right next to it! And nobody around, the Rosses' all shut up, and I can't go over to Mrs. Hempel ... and all those police ..."

"Well, the police are an advantage, aren't they? And you're just as close to Maggie, and to Lou, as you are to your side neighbors. You're really not being fair to Bob, you know, leaving his home this way."

"You just don't want me here, that's all," said Dee, ending it. She pushed back her chair and ran out of the room.

Mark, entering, had to stand aside rather quickly.

"What's all that?" he asked indifferently.

He got no answer, except a clearing of his father's throat. Mark shrugged and came in, had his hand on the back of his chair, when his mother said to him:

"You're too late for luncheon, Mark. I'm sorry, but we're almost finished."

He stood and looked back at her, an almost tranquil regard. Carl cleared his throat again.

"Well, I don't know, Clare. It's been an upsetting day for everyone—"

"I don't think Mark is particularly upset by our troubles. Or even very interested. Are you, Mark? And it's hard to see what else could have kept you so long—you haven't even attempted to tidy up. I'm sorry, Mark, but you can't expect us to sit on with you when you've kept us waiting all this time for no reason. Or to leave you eating here alone, like a savage. I'm afraid it's a situation you've made yourself. I don't like it any more than you—but there it is."

"I'm rather hungry," he remarked, in the same tranquil way.

"Then I hope you'll be with us for dinner," Clare replied.

Carl got up, as if to release his son from standing there.

"Well, I'll clear off, if we're all finished. You can give me a hand, if you like, son."

"No—please, Carl. I don't want Mark in the kitchen anymore. Otherwise this cycle could go on forever. We aren't any of us enjoying it."

Mark left the room—the downstairs—without further demonstration, and his father went into the kitchen.

Clare said to Maggie, "I apologize for this—and I'm afraid I used your presence deliberately, Maggie. I just wanted him to see himself through someone else's eyes, for once. This furtive eating doesn't seem so strange to him when it's just us. Although, of course, it's against us."

"Yes," said Maggie, and got up. "Glad to participate, Clare. Now I'll help Carl, if that's all right with you."

"It would be very nice of you."

And her gaze followed Maggie from the room, in awareness of her anger, and no doubt in understanding of it.

Carl didn't have anything to say, out in the kitchen, nor did Maggie attempt to talk to him. They simply cleaned up. Clare and the cane could be heard passing by, going upstairs.

Presently Carl said, with his back to her, "He wants to live down in the city for a while. Near his analyst, he says."

"I see," said Maggie.

"Of course that isn't the real reason—he only sees the man twice a week. It's the reason he gives."

"Could you swing all that, Carl?"

"I could see that he worked, I think, if he were down there. Or went to school again. Yes; I could swing it."

"Perhaps it might ..." She let that die, and so did Carl.

Later he said in a more usual voice, "Perhaps when he comes to the point where he can give us the *real* reason. That's what Clare's waiting for, and I suppose it is very important."

"I just don't know, Carl."

Leaving, as soon as she decently could, it occurred to Maggie that Mark might not be allowed to move to New York, even with his parents' permission. The crowd of more-or-less official cars surrounding Ralph's house put this unwelcome idea into her head. She herself hastily put it out. The police had not attempted to restrict the movements of any of them, except for turning back the Halleys right at the beginning, and perhaps that had been some sort of confusion. No doubt Mark could go wherever he liked, subject to his mother's approval.

CHAPTER TWELVE

"You did that very nicely, old girl," Sam said that night with a generous lack of surprise. A film of Maggie against the background of their house had just disappeared from the television screen.

They were both as stirred as children by the brief, alien glimpse of their life. And Maggie was pleased by her own dignified behavior. They had caught her on the way home from Clare's, in worried thought; she hadn't really had time to get flustered. Someone had wanted to know if she herself had been visited by the "murderous prowler" and she had admitted that she had: he had simply looked through the house and gone away again without taking anything or noticing her presence.

"I was upstairs at the time," she said, to Sam's smothered delight.

That was about all. She had declined to discuss Inez, denied that they planned to leave their home, didn't know of any of her neighbors with such plans. The camera followed her back while commentary went on. Her winter coat was definitely too long.

But it was really very exciting.

She said guiltily, "I wonder if any of the children saw it?"

"They'll call if they did," Sam assured her; and had hardly spoken when the telephone began to ring. It was Susan Squires, rather incoherent, with Jack shouting something in the background. She thought Maggie had been marvelous, but what had she said about leaving? Jack had been talking so much she hadn't understood clearly....

"We're not going anywhere, Susan. I don't know of anyone who is. Do you?"

There was some disorder at the other end, and then Jack's voice blared into her ear.

"Why didn't you smile, girl? Dammit, you're a good-looking woman, Maggie—give yourself a chance! You don't want to let those guppies throw a scare into you, they're just chore boys with their mikes and cameras...." She had hardly got the telephone back in its rest when it rang again ... and again. And again.

After nearly an hour of this, Sam turned off the bell. "Enough's enough," he said. "It must be hell to be famous, you know that?"

"Awful."

"Who was that Mrs. Grandy, Brandy, anyway?"

"I don't know. Church, maybe. Sam, do you suppose Ralph is getting this too?"

"Lord, I hope not."

They considered this; and Sam added: "Probably the police still answer the phone over there, anyway."

"Do you think so?"

Curious, she tried Ralph's number. A man answered.

He just said, "Yes?"

"I'd like to speak to Mr. Webb, please. This is Mrs. Leavis, across the road."

"Just a minute."

There was an interval, faintly resonant. Then Mrs. Hempel came on the line.

"Mrs. Leavis—I've been trying to call you. Mr. Webb had said you might want to look through Mrs. Webb's things ... for the funeral? Would you like to come over here, or would you rather I brought some things over to you?"

Maggie had forgotten this melancholy part of her duty. She said cautiously, "Perhaps I'd better check with Mr. Webb about it, Mrs. Hempel. Is he there?"

"I think he'd prefer to leave it to us—to you, that is."

"Well," said Maggie, "just let me have a word with him anyway, would you?"

Reluctantly, Mrs. Hempel then had to admit that Ralph wasn't there. He was over at the Morgans'. She sounded defensive about this.

"Just until things quiet down here, he says. It's been a madhouse, Mrs. Leavis."

"I can imagine. Do you mean that he's staying there?"

"Well," said Mrs. Hempel, now in open discontent, "he says he'll be home to sleep."

Was this why Maggie had heard nothing from Lou all day? She went back to Sam, thoughtful.

"Sam, do you realize what a bunch of displaced persons we've turned into? Now Ralph's over at the Morgans'—he just comes home to sleep, Mrs. Hempel says. And Dee's down with Clare. And Georgia's here—when she's here. Mrs. Ross over at the hospital, Dee's children in with her parents ... Why, we're completely—"

"Displaced," he agreed. "That's right." He gave her a measuring look. "You wouldn't like to go in to the city and stay with Don and Mary for a while, would you? They suggested it themselves. I think it's a nice idea—have yourself a little fling with the kids. How about it?"

She was only bewildered.

"Don said that? But when? I just talked to him, he didn't—"

"He called me at the office. I said I'd talk to you about it. The thing is," he said, "they may get this cleared up in a few days, and meanwhile there's no use in your sitting around here all day alone. Or we could both go down—stay in a hotel, live it up. I'd just have to commute the other way for a while. Make a change."

For Sam only went as far as Stamford each morning, where the Leavis Hat Factory was, and had been for three generations.

Maggie found no comfort in his proposals. Only new bewilderment.

"Why, I don't want to do that—close up the house? What would we do with the cats? What about Georgia?"

He looked at her patiently.

"We've taken vacations before, Maggie. Georgia isn't here much, she might as well stay down too. And the cats would be all right, we'd leave the house warm and food around. I'll come up and look in on them. Why shouldn't you have a vacation?"

"Because it wouldn't be a vacation! Why, I'd feel like a refugee, Sam, I wouldn't have a minute's peace down there, thinking about everything.

And it might go on indefinitely, I don't know why you say 'a few days.' You haven't heard anything, have you?"

Sam said No, he hadn't. But he then confessed that the police had been in to see him that day.

"In *Stamford?*"

"That's right. Our local chief, and another fellow—they seem to be going about things pretty efficiently, Maggie. I wouldn't be surprised if they get this cleared up before too long. They've got five specific times to clear each one of us on. So apparently they connect Inez's death with our other incidents—which gives them quite a lot to go on."

"You mean they asked you for an *alibi?*"

"Why not?"

"But then they—that means they think it's one of us, Sam. It must mean that. Have you got one?" she asked suddenly.

He wasn't to be hurried, now that he had finally got round to telling her. He got up and sorted through the papers in his coat pocket, hanging on the door.

"Well, I jotted it down after they left. They seem to have a fairly precise timetable on our troublemaker—which was more than we ever bothered to make. Here it is," he said, settling himself again. "Tuesday, February eleventh, approximately seven p.m. That was Susan, out in her garage. No alibi. Next, Wednesday—"

"What do you mean, no alibi? You were right here with me!"

"Now, Maggie, you know better than that. You don't count; you're my wife. Next was Wednesday, February twelfth, between nine and nine fifteen p.m. No alibi again. That was Lou," he added.

She said nothing, accepting her legal worthlessness to him.

"You're next," he said then. "And this is where I clear, so cheer up. Approximately four p.m. on Thursday, February thirteenth—and I was still at the business, at least three people confirm it. No relation. Not even illicit."

"You're still clearing through me," she pointed out. "I might have just made that up so you'd have an alibi."

"No doubt they'll think of that," he agreed. "Now there's nothing until Sunday, the sixteenth, around noon, when Mrs. Ross saw the person in her barn. Just you and me again—we were getting ready for the meeting, remember?"

"I remember. And I remember I did the telephoning, too. You could have been anywhere."

"Very true. And by the way, they asked me if I knew of anyone who wears a red coat. Or jacket. I assume Mrs. Ross must have caught a glimpse of red through the barn window, though they carefully didn't ask me about the coat and Mrs. Ross at the same time. But I can't think of any other reason. Neither Lou nor Susan mentioned seeing anything. You certainly didn't. Unless it's something about Inez we haven't heard."

Maggie was silent. Mark had a red turtleneck. The information leaped into her mind, and she quashed it with an impatient gesture, which Sam passed without comment.

He himself had a red plaid lumberman's jacket. So did Carl. Jack Squires sometimes wore a heavy red flannel shirt. Even Geoffrey had a red velvet smoking jacket, given him by Lou, which he actually wore. He was probably the only man they knew who could have done so. Even the men seemed to enjoy seeing him quietly smoking his pipe in the rich coat.

Maggie suddenly smiled at her husband.

"It must have been Geoffrey, in his smoking jacket," she said.

"Banging on the washtub."

"With his pipe."

Her smile died away. She was quiet again.

Then she said, "Well, that's four. And with Inez, it was just you and me again."

"Right."

"What about Dee's cake, though? Didn't anybody mention that? It makes six."

"No, I don't believe they know about that," said Sam. He added, "And they're not going to know about it from me, either."

"Why not?"

"Too damn silly. Dee probably dropped it herself. Sounds just like her. She probably does some of that damage the kids are blamed for, too, the way she drives that car."

Maggie glanced at him in passing surprise; Sam wasn't usually annoyed at pretty young women. Then she said stubbornly: "Well, it does sound silly, but so does all the rest of it except Inez. I think the police ought to know about that cake too, Sam. They can decide for themselves how silly it is."

"All right, tell them, then."

"I'll remind Bob," she decided. "It's no wonder he forgot, with the children in town and Dee at Clare's. He must be rushing around like three people."

In his red corduroy zip-jacket, her tiresome mind added. But he almost never wore this. Around home, he was attached to an old leather flying jacket. Dee had attempted to replace this with the red corduroy; but unlike Lou's, her gift had little success. Bob appeared in it a few times and then out came the flying jacket once more. Dee didn't seem to mind, she took to wearing the red one herself. Perhaps she had bought it with the idea of sharing; they were much of a size.

"Sam," said Maggie.

He looked up from his notes.

"It isn't only men that take against women, you know."

He remained blank.

"Why don't they ask where we women were? And if we have red things? Most of us have, I think."

He seemed relieved.

"Thought we were going back to the poltergeist," he said, and grinned.

"No, I mean it. We're not exactly a delicate lot around here. We wouldn't survive if we were. And women's quarrels can get pretty fierce, you know."

"Lord, don't I! We've got one going down at the business right now. You wouldn't believe—"

"Yes, I would," she said, blocking this.

He moved in his chair, then accepted the fact that she was serious.

"All right," he said, with distaste. "Who's quarreling then?"

Maggie then had to admit that nobody was, particularly. "But the trouble isn't exactly a quarrel is it? More like a grudge—some old grudge. I suppose there must be lots of those, if we could remember. Something we've all forgotten about, except—except the person who hasn't."

"Well, then," said Sam.

"But it doesn't change the point, Sam. It could be a woman as well as a man."

"All right. You'd better tell the police about it, Maggie. When you tell them about Dee's cake," he added gravely.

She abandoned the discussion and got up. He called after her, placative, "Forgot to tell you—our police chief was very upset that we hadn't reported our prowler to him. Said he certainly would have looked right into it, reminded me we were valued citizens of the town, even away out here. So on."

"Tell him to look at our road and see how valued we are."

"Believe me, I thought of it."

Comfortable now, Sam moved to his basket chair and the paper. Maggie went on thinking. Lou was the person she needed for her queasy new ideas; and that meant waiting until morning.

CHAPTER THIRTEEN

But morning brought new disorder, which began when they were scarcely out of bed.

Sam was still upstairs, and Maggie frowsily alone in the kitchen, when Jack Squires came pounding at the back door.

"Something's wrong with your phone," he announced; and strode away to fiddle with it before she could say a word. In fact, she had none to say, and simply went on getting breakfast until he came back triumphant.

"Your bell was turned off. Shouldn't leave it like that, you know. Well, never mind—the thing is, can you pretty up fast and drive us to the station this morning? There's nobody else but Lou, and she's got a cold."

"Has she?" said Maggie, dismayed. It began to seem weeks since she had known anything of Lou except by rumor. Almost like a mysterious estrangement. She pulled herself together.

"All right, I guess so. Susan sick?"

It was Susan's week to drive.

"No, she's leaving me," he said, sharply smiling. "Taking the kids *and* the car. So it looks like you're stuck for the rest of the week, Madam Maggie."

She continued to fry eggs.

"Going to her mother's?"

"Nope. Can't take the kids out of school. No, she's moving into one of those furnished efficiencies on Gorton Road—money no object, naturally. So you haven't lost your friend, dear."

"I didn't suppose I had. Well, that's sensible, Jack, if she's nervous out here. But why aren't you going too?"

"Because I happen to live here," he replied with savage cheer. "Among the rest of you who are staying and looking after their property. Not to mention the fact that we have probably got more police protection out here right now than the whole town put together. She'll be a sitting duck on Gorton Road, if anybody's after her."

"Well, don't tell her such a thing," said Maggie. Although he undoubtedly had. "All right, I'll drive.... Have you eaten?"

"Certainly. And fed the kids too. I wouldn't say no to dinner tonight, though."

"Well, I would. You go by and eat with your family, Jack. For goodness' sake!" He gave her a mysterious hard smile, indicating some unshakable resolve, she supposed, to open cans in his deserted house.

"What family? Well, you're right—you gals stick together, you'll win the battle yet. See you in, um, twenty-five minutes. Right?"

He stamped off, leaving Maggie with her adrenalin slightly up, as usual after Jack. The revived telephone then rang. It was Georgia.

"I tried and tried to reach you, Maggie—they said there was nothing wrong with the phone, why didn't you answer? I was so afraid you'd leave the door unlocked for me, or something, and I just couldn't make it last night, we worked so late."

"It's all right. Sam always locks up now. You've got your key, haven't you?"

"Oh, yes—but I did say I'd get there, and then I just couldn't get away, things dragged on and on, and there's that hotel room just sitting there...."

"Oh, Georgia, will you stop. You're beginning to make me feel like your mother." That was the adrenalin left from Jack. Maggie took breath, and said into the silence: "Look, it didn't matter a bit, really. We lock up, you've got your key, no harm done."

"I really was working."

"All right, love. Forget it."

"But there's something else.... I can't get out today, and I missed yesterday too. I hate to ask you, but could you possibly take Mother's bed jacket over to her? It's up in my room, I had it all ready."

A glorious morning, it was going to be. A visit to neglected Mrs. Ross; a session with Mrs. Hempel going over Inez's clothes—and to begin with, a hag-like appearance among the men going to the station. There was no time left for "prettying."

Ralph was in the little group that silently gathered to the white-breathing car. When she said, "Good morning, Ralph dear," he explained himself at once.

"Just going in for a few hours—things pile up."

"I think you should."

"Absolutely," Jack agreed. "Well, let's make up a pot—can we get him past the police barrier or not?"

It was rather a Ralph-like joke, and Ralph himself smiled faintly, but none of the others responded. Geoffrey Morgan came out his door, immaculately handsome and just not late, and they started off.

At the foot of their road, there was no police barrier. Uneasiness rippled among them at the discovery.

Jack grumbled, "I see we get up earlier than our protectors."

"It may be off entirely," said Carl Hoffmann. "I believe the barrier was only to keep out the usual visiting ghouls. But we still have men up by the houses."

"Doing what?"

"I'm not sure. Mark and I ran into them yesterday down, uh, down back," he said delicately. "We just went around them."

"They pack up and leave with the television crews, probably," said Jack.

Aware of Ralph, none of the others spoke. Ralph himself said, after a brief silence, "I would like to do something on my own, if it's agreeable to the rest of you. Inez wanted a professional twenty-four-hour guard hired until this business was cleared up, and I think it's obvious now that she was right. I'd like to make arrangements for a man to start as soon as possible. It's a reasonable expense, and I'd prefer to assume it. Mrs. Hempel's going to be there alone now," he added.

He had for once succeeded in silencing them all.

Dangerous tears came into Maggie's eyes; she kept driving, and blinking. Sam was the first to speak.

He said, "I think it's an excellent idea, Ralph."

The rest of the men murmured into life.

Geoffrey remarked, "I've been thinking seriously of something of the sort myself. Lou refuses to leave, but I don't think she's set foot out of the house in days. I'd appreciate going halves with you, Ralph."

"Thanks, but I'll do it. Just so none of you objects."

Jack grumbled, "You're a brain, wish I'd thought of it. Be a hell of a lot cheaper than what Susan's cooked up, moving into that gold-plated trap on Gorton Road. Damn it, that's strictly expense account—I never heard of anybody yet that paid out his own money for it. Except my dear wife. You're supposed to hole up there while the company finds you a new house, right?"

He meant well, he was offering them something passably ordinary to chew on. Maggie left them in desultory talk on the station platform.

The beginning day was another grey, windless vacuum of raw chill. Old snow still lay patchily at the roadside and shallow in the woods: pocked, trampled, dirtied. They were in a February interval in which all life seemed to have departed, not only from the earth but from the air; and the most one could hope for (secretly) was the liveliness of a new storm. Not a soul was in view around the houses, not even Dee's little red clad children. Really a total vacuum.

If this were privacy, Maggie perceived that it could lose its savor. She thought almost wistfully of yesterday's invasion—the crowds and cars and arm-catching strangers that had made her so indignant at the time. Today, not even the police seemed interested in them.

She was wrong, of course. Georgia's trooper friends came to see her before she could leave on her dismal errands, and she helped them with a community timetable that they seemed to be making. The Dick Appleby friend (known to Maggie as "you" or "Officer") willingly explained their interest to her. It was not, he said, as though all the attacks had taken place at night. Mrs. Ross had been invaded at noon on a Sunday, Maggie herself in the late afternoon of a weekday. This suggested some familiarity with their routines. Mrs. Ross, for instance, had been home early from church, since she usually stayed for a social hour after services. What about Maggie's habits?

She did her best to explain these, and any others which interlocked—such as the morning and evening car pool. She told them about Dee's cake. She showed them an old red slicker which had belonged to Dolly and was now used for wet days in the garden by herself.

"Since you're interested in red clothes," she said.

They didn't deny it—would, in fact, have liked her to tell them about any other red clothing that she happened to know of. She didn't like the idea, any more than she had when Sam had started her thinking about it. Most of them had something red, she said; and left it at that.

Later, having coffee with Mrs. Hempel, she stood at Ralph's back windows and stared down through trees toward the creek.

"The ground's still hard, I know," she said, half to herself. "But there's so much leaf mold down there, I should think it would tell them something. And those little patches of snow."

"Perhaps it has," said Mrs. Hempel. "They've certainly been over and over it. I still see men down there, now and then."

"You don't think of leaving, I hope?"

"Oh, no. These things can happen anywhere," said Mrs. Hempel practically. "And I'd think we were much safer at the moment than we've ever been before. Mr. Webb's putting in a round-the-clock guard, you know. With a dog."

"Yes, I know."

"Anybody'd think twice before they came sneaking around here now. I think some bad fellow was probably holed up in one of the barns or outbuildings. It's a pity we didn't have the dog before."

Maggie listened with surprise, with gratitude almost, to this sensible voice. Mrs. Hempel seemed to feel no doubt at all that Berry Hill's troubles had come from outside—and were over. But then Mrs. Hempel had not sat trapped in the bathtub while that most personal, most unfriendly appraisal was made of her intimate belongings.

She said with light caution, "You're still careful to lock up, though, aren't you?"

"I've always locked up, wherever I am. In fact, it surprised me when

I came here and found that most of you didn't. The world's not the way it was, Mrs. Leavis."

You were supposed to agree with this; Maggie did. She wished she could also agree with Mrs. Hempel's belief in the bad fellow who had gone away.

CHAPTER FOURTEEN

The radio, the newspapers and, to a smaller degree, the television spasmodically reinforced Mrs. Hempel's idea in the days that followed.

The Nature Preserve behind Berry Hill appeared briefly as a haunt of Dracula when the local police said that they had uncovered evidence of night trespass and some slaughter of the protected animals. But this turned out to be two local boys who had received bows and arrows for Christmas and wanted to shoot something that wasn't a pet.

At the same time, the local Institute for Nervous Disorders lost a patient, a male, with some history of violence. The fact that he was seventy-eight years old and had been discovered in a terminal coma within the grounds came out in later bulletins.

A local housepainter was held for questioning. Maggie knew all about him, and her heart leaped with a terrible hope. He was an unbalanced person who had given Ralph a great deal of trouble over painting the upstairs. In one unsupervised day he had managed to turn the walls and woodwork into such a ghastly mess, and to do so much damage to chandeliers, wall fixtures and floors, that Ralph had ended up by getting a court injunction against him. For some legal reason the Webbs had had to live with their disaster until the affair was settled. Ralph, understandably, wouldn't let the man back in the house; and he had haunted them for a while in his truck, ferociously blowing the horn and yelling. Then the court injunction ended that. Eventually the damage was repaired, and the town character had found some other way to pass his confused days. But he had carried this grudge among his others, and referred to Inez as "that snotty bitch." The police had picked him up.

Nothing came of it. He must, like Sam, have been able to prove his alibi.

A couple of days sufficed to run through these alarms, and then Berry Hill dropped from public interest. Strangers paid them fewer visits, their telephones became available for normal use, they were no longer caught at by people wanting their stories or their smeary photographs.

Fortunately, this quietness fell in time for the funeral. Inez was buried from the local Episcopal church, which Ralph subscribed to and even sometimes attended. All of adult Berry Hill except Mrs. Ross came to the services, as they had all come to the funeral home, and would all go on to the cemetery.

In this solid unity they had never seemed a more diverse and unrelated group. We really are like a family, Maggie thought, remembering the last years of gathering at her parents': the uneasy looking round among one's own whom the years had altered and increased, finding not much kinship but that most inescapable of all: name and blood. But what held these families together?

There was Clare, absolutely expressionless as she got up and went down with the rest of them, shared her books attentively with Carl, never opened her mouth. What did she do instead of kneeling? Maggie could not help peeking to see. Clare knelt. Very gracefully too. Carl, more awkward, his voice sometimes audible in the wrong places, seemed wholly engrossed, and moved. He was, of course, a freethinker too; but he seemed to have forgotten the fact. What would Clare do if he wanted to come again? (Allow it, of course.) They had not brought Mark.

Behind Maggie, Jack and Susan Squires bumped and shuffled and had low-voiced squabbles over the kneeling pad. But on one of the hymns, which they both seemed to know, their united voices suddenly soared out in perfect accord, Susan's very sweet, Jack's resonant and full of vibrato. It got rather out of hand at the end, Jack becoming a little too loud and attempting some unsuccessful descant, and Susan wavering with him. But it had been an astonishing performance while it lasted. Maggie glanced at Sam, but he was absorbed in producing his one note at the right times. Georgia, on her other side, raptly watched the candles and wept. Maggie looked away.

Two rows ahead, Ralph sat between Inez's sons and the Morgans. Five perfectly tailored backs rose and descended together, five perfectly brushed dark heads—Lou's covered with a tiny veil—bowed and lifted in unison. They alone had some appearance of being related, at least in species. The rest of them, Maggie thought, might have been collected from all over the zoo and dressed for the occasion. At least Inez's rather splendid looking friends, with whom the church seemed to be filled, would find Ralph in presentable company. If he cared.

She did not see the Halleys until they came out of church. Either they had come late and sat at the back, or had not got there at all. Since Dee, sullen and bewildered, seemed to have just been stuffed into her red fox coat and Bob was jittery, it was probably the latter.

Dee's parents were with them, and Maggie stopped to shake hands.

Mr. Kiley, a prosperous local builder, held on to Maggie's hand and kept her eyes fixed by his.

After perfunctory mention of Inez, he said earnestly: "We certainly appreciate how nice you've been to our little girl, Mrs. Leavis. DeeDee's told us lots about you, she certainly does admire you."

Did he think she was Clare? Nobody else said a word. Mr. Kiley went on, over her murmur: "Now if you could just persuade her to come on home for a while, till this nasty business gets cleared up, we'd be mighty happy. Those kids miss their mother, and we'd love to have her. Bob too, of course. Got that great big house, just waiting."

What was there to say? From the look on Dee's face, nothing. Flashbulbs went off, at the end of the walk, and galvanized the slow groups into movement. But all that was wanted was pictures of Ralph and the sons; and when their car moved away the disturbance stopped. At least there were no television cameras.

Snow was beginning to come down.

By the time the cars found their way back, individually, to Berry Hill, it was falling heavily, in windless air. Perhaps because of this, and the threat of difficulty in getting away again, the Berry Hillers were not so outnumbered by strangers as they had been in church. Lou and Mrs. Hempel had arranged the homecoming; and Maggie saw, coming into the Webbs' house, that the arrangements were elaborate. Apparently this was something else that Ralph had wanted "done well." The dining room was arranged for a buffet, with white-jacketed attendants. Another attendant presided over the bar. A strange maid took their coats. The Leavises, numbed and saddened, allowed themselves to be absorbed. It was like a sad echo of one of Inez's parties, underlining the fact that she was not there.

After a time, almost furtively, the Berry Hillers began to clump together. It seemed a smallish clump to begin with; but as the rooms grew more empty under the snow's continuing threat, they began to find themselves a majority. Ralph himself was with them oftener, too. He had begun, on returning, to thrust an arm round Georgia, or Susan—to keep a hand on Sam's arm, or Geoffrey's.

"Stick it out," he muttered finally. "They're going."

Stick it out for what? Till he passed out? Clare's clear blue eyes followed him speculatively; and Dee giggled.

Like Ralph, most of them had drunk more than they meant to. After the cold, the emotion, the long-enforced sobriety of church and cemetery—and now this endless, overheated idleness—they were beginning to show one another the familiar and ragged signs of too much to drink. Some of them could barely keep awake; Susan was comatose in a chair, with her shoes off, and Sam had been looking at the same picture for fifteen minutes. Jack was trying to develop an argument with Carl, who kept saying with belligerent slowness: "Now just a minute, there, fella ..." Clare was telling Lou something long, sharp and explicit, with Dee's arm wound in hers. And Maggie was frankly leaning on her husband's back—or he on hers. Only Georgia still circulated, and even she looked tired. She stood linked to Ralph, both of them smiling fixedly at a talking woman.

It wasn't like one of Inez's parties after all—not even an echo of one. As if he himself realized this, and wished to be done with it, Ralph escaped to them again.

"Come on, let's get out of here," he said abruptly. "This air isn't breathable any more, the boys can take over these diehards—I don't know who they are anyway. Come on."

They roused each other and wandered away after him—a considerable exodus, in fact, which Inez's grown sons watched with some interest. Ralph led them back to his study, which was a television and napping retreat, and waited by the door to shut them in. His day-long air of decorum had left him, and he faced them with a profound, an almost ferocious gravity when he had them corralled.

"Now everybody sit down," he commanded, waving his arms. "Lie down—throw the pillows on the floor, relax a minute. Then we'll break it up."

"We're in no hurry, Ralphie dear," said Susan, who no longer was. He nodded at her.

"No—'nough's enough. But we did it, for Inez. Didn't we? We did it right. Thanks to you, Lou. And Maggie. All of you. You're fine people, I'll never forget this. I'll never forget it."

"Oh, dear," said Clare, barely audible.

He was certainly suspended. But then, most of them were. A faint, uneasy awareness of this passed through them.

"Fine people," said Ralph, with growing aggression. "Won't say any more about it, ever. But you'll know. I won't forget. And I'll tell you something else—this house is not going on the market, I am not going anywhere. This is where I live, this is my home—and I'll tell you something else, the first home I ever had. Going to be the last, too. Like poor little Inez, never did any harm to a soul."

He swayed, staring. Georgia lurched up and threw her arms around him.

"Good for you, Ralphie," she cried. "Good for you...."

Ralph embraced her in return, but as if she were a pillow thrown to him. He raised his voice again, over her head, over the rise of other voices.

"Lots of property, but no home," he said firmly. "Now that's the truth, and you can believe it. And I'll tell you something else—one rotten apple isn't going to spoil this basket, no matter what. I'm the one that's saying it, and I'm the one that's—the one that damn kook—that lousy, rotten kook—"

In Maggie's ear, Lou's voice breathed: "We'll stay here with him—can you get the rest of them started?" Then she brushed by, on her way toward Ralph. He and Georgia were staggering slightly, one of them having lost balance. They seemed unhappily attempting to dance.

Maggie looked round on a mixture of expressions that ranged from fierce agreement (Jack) to Clare's discreet reserve; that encompassed sympathy, bewilderment, stupor, even dismay, as Dee hunched against her husband like a child who suddenly doubts the magician and the party.

It was time they all went home.

Ralph was led away, muttering, by Geoffrey. The rest of them straggled out and took leave of Inez's sons and the few old friends of Inez who were still there. By the time they were given their things and prepared to leave, Ralph was back among them. His thinning hair had been brushed down again, his clothing straightened. He took their embraces and handshakes numbly, nodding all the while: saying "Thank you ... thank you ..." over and over. But nothing else.

They came out, still a group, into growing darkness and ankle-deep snow. Sobered, even appalled, they clung together briefly in their inadequate clothing. There was nothing to do but to begin wading, the sooner the better; yet they moved very little and in a slow huddle, as if reluctant to part.

Carl Hoffmann was saying, with innocent interest, "Quite an aggressive side to Ralph, isn't there? Very healthy reaction, I was glad to see it, but I was a little surprised too."

"Well, I don't know why, dear," his wife replied. "Ralph's jokes have been clueing you in for years.... For goodness' sake, let's get out in the car tracks," she added, pushing him. "This is absolutely dreadful!"

Their road was churned and tracked by departing cars, and one of these, askew, had even been abandoned. But over the lawns and fields, the approaches to each house, snow still lay complete. The houses themselves, left hours before, stood dark and random in the gloom. They might all have been untenanted. Even abandoned.

No car tracks were available to Maggie and Sam. They picked their way over the ruts and then started, alone, up their long, unbroken drive. Maggie paused a moment and looked around her, after the retreating others.

Then she said, wistful, "They say this was a thriving community, years ago."

"Rotten apple in the basket," grunted Sam, "Come on—stay in my tracks."

She followed him, squaw-fashion, toward the locked darkness that was their home.

CHAPTER FIFTEEN

Normality returned to Berry Hill with eerie abruptness after the funeral. The heavy snowfall, which reached sixteen inches, undoubtedly had much to do with this; but it was hard not to conclude that Inez's burial somehow helped.

Susan came home with the girls. She seemed revived by her expensive gesture and not at all nervous about returning. It was true that Ralph's guard (or guards; they relieved one another) changed their situation—or changed their feelings about it. A large dog went with the guard; and there was some difficulty at first with the Halley's Dukie, who was even larger. Bob had attended to this. Dee was apparently back in her own house, although she was never seen and the children were not with her. And Mark Hoffmann vanished from among them. His father had found him some sort of job down in the city after all, and he was living with a friend.

These bare gobbets of news were all delivered to Maggie by Sam, who had taken over the community driving and the car until driving improved. Maggie was grateful for his bits of news, which he conscientiously brought home as soon as he acquired them, but he never knew any more than the bare facts.

"*I* don't know," he would say, when she pressed him. "Call up Clare and ask her." Or Susan; or Dee. But she did not like to do this, and waited for someone more informed to come visiting. No one did.

Until one morning, some days after the funeral, someone came to her back door.

She had almost forgotten she had such a door. Thawing, freezing, and more snow had made it a chore to keep even the front drive passable; the delivery men all used the front now, and Sam had even moved the garbage cans around there. Her heart leaped at the first sound, which was so modest as to seem almost furtive. Then, assuring her that he meant to be heard, her visitor rapped again. She went with caution to look out, and saw Bob Halley.

For a moment she scarcely recognized him. In his flying jacket and laced boots, bareheaded, wind-beaten and smeared with snow, he had the unfamiliar look of some rough stranger, frowning while he waited to be answered.

But it was Bob, of course. She pulled back the bolt to let him in.

"Where in the world have you been?" she asked, as soon as they could speak. He didn't come in, but began brushing and beating at himself, in some new awareness, while cold air blew past him.

"Never mind all that, just come in," Maggie said, "Hurry up—it doesn't matter, you aren't the first snowman we've had in here."

He had barely stepped in when the front doorbell rang, startling them both.

"Perhaps I'm having a party. Take off your things, I'll be right back."

She hurried away. Ralph's guard waited at the front, his leashed German shepherd dog looking up at her as alert and intelligent as another person. Almost as large, too.

He only wanted to make sure she was all right. Someone had been crossing the backs of the properties; they'd lost him for the moment.

"Why, it's Mr. Halley," she said. "He's here."

"Oh, then that's all right."

She had an impression that he knew perfectly well it was Mr. Halley and he was there. Puzzled, she added: "Would you like to come in have some coffee? You can bring the dog, if he won't chase cats."

"Oh, he'll chase anything he's told to. Nothing he isn't," the guard said.

Maggie looked down again, and believed him.

"Well, come in, then."

But he declined. They had their own billycan, he said. But thanks all the same. She watched them go back down the drive, in perfect accord, and had a vision of the two of them sharing their billycan of coffee.

Bob had taken his flying jacket off and stood holding it, still by the back door. She took the jacket from him and hung it up.

"Who was that?" he asked.

"Ralph's guard. Someone was crossing the backs of the properties."

He stared at her.

"Someone—where? Just now?" Then he saw her smiling. "Oh. I see. I'm lucky I didn't get my arm torn off, is that it?"

"Come and sit down," she replied. "Never mind the chairs, they've survived years of wet bathing suits. Why are you crossing the backs of the properties, anyway?"

"I've been to Clare's," he said shortly, as if this made it all clear. He continued to stand while she brought coffee to the table and put out a plate of the elaborate cookies she had baked to pass the time. They seemed to catch his attention.

"You make those?"

"Yes. Nothing much else to do, is there? Except that Lou and I got fed up and took off for New York yesterday. Matinee and all. Mainly because it makes home seem like heaven when you get back," she added ungratefully.

He didn't answer; yet he was attending closely, as if to something important. It occurred to Maggie that she and Lou hadn't asked Dee to come with them—not that they had thought of it, but something about Bob suggested the omission. She tackled it.

"Do you suppose Dee would like to come in with us, sometime?"

"I don't know," he answered. He sat down then with a sagging suddenness that was more like collapse. "I just don't know. I'm worried about her, Maggie. That's why I came."

"She's not ill?"

"I don't know," he said again. "All she does is stay shut up in that house, and sleep, and watch television. Except she doesn't really watch it. I don't think she'd eat if I didn't bring home food. She won't order, she doesn't have the cleaning woman anymore—and God knows when she'll let the kids come home again. She's like a kid herself," he said, "with the covers over her head. All the time. And I can't get her out of there, either. She won't leave."

"Oh, dear ..."

"I'm not trying to unload this on you," he said then, looking up. "I know it's my problem. Not even her parents'—God, they're the last thing we need. But I did go and ask Clare what she thought about it. Her dear, good friend Clare," he said slowly.

His eyes warned her to be careful, but she did not know of what. Nor was there time to speculate. "Well?" she said.

"Dear Clare says, get her to the psychiatrist."

Maggie said briskly, "Well, of course she does. She isn't giving you any advice she doesn't follow herself, Bob."

He continued to stare across the table at her, with dog-like steadiness.

"I mean, some people call the doctor, some people call the minister—Clare calls the psychiatrist. What did you expect?"

His eyes went down, then. She gave him time.

He said at last, "I expected her to care. I expected her to know something about Dee, after all this time—some kind of thing a woman would know, that I wouldn't. But she doesn't know anything about anybody, that one. All she can do is look it up in the book. No wonder even her own kid won't talk to her."

"Bob."

He shrugged, didn't look up. She had to talk to the top of his dark head.

"Bob, forget about Clare. I'm sorry you were disappointed, I know you were—but it isn't that important. What's important is Dee, isn't it? The thing to do is to try and figure out what kind of help she does need. Don't you think she needs some? Isn't that what you want for her?"

"I know what's the matter with her, all right," he muttered. Still head down, he began to poke at the things on the table before him. "I don't need anybody to come in and tell me that. And I guess I don't need anybody to tell me what to do about it."

He gave his cup a final push. Looked up.

"We're going to sell that place. I'm giving you all notice, right now. We're going to sell, and find someplace where there's other girls her age, with young kids like ours. Young people like us, that go bowling, and babysit for each other, and go dancing ... whatever. That's where we belong. Someplace like that. Not here, with a bunch of middle-aged eggheads. We never did."

Then he saw her.

"I don't mean you, Maggie. You and Sam, you're different. You know I don't mean you."

"Well ... we're certainly middle-aged, Bob. You might as well let us be eggheads too...."

He wouldn't smile.

"No, you're the only ones we'll really miss, I didn't mean you. And I'm sorry I blew off at you like this, just forget it. It'll be all right."

He was now preparing to escape physically. Maggie leaned and put physical restraint on him—her hand on his arm.

"No, wait, Bob. Don't go yet. I'm really upset to hear about Dee. And I'm not quarreling with your feeling that she might be happier somewhere else, maybe she would. But don't go home and spring it on her until you've thought it out. She was the one who was set on coming here, wasn't she? Or was it her parents?"

"Lord, no. Mr. Kiley wanted us to build—and it would probably have come a lot cheaper than what we ended up doing. You know we practically had to gut that place."

"I know. We all envied you."

"Well, don't. I think we spoiled it, myself," he said impartially.

"Nonsense. You could sell that place tomorrow, and you know it. If you decide that you want to."

This time he did get up, but only to start a restless walk around the room.

"Yes, we could sell. But we could sell because we're on Berry Hill, that's why," he said. "What is it about this place, Maggie? I'm not a local boy, I don't understand the big attraction. Sure, it's pretty, it's private—but what else? Dee's lived in this town all her life, and this was where she wanted to come. Why?"

"I don't know what it was for Dee, Bob. You'd have to ask her that."

"Well, what was it for you?" he demanded.

"Oh, lord. Twenty-six years ago … I don't know. Pretty, and private, I guess. And we knew some people here. It was more like a family compound then, with lots of children…. But it's true, there's something about it that doesn't change much. Perhaps that's what Dee liked."

He had stood still to listen to her, head on one side, eyes down. With his open-necked wool shirt and roughened hair, he seemed perfectly appropriate to her kitchen, someone she might have gone on talking to—if it had not been for his expression. He had no look of a man who had come for conversation, or advice. He had something to say.

He looked up at her, and said it.

"You're all fooling yourselves, Maggie. I think Dee knows it now. You'd all know it if you'd be honest. This happy family act isn't working. How many of you have to get roughed up before you'll admit it?"

She didn't try to reply. It was a time to listen; he hadn't finished. Coming closer to the table again, he stood and stared down at her. "The police aren't even looking for an outsider anymore—don't you know that?"

"Who told you so, Bob?"

"I don't need to be told. Do you? Haven't you and Sam had all the questions, and picking over your clothes, and God knows what? What do you think it's for?"

Nobody had picked over Maggie's clothes, that she knew of. She said uneasily, "Oh—you mean about that red—?"

Uncertain if this had been a confidence or not, she stopped.

"What?"

His tone was both sharp and absent. He really seemed very different, almost beside himself with what must have been intolerable strain and worry.

She said, "Bob, don't go and talk like this to Dee just yet. Wait and talk to Sam tonight, won't you? At least blow off a little steam on him before you do anything. You may be quite right about taking Dee away, but you don't want to tell her in a way that will frighten her even more, do you?"

"I'm not the one she's afraid of," he muttered. "No, I didn't mean that—"

A pause fell between them, uncertain on her part, intent on his.

"You and Sam ought to get out of here too," he said, "You don't need this big place anymore—and you sure don't need this inbred bunch around here. Why don't you get out?"

"Oh—Sam would never give up his house...."

He continued to stare down at her, as if this were a most unsatisfactory answer. As in fact it was—he was in no mood for discussion. All she hoped was to quiet him a little, after the exasperations of Clare, to keep him from going home in his present mood.

"You could go down and talk to Sam in Stamford," she suggested. "Why don't you do that? Go down and have lunch with him. I'll call him for you."

The front doorbell rang again and she rose reluctantly. Bob moved away from the table, and from her.

"I'd better beat it. Thanks, Maggie—and forget all this. I'll work it out somehow."

"Bob, please wait. I won't be a minute."

"No, I don't want to see anyone else."

The bell rang again; she had to leave him, taking down his flying jacket in morose abstraction.

"Please wait...."

She hurried through the house, and found without pleasure that her callers were uniformed policemen—vaguely familiar, as they all seemed by now.

She said, "Well, good morning," in modified welcome.

"Mr. Halley here, Mrs. Leavis?"

"Yes," she admitted. "But have you really got to see him now?"

"Why?" one of them asked, in sharp interest.

She decided she was only making things worse, and held the door wider.

"He's worried about his wife, she isn't well. But come in."

They came in, and went past her—kept going, so that she found herself following these strange men through her own rooms.

Their rapid glances made her say, "We're in the kitchen"; but at that doorway some wordless divergence between them ended in the second man doubling back suddenly. He nearly bumped into her.

He said, "Pardon me," and went rapidly back through the house. She looked after him in confusion until the hard slam of the back door swung her attention round again.

She went on into the kitchen. No one was there.

The door curtains still swung.

By the time she got to the window there was nothing to be seen. She threw on Sam's jacket, which always hung in the entry, and went outside herself. The "back properties," except for some churned snow, offered only a view of February desolation.

She came inside again, stood indecisive, then ran through the house and out onto her front steps.

Far down the road, near Clare's, three men made a close group. Bob's station wagon was pulled up there. She saw him start away toward it, and the men move with him—or after him, it was too far away to be sure. They paused again by the car; then all three of them started back in her direction. She retreated into the house.

From the windows, she watched the three of them get into the police car, which stood in the road still emitting vapor from its exhaust. The car turned, and took off toward the highway. It all happened very quickly, like some slow sleight of hand which she still could not follow. Then the car was gone, and that was all.

It seemed to Maggie, as she reached the telephone and began to dial, that she had never been calmer in her life—except for her breathing and a kind of long countdown which her heart was doing. When Sam came on the line she said distinctly, "Sam, I think they've arrested Bob Halley. Just now. He was here with me, and two policemen came, and he went out the back way, and they chased him down the street to Clare's, and they put him in the police car and drove him away!"

Dead silence from Sam's end.

"Sam, it's *true!* His car is still sitting down there by Clare's."

"All right," he said then. "I hear you. What do you mean, they chased him? He *ran away?*"

"Of course not, he just—" She made herself pause, to sort out what had happened. Indignation rose in her. "Certainly he didn't run away! He just didn't want to see anybody else, he was very upset. He left when I went to answer the bell, he didn't even know who it was! And then they started running in all directions, they didn't give me a chance to—"

"All right," he said again. "All right. What was he doing there, anyway?"

"*Nothing!* Having coffee, talking … He's worried about Dee!"

"You go over to Lou's," he said suddenly. "Maybe I can get away early. Don't stay alone, now."

"Oh, for goodness' sake, Sam—there's nothing the matter with *me*. It's Bob that's in trouble, and it's all some kind of crazy mistake. He came along the back way to see me because he didn't want Dee to see him, I suppose. And the guard got excited about that, and came and rang the bell, and then I guess he must have told the police ... I don't know, it's just an awful mix-up, and we ought to *do* something!"

"Well, I don't know what," he said; and paused. "There must be more to it than his coming in the back way, though."

"But what? Sam, can't you call somebody? Can't you find out?"

"I don't know. I'll try. You calm down," he said unfairly. "Go over to Lou's. I'll try to think of something, and call you there."

He fell into silence, which she no longer interrupted. They sat in equal, linked silence, in distant rooms, until Maggie spoke again more quietly.

"Well, see what you can find out, Sam. Call me. It was an awful shock."

"I know, dear. Go over to Lou's."

"I will."

Subdued, they hung up.

CHAPTER SIXTEEN

Barely an hour later, Mr. Kiley came and took Dee back to town with him. Clare, unable to get her own car out past Bob's station wagon—and unaware of his dramatic leaving—had limped up to the Halleys' just as Dee was being bundled into her father's car.

Mr. Kiley had been rather short with her, Clare reported without offense, and was going to "send someone to get Bob's car." Dee hadn't a word to say. They had just driven off and left Clare standing there. She said she had found it all rather mystifying. Then she came over to borrow Lou's car, to keep an urgent appointment, and was told what had happened. She listened seriously, without comment, and went off to keep her appointment.

One of Mr. Kiley's local contacts must have told him the news. Or had Bob called him? In either case, the news must be serious.

Sam called at last, but he could only tell them that Bob had been taken in for questioning. Whether this questioning would end in his being arrested (or "charged," as Sam's lawyer put it) or whether he would be released, one could only wait to see. There was nothing to be done at the moment. Naturally, the police were not giving out any information about the "questioning." Sam's lawyer admitted it could be serious.

A man from the local garage came and got Bob's car.

Nothing else happened.

Maggie went home again. She wanted to make a furtive call to

Georgia, in New York, who must know more than any of them about arrests and questionings. Who might even know of something that they could do. But she could not reach Georgia.

The radio chattered and sang to her, but it said nothing about Bob, or Berry Hill.

She tried Georgia twice more.

Eventually Sam came home.

She was inordinately glad to see him, as he seemed to be to have got there. It was as if each of them felt that now, at last, they would make some sense of this thing. But that was an illusion, of course. Past the first flurry of fixing drinks, of being able to see and touch one another, there was nothing new to say or learn from being together. Sam wanted to hear the complete story of Bob's visit to her, and she told it to him in conscientious detail. Since their present had come to this appalling standstill, they could only pause over what they knew of the past.

"He's really been having an awful time, Sam. And he never said a word about it, to anyone. I wish he had, before he got so bitter. I wish we'd taken the trouble to find out."

"Well, you went all through that, don't forget. He's had his troubles all along with that girl. There's something the matter with her."

"Just too much doting parents. It probably would have been much better if they'd started out someplace the way Bob said, with other people their age. Instead of all of us doting over her and the babies. We did, you know."

"Well, it still should have worked out," Sam said glumly. "Other kids go through it and take hold of things. She never did. Must have been something funny there all along."

But this was as far as they wanted to speculate, even to each other. Thoughtful silence fell between them. Maggie got up, with exaggerated movement, like a dog shaking itself.

"Well, let's have dinner," she said. "Time for the news."

Sam began to replace his shoes with slippers.

Presently the grave, reliable voices of the news-tellers rolled out into the room, the explicit pictures began, soothing them into inattention. Maggie was at the stove when Sam's exclamation made her turn. She needed a moment longer to refocus her thoughts, her vision, and saw only a grey little group of men vanishing from the screen. A confusion of half-understood words hung round her—and then the voice stopped, the picture ended.

She stammered at Sam, "But what—did they say he was *arrested?*"

"No—same thing. Just what we know ..."

"But—'home of a neighbor,' Sam—that's here!"

"Well, I know that!"

"But they make it sound as if he were over here *attacking me*, or something!"

He didn't reply. Rather strangely, he had begun to change back into his shoes. The telephone started to ring, and he said explosively: "Turn off that bell!"

Before she could move he went to answer it himself, Maggie trailing. Jack's voice blared out, audible even to her. Sam cut him off short.

"Of course she's all right. I don't know, nothing at all ... Yes, we heard it.... I tell you, I don't know."

Then he hung up and turned off the bell.

This meant that people had to come to them, as Sam might have foreseen. Fortunately, the first to arrive was Geoffrey, whom Sam greeted with a kind of relief. Carl Hoffmann came soon after. Clare was not with him; he said she had a meeting to attend and, in fact, had eaten somewhere else. The Leavises understood that Carl was having a period of isolation at home because of letting Mark go down to the city; but he seemed to be bearing up calmly.

Sam built a fire, and the three men sat round it to consider the situation. To Maggie, it seemed a conspiracy of dullness. Not the slightest shade of opinion was expressed, or surmise. She saw that Sam was wearing one shoe and one slipper, but it didn't seem to bother him. She wandered off from them, secretly turning on the telephone bell as she went.

Then Jack Squires arrived. At least he livened them up; she could hear him clear out in the kitchen.

"I'm not asking you what you think—I don't give a damn what you think, it doesn't matter what any of us thinks! What matters right now is seeing that this guy gets a fair shake—and if you think Old Man Kiley is going to look after that, you're out of your minds. All that old bastard wants is to get his baby girl home again, and they can cut Bob up in little pieces and stew him, for all he cares!"

Some sort of argument began; Maggie, lost in fatigue and a morass of old thoughts, went upstairs and left them to it. She tried to read, turned out the light—turned it on again. Downstairs, the men were beginning to sound a little high, though without merriment. Was this the way one met the absolutely incomprehensible? Grouping without resolution, or wandering off alone and unable to rest? Or were they really, as Bob thought them, rather strange people?

It seemed to her that she would never sleep. In fact, if Sam had come to bed sober, she would have known nothing of it. As it was, she was conscious enough to hear Georgia come in, and the temptation to go and talk to her, at last, finally dragged Maggie out of bed again. Sam knew nothing of that.

Georgia was huddled in bed, doing a rapid massage with some face cream, when Maggie peered round the door. She looked wide awake and thoughtful, and beckoned Maggie in.

"Did you hear about Bob?" Maggie croaked.

Georgia nodded.

"What a mess. And to make it worse, he's retained Frank Sull. Or maybe Kiley did—it sounds like him."

"Who's he?"

"Oh, you know—in town, here. The one that's always fighting with Clare at meetings. Old Save-a-penny Sull."

"I tried and tried to call you."

"I know; I'm sorry. But they seem to have got hold of Sull right away, it wouldn't have made any difference. Sull won't give up a plum like this in a hurry. Of course he's going to have to have help, but you can bet it won't be any spotlight-stealer like Himself."

Maggie struggled with disappointment. She had not known how much she had been counting on Georgia and the half-mythical, all-powerful Himself.

"You mean there's nothing we can do? If they really arrest him?"

"They'll hold him, all right," Georgia said tightly.

"They wouldn't have gone this far if they didn't mean to. Well, we'll see. I'm going by in the morning and see if I can pick up any unofficial crumbs from the boys at the barracks. And I can tell you right now, I don't believe for a minute Bob's been ghouling around here playing nasty tricks on people. He's just too damn busy, for one thing,"

"Oh, Georgia—I'm glad you're back," said Maggie.

"So am I, love. To tell you the truth, this free-wheeling isn't all it might be—or not at my age."

It was the first time Maggie had heard her friend use this ominous phrase.

"Why, you're no age at all," she protested drowsily. "You're you, that's all."

"That's right. And you're dropping asleep. Go back to bed—there's nothing more we can do about it tonight."

She gave Maggie a creamy kiss and turned her round. Maggie, comforted, made her way back to oblivion.

CHAPTER SEVENTEEN

Dee's father called Maggie the next morning. With unusual brevity, and hardly any compliments, he asked if he could take the liberty of requesting a big favor.

Maggie committed herself at once to whatever it was—feed Dukie; collect mail—and then added that they were all very distressed about Bob.

"We feel sure this is a mistake," she pressed on, not giving him time to take over, "and we do hope Mr. Sull is the right person to help Bob. If he—"

But her turn was over. Like one of his own large machines, Mr. Kiley moved in.

"Why, Frank's the best lawyer in town, Mrs. Leavis," he said reproachfully. "Wouldn't have handled my affairs all these years if he wasn't, I can tell you that. He's known DeeDee since he used to keep lollipops around for her, too, and you can bet there isn't anything he won't do to help. You're mighty kind to mention it, though—we appreciate it. Now I hate to bother you this way," he went on firmly, "but I guess I made a little mistake sending DeeDee's dog to the vet yesterday. We aren't really set up around here for a big fellow like that, you understand, especially since he still has a little trouble about his manners, if you get what I mean. But if she really feels that—"

Maggie couldn't bear any more.

"What do you want me to do, Mr. Kiley? Get Dukie?"

There was a pause.

"Why, no," he said, in some unusual state of doubt. "That wouldn't be necessary, Mrs. Leavis.... I understood DeeDee had already picked him up. Isn't he out there with her?"

"I don't know. Do you mean DeeDee—she's back home?"

"You haven't seen her?" he said sharply.

"No, I haven't. But I haven't been out yet. When did she leave there?"

Another small pause; then Mr. Kiley said very politely: "Mrs. Leavis, I wonder if you would mind just glancing over the way to see if her car is there? If you would just take a minute and do that. I'll hold on."

Maggie took a minute and looked. The car was there. She came back and said so.

"Yes," said Mr. Kiley, concealing in this monosyllable whatever he felt. "Well, now, Mrs. Leavis, I haven't been able to reach DeeDee by phone—you can understand she probably doesn't want to answer, right at this time—but I thought if you could give her a message from us—?"

"Yes, certainly."

"If you would just tell her to come on back home and bring her doggie with her? Tell her he's perfectly welcome, it was just a little misunderstanding on my part. Would you tell her that?"

"Yes," said Maggie. "Mr. Kiley—where are the children?"

"Oh, they're fine," he said, hearty again. "Playing out in the yard right this minute, happy as can be. You don't need to worry about them. But you tell DeeDee they're asking for her," he added, as if he were slipping her another card to play.

After one fast cup of coffee, on which she burned her tongue, Maggie accepted her mission. She was going to have to go over there and do something about Dee, as she had neglected to do during the past week. Or weeks—or months. The time had come to participate.

Picking her way across the road, through the slush of a beginning thaw, Maggie thought the Halleys' house seemed different already. It wasn't just the absence of the children—she was already accustomed to that. Was it the blinds? Every window had venetian blinds, and all of these were down. Surely that wasn't usual. Dee's lonely presence inside took on added poignancy from this look of hiding; and Maggie thought: I'll have to take her home with me. She can't possibly stay there alone....

Some long moments at the front door suggested to Maggie that this was the wrong approach and would not be answered. She picked her way around back.

The back of the house was equally unresponsive. Dukie was barking his head off somewhere inside, so Dee must be aware that she had a caller. But she did not answer.

Maggie stepped back so that Dee might see her from a window, and called. Her own voice sounded thin in the open air, not capable of penetrating the locked and blinded house. Maggie wandered around, calling at intervals, but the house gave back no echo of life. Except for the frantic, enclosed barking.

This began to get on Maggie's nerves, as it must surely do on Dee's, and at last she turned away and began to cross the ground between the Halleys' house and the Webbs'. Beneath its melting crust the old snow was treacherous, and she had difficulties that filled her boots (and one glove) with wet slush; but Mrs. Hempel saw her coming and held the back door open.

She was sympathetic, stripping Maggie of her outdoor clothes at once and shaking them out to hang.

"Isn't it nasty? This is the time when I just hate snow, I never want to see another flake. I heard you calling," she explained, "but I didn't think she'd answer you. She wouldn't answer me."

"I'm worried that she's in some trouble," Maggie said. "There's no reason for her to keep us out ... and she must have heard, Dukie was barking his head off."

"Well, I was worried at first too," Mrs. Hempel agreed. "But she seems to be all right in there—the lights go on and off in different rooms, and she let Dukie in this morning. It sounded as if he was running loose all night."

"How long has she been back?" Maggie asked, surprised.

"Since last night. Around seven or eight. I called her when I saw the car, but she doesn't answer the telephone either."

"I know.... Do you suppose the guard could be any help?"

A kind of stolid embarrassment altered Mrs. Hempel's expression.

"Well, we don't have the guard now, Mrs. Leavis. Mr. Webb let him go yesterday."

The news shocked Maggie. It was the first overt acceptance any of them had made of the possibility of Bob's guilt. And it was so prompt, and blunt—as if Ralph had simply said, Well, that's that; the matter's closed. Almost as if the arrest had confirmed some private and unexpressed belief of his own! She recalled now that he had come neither to their house nor to the Morgans' last night.

Perhaps he had not come home?

Mrs. Hempel said Yes, he had been home around the usual time—before Mrs. Halley arrived, in fact, because she had remarked on the fact to him. He had not, said Mrs. Hempel, suggested that she do anything about it.

The two women stopped at that, equally unwilling to discuss Ralph's behavior. Mrs. Hempel probably knew more about his feelings than Maggie—who really knew very little; but that was her business.

"Well," said Maggie, "I think I'll slip a note under the door, that's all I can think of. If you'll let me have some paper?"

Mrs. Hempel was very glad to find paper and pen, and Maggie wrote a small letter that rather surprised herself. Why was it so much easier to sound cordial on paper?

"I was thinking of putting a note in their box," Mrs. Hempel remarked, "but then I thought, she probably won't bother picking up mail."

Their mailboxes stood in a row down by the highway. Reminded, Maggie decided to go down and clean out the Halleys', putting their mail and her note inside the back storm door. If Dee was letting Dukie in and out, she could hardly overlook it there.

It was a damp journey, in clothes that had not begun to dry out. A half-hour later, in poor condition, Maggie made her way again to Dee's back door and discovered that everything was locked, even the storm door. She left the mail in the milk delivery box, along with the milk, and thankfully went home.

Mr. Kiley was ringing her as she came in the door. Shifting from one wet foot to the other, Maggie explained the situation to him. He listened in unaccustomed silence; and then spoke decisively.

"Now I don't like that one bit, Mrs. Leavis. She shouldn't be shutting herself up like that. I wonder if you'd mind just going in if I bring the key out to you? Once she sees it's you, she'll be all right," he added encouragingly.

Yes, I would mind very much, Maggie said silently. She shifted feet.

"I think if anyone goes in, it should be you, Mr. Kiley," she said at last.

"Well, I don't agree with you there, Mrs. Leavis—she's a little touchy with me right now, like I told you. It would be a lot better if you went in."

"I don't think so. I think she might very well resent it."

"Oh, not from you—she thinks the world of you," he said quickly.

"From anybody," Maggie said firmly. "I think we'd better let her read my note and then make up her own mind."

"I could bring the kiddies out," Mr. Kiley said thoughtfully. "You could let them run on in ahead. Once she's got some company, I know she'll be glad—she must be pretty lonely all by herself in there, Mrs. Leavis."

Maggie still thought they should give Dee time to respond, and said so. The argument might have gone on if she had not been in such physical discomfort—Mr. Kiley did not give up easily. But she had begun to sneeze; and on this evidence, escaped. Even then, it was rather like hanging up on him.

She had barely changed into dry clothes when he showed up at her door with the little red-coated children. They looked so small, so impassive under the fluctuations of their life, that Maggie was distracted from firmness. Somehow they all came in and the children were undressed. She discouraged by silence any discussion of their mother over their heads.

He accepted this condition, presently. His presence among them became a waiting presence, portentous with plans. The children grew silent again too, acknowledging in this way the strain of their grandfather's self-restraint.

Maggie lost patience.

"Why don't you leave them with me awhile?" she said. "There's plenty in the house to amuse them, and they're used to playing around outside. Would you like to stay awhile?" she asked them.

But they waited to be told what would be done.

"How do you mean?" Mr. Kiley asked cautiously. "How long would you want to keep them?"

"Oh, for a real visit," Maggie said recklessly. She smiled at the children. "With pajamas and toothbrushes and everything."

The little boy smiled back; the little girl began to kick her heels.

Mr. Kiley said quickly: "Oh, I don't think Grannie would want us to stay away so long, would she, scouts? Maybe if we just took a little hop across the way and said hello to Mother, then we could be on our way back to Grannie again. Maybe we'll even bring Mother with us—how would that be?"

A real rage swelled in Maggie. She got up and affected a bustle of cookie-passing to conceal it from the children.

"I think we'd better not bother her today, don't you? Let her have her rest, and then when she calls us up we'll go to see her."

And she gave Mr. Kiley a look that silenced him.

That ended the visit. Without offense—indeed, with a return of his placative compliments—Mr. Kiley discovered that it was time for them to go, and the children were dressed again.

He put out a hand, at the door, and with it pressed a key into her palm. Her startled withdrawal let the key fall to the floor. He stooped for it and groped to press it into her hand again, murmuring: "Just see that my little girl's all right—please. It's the back door," he added; and was gone.

Maggie turned from the door and threw the key hard, out into the dining room somewhere.

Then, of course, she had to go and hunt for it on her hands and knees.

CHAPTER EIGHTEEN

That night Dukie was loose again.

Waking at intervals, from what seemed no more than a long half-sleep, Maggie heard him in the distance now and then, and once close by the house. His voice had the excited note of a dog released, not quite sure of himself or his surroundings, but full of pent-up energy. Later in the night he must either have fallen silent or gone home, for she was awakened no more until morning. Then all was light and silence.

Sunlight, in fact. Heavy and yawning, hearing Sam already

downstairs, she padded over to look at the outdoor thermometer which the morning sun warmed—an optimist's thermometer, Sam called it. It stood at a rather promising 36° already.

But her spirits did not rise with it, nor with the implied promise of a real and continuing thaw. With the back of her mind still filled by a dog's wild voice, she was disturbed by the morning silence. While she had slept, Dukie had been called home again, apparently, and shut up once more in the shut-up house.

It wasn't a situation that could go on. She would have to use the despised key; she acknowledged that. Soberly she came downstairs to find Sam in possession of the kitchen.

"You should have waked me, Sammy," she murmured.

He gave her a proud look.

"Why? I'm not helpless."

Far from it, he had one pan filled with chunks of frying ham and was making griddle cakes in another. Control of the kitchen sometimes went to his head.

She poured some coffee and sat down.

"It was that dog.... Didn't you hear it?"

"Of course I heard it. What's the matter with the fellow? It never used to make a sound. Must be a new guard."

"That was Dukie. The guard's gone, Ralph let him go."

"Did he?" said Sam; and paused. "When?"

"Day before yesterday. As soon as they took Bob in, it seems."

Sam removed his griddle cakes and poured more.

"Odd," he said finally. "Looks like he had his own opinion all the while, doesn't it?"

"It must have been a pretty strong opinion. And he never gave the slightest hint of it."

"Well, he wouldn't. That's Ralph," said Sam, defining the situation.

Not, however, to Maggie's satisfaction. She moved to the stove, so that Sam could retire and eat, and shifted to a more immediate concern.

"Dee's back. She's been holed up in that house since night before last, and she won't answer anything. Her father's frantic about it."

"Should think he would be. Hell of a situation for her. She'd be better off with her people. Or somebody."

"He says she resented his putting Dukie at the vet's. He wants me to go in there and tell her he's sorry, she can come home and bring her doggie. He gave me a key."

Her voice, more than her words, made Sam stop eating and examine her.

"Must be more to it than that," he decided.

"I think so, Sam. It's hard to know what to do."

Sam went on with his breakfast. But she had his attention now; he was considering. She let him do that.

He said presently, "You mean she doesn't answer the door? Or the telephone?"

"More than that, Sam. We've even tried calling under the windows, Mrs. Hempel and I. So she would know it wasn't reporters ... or her father. But she doesn't answer. I put a note in with the milk, too."

"She take it in?"

"I don't know. I got their mail and put everything in the milk box. She couldn't overlook all that."

"You're sure she's there?" he asked suddenly.

"Well, the car's there. And Mrs. Hempel says lights go on and off. She's letting Duke in and out, too. Of course she's there!"

"Or someone is," said Sam.

She stared at him. "But who else could it be? Nobody else would go and get Dukie from the vet, anyway!"

But Sam had made up his mind. "Well, I don't want you going in there. If Kiley doesn't want to go in himself, let him call the police. He's got a hell of a nerve, handing you that key!"

He got up from the table. Apparently breakfast was over. She turned off the stove. But neither of them moved.

"I think it's Dee," she said after a moment. "But someone could be with her, Sam."

The idea was in his mind, too—perhaps that was where she had got it. Someone could be with Dee who kept her from answering her door or using her telephone.

"That dog makes friends with anyone," Sam remarked, still standing in place. "He'd be no protection. Even if someone was hiding there when she came home."

He started for the telephone. Maggie went after him.

"Who are you going to call, Sam?"

"Police."

"Oh, wait ..."

Her dismay was instinctive, perhaps an echo of that experience with Bob's captors. Perversely, she felt at once sure that Dee was in her house alone—unhappy and unwilling to face even her neighbors. A uniformed invasion would finish her.

"Sam, wouldn't it be better to call Mr. Kiley? Tell him what we're thinking—?"

It wasn't a message she would have wanted to deliver herself, so Sam's expression didn't surprise her.

He said briefly, "Kiley knows how things are over there. His solution is to pass it on to you."

She said nothing more, but stood beside him unhappily while he called the State Police barracks. Her first flush of fearful surprise past, she no longer believed in Dee as a hostage, or a prisoner. It simply did not seem possible. But she had taken lessons enough in the impossible, these past few weeks, to remain silent and swallow her disbelief.

One advantage of living on Berry Hill, by now, was that all the police knew who they were and leaped to answer the mildest complaint. Besides, Sam put it rather well.

"Someone's occupying the Halleys' house, the past couple of days," he said, dispassionate. "It's possible that it's Mrs. Halley, but we're beginning to wonder. There's no sign of life except at night, and we can't make any contact at all. I think you'd better send someone to look into it."

"The key," Maggie whispered.

He ignored this until he had hung up.

"I'll tell them about the key when they get here," he said. "Meanwhile, I'm going over to see if that mail's been taken in."

He made no objection to her coming too. In sober silence, they dressed and went out of doors.

The air was almost spring-like. Windless and warmed by steady morning sunlight, their world lay beneficent around them. The eaves and porches dripped steadily, rivulets ran shining in the street and drive. The tired snow-heaps which yesterday had mysteriously diminished would sink much farther today if the thaw continued. Across the road, Dee's house stood totally blinded and unresponsive to the change.

Halfway across the road, Sam asked her if she had brought the key. She said an unladylike word, and went back to get it.

The State Police car was drawing up as she came out her door again, and she waved to the emerging two men. They waited for her.

"My husband's around back," she explained, hurrying up to them. "Back of the Halleys', I mean. We have a key to the back door."

She proffered it.

"But you haven't been in, Mrs. Leavis?"

"No. The storm door is latched," said Maggie calmly.

This was true. It was also true that she had forgotten about it until this moment. Relief let her smile at them.

"We wouldn't like to take the responsibility of breaking the latch, you know."

If only she had remembered to tell Sam! But no doubt he had by now discovered the latched door for himself. She waited, conscience clear, while the two men split up as they seemed to like to do: one of them going up to the front of the house while the other started around back. She stayed with this one, explaining as they went how she and Mrs. Hempel had attempted to reach Dee, and what various signs of occupancy had led them to do so.

They rounded the house and discovered Sam standing inside the open storm door, peering into the kitchen. He turned to meet them, holding up the damp mail. Dukie could be heard frantically barking inside.

"Here's everything—your note, too," he said. "No milk, though. Did he deliver today?"

Maggie peered into the box.

"He must have. The bottles are gone. And that storm door was latched, yesterday."

Sam looked at her, but forbore comment. He stood aside, and the trooper put the key into the lock. It was a new key, a new lock, and in fact a new door which opened easily—but not far. The sound of Dukie's frenzy swelled out at them, but the dog himself did not appear. The trooper waited several moments, with commendable caution. Then he turned to them.

"Shut up somewhere. Will you wait outside, please?"

He pushed the door wide and went in. Sam let the storm door close once more. In the ensuing quiet, he handed Maggie the mail.

"I've got to find someone else to drive to the station," he said. "You'd better come with me. They know where to find us."

"He told us to wait."

"All he meant was, don't come in. We don't have to hang around."

He felt foolish. So did Maggie, a little. But she wasn't leaving. Perceiving this, he said: "Well, wait here then. I'll come back."

"You don't need to, Sam. Go on—I'll call you up. It looks like everything's all right after all, they'll think we're crazy."

"No they won't," said Sam. He hesitated. "You stay out here till he comes back, though."

"Oh, I will. But poor Dee—how embarrassing—"

"Never mind that. She could have been in real trouble."

Why were they so sure that she was not? As if the presence of the troopers, the easily entered house, even the sunlit morning air had worked together to dispel like a dream their sudden, common notions of hostage, of invasion. Sam was even looking at his watch—clearly thinking about the 8.15 train to New York.

"Go on, dear," she urged him. But he could not quite bring himself to leave, he muttered that he supposed he could hail Ralph when he came out and get him to drive. They could see the Webbs' house from where they stood, and Sam moved for a clearer view and waited there.

Nothing except the calling of birds—and the stifled, tireless barking indoors—engaged their attention until the trooper appeared once more. He seemed much less business-like. Maggie thought he looked a little embarrassed.

"All clear, folks. Afraid we woke Mrs. Halley up. You want to go in now?"

"Is she all right?"

"Seems so—she was pretty sound asleep. You want to go in?" he repeated.

Suddenly Maggie did not. The plain truth, then, was that Dee did not want to see them ... and here they were, complete with police. She would at least have to go in and apologize.

"Yes, I'll go in," she replied.

Sam waited to make sure that the trooper went with her. Then he hurried off to catch the 8.15.

CHAPTER NINETEEN

Dukie was shut in the cellar; and it seemed miraculous that the door could withstand his frantic clawing and leaping. Maggie was very glad of the trooper's ushering presence through the kitchen. He shut this door behind him, and they were in the quiet of the hall. There, he walked with her to the foot of the stairs.

The house was extremely quiet. Not only did no sound come from upstairs, there was no sound anywhere. Every floor was carpeted, even the stairs. The refitted windows shut out sound, the new furnace made none. The house had been deadened to sound; and deadened was the word for it. Except for Dukie's muffled pleas, Maggie could have imagined herself gone deaf.

The trooper allowed her to go upstairs alone; and when she came into Dee's bedroom she understood why. Dee was on the bed, huddled against the headboard, with an obviously snatched-up cover clutched against her. Otherwise she seemed naked. She must have made one of her waking bounds from bed when the door had opened and found herself standing there facing a uniformed policeman.

She still seemed frozen with shock. Maggie's appearance brought no sign or sound of recognition. Dee only shrank farther back, staring blankly at this new apparition.

Maggie had seldom felt more embarrassed.

"I'm terribly sorry about this, Dee," she said. "We really didn't mean to invade you this way. But we've been so worried...."

Dee said nothing. The air was stiflingly warm, the light very poor. No sunlight came past the tightly shut blinds.

Maggie's tone changed, from one of adult communication to the child-comforting sounds that Dee often seemed to evoke.

"Don't be frightened. We only wanted to make sure you were all right. Are you?"

She began to move forward, and her foot caught in some tangle on the floor. A pair of pants, or jeans. She stooped and picked them up, as she would have done in a child's room—seeing as she did so that the carpet was littered with more clothing, as if Dee had flung off all she wore on her way to bed.

Then, very hoarsely, Dee spoke.

"Who's that man?"

"He's a trooper, Dee. I'm sorry, but your father gave me a key to come in and see if you were all right. He's worried about you, we all are."

"Make him go away...."

The jeans Maggie held were more than damp, they were uncomfortably wet—and the roughness of Dee's voice was more than a waking roughness. She could barely speak—and had obviously been out in the wet, slushy night with her dog. Maggie looked down at her with compassion and despair. It was hard to believe that this crouching girl was anybody's wife, or mother. A daughter, yes—but Dee herself had fled this definition, and Maggie could not honestly blame her. Yet she needed someone's care; that was clear.

The terrified croaking came again.

"Make him go away...."

Maggie nodded. "Yes, I will. But lie down, Dee. It's all right. I'll be back in a minute."

She gathered up the rest of the wet clothes and carried them back downstairs with her. The trooper still waited at the foot of the stairs. Maggie approached him with some constraint, but he said kindly: "Everything all right?"

"Well, no. She doesn't seem to be very well. But at least we can look after her now. I'm sorry we had to trouble you...."

"No trouble. Anything else we can do? How about that dog?"

"I suppose he'd better stay where he is. She seems to set great store by him."

"Well, you'd better let her handle him, then," he said, and grinned. Maggie assured him that she would.

She saw him out the front door, where his fellow waited—saw them grin again, exchanging some comment as they drove off. They probably didn't have much occasion to startle naked girls out of bed. But at least they had searched the house; and Maggie was frankly glad of that.

She left the damp bundle in Dee's splendid utility room, by-passed poor Dukie again with a timid word, and went back upstairs.

Dee was huddled as Maggie had left her, but with her head fallen to one side. The hand holding the cover had slid down. Was she asleep once more? In the dim light, Maggie could not tell. As she approached the bed, Dee's head came instantly, warily up again. She stared as if nothing had taken place between them—as if this were a first, incomprehensible invasion. She made no sound.

"It's just me again," said Maggie, not encouraged by this blankness. "I think you've got a fever, Dee. Let me see."

She put out her hand. It was at once caught at the wrist, and held in a hot grasp of steady strength. Maggie made no attempt to free herself, but her spirits sank.

"Dee—Dee, it's only Maggie. It's all right. Look at me, it's only Maggie."

Dee already was looking at her—or, rather, staring with intensity through the shuttered light. But it was impossible to tell what she made of what she saw. Maggie put her other hand over the hand that grasped her wrist. Her own fingers felt icy against Dee's flesh, and she worked them gently to persuade the taut fingers to loosen.

"Lie back," she said. "Lie down, Dee. Let go and lie down."

When there was no response she took her free hand away and put it across Dee's forehead; and as if this had been a blow, an icy blow, Dee gave a great gasp and fell curled upon the bed, turning her face away. She snatched back her hand, too, and Maggie's fell free.

Where would an icebag be? Or rubbing alcohol—would Bob have that? Throwing off her coat, Maggie went into the bathroom and turned on the water to run cold while she looked. All she found was towels—a litter of towels on the floor, thrown over the fixtures, mixed with more abandoned clothing. Dee could not possibly have achieved all this disorder since last night. She had been living this way for days.

From the bed, Dee watched Maggie's return. She watched the cold towel descending, then turned her head at the last moment. Maggie turned it back and pressed the cold cloth into place. Dee's mouth fell open and her breathing became audible.

Maggie could hear no rales, but she knew there was more trouble here than she could cope with.

"Dee, I'm going to call the doctor. Can you tell me which one? Is it Dr.

Sanders?"

"No—no—"

The head moved, the towel fell off. Maggie replaced it. Like separate small animals from an inert parent body, Dee's hands came up and fastened, one on each of Maggie's wrists.

The grasp was loose but complete. Ready to tighten.

Maggie said softly, "Dee, lie still. Put your arms down, and lie still. This will help you."

Dee shook the cloth off once more. Then she went on staring up at Maggie. Her hands still kept Maggie's wrists; and when Maggie pulled to free them the grasp hardened.

"Dee, let go. Lie back."

For she had raised her neck slightly, as if to stare better through the poor light. She seemed neither to hear Maggie nor to be aware that she was speaking.

The posture was awkward, leaning over with her wrists held. Maggie sat down on the edge of the bed, and with this better leverage made another attempt to withdraw her wrists. Dee held on.

Perhaps it was the unmoving stare that Dee kept upon her, or perhaps only an instinctive reaction to pain—for the grip was becoming painful—that made Maggie give a sharp, sideways jerk to both her arms.

It did her no good. Not only did Dee's fingers stay clamped in place, but Dee herself came up farther in the bed, bracing her own arms to meet a struggle. Her staring face, closer to Maggie's now, began to appear triumphant. Maggie saw that Dee imagined herself to be at grips with an enemy—and determined to win.

Sick or not, she was strong.

Maggie was a large, strong woman herself; but a wrestling match was the last thing either of them needed. She took a long breath and said into that near face, at full volume:

"Dee! Stop it! Stop it!"

At the same time she brought her arms sharply together and then flung them wide to shake off that grip.

Dee won again. Her teeth began to show.

Staring at Maggie still, she began to mutter: "… stronger than you! And you're old—you're all old, and stupid, and mean—and I hate you! I hate you!"

They suddenly burst into motion again. Whether her own impulse matched Dee's or triggered it Maggie did not know, but she found herself on her feet, wrenching backward, while Dee was swinging round upon her side and scrambling to her knees.

She let go of one of Maggie's wrists. Gasping, Maggie lost balance for a moment—and as she did, both Dee's hands took a fresh grip on her still prisoned arm and jerked downward. Maggie fell.

She fell legs asprawl, whirled round, her back hitting the side of the bed with a thud. Her held arm felt as if it had been wrenched from the socket, and the pain dizzied her for a moment; she could not even cry out. Dee was close at her back, breathing harshly, still muttering words that held no more meaning for Maggie, if they held any at all.

A strong bare arm crooked round her throat and pressed her head back against the edge of the mattress. Maggie's breath was shut off; she fought without thinking—arched and bent her body, clawed at the bare arm until her own nails painfully tore. But the hard edge of the mattress pressed inexorably at the back of her head; hard muscle and flesh held her throat like a vise.

The arm gave a sharp jerk upward, to snap her head back. Like Inez … like Inez … Maggie knew with horror what the struggle meant now, but she could do nothing against her imprisonment that would end it. All that saved her for the moment was the mattress edge that braced her head; and recognizing this, she tried with all her weight to slump lower, to wriggle down.

But the woman at her back would not have it. She knew as well as Maggie what blocked that victory she meant to have; and her squeezing arm changed its pressure, began to drag upward. She was in a fury now—furious at the unexpected weight and strength that opposed her this time. She had fallen silent.

The world fell silent. Dark, and silent. Except for a hard, sobbing gasp of breath, the room held no sound at all. But somewhere down in the house, another sound began to reach Maggie.

She was lying crumpled on her side, her face against the carpet. No one held her. No one touched her. The breathing was her own, miraculously restored. What had happened to Dee she did not know.

Downstairs a voice went on calling, with cautious cheer.

"Company's coming!" it insisted, into the dead house. "Where is everybody? Company's here!"

CHAPTER TWENTY

With the arm she could still use, Maggie pushed her body slowly up from the floor. Sitting there, dazed and aching and breathless, she turned her head and saw Dee.

Dee was crouched as far back against the headboard as she could get. Her eyes were fixed on the open doorway; they turned to meet Maggie's.

"Don't tell ..." Dee whispered then. "Don't tell ..."

The amazing thing to Maggie was that she recognized the woman on the bed. It was simply Dee again. The fighting, murderous creature that had held her, tried to force her death upon her, might have been some succubus. Vanished. There knelt the large, flushed, pretty young woman she had known for years now as Dee Halley. The only strange thing about her was that she was stark naked.

Under Maggie's eyes, Dee sat as fixed as a rabbit suddenly come upon. Then she bolted like one. Off the bed, round it, into the bathroom. The door slammed. Maggie followed with her eyes this disappearance. Her breath still came like wind through a ragged hole.

Someone else had heard the slam. The voice began again, less confidently, from the foot of the stairs.

"Hey, Mommie—there's some people down here to see you. Want us to come up?"

Maggie began to drag herself up from the floor. Her legs had lost their bone—or seemed to. She made it to the door in a perilous stagger, and stood leaning there to try for her voice. It came out hoarse and deep, stopping the little party that had begun to mount the steps.

"No—don't come up," she said.

They all stood still—the children checked by their grandfather's hand, Mr. Kiley himself staring hard at her.

Then he began to speak, in a random voice that did not match his rapid eyes.

"Well, I thought you might be here, Mrs. Leavis—nobody at your house, and our back door open. We thought we'd just look in too...."

She tried twice; then said: "Children, go over to Mrs. Hempel. Tell her I'm coming.... Tell them to go," she said in exhaustion to Mr. Kiley.

He considered her a moment longer. Then, subdued, he said without looking at the children, "Okay, scouts—I guess that's what we'd better do right now. You run along, like Mrs. Leavis says."

Without protest, slowly, they turned and went back down the few steps they had mounted. Down the hall, the little boy looking back several times. Into the kitchen, where the dog still suffered behind his door.

Maggie waited. When the storm door could be heard to shut she turned her attention back to Mr. Kiley. He had come several steps higher, a tentative approach.

"What is it?" he whispered. "DeeDee not well?"

"No," said Maggie. "Not well."

She began to come down, with care, holding the rail. When she went to pass him Mr. Kiley took her arm. The touch made her cry out with pain. He dropped his hand at once.

"Mrs. Leavis, what is it? What's the matter?"

She looked at him from miles away, with total disbelief.

"You don't know?" she said. "You're her father, and you don't know about Dee?"

"Now just a minute," he said, turning to accompany her slow descent. He carefully did not touch her again. "Just what is it you're trying to say to me? What's the matter here?"

She kept going, an act of concentration. He got slightly in front of her.

"Mrs. Leavis, I don't know what's wrong here, but I can assure you that, whatever happened, DeeDee doesn't mean it. You said yourself she isn't well, and she'd been under a big strain. I'd appreciate it if you wouldn't hold a little temper or whatever it was against her...."

She went around him, part of the long slow progress that must be made—out of here, back home.

"Go upstairs," she managed. "She's up there."

He stayed where he was, watching her go. When she reached the front door he spoke again.

"I wouldn't like to think you'd be a person to try and make trouble, Mrs. Leavis. For a girl in her position. In her own house. That's the kind of thing that might rebound on you, Mrs. Leavis."

She got the door open and went outside—into sunlight, into open air that struck like ice at her sweat-soaked body and clothes. Her coat was upstairs; she didn't care. But turning carefully to close the door, she saw Mr. Kiley still standing on the stairs, still watching her. Alert, sharp-eyed. Terrified.

She met his eyes a moment. Then shut him in.

When she achieved her own house once more, she thought at first that she had come to the end of what she could do just then. Weakness and relief together almost finished her. She did not dare let her suddenly trembling body sink down anywhere until she got to the telephone. Then she leaned over it, useless.

A big, strong woman like you, Maggie.

That was why she was alive.

And why Inez wasn't.

She pushed up and raised the receiver, dialed Operator. Asked for the State Police barracks. To the eventual answering voice she did the best she could with her own voice that seemed to be vanishing by the minute—and kept wavering and breaking as well. The man who answered seemed to feel her difficulties, and helped.

She didn't try to remember names, or to ask for anyone. She said she was Mrs. Sam Leavis of Berry Hill; and waited till he got that. Then she said she wanted to report an assault on herself, and to please send someone. A couple of questions went by her—she heard them, but no answering impulse rose up in her. From that rest she got enough purpose to say, "I'm at my home. Please send someone." Then she hung up.

And sat there. Her hanging arm throbbed unbearably; she tried to shift it. There were other calls to make. She knew this; but her consciousness had slipped from her control and gone backward—reliving, reaffirming what had happened up in Dee's room. Her eyes were wide open; all the time she could see her own curtains hanging in sunlight, with clear air out beyond; but this was a backdrop to what she really saw. Or felt, or tried to comprehend. That silent, hot room across the street, and the unreachable woman who hated all of them.

At some point the telephone rang and she picked it up after a while. Mrs. Hempel was sorry to bother her, but she had just seen Mr. Kiley help his daughter out to the car and drive her away. Was there anything wrong? Did she know if there was any arrangement about the children?

"Yes," said Maggie—only a croak by now. "Very wrong ... Can you keep them awhile?"

She certainly could, Mrs. Hempel said quickly. No trouble at all ... but was Mrs. Leavis all right?

"Yes," said Maggie. "All right."

And thought in wonder, It's true. I'm alive. I'm all right.

The men came. They pushed open the door she had not relocked behind her and met her still in transit through the room. She began talking to them at once, with the last of her voice, before it should vanish entirely.

"*Not Bob Halley*," she wheezed at them, clutching one-handed at sleeves, hands, whatever came toward her. "His wife—she tried just now, in her house—with me, her arm around my neck—*tried to kill me*...."

Nothing would stop her; she went on making recognizable sounds while she might; making them listen.

"Her father came, he took her away— Don't touch my arm!— Be in town, his house. He gave me key, go in see if she was all right...."

Were they still understanding? Tears of weakness, of exasperation, began to run down her face, she kept fending them off her hanging arm every time they moved—wheezing and croaking away, aware that she was not behaving rationally, and desperately indifferent to the fact. There was so little voice left to her, and so much to make clear!

Then there was no voice left. She stood in dismal, rasping defeat while one of the men raised her good hand and looked at it, showed it to his partner. She looked at it too, seeing how broken and dirty the nails were. Dark-dirty.

Blood?

"Well, you put up a good fight, Mrs. Leavis," they told her. "That left marks."

They found her a coat, and took her out to their car—driving her to a doctor, they said. Beyond this they were mainly silent—and she enforcedly so. Tears continued to run down her face all the way, perhaps in exasperation. It was her right arm that was gone, too. She could not even write.

CHAPTER TWENTY-ONE

Mr. Kiley struck back hard in defense of his daughter, as he had implied that he would. He laid a complaint against Maggie through his lawyer, saying that she had used a key he gave her in the belief that she would help DeeDee, who was ill; and that instead she had come in and treated his girl so roughly that she, out of her head with fever, had had to defend herself as best she could.

It was true that Dee was ill. She was, in fact, in the hospital with a high fever, which meant she could not be communicated with. It hardly seemed to matter. The commotion of which she was the cause went on without her—swelled and spread beyond her as it had done before, while she lay endlessly sleeping. For the time.

Frank Sull had lodged his complaint very reluctantly, acting—as he repeatedly said—against his own advice. Before many days had passed he gave up saying anything at all, and rode out his blunder in silence, as a man learned to do. For the truth of Maggie's story lay indisputable in the bodies of the two women ... and the history of Inez. Maggie's bruised and injured throat, and the frantic long gouges in Dee's arm—naked this time—were there to see, and were carefully seen.

In the case of Inez, the nails had worked with less vigor, less time; but a red fuzz under them had been matched at last to Bob's corduroy jacket. And this, found hanging in the Halleys' cellar, still bore on its right sleeve the traces of clawing.

They could only wonder what had led to the attack itself. Clare thought it unlikely that Dee would ever tell them, or even admit her guilt. Maggie, forbidden to speak, silently imagined Inez's headlights picking out the solitary, prowling figure in her garage as she drove up. Then she would have seen with relief that it was only Dee. Looking, perhaps, for her children. Had her relief diminished as Dee turned and came out, with something of that blind, hostile look that only Maggie had seen besides? Or, realizing it was Dee, had Inez got out and gone to help in whatever her present dilemma might be?

Clare was probably right, and they would never be sure of the details. Maggie for one did not want to know them. She already knew more than she could put from her mind.

Her arm in a neat sling to keep it quiet, so that the wrenched and dislocated shoulder might heal; her voice denied her, Maggie waited for two things only: Bob's release, and his return to Berry Hill. She had something she wanted to say to him, and she would find the voice for that. Meanwhile she silently accepted the invasion of her unlocked house.

At least one of the women was always with her in the daytime, to keep her house and feed them and be her voice. The men came around in the evening to keep Sam company since his wife could not talk to him. All except Ralph. He had sent her astounding flowers, and asked Sam about her every morning, but she understood why he kept away. She was too much of a reminder. A living reminder. Sam said he never mentioned Dee, or Bob either.

Everyone else did. Georgia brought them the only real news they got—aside from the police, who were unexpectedly open in telling Sam about things like the red corduroy jacket whose fibers had matched the scrapings from Inez's nails. But Georgia collected unofficial information. She knew about Frank Sull's tribulations, she heard about Dee's condition, she even brought them some interesting bits of Dee's history.

Among the discreet ladies of her mother's acquaintance it was apparently well known, though never mentioned, that Dee had been "hard to raise." When Dee was in grade school she had so badly beaten a friend that the parents had won a good-sized settlement over it. Apparently the friend had teased her. Later she had been suspended from school for knocking a teacher over backward in her chair. No damages this time, for some reason, but a change to private school. The settlement had been handled quietly by Sull, the two incidents had been kept off record; but the ladies remembered. And now, in confidence, they revealed what they remembered.

"That's the disadvantage of living in one town all your life," Georgia said, mock-sighing. "The underground knows your whole history. Like me. In New York, I pass for normal."

She was the first to call up and tell Maggie that Bob had been released. But that was as much as she knew.

He didn't come back to Berry Hill. God knew, there was little to come back to in his own house. His father-in-law had his children, even poor Dukie had long ago been taken back to the veterinarian. But there were all the other houses where he could have gone, for rest and help and sympathy, too, if he wanted it.

But he didn't come. No one knew where he was, or no one who told Maggie. He didn't go to the hospital to see Dee; his children were still at their grandparents'. A week had gone by since the morning in Dee's house, and Maggie had most of her voice back (though she still wore the sling), before she heard of him.

Then it was from himself.

He came to her back door. She was drying silver that Susan had washed, the two of them idly talking—not even about Dee, or the troubles—when he came up and rapped.

It seemed to Maggie that she knew at once who was there—though the curtains hid him, though the back way was cleared now and others came there. But she said to Susan: "I think that's Bob."

Susan put a dirty pot back in the sink and began to wipe her hands.

"Oh, I knew he'd come! Jack said he'd be off like a scalded cat, but I *knew*—"

"Susie, go upstairs? Let me talk to him first. Come down later."

Susan's face fell, but she nodded and left.

Bob looked as his own older brother might. If he were a quieter, indoor type of man. He was nicely dressed in a dark suit, and he took off the first hat Maggie had seen on him. But he didn't expect to be welcome. His glance jumped to the sling and away again.

"I wonder if I could talk to you a minute?" he said.

Like a novice salesman.

Maggie drew him in with her good arm, looked at his face on a level with hers, and began to smile out of sheer relief.

"I was beginning to think I'd never see you again, Bob," she said. "Sit down. Where were you?"

He looked taken aback.

"Upstate," he said, stammering slightly. "Upstate New York. I come from there. I went home."

So he had a home. Maggie's relief expanded.

"Parents?" she asked.

He looked at her doubtfully. "Yes."

"Then you have someplace to take the children? Bob, you must take them—you have every right to take them. We'll all help you if there's any trouble with Mr. Kiley. Can you take them? Are your parents able to have them?"

Now he sat down with her, pushing his chair out and leaning forward, with his forearms on the table. He began to look like the younger brother again.

"That's mostly why I came, Maggie," he said. "Don't worry, I won't need help." He looked at the sling again, and back at her face. "You must be thinking there was a lot I didn't tell you," he said then. "That I ought to have told you."

"Like what, Bob?"

"Like keep away from my wife."

She couldn't find an immediate answer. He wasn't expecting one. He leaned closer to her across the table, frowning with effort.

"You remember that morning I came here, Maggie—that morning they took me in. All that stuff I told you about how rotten it was here."

"Well," she said, "yes."

"This is sort of hard to explain. The best way I can tell it is, when you know things are worse than you think—and you don't want to know it—somehow it begins to seem to you like it's everything around you that's gone bad. Not in the center, but around. If you could get away, things would be all right again."

"I know what you mean, Bob. I had a feeling, that day, it was something like that."

"But I never thought she would hurt anybody. Even the things you talked about at that meeting—my God, I never thought Dee would do anything like that. I never thought she'd *bother*," he said with despair. "She had sulky spells, sure—I guess everybody knew that. But she'd go off by herself, if you left her alone awhile it seemed like she forgot about it. She didn't like you to talk to her about—anything, and, to tell you the truth, I was so darned busy that I didn't try much. I keep thinking, maybe if we hadn't had the kids right away, if I could have spent more time with her …"

But she saw in his face, heard in his diminishing voice, that he didn't believe much in this idea.

Maggie said, "The trouble was long before you, Bob. Did you know about the things that happened when she was in school?"

He hadn't known; and he listened with taut attention while she told him. Then he took a long breath.

"It's something about that old man of hers," he said. "I don't know—sometimes I thought she really hated him. Maybe Clare's the one I ought to be talking to, she can always explain this kind of stuff. Afterwards."

As if in apology for his brief bitterness, he got up. Took up his hat.

"Don't go," she said. "Aren't you hungry? Isn't there anything we can help with?"

"Oh, I'll be back. After I get the kids home, I'll be back for a while. To close up the house, and—and see this thing through, about Dee. They're transferring her to the prison hospital today," he said briefly.

She rose and followed him to the door.

"Do you want to come back here, Bob? You can't stay over there alone."

"Now wouldn't that give people a laugh," he said soberly.

"I don't think so."

He didn't reply; he didn't leave either.

Then he said: "Something else I've been thinking, Maggie. She wouldn't have wanted to go live with a bunch of other people like us. Our age," he corrected himself, after a moment. "I can see that now. Then there wouldn't have been any reason for her to be different, like there was here."

She thought he was probably right. And that he had spent a long week, thinking. With more to come.

"You get those children, Bob," she said. "Take them up to your people, I won't feel easy until they're gone from here. Then you come back."

He answered her with a thoughtful look that she couldn't read. Then he said, "Goodbye, Maggie," and went out.

With a rush of release, Susan began coming down the stairs.

THE END

A NIGHT RUN
Elizabeth Fenwick

CHAPTER ONE

When he received the news that Buffy Oliver had been arrested in connection with Mrs. Kavanaugh's death, Waldon received at the same time—in absolute immobility—one of the greatest shocks of his life.

He didn't even want to hear details, then. Nor did the faintest sense of protest mar his stillness. He saw his mother look at him, and put a silencing hand on Martha Mary's arm; and as if that had been a signal he turned and went up the back stairs again, leaving them there together in the kitchen.

In his room, sitting on his bed, he could begin to examine the blow he had taken. It was not a wounding blow, or a paralyzing one, after those first few seconds. On the contrary, his mind felt clear enough to acknowledge that the shock had been one of confirmation rather than surprise. As of something he had been expecting without knowing what he expected. Like—though less than—the shock of seeing Buffy run at night. Alone and swift and barely glimpsed, at midnight, running across their bottom field. He had never told that nor discussed it; and he certainly didn't want to discuss Buffy's arrest now. Not with anyone—and especially not with his mother, or Martha Mary.

He got up and went to the head of the back stairs. A continuous murmur of voices came up them—his mother usually stayed in the kitchen with Martha Mary for a while each morning, after she came to work. They were supposed to be planning menus, how absurd. Josephine was still doing the upstairs. He could hear her, in his mother's bathroom. Waldon went silently down the front hall and stairs, and out of the house.

For the first time in a week he gave no thought to his morning appointments. Whoever called would simply be told (after his mother had ascertained the fact) that he was not in the house and had left no message; that would have to do. In his blue jeans and open-necked plaid shirt, he went around the house and got into his new Volkswagen pickup, starting it as quietly as possible. Martha Mary's collapsing Plymouth was left sticking out into the turnaround, as usual, and he lost a little time avoiding it—he saw, in fact, a light dress appear behind the screen door. But before anyone could challenge or question him, he shot down the drive and turned into the main road, towards town.

In ten minutes he would have the New York papers, delivered to this part of Connecticut in good time for early morning readers. He had no doubt that an arrest of Dr. Boes Oliver's granddaughter would make the New York papers—the Kavanaugh had made them all by herself, when she died, and she wasn't even locally well known.

The morning was already very warm. He opened up the windows as he drove, watching ahead all the time for a sight of the Olivers' roof, although he knew to a certainty where his first glimpse of it would occur. And there it was—slate blue, through leaves, among unpeopled fields. Dr. Oliver had quite a lot of land, even for this semi-rural appearing country; he had bought many years ago before the New York influx had made prices shoot up. It occurred to Waldon now that Buffy's arrest (*if* it was true, *if* it was true) might involve considerable expense—perhaps more than Dr. Oliver could meet at once. It might be another way in which he, Waldon, could be useful.

A little pulse beat in his throat, and he slowed the pickup to peer up the long, "English park" stretch of ground to the house itself. In spite of its opened windows, it looked deserted, untenanted, somehow—perhaps because Buffy was gone. It was all he could do to keep from swinging into the drive, going up to the house right away.

But not yet. Not until he *knew*. Behind him, some idiot blasted on his horn—the road was busy this time of morning, with local people going to work—and he started, changed gears, shot ahead in a contemptuous burst of speed. He kept it up the rest of the way, passing constantly in quick swoops, taking a savage satisfaction in unnerving the drivers he cut in front of. No doubt they were all, like Martha Mary, chattering happily about the new local scandal on the way to their little jobs. Glad to be able to paw away at Buffy and her grandfather.

In town, he wove expertly through back streets, avoiding the stop sign congestion of Beecham's center. He was heading for Marty's, which specialized in newspapers and magazines—Marty even had Boston papers, for the few Massachusetts outcasts around here. The standard papers, local and New York, were always displayed on wire racks in front of the store, weather permitting; this morning he saw them from a block away and rushed towards them as if they were a kind of beacon, swerving around any obstacles in the street. He pulled up with a slam of brakes and jumped out, going at once to the racks.

The morning bustle of the side street washed around him as he stood there devouring print, his glance leaping from one set of headlines to the next. People brushed against him, going in or out of the store; someone said "Morning, Waldon," and he replied "Hi, there," without raising his head.

There wasn't a word about it. Not one word. He took the local paper out and turned it to see the foot of the front page—if it wasn't on the front page, it certainly wouldn't be inside anywhere. Not something as important as this. With the tabloids, of course, it might be inside. He took a copy of each, hesitant, thinking that if the news were too recent for the local, it could hardly have reached New York. Or could it? Was there even some reason for local caution? Or was it all some crazy, mixed-up mistake of his mother's cook?

He knew a moment of sheer rage, standing there with the probably useless tabloids in his hand. All this for nothing—all this for some malicious gabble out of that mush-brained Martha Mary!

But he realized at once that she could hardly have made up a thing like that. Either she had the news very fresh, from some local connection, or she had exaggerated a less startling fact. In any case, he might as well look through the New York papers carefully, now that he had them.

Controlled again, he went inside to pay. Waiting for change from his quarter, he was seen and hailed by Marty, at the back of the store.

"Hey, Waldon—come here a minute!"

He didn't reply. But when he had his change and had pocketed it he walked back, unsmiling. He wasn't in the mood for Marty this morning.

"What is it?" he said.

Marty, busy sorting and unfastening bundles of magazines, grinned at him briefly.

"I got those filter-holders in, that your father wants. You want to take them?"

"No, certainly not. If he wants that kind of pablum he can pay for it himself."

Marty raised his head, grinning again.

"All right—don't get sore! What's the matter—you had a fight with the old man?"

Waldon had to answer this.

"You know perfectly well what my position is, Marty. Anyone who's frightened by all this cancer-scare had better just give up smoking. If they can't do that then they'd better give up reading things that frighten them. These in-between measures are simply ridiculous."

"Okay, it's not my problem—I got no time for smokes. But tell him, will you, when he comes up this weekend. He's been waiting for them." And with no pause, he went on: "What's all this stuff about Doc Oliver's girl, you heard it? I heard she's supposed to confessed she knocked Rosie K. off."

For a minute, Waldon thought his heart had stopped. Permanently stopped. Standing there in that pause of death, he was nevertheless aware of the rapier-thrust of Marty's eyes as he finished speaking. It was Marty's system—the verbal impalement that made people give themselves away, that made Marty one of the richest gossip mines in town. Ordinarily Waldon was more than a match for it—but not this time. When his breath came surging back he had to take it in, Marty or no. He could tell how his face must look, from the way it felt, but there was no help for that either. It was all he could do just to turn around and walk out of the store—leaving Marty the satisfaction of his victory, whatever he made of it.

In the pickup again, however, Waldon's mind continued to work in spite of the physical distress he still felt. His first thought was that the papers beside him were useless. If the news about Buffy were still in the stage where Marty wasn't sure, it couldn't be in print. Or available anywhere except at the source. This meant he had a choice between going over to the Beecham police headquarters and hunting for Dick Riley, or going back to the Olivers'.

He didn't hesitate. He was no Marty, to go sniffing around other people's concerns. If Buffy were in trouble—as there seemed no doubt; and if that trouble were his business—as he knew it must be; then he would go directly to her people.

The decision, although firmly made, didn't help to calm him. He felt quite sure Buffy wasn't at the house; but there was always the chance that he might get Dr. Oliver instead of his sister, Miss Min.

It wasn't anything against himself, Waldon, to admit that he wasn't at ease with Dr. Oliver—almost nobody was, including Buffy. As somebody had once said, rather cleverly, Dr. Oliver was so august that most people thought he was dead. His music was never attacked anymore—actually, it wasn't even played very much, but his name was solidly established as one of influence in American music. The men he was supposed to have influenced were themselves middle-aged, some of them even *passé*, so it was probably true that outside of Beecham people might be surprised to learn he was still alive. But in Beecham there was no doubt. Although he lived so quietly, Dr. Boes Oliver (if possible, in person; if not, his house) was one of the first landmarks to show any visitor.

The constraint Waldon and many others felt in his presence was certainly not due to Dr. Oliver being unpleasant. He could be, of course, but he seldom troubled. No, it was his perfectly genuine remoteness from them all—in time, in preoccupation—that gave even insensitive persons a feeling of awe, of being in touch with ancestral mysteries. To someone sensitive to this atmosphere, as Waldon knew himself to be, the effect was often, unfortunately, overwhelming.

Nevertheless, he drove the Volkswagen away from town almost as rapidly as he had approached it. He had to know. And he had to know the truth. No more of these shocking, heart-stopping rumors. He had to know.

He swung for the entrance to the drive, and then braked to a screaming stop. The gates were closed. For the first time in Waldon's memory, the delicate wrought-iron gates to that leafy drive were drawn firmly together, barring the way.

And padlocked. He could see the padlock from where he sat.

Afterwards, Waldon felt satisfaction with the way he met this emergency. At the time, he was not even aware of planning. He simply backed and pulled the pickup in close to the hedge. Then he got out, put his trembling hands on the iron curlicues of the gate top, and in one desperate thrust flung himself over.

CHAPTER TWO

There was no sound or sign of movement, from house or grounds, as Waldon came limping up the drive. He had twisted his ankle and skinned one arm in vaulting the gate, but this reflected on his emotional rather than his physical condition. Ordinarily he could take a four-foot vault without difficulty ... certainly without falling down in landing. He shut the incident firmly from his mind.

The house ahead of him was of grey stone, kept clear of creepers, with weathered blue shutters that blended with the slate roof. He was very fond of it—considerably fonder than of the much larger and much better kept house of his parents. He wished, in his most secret heart, that he could live here. Often he had almost a feeling of coming home, when he came to the Olivers'.

On ordinary days the back door was unlocked and he came directly in, calling out his name to whoever might hear. Perhaps it was unlocked today, but he would not have dreamed of going in. He rapped and stood waiting, not touching his long, full moustaches as he waited— that was a nervous habit of which he had broken himself, since some people considered it humorous, and only in moments of stress did the impulse return. He stood quiet and erect, ignoring the yapping of Buffy's dogs inside.

The yapping went on, increased. From the sound, they were flinging themselves against the door. He prepared to catch any that might slip out when the door was opened, and thus did not hear for a moment the tapping on the windowpane by the door. When he did hear, and turn, Miss Min was struggling to get the window open. She could raise it only a little (he ought to fix that again for them), and had to stoop to speak to him, as he did to listen. The dogs went on making an awful din.

Her sad little voice floated out. "Not today, Waldon. (Oh, hush—hush!) I said, *Not today, Waldon.*"

He was flooded with shame, to be so misunderstood, and he called back a little too loudly: "Why, we didn't have an appointment today, Miss Min!" Then, receiving direct inspiration, he added clearly: "I came to see if you'd like me to take the dogs for you!"

She disappeared from the window and he thought she had not heard. If it were not for his idea there would have been nothing to do but turn away, discomfited—but the idea gave him courage to rap again, because actually it was a very good idea. He had his hand firmly raised when he heard her fumbling with the knob; she had heard him after all. He prepared to squeeze in without letting an animal out, and was presently successful, standing over her at close range while she locked the door again (Miss Min was very small, and he above average in height). The three dachshunds leapt around them, madly noisy, and when Miss Min turned back to him she made no attempt to speak but put her hand on her heart and raised her eyes, showing despair.

At once he sank down, drawing the little dogs towards him and allowing them intimate investigation, which quieted them. Then Miss Min's sad little voice said: "What I should do without you, Waldon, I really don't know."

He smiled up at her, and then, embarrassed, dropped the smile.

"I'd be glad to take them, if it would be any help," he said.

"I can't tell you what a help it would be. They are really a last straw," she said. "A last straw."

He saw that she had begun to cry, and stood up.

"Miss Min, I would do anything," he said, "*anything*...."

"Oh, Waldon—what can anybody do? How can one even understand a thing like this? All our *years* in this community—a man of the Doctor's standing and reputation—and it seems to count for nothing, just nothing!"

"You know that isn't true," he said.

"It's worse than true," she exclaimed, illogical and fierce. "Sometimes it seems to me those town people look for ways to insult him, to bring him down to their level, just because they can never aspire to his ..."

She was controlled again, wiping her eyes with a dainty handkerchief. Unlike many old people, Miss Min was always very dainty about her person.

She said quietly, "I'll go get their leashes, if you really mean this kindness. Buffy left a note about their feeding, but I don't know where it is. I'll look."

"Don't bother about that, I know how to care for them," he said; but she was already pushing through the swing door.

There was an interval, in which he stood where he was, his heart beating hard. The dogs abandoned him, going to whine at the swing door, where they would be struck by anyone trying to enter. He whistled softly, to call them back—then stopped as the door did open a little and a head poked through. It was Dr. Oliver's head—white-haired, deep eyed, with its usual stern expression.

Dr. Oliver withdrew his head without speaking, and Waldon had not thought of anything to say either. A moment later he heard the Doctor's voice saying:

"… won't have that boy whistling around here today …" and Miss Min's instant, sharp rejoinder, driving him away.

Then she returned, carrying a lot of thin leather straps and a sheet of paper. Waldon was trying to control a surge of resentment—not, of course, for her. It was true he did sometimes forget and whistle near the Doctor's windows, and it was also possible that twenty-nine to eighty-odd might justify the word "boy." But the total picture evoked by the words was neither friendly nor fair, and he had to struggle to forgive it.

Miss Min was obviously annoyed too, and thrust the leashes at him quite sharply, as if he were the Doctor—saying, "Here." Then she added, "If he would only *keep out of my way*—!" Then she said, quieter still: "Now there's some special sort of food they have that I will give you. Just bear with me a moment longer, Waldon."

"Please don't hurry, Miss Min," he replied; but she was gone again, this time into the pantry.

He untangled the leather, which was coral and yellow, and entwined—the coral being a double harness for the two females and the yellow a single harness for the male. The dachshunds came willingly to be harnessed, and then made this difficult by wriggling constantly. He was still struggling with them when Miss Min returned with a covered basket.

"I'll put this in the car for you, Waldon," she said. "You'll have all you can do to get the dogs in."

He started to thank her, and then remembered where the pickup was, and explained. He could not resist asking, with a small stir of jealousy, who had fastened the gate for them.

"The Doctor went down and did it himself," said Miss Min, impressively. "Last night, after they left. He found the padlock himself, and put it on. And now he's lost the key."

"Last night?" said Waldon. "They took her last night?"

This seizure upon her words, which he could not help, made her pause and look at him differently, he thought. He apologized.

"I'm sorry—I don't mean to pry."

But there was no rebuke in her voice, as she answered readily: "I know you don't, Waldon. But I was wondering what sort of story has got around, and where you heard it, if you don't mind my asking you."

Waldon simply told the truth.

"Martha Mary told my mother, as soon as she came this morning. I didn't stay to hear everything she had to say—I didn't want to. But she did say that Buffy had been arrested ... about Mrs. Kavanaugh...."

He couldn't make it any clearer; he didn't have to. Miss Min was already nodding.

"Quite wrong, of course. She hasn't been arrested—even *they* wouldn't dare to do a thing like that, for such a nonsensical reason. She's been taken away for questioning," she said, in precise quotation, "which is quite offensive enough, considering they could very well have questioned her here if they had only behaved themselves. I hope you'll correct anything more you hear about Buffy being *arrested*."

"I will," he said, earnest.

"The Doctor was quite within his rights in telling them to leave," she said, "whatever story they care to tell about it. *You* can furnish the correct story, Waldon—I'll tell it to you. Come along," she said, opening the back door. "I'll walk down to the road with you. If the Doctor hears us talking here in the house he'll be out here sure as day. He's still very upset," she added.

Waldon said he thought that was natural; and privately he regretted his own private loss of temper about the whistling boy remark. It was almost impossible for them to talk, however, once the dogs got outdoors. Either no one had remembered to air them that morning or else they thought they were going to find Buffy out here in the grounds. They got into complete and active disorder among themselves and Waldon's legs; until he said: "Look—let me take them down and put them in the pickup, and then I'll come back. Will you wait?"

"Yes," she said. "You're invaluable, Waldon."

Suddenly almost gay, he ran down the long drive with the little dogs streaking happily along beside him. The closed gate brought them all up—it could have been an awful problem, but fortunately by squashing them a little he was able to push the dogs underneath. Then he carefully transferred the leashes to the top, and still holding them vaulted over himself—more successfully this time. The dogs were by this time quite wild; so after shutting them into the pickup he rolled up the windows so their barking would be muffled. They began to pant heavily at once; but he did not intend to leave them that way long.

He vaulted again—better every time—and ran back up the drive. Miss Min had seated herself on the fieldstone wall, out of sight of the house windows, and motioned him to join her. He tried to control his breathing, and Miss Min patted his arm.

"You're a loyal friend," she said. "Buffy will appreciate it one day, never fear. I know she hasn't seemed to in the past, Waldon, but frankly that isn't the only thing she hasn't appreciated. God knows I would never wish a thing like this to happen to her, but as long as it *has* happened, I hope it will make her a little more thoughtful. I can't begin to tell you how awful it was last night. She made no attempt to show consideration for her grandfather's feelings. None."

"What did— What happened?" Waldon asked. His hard breathing would not diminish; excitement added to exertion made it hopeless. But Miss Min was luckily too intent to notice.

"It's true we had no warning at all that they were coming," she said. "Someone—I don't know, I can't imagine who would do such a thing!— after all this time, reported to the Beecham police that they had seen Buffy *hanging around* Rose's house last week—the very night she was so *terribly killed*, you know. Well, of course, I didn't have the slightest hesitation in telling them it wasn't true—you know that none of us here, so nearby, has been able to think or speak of anything else all week, an absolutely incredible thing like that happening *here*, so brutal and savage—and to poor Rose, who was after all a neighbor—a person more or less like ourselves—"

"Rather less than more," Waldon could not help saying. He was disconcerted to find that his pent-up breath came out in a rush, surprising Miss Min; but he went on doggedly: "Of course I didn't know her very well—I had an appointment with her when she first took the millhouse, but it was pretty hopeless. She wasn't willing to do any of the things I recommended—an absolute minimum—and I certainly couldn't get order out of that wilderness without some—"

He broke off, with a gesture: why should they talk of that, now? Miss Min nodded sad agreement.

"Poor Rose," she said. "A really difficult person, we all found her so. But to hear of her dreadful end—well, I haven't had it out of my mind all week, and I'm sure you haven't either. *And yet it was true*," she said, a little wildly. "All week in the same house, and not a single word to her grandfather or to me! And then simply, calmly, to sit there and *admit* it, in front of those people—!"

He stammered, "I don't—what do you mean? What—"

"Waldon, *she was there!* She didn't even attempt to deny it! Wouldn't you think she would tell me a thing like that? Or if she was ashamed to tell us, oughtn't she have had the decency to deny it to those *people?* Her grandfather tried to save her—that was when he forbade Buffy to say another word! He told them, he was absolutely right, that she knew nothing about Rose, and that it didn't concern them how she took her exercise.... What else could he call it?" she said, turning up her little hands in her lap in a helpless gesture, her sad little voice trailing away. "What else could he have done?"

There was silence between them, with the warm country sounds rising murmurous all round. The enclosed little dogs, far down the grounds, still faintly barked.

Then Waldon said, "She was running...."

Miss Min echoed him.

"She was running. For no reason. In the middle of the night. And she *told them so*."

Waldon suddenly put his face down in his hands. He couldn't help it. It felt as if it were going to burst, to burst in heat, like a sausage skin, and spill his essence irretrievably out. The movement brought on a swift dizziness, too, so that his ears rang, and for a while he heard nothing.

Then Miss Min's voice, in course, began to come through again.

"... and got hold of that silly quarrel, too, which just made it all the worse. But they did leave, when the Doctor told them to. Only they took Buffy with them."

What quarrel? Dizzy still, he did not ask; he felt that the answer to this was somewhere in his own knowledge, could be sorted out later. He made himself lift his head, swallowed a rush of nausea, and then asked:

"Where? Where is she? When will they bring her back?"

"I don't know, Waldon. I don't know. Of course it can't go on this way, the Doctor called Mr. Friend last night, so I expect he'll do something about it very soon."

"Friend? Mel Friend? But Mel's in New York all week, he isn't here!"

"Then I expect he called him in New York," said Miss Min sadly.

Waldon got up. His hands were clenching themselves tightly, his throat was clenched too—but he managed to get the words out in a voice that sounded calm, almost normal.

"Miss Min, she wasn't there. I don't know why she said that, but she wasn't there. I saw her. She was running, yes, but she was running across our bottom field, I saw her out of the upstairs bathroom window.

She wasn't anywhere near the millhouse that night."

Miss Min got up too, looking at him doubtfully.

"Waldon, what are you saying? Are you sure?"

"Yes. I'm sure. It's a good five miles away from the millhouse, she couldn't have run all that way, not that fast. She was running very fast."

Miss Min stood still, continuing to regard him. He met her eyes steadily. Then she said in a new, excited voice: "I think I had better tell the Doctor about this. You wait here, Waldon, please."

He nodded once, and she started rapidly back to the house. Then, as rapidly, she swerved and came back to him again. She looked very small, very bewildered, standing there gazing up at him.

"Waldon—you're really sure of what you're saying?"

"Yes," he said. "I swear it. It's true."

She looked up at him a moment longer and then set off again, at an unsteady trot. He watched her go. The moment she disappeared into the house, exhaustion, like a friend, gently overpowered Waldon and pressed him downward to the grass—to lie prone, thoughtless, almost careless of what would come next. He thought of nothing; but let the summer air, the muted liveliness of an August morning, wash upon him like mild waves until an answering life began to stir in him.

Then he sat up. He drew up his knees and wound his arms about them and sat so, dully watching the kitchen door for Miss Min's return. When he saw her emerge, he got to his feet.

She seemed changed by the time spent in the house. Her expression was hesitant, perhaps embarrassed, and before she spoke at all she came and put her hand on his arm.

"Waldon, dear," she said. "I've been speaking to the Doctor about what you told me...."

"He's got to believe me. It's true."

"He believes you, dear, and he's most grateful to you—we both are. But you see, Waldon, he feels that he—that we have put ourselves completely in Mr. Friend's hands now, and that we mustn't act except through him, or else we may do more harm than good to Buffy. You can understand that, can't you?"

"Do you want me to tell this to Mel? I will."

"Well, let the Doctor do it, Waldon," she said. "He will, as soon as he can. The Doctor is just waiting to hear from him now, and then he'll tell him. And meanwhile he doesn't want you to—he says he will appreciate it if you will just not do anything, Waldon. Not say anything, you know. To anybody."

This stern injunction, although Miss Min was softening it as much as she could, struck immediate silence upon him. He could make no reply.

After a moment Miss Min said softly to him: "'They also serve,' you know, dear."

Who only stand and wait.

Tears came into his eyes, and he averted his head—turned wholly from her, and stumbled towards the drive.

"Goodbye, Miss Min," he managed to articulate.

She said behind him, "Goodbye, and thank you, Waldon. I hope the dogs won't be a great trouble to you."

A little later still she called: "Give my love to your mother, dear."

He did not even glance back in acknowledgement.

CHAPTER THREE

He went steadily downwards between the close press of leaves, beneath the random shading of the elms that lines the drive. When he came to the gate it seemed insurmountable—he wished only to open it, to push the barriers apart. But the padlock held them. He thought for a moment, unclearly, of striking it open with a stone—was even glancing about for one, when he recollected himself. There was nothing to do but lean and put one leg over, and follow it as best he could.

The dogs were quiet now, even when he opened the door to get in. They were all panting heavily—slavering, really, so that he was grateful they were on the floor in the back, instead of drooling on the seat that way. The car was too hot to get into at once—it had been standing in the sun—so he opened both front doors and let air circulate through while he waited; and the idea of a cold beer came into his mind then. An idea that was a refreshment in itself.

He got in and drove away, wondering where to go for a beer. The closest place was home, but he did not want to go there yet and run the risk of getting involved with his mother, or hearing of telephone calls that might have come. He had a refrigerator in his workshop, but it wasn't dependable, and the beer there might not be cold. However, if he went to his workshop he could get the dogs installed and have them off his mind—and the refrigerator might be working. He decided to stop by and see.

Quite soon he came to the little road he was making to his own part of his parents' property, so that he would not have to use the driveway every time he wanted to go to his workshop. This was well out of sight and hearing of the house, so that the house and workshop noises should not intermingle, and it really gave him quite a sense of being on his own—which was the approved purpose of his workshop. His spirits rose, in fact, only to be going there.

The Volkswagen took the ruts easily, pulling with controlled power, as he liked to feel it do; and presently he came into his clearing and stopped. He got down and opened the garage—separated by a partition from the workroom itself—and glanced round to see if there was anything to be removed before the dogs went in. It seemed a little untidy, but he saw nothing the dogs could hurt, so he went back to get them.

They came plopping out upon the cool grass and stood or lay there, panting and wagging their tails faintly. He stooped and patted them, speaking kindly, and they seemed grateful—Buffy's dogs had very sweet dispositions.

Like Buffy. Like her own dear self....

He spent a little while caressing them—until they began to revive and mill around him, pulling at their leashes. Then, consciously postponing his own need for a cold beer in favor of their needs, he walked them slowly around the clearing for a while.

After that he shut himself in the garage with them while he made their arrangements—setting out pans of water, of food; removing and hanging up their harnesses. The garage was a little stuffy, but he decided against opening the windows. Ordinary sounds from here would not reach the house, but barking or howling would, and his mother always rested in the afternoon. He was experimenting with a home-manufactured room cooler in his workroom, and went in to see if he could not fix something up by using that, and leaving the door between workroom and garage open—with some sort of wire mesh across it, of course. For the present, he closed the door.

The refrigerator had stopped, but recently enough so that the beer inside was at least cool. He drank gratefully, with inexpressible pleasure. Then he lay down upon his studio couch and fell asleep.

He had not intended to sleep—had not realized he might do so, until he found himself engaged in the chagrin of trying to waken. It was hard, unpleasant—he was so hot, and limp, and some dream urgency clung which he could neither get back to grasp nor forward to escape. He got off the couch and staggered over to the sink, running cold water into his cupped hands and plunging his face into it again and again. Then he stood and ran the cold water over his wrists—one of the few pieces of good advice Martha Mary had given him, in her years of persistent advice-giving.

By then he was awake enough to be aware of the dogs whining next door, giving tentative yelps. They had heard him moving about. He supposed he ought to go in, but he was too tired, too hot, to become involved with them now. Instead he went outdoors and flung himself down on the ground to recover further.

Even out here, lying in shade, it was unpleasantly warm; and he could still hear the annoying, nagging sound of the little dogs. He sat up and ran his pocket comb through his hair, then carefully over his moustaches; then he sighed and got up, and went over to the pickup.

Jolting back down his half-made road, he was not sure where he meant to go. With returned wakefulness, his morning sense of urgency had returned; but he had not decided which, of several actions, he ought to choose. One trouble was that he was hungry; it was far past noon.

He did not even consider going home to eat. Several miles away, near the lake, was a roadside restaurant where he could pick up a couple of hamburgers and some iced coffee, and he made for this, driving fast to complete his waking up.

The restaurant—with a long, old-fashioned bar down one side which served only beer—was run by a German family who served interchangeably at any task; behind the bar, waiting table, cooking. The son could cook as well as his mother, and the sister drew beer as carefully as her father, and they all worked incredible hours, with unshakable slow good nature. Waldon was very fond of their place—dark and roomy, filled with all sorts of Bavarian *gemütlichkeit*—but as he came in today, he saw that practically the only customer was Kurt Schroeder.

He didn't dislike Kurt—actually, he liked the idea of Kurt better than Kurt himself: a man holing up in romantic-looking countryside to paint nothing but slum doorways—and he admired his painting very much; but Kurt was hard to talk with at the best of times. No person to run into when you didn't feel like talking to anybody.

However, there he was, lolling all over the big corner table, and he wasn't too far gone to spot Waldon at once; so Waldon went towards him.

"Well, Waldo," Kurt said, as he pulled out a chair and sat down. "How's Waldo today?"

"Someday you're going to sober up enough to find out what my name really is, Kurt," said Waldon. "You better put that bottle down on the floor—unless you're trying to get the place closed up."

Kurt had brought along cheap whisky to go with the beer; he didn't even attempt to hide it. Well, it wasn't Waldon's worry. He turned and held up two fingers to the son, behind the bar.

"Well done," he said. "And iced coffee, Max."

He watched Max disappear into the kitchen. Probably alone here, at this slack time of day. Then he turned back to Kurt.

"Honestly, don't you give a damn about these people?" he asked, indicating the bottle on the table.

"I don't give a damn about what you give a damn about," said Kurt. "Why the hell aren't you out mowing lawns? And why the hell don't you ever lie down and let the lawn mower mow all that hair off your face—hey? Zoo-o-oop!" said Kurt, mashing his hand across the lower part of his face to show how the lawn mower would go. Then he laughed.

This was the way conversations with Kurt went, when they got out of hand. You had to be pretty drunk to enjoy them. Waldon let a little time go by, and then took things into his own hands.

"How's the painting going, Kurt?" he asked, in a pleasant, serious voice. But Kurt was pretty far gone after all. He just sat, owlish, and let the words go by him.

Max came up with the hamburgers and iced coffee—nicely served from a tray, with the ketchup bottle, the sugar shaker, napkins, spoon. The tabletops were always cleared in between customers, and left with their scrubbed wooden tops shining light and clean. It was really a very nice place.

He smiled at Max, who inquired as he served him: "You heard anything about the police being up to Dr. Oliver's, Mr. Coutts? Seems kind of hard to believe."

It was impossible to answer this because of a big roaring sound Kurt began to make, and then he yelled: "That's not Mr. Coutts, Max—you dummkopf! Mr. Coutts doesn't hang around joints like this! Mr. Coutts is the president of all the money in the world—don't you know anything, big stupid? This is his little boy Waldo," he yelled, half rising, so he could drop a hand like half a ham on Waldon's head. "This is LITTLE WALDO HE'S GOT HAIR ALL OVER HIS LITTLE FACE! See it? See it?"

In a purely instinctive reaction Waldon rose too, knocking the hand off his head and reaching forward furiously, when Max caught his arm.

He didn't need a second reminder. Still standing, still breathing quickly, he presently managed to smile and say to Max: "It's all right." Then he looked down at Kurt, sunk into his chair again and laughing foolishly. "Get hold of yourself, Kurt," he said quietly. "You're too big a man to act like a drunken clown."

"I'll get you another glass right away, Mr. Schroeder," Max said. "It's all right, sit still." He began picking up the pieces of the one Kurt had just broken, with Kurt watching him.

"I am a drunken clown, who says I'm not?" said Kurt, and this time dropped his hand on Max's head—but luckily, quite gently. Evidently he wasn't too far gone to be rather ashamed of himself. He was smiling, and Max smiled back.

Waldon admired Max more than ever—kneeling there, picking up the glass as neatly and quickly as he did everything, and still able to smile with genuine friendliness.

To him, Waldon said clearly: "I'm sorry I wasn't able to answer your questions, Max. Yes, it's quite true they've been to Dr. Oliver's, but they only wanted to ask Miss Oliver some questions. About Mrs. Kavanaugh, you know. They wanted her help."

"Rose," Kurt mumbled. "Poor Rosie. *She* can't help anybody."

He was at the stage where he could neither shut up nor make sense, and Waldon decided to ignore him.

"I guess they're pretty hard up for help by now," he went on, to Max.

Max, getting up, shook his head.

"That was a terrible thing, Mr. Coutts. I guess nothing like that ever happened around here before—to beat a woman to death like that in her own house. Everybody's locking their doors around here since it happened, nobody ever locked doors around here before."

"Oh, I expect whoever did it is miles away by now, Max," said Waldon. "Some tramp, after her money, I guess."

"Poor old Rosie," said Kurt. "The Desperation Kid...." And turning his face up to Max, he demanded: "You ever have her, Max?"

Max wasn't embarrassed by this but just smiled, shaking his head.

"She never came here much, Mr. Schroeder. Not after she first took the millhouse. She wanted us to deliver beer to her, but we can't do that—we don't have the time. I guess she didn't like it because we couldn't deliver to her."

"HAH!" said Kurt—an enormous, explosive sound. He kept on looking up at Max, as if newly interested. "No, she wouldn't miss you, would she, Maxie? But by God, you knew enough to miss her, didn't you, boy? Didn't even need to make one teeny weeny delivery to catch on to poor old Rosie."

He sat there shaking his head, a pretty disgusting sight, but Max didn't seem to mind. Probably he was used to it by now, and knew just how to handle him.

"She was a nice-looking woman," he said now. "The papers said she was forty-seven, but she didn't look that old. Did you think so, Mr. Schroeder?"

"Maxie ..." said Kurt; and then he didn't go on with whatever it was, but began lurching to get out of his chair. "I'm gonna get some beer."

"I'll get it, just sit still," said Max. He took the carefully gathered glass away with him, and disappeared into the kitchen.

Waldon ate his hamburgers, a little embarrassed to be left holding one half of this conversation. But Kurt just sat and stared at him.

Max came back with a mop and began cleaning the floor. Kurt still didn't say anything, and neither did Max, except when he apologized for not bringing the beer first.

"I'll get it in just a minute, Mr. Schroeder," he said; and Kurt didn't even answer.

In that lull, Waldon finished his hamburgers and drained his iced coffee glass—a little quicker than he would have done, if Kurt had not been spoiling the place with his moods. He took a dollar from his jeans and put it under the hamburger plate, which paid for everything and left a tip for Max, in an unobtrusive way. Then he pushed back his chair; and as he did so, Kurt began talking again.

"What about you, Waldo?" he said. "Did Rosie ever get around to you? Or wasn't she scraping the bottom of the barrel yet?"

All of a sudden, Waldon had taken all the dirty, drunken talk that he could take. He lunged over the table and had his hands buried in Kurt's jacket before he knew what he was doing, and had him half out of his chair before Max caught his arms from behind and broke him loose. He could hear his own voice sobbing out, "Dirty, drunken swine! Filthy loud-mouthed swine—" all the time Max was bundling him towards the door. And Max was talking too, while they were struggling together across the floor: "He's drunk, Mr. Coutts—Mr. Coutts, you don't want to hit a man that's drunk—"

Well, that was true. He didn't. But it wasn't till the screen door banged behind them and they were standing together outside, in hot sunlight, that he could get hold of himself enough to drop his hands. Right away, Max dropped his too, and apologized.

"I'm sorry, Mr. Coutts, but I don't want you to do something you'd be sorry for."

"No. You're quite right, Max. And thank you," he managed to say. He held out his hand, but Max was already going in and didn't see it. Kurt was still roaring away in there, probably Max was afraid he'd break something. It was really intolerable, and he didn't see how Max stood it, or why he should.

CHAPTER FOUR

Driving away in the Volkswagen, he was relieved to find that this disagreeable incident hadn't really upset him at all. In fact, he felt better than when he came. Partly, of course, this was due to his having eaten; but he also thought that momentarily grappling with Kurt had filled some day-long need of his own. Because what he really wanted, probably, was to *fight* somebody on Buffy's behalf.

He wished he could. He wished it were that simple.

But by now, with the first shock passing off, he realized that Dr. Oliver had been right in choosing, for Buffy's champion, someone like Mel Friend. Mel wasn't, it was true, the exact choice of lawyer that Waldon himself would have made. Mel was a big name, but rather a flashy one—you almost expected anyone Mel was defending to be at least a little bit guilty. Or shady. Perhaps shady was the word he meant.

God knew, there was nothing shady about Buffy. Yet he could understand the old man turning, in the first trembling confusion of the moment, to one of the hardest, smartest fighters in the legal profession—who also happened to have become a neighbor. It was probably, on the whole, a good choice; but whether it was or not, the choice was made and he, Waldon, would have to go along with it if he wanted to be a part of her defense.

If he wanted to! He *was* a part. Nothing, no one—not Buffy herself—could have deflected him from his purpose. He had never felt such closeness with her as now—now, when he did not even know where she was, nor how he could see her or be near her. The only outer nearness he could achieve was to stay within the circle of her concerns, and those who shared them; and that was what he meant to do.

He was on his way to the Friends'.

They had bought the old Holcomb place, on Rock Hill Road, and had spent quite a lot of money fixing it up. Will Richmond, right in Beecham, had done the house, although except for the big plate-glass windows there hadn't been much to that except cleaning it up and making it sound. But they had brought some man up from New York to replan the grounds. Anita had been quite nice about it, explaining that she had worked with this man before and they "understood each other"; but their mutual understanding hadn't produced very spectacular results. Waldon still offered her suggestions, from time to time, and she had taken some of them.

Nevertheless, when he came around to the flagstone terrace where they were all sitting, and Anita rose to meet him, she didn't seem terribly friendly. It was true that he had missed a couple of appointments with her, but not without reason; and the lawn looked perfectly all right.

Commenting on it as they shook hands, he said: "I expect you used that crab grass spray, didn't you?"

"You never brought it around, Waldon," she replied; but he wasn't going to accept that.

"Good heavens, Anita, I don't sell the stuff!" he said, good humoredly. "I only mentioned it, as a recommendation."

"Oh, then I misunderstood you," she answered, and raised her eyebrows a little.

Another odd thing about Anita was the feeling he had, when using her first name, that she didn't quite like it. Which was absurd. He always made a point of using first names with all their neighbors, unless they were of an age to require the respect of a title, which Anita certainly wasn't. She was probably not used to country ways; and he felt, in firmly continuing to use her first name, that he was providing at least one little hint for her, which she could take or not.

There were several others on the terrace—mainly the Hunts. He was very fond of Marcie Hunt who wrote children's books, and he greeted her next after Anita. She asked, as she always did, after his "mama," and he replied as always that his "mother" was quite well, and longing to see her. He only nodded to Marcie's sister Edith, whose hoarse, cawey voice grated on his nerves; fortunately she spent most of the year in New York. Then he said hello, with kind brevity, to their father. Old Mr. Hunt shook quite badly out here in the clear light and mercifully didn't even try to get his hand up.

After that Anita introduced him to a Mr. Krieg (no first name mentioned) and for some reason seemed to expect that Waldon would sit down beside him. He had no objection to that, and did, accepting a gin and tonic and looking pleasantly at Krieg to size him up. He seemed young, quiet, New Yorkish. He was sizing Waldon up, too.

"Just out for the day, perhaps?" Waldon suggested. Before Krieg could get his mouth open, Edith cawed across the terrace at them: "That's Buffy's *savior*, Waldon—he just got her out of the clink, wasn't that sweet?"

A confusion, almost a dizziness, made them all disappear momentarily from Waldon's sight; but it was a very slight distress and even in the midst of it he could hear Anita's cool voice saying to him:

"Mr. Krieg is one of my husband's associates, Waldon—he couldn't get away himself today, so Mr. Krieg very kindly came up."

For some reason—just until he became more collected—Waldon didn't feel like addressing Anita or the "savior." He said sharply to Edith instead: "I wish you wouldn't say things like that, Edith—Buffy wasn't in *jail*."

"Well, as a matter of fact, she was," said Krieg's quiet voice beside him. "Special treatment and all that, of course, but still jail."

He couldn't believe his ears. He turned to stare—rude or not—at this "associate." Marcie Hunt's soothing voice reached him, speaking quickly.

"I think that was just unforgivable," she said. "I don't care how difficult Dr. Oliver is—surely they could settle their silly old zoning or road building or whatever it is without hitting below the belt like that. And at poor Buffy, too!"

"It really didn't have anything to do with zoning or road building, Marcie," Anita was replying. "Apparently Dr. Oliver refused to let them talk to Buffy and ordered them out of the house. And their answer was to take Buffy with them—which they had a right to do."

"A right!" Waldon cried, hardly able to believe his ears. "A right to take a young, well-brought-up girl out of her home and *throw her into jail?* Anita, are you out of your mind?"

She began to answer, "No, Waldon it's—" but everybody was talking at once.

Marcie's low, stubborn voice insisted: "Absolutely disgraceful, I don't care. They—" And then Edith cawed her down, bursting with horrid laughter: "Oh, don't be such a prig—how could they possibly *resist* it? After all these years, to catch that old monument with his pants down—of course they took her! Why not?"

"But they had no right to put her into the jail!" Marcie protested.

"Well—had they?" demanded Edith; and her rather crow-like eyes were dancing, Waldon thought for a moment, directly at himself. But she was asking Krieg, who said, "Well, of course, that's a point"; which made Edith start cawing again.

"So he's going to *sue!* How absolutely delicious! This can go on *indefinitely*—and we'll have something to talk about besides poor old Rosie-pants, because that's really too dreary, I don't even like to think about that."

"You're being pretty dreary yourself," said Waldon suddenly. He had never so much disliked her affected way of talking. "It's hardly so 'delicious' for Buffy, you might remember that."

"Well!" said Edith, considering him brightly. But her sister broke in quickly again.

"No, really, Edie," she said, "it isn't a joke—we mustn't treat it as if it were."

"*Is* he going to sue?" said Edith, ignoring this, and fastening avidly on Krieg again.

He said, rather commendably, "Dr. Oliver? Why don't you ask him, Mrs. Kane?" but Edith wasn't in the least abashed.

"Oh, he doesn't even *talk* to me anymore," she said. "I'm the *bad* sister—didn't you know? And as for Buffy, my love," she said, returning to Waldon, "I imagine that poor child was rather pleased to get a night off—for any reason! One jail or the other, it can't have been so awfully different from home, now can it?"

From the disagreeable way her eyes were sparkling at him, Waldon was aware that she rather hoped to make him rise and walk away, because that was an answer he had once made to her vulgarity. He would have done it again, too, except that he was determined not to oblige her in any way. So instead he began to address Marcie, just as she began to speak to him, and that made an unfortunate pause which Edith broke right into.

"Although from what I hear she does manage to find some amusement—or does she really run around naked in the fields at night?"

This time, Waldon was almost the only one who did not protest. He waited until he would be heard, and then said clearly: "You're a filthy-minded old liar, Edith."

She at once rejoined, "And you're a neurotic little pansy, darling. Grisly, isn't it?"

"There's a lawyer present to hear what you say," said Waldon.

"Uh—no, I'm afraid not," said Krieg.

Anita rose at this point (rather belatedly, perhaps by intention) and came to stand beside Waldon, who found he had got up after all.

"Would you mind talking with Mr. Krieg a moment?" she said. "Give me your glass, and I'll bring you fresh drinks indoors."

Krieg was standing by him too; for a moment Waldon felt almost hemmed-in. But this was a reaction from the adrenalin-rush engendered by Edith, and he spoke past it, pleasantly.

"Certainly—you'd like us to go in? Please don't bother about any more for me."

"I'll pass, too," said Krieg, and with a rather nice smile, which Waldon hadn't noticed before, he gestured Waldon before him, through the French windows.

As soon as they were inside Waldon said emphatically: "That was an absolute, malicious untruth about Miss Oliver. Edith doesn't even believe it herself, although I'm sure she'd love to."

"I realize that," said Krieg, still with the nice smile. So Waldon went on: "She's really quite pathological, you know. Edith. For instance, she and Mrs. Kavanaugh—who died—were almost inseparable, and you heard the way she spoke about her just now."

"Yes," said Krieg. "Well, it really wasn't Mrs. Kane I wanted to talk to you about—it's Miss Oliver, if you don't mind."

"I don't mind at all," said Waldon. "Let's sit down, shall we? It's quite a nice room, isn't it?"

It was more than that, it was a really lovely room, done in various very subtle greys, with touches of peacock and Chinese red, and black of course. He happened to know that Anita had done it all herself—and it was rather like her, with that coolness he found most restful. (Even though they didn't seem to be on the best of terms at the moment. Well, that would pass.)

"I expect the Olivers have passed on to you what I told them this morning," said Waldon, rather bravely, for he did feel a certain inner tremor about "making a statement"—even though he wanted to make it, and meant to make it, and had every right to make it.

Krieg said, "Yes—you said you'd seen Miss Oliver the night of the murder at a considerable distance from the millhouse, wasn't that it?"

"Yes, I did," said Waldon. "I saw her absolutely distinctly, from my bathroom window, and I can take you there and show you—"

Krieg interrupted him; he had taken out a notebook and pen. But that was, after all, understandable.

"Let me just get squared away first," he said. "Now—Waldon Coutts. That's two t's?"

"Yes. It's A. W., Jr., really, but my father has dibs on the Arthur—to which he's entirely welcome, I might add."

"You're A. W. Coutts' son?"

"Yes. Our address is just R.R. 3, Beecham—unless you want to put 'The Elms,' which I hope you don't."

"R.R. 3. Right," said Krieg, writing. Waldon watched, liking him better all the time. "Profession?"

"Grounds planning and care," said Waldon, promptly. "I can't bear 'landscape' for a word, can you? And in my own defense, I must say that I did not do Anita's—though I do help her struggle along with what's there."

"Right," said Krieg again. "Now the date we're talking about is August third, running into August fourth. Friday night into Saturday. You're clear about that, are you?"

"Absolutely. For one thing, of course, we all heard about Mrs.

Kavanaugh on the Saturday, which pretty well fixed that date! And for another, in case you want corroboration, my mother was giving a musicale—really she was, people still do—and I had to hang around to drive people home. Some of them come in town taxis, and then I chauffe them back afterwards."

"How about time?" Krieg asked. "Any way to fix that?"

"There certainly is, thanks to the dear old musicale. The fiddling stopped at eleven, and then everybody had to eat, and I started chauffing at eleven-thirty. That was just the Fosses, who always rush home early. They're not too young. Then—"

"Foss?" said Krieg, a little sharply. Waldon paused, not understanding why.

"Yes, Foss. F-O-S-S. Why? Oh, you want to check with all these people?"

"I don't think that'll be necessary," said Krieg. "Then what happened?"

"Yes, but what sort of bell did the Fosses ring?" said Waldon. "I mean—what sort of bell *could* they ring?"

Krieg's nice smile returned.

"Are they that dim?"

"Well, pretty dim. I never saw anybody jump when I said Foss before."

"I don't think I jumped, did I?" said Krieg, still smiling. Waldon was beginning to think him rather evasive; but as if Krieg himself agreed, he said abruptly: "I just thought I'd heard the name before, in connection with the Kavanaugh murder. They were her next-door neighbors, weren't they?"

"Yes, they were," said Waldon. And then a bell, quite clearly, rang in his own mind. "They're the ones who saw Buffy, aren't they? *Said* they saw her."

Krieg looked back at him a little too steadily, a little too long; and Waldon added: "Oh, I know you're not supposed to say. I'm not trying to embarrass you. It's just quite obvious, now—I don't know why it wasn't all along. Pious old devils! I wish I'd run them into a tree."

"Oh, come on," said Krieg, smiling again. "In the first place you're condemning them without any evidence, and in the second, even if they were the ones, it wasn't exactly a malicious report—Miss Oliver herself says she was there."

"But she *wasn't*," said Waldon. "I *know* when she thinks it over she'll realize she's mixed up about that—she couldn't possibly have run all that way in one night, not as fast as Buffy runs—it would just be superhuman."

"She runs fast, does she?" said Krieg. He looked interested; and all at once Waldon wanted to tell him about it.

"She runs beautifully," he said, in a low voice. "Like a—like a Diana through the woods." Then he added quickly: "She wears a kind of tracksuit, or shorts, or something, of course. I couldn't quite see what, but it was some dark cloth, very clearly clothing. Only a pathological mind," he said, suddenly enraged, "could imagine that she ran—without clothing, because that would *be* pathological! What Buffy does is simply a wonderful, free expression of her youth, and health, and strength—and she needs something like that, it's a rather confining life there, you know. Of course they're terribly fond of each other, but the Olivers are pretty old, and Buffy's only twenty-one, and they really do keep her pretty close. She's awfully fond of her grandfather. He doesn't even like her to go away to school, so she doesn't."

Krieg, listening thoughtfully with his eyes on his notebook, did not speak at once when Waldon had finished—which showed, Waldon thought, a nice sensitivity. Waldon was quiet too. This sympathetic conversation, in Anita's lovely room, was completely wiping away the unpleasantness of Edith for him. And of Kurt.

Then Krieg said, "Well—now about what time do you think it was, when you saw her?"

"It was about a quarter of twelve," said Waldon at once. "Between quarter to and ten to. I've figured it out by timing the drive back from those cursed Fosses and then going up to the bathroom, which is what I did that night. Possibly five to, but I don't think so."

"And you saw her clearly, running across your land?"

"Unmistakably. In the first place, it couldn't have been anybody else—and in the second place, I know Buffy terribly well, I've known her for years. I couldn't mistake the way she runs for anyone else in the world."

"I see," said Krieg. He closed his notebook, putting it away, and gave a little sigh. "Well, thanks—very good of you to tell us this. The trouble is, of course, that both Miss Oliver and the person who saw her say that she was at the millhouse later than that. Sometime later. So she could have been both places, you see. Although she says she wasn't."

"But if it was *later*—" said Waldon; and excitement rose up in him: "but *later* doesn't make any difference, does it? Wasn't Mrs. Kavanaugh already—didn't she die *earlier?*"

"Well, those estimates have to be flexible, of course," said Krieg. "Especially since the body wasn't found until mid-morning the next day. However, 'before midnight' is certainly not one-thirty in the morning, is it?"

Waldon suddenly put out his hand, and Krieg, with his pleasant smile, presently took it.

"I'm terribly glad you're here," Waldon said. "To tell you the truth, I'm glad it's you and not Mel! Oh, it's nothing against Mel, please don't think that. But I feel that you, as a person, have Buffy's interest really at heart. Isn't that true?"

"She's certainly a most appealing young woman," said Krieg.

Going back out to the terrace, Waldon almost felt as if he were walking on air. He didn't even mind seeing Edith again—although as a matter of fact he didn't, since Marcie had taken her and their father away; and he took Anita's hand with a real surge of affection for her.

"You're wonderful, Anita," he said. "And I adore your room. I hope Mel knows how lucky he is. I do."

She smiled back—gave quite a cheerful laugh, really—so that was all patched up, too.

It had been a real stroke of luck, coming here. He leaned out and waved at them, as he drove the Volkswagen away.

CHAPTER FIVE

He felt so calmed by all this that he decided just to go home. Anyway, it was getting on towards time to clean up for dinner. He and his mother had their dinner early during the week, when they were alone. "Keeping country hours," his mother called it—and then it made a nice long evening, too, which she enjoyed. Driving by the Fosses, he almost changed his mind and stopped, and went in to have it out with them. But he had hardly begun to slow before he put the accelerator down again. No. Not now. He was too much drained by his long day of excitements, and he wouldn't handle it well. He hadn't even formulated clearly to himself just what it was he wanted to handle. At the moment, he only wanted to knock their silly old heads together for them—which wouldn't be much help to Buffy!

Smiling, he drove on, enjoying the speed of his sturdy pickup and the way it answered to his handling, however sudden. There were no cars in their driveway, thank goodness—he went round the back, dodging Martha Mary's Plymouth, and ran the Volkswagen into the garage.

But once in, he sat frowning, wondering if he really wanted to put the pickup away for the night. It was impossible to get it out again unnoticed, which always meant questions. Should he take it on back to his clearing, just in case? Thinking of the clearing, the workshop, reminded him suddenly of the dogs. He said aloud, "Oh, Lord—" and started to back out again.

But there was his mother, already coming across the gravel with that worried look on her face! He leaned and called to her:

"Can't stop now, mother! I'll be back soon—Buffy's dogs are frying down in that damn' workshop!"

She didn't seem to understand any of this, but at least she did stop, and he shot away.

The sun was off the aluminum roof of the garage by now, but the air inside was awfully uncomfortable. The dogs didn't even get up when he came in, but they did make faint noises, and move their tails—he was starting to pat one when he noticed it had been sick, very messily. He groaned, and then picked it up anyway and carried it out on the grass. They probably wouldn't start running around until he could leash them up out here, and he didn't want to spend any more time in that smelly oven of a garage than he had to.

They started walking around pretty soon, making prolonged puddles right in front of the door, but he let them. Then he tied them all up with a long, rather cleverly arranged length of rope and left them outdoors while he went back inside to see about their pans, and the mess.

It really was a mess. He couldn't even think how to begin dealing with it; and finally he decided just to let Josephine come down and give the place a good cleaning tomorrow—his mother had been wanting him to, anyway, and it would please her. He also decided to feed them all outdoors, for a treat, and even to leave them there until later. They'd be perfectly safe, and he could lock them up before dark.

He mixed up their mush, or whatever it was, with water, the way the directions said, and then took the pans out and put them down in a row. Two of the dogs seemed fine, and came right up to eat; he sat down by the one that didn't and petted her for a while—even offered her some food on his hand, but she wasn't ready.

It was nice in the clearing, in the late afternoon, just sitting there with Buffy's dogs. He lay down with the droopy one in the circle of his arm and stroked her, and looked up through the leaves at the sky, thinking about Buffy. Or starting to—because when he put his head back on the ground the other dogs came running up to nuzzle his ears, and when he tried to push them away they thought he was playing.

He sat up again, and took the sad female on his lap, talking to her. She tried to lick his face, in return. Dachshunds really had awfully sad eyes. Her nose felt cool enough, he thought she would probably perk up all right and get hungry later.

He was certainly hungry! The two hamburgers he had had to gulp down on account of poor old Kurt were just a memory now, and Anita's delicious gin had made him quite interested in food. He said goodbye to the dogs, and was pleased to hear them whining after him as he walked away. He turned round a couple of times and called out to them reassuringly, but that only made them begin to yelp, so he went on.

His mother, good Lord, was still standing there at the back of the house, looking around rather foggily as if she thought he might drop down from anywhere! He felt a surge of affection for her, she looked so helpless and patient, and quite pretty, really, in her nice green chiffon. He waved, to fix her attention, but she didn't smile—just went on looking anxious.

"What are you frowning about, sweetie?" he asked; but of course she wouldn't say, just got self-conscious, and tried to smile back at him. One of the more hopeless aspects of parents was the way they couldn't change, with the best will in the world; in some ways he thought it would have been better just to let her go on pouring anxiety all over him every time he came home, instead of standing there holding it in.

He said, to help her out, "I know you've had dozens of phone calls, and you didn't know where I was, and you're cross as a witch, and I don't blame you! Now—better?"

Even then she shrank a little from his arm. He looked at her questioningly, and she murmured: "Darling ... such a funny *odor* ... whatever is it?"

He said a little shortly, "Oh—sorry. One of Buffy's dogs was sick. I'll go clean up."

He couldn't smell it himself; but the idea was rather disgusting. He took the back stairs two at a time and was in his bathroom, stripping, by the time she came. He could hear her moving about in his room, pulling out drawers, and he called to her: "Just a white shirt, mother, and those midnight-blue Bermudas—I'm not going out again."

He spent a long while under the shower, sluicing himself from head to toe and enjoying, as always, the water's cool renewal of all his parts. His mother handed him clean underpants through the door; and with these on, and his hair and moustaches sleekly brushed, he came cheerfully out to join her.

She was sitting by the window, and her body looked relaxed, but her face didn't. As if aware of this, she looked out towards the garden as soon as he came in.

"Well, what a day I've had," he said, deciding to overlook this. He made his voice a little cheerier than he felt. "Every bore in Beecham, one right after the other. I really don't understand how Marcie and Edith Hunt came out of the same box—if they did! What on earth was old Mrs. Hunt like? I really don't remember her at all."

"Oh, quite nice, dear. Very nice."

It was such a flat, sad little reply, leading nowhere, that he gave up and went on dressing in silence. Then, of course, she began to fidget.

"Oh—Mr. Foss called, Waldon. He was just wondering if you'd got their power mower fixed."

"No, I haven't," he said. "And if they're going to hang on my neck about it this way they can just take it into town and pay Holland a fortune to ruin it for them. I'm only doing it for a favor, after all."

"I know, dear."

He was silent, thinking of the Fosses, and she was silent too—thinking about whatever it was *she* was thinking about. Luckily, just then, he noticed the belt she had put in his shorts and gave a cry of pleasure.

"My Guatemala belt! Where did you find it?"

"On the closet floor," she said, "away at the back. I knew it had to be somewhere."

In this mutual pleasure, they had their first moment of real contact; and with a little effort he made it last them downstairs. Ordinarily at that point she would have gone out to Martha Mary, while he made their Martinis; but tonight like an awkward wraith she hovered behind him in the living room.

He looked at her inquiringly, and she was looking away from the *Beecham News*, unfolded on the couch. Ordinarily this distinguished journal lay unopened on the hall table until Josephine threw or took it away the next morning—unless someone wanted to look up a local movie—and for a moment he didn't follow.

Then he did. And without a word sat down and picked it up. His mother didn't make a sound.

The story about Buffy was on the top half of the front page, under one of the awkward headlines of which they seemed to be masters: Miss Eleanor Oliver Questioned About Kavanaugh Death. He began to read the story with serious care, forming his opinion as he read; on the whole, he thought they had handled it well—for them.

He read: "Miss Eleanor Boes Oliver, granddaughter of Dr. Boes Oliver, world-famous composer and a longtime resident of Beecham, was questioned today by Police Chief Edgar Egan for possible information regarding Mrs. Rose Kavanaugh, whose brutal murder on the night of August 3 still remains unsolved. Miss Oliver, 21, is understood to have been in the neighborhood of the Millhouse on Fern Hollow Road, Mrs. Kavanaugh's residence, near the hour at which the crime was committed.

"Interviewed by this reporter, Miss Oliver (known to her many friends as 'Buffy') stated: 'I want to help in any way I can, but there is nothing

I can say except that I did not see Rose (Mrs. Kavanaugh) or anyone else near the house that night. I was not in the house or on the grounds, I was only passing by.'

"Miss Oliver, well-known locally as a fancier of thoroughbred dachshunds, was accompanied by Mr. Gavin Krieg, attorney, of New York, an associate in the well-known firm of Bechman and Friend. Mr. Melvin Friend, partner, resides on Rock Hill Road in Beecham.

"Dr. Oliver could not be reached for comment."

Waldon put the paper down feeling, on the whole, quite pleased. He said to his mother, with a little twinkle, "Well—nothing about *jail*, anyway!" but she stood there absolutely unresponsive.

Beginning to be a bit annoyed—what on earth *was* it?—he added, sharper: "Do you want a drink? Or would you rather just eat? I'm starving."

"Oh—I'll tell Martha Mary," she said, and went away in a hurry. If she was going to be like this all evening, he was in no hurry to have her come back!

At the table, he let her see he was tired of it; so of course she began floundering around trying to find some way out. First it was Martha Mary, and how sorry she was that Martha Mary had come in with that nasty gossip before he was really awake, she knew how it upset him. He let that pass. Then it was something about Marcie Hunt, and how she, his mother, really hadn't understood what Marcie was talking about but whatever it was Marcie did want to apologize, and she (Marcie) also wanted him to know that he mustn't pay any attention to Edith because of course nobody believed those stories about Buffy. "Those stories about Buffy ..." said his mother, in a failing voice, "Buffy ... running, without ..."

Her face had gone quite strange. It took him a moment to realize (because of the deceptive candlelight) that she was blushing! That was really the end. He put his napkin on the table and said in a cutting voice: "It really isn't an indecent subject, mother. Unless, of course, you believe it."

She only began to cry. For a moment he was too much taken aback to do anything—and then, of course, he realized there was nothing to do. Either she would stop, or she would get up and leave the table; on the whole, he was relieved when she got up and left. His own eyes stung a little too—mainly from unbearable annoyance—but he put his napkin back and did his best to go on eating, until Martha Mary came in. She didn't say anything, but she didn't go away, either, until he told her to, quite sharply.

But after that it was hopeless. He got up and went into the music room after his mother, feeling almost ugly, what with the unreasonableness of it, and his lost dinner, too.

The room was shadowy, and she hadn't turned on any lights, of course, but was sitting with her head down on the piano, sobbing away. He sat on the bench too, but not close, and he didn't touch her. She knew he was there.

After a while he asked, in a low voice, "Are you *trying* to hurt me, mother?" At once she turned and flung herself upon him, and he did hold her then, gently stroking her back. His anger was going down, but he felt terribly sad, it was so hopeless.

"Oh, my darling," she sobbed, "don't you know I would *die* to keep hurt away from you? Don't you know it *is* death to me, to know that these things can touch you—that I can't hold them away—that it's like watching you drown in deep water when I can't reach you, *I can't even swim?*"

He didn't understand this one at all; but he did begin to feel a little frightened, she was so terribly vehement about it.

Feeling totally inadequate, he could only go on holding her, and ask: "But what *is* it, mama? I don't even know what you're talking about! What's wrong?"

He was holding her quite tightly by then, but she began separating them—straightening herself up, and pushing back her hair, and wiping her eyes. He didn't look at her face; he didn't like to, when she cried like that, and she seemed to know it. She turned her head away.

He said in a less subdued—almost a coaxing voice: "Honestly, mother, I just haven't a clue, can't you tell me what it is? You know I wouldn't do anything to make you feel this way. Don't you?"

"I know dear," she said, quiet again. She put her hand over his and held it tightly; but her fingers couldn't stay still, she kept working them upon his hand. Her fingers were very strong, from the piano.

"Well, then, what is it?" he said, a little less patiently. She surprised him then with a little smile—almost a real one, quite natural.

"Nothing, darling," she said. "Just my foolishness."

"Well, your foolishness is my foolishness," he replied, light. "Come on—what is it?"

She just went on looking at him, smiling faintly, and shook her head.

"You don't really believe those stories about Buffy, now, do you?"

He hated even to ask her; but he had to begin somewhere. Otherwise they could just go on sitting here all night. She didn't make either a yes or no gesture in reply, but she did turn her head a little, so that they were no longer looking into each other's eyes. He felt relieved enough to let annoyance back into his voice.

"Oh, really, mother—that's fantastic! What's got into you?"

She said then in a different voice, listless, almost indifferent: "She does run at night, Waldon. I've known it for some time."

"Well, of course she does! I know it too, I've seen her! But what's wrong with that? She has all her *clothes* on," he added; but for some reason his throat constricted as he spoke—he couldn't imagine why, because she *had* been clothed, the time he saw her.

Had there been other times? Did his mother know of these? Or was it just some more of her damned mystification? He would never know; experience told him that much. And in the face of this knowledge, he began to feel a total fatigue for the whole subject. And an unreasonably deep depression, that added to the fatigue.

As if his mother had sensed this, she rose, but still kept his hand.

"Come on, darling," she said. "Forgive me, and come back and eat your dinner. Please, darling."

Her voice broke slightly on the last words, so he did get up and go back with her, but he certainly didn't feel much like eating now. However, he sat down and replaced his napkin. Then, as if *he* had been the one to leave the table in tears, she now set herself to cajole and placate him, and to make innocent conversation, and to urge him to eat. Actually, once he began, the food did revive his appetite; but it was longer before he could take much interest in what she was saying.

As if she understood this, and were bravely determined to engage him at any cost, she began in a light voice to speak of Buffy again.

"You know, when I heard Buffy's dogs this afternoon, I really got quite worried for you," she said, smiling.

He looked up.

"Oh, could you hear them? I'm terribly sorry, I thought—"

"Oh, they didn't disturb me," she said. "Actually they sounded so far away I couldn't imagine where it was coming from, and then Martha Mary said she thought it was from your workshop, so I put two and two together. I didn't go down, of course," she added quickly.

"Why, I don't care, mother. Go down any time you like."

"No, darling, that's your own place—no one goes near it unless you say so. But when—"

That reminded him; and he interrupted her to say, before he forgot: "By the way, I wish you would have Josephine go down tomorrow and sort of swab the garage out. Or is that something she's likely to get balky about?"

"No, no, dear—I'll be very happy to get it cleaned up for you. What time would you like us to go down?"

"Oh, any time, I don't care." Then he caught, in retrospect, the "us."

"But I don't want you doing it, mother! If Josephine needs help, let Martha Mary help her—surely she doesn't need all day to prepare the little we eat!"

"Oh, Martha Mary's very useful to me," she said. "Though I must admit I get rather weary of all her gossip. For instance, when we heard the dogs this morning, she said—"

"Or how about McKinnon?" he asked suddenly, remembering this dour unhandyman of theirs. "Where on earth is the man, anyway? I haven't seen him in days."

"Well, darling, *he's* been here, it's you that hasn't," she replied; and her rather turned-away expression reminded him that he had interrupted her.

He said, "I'm sorry, what were you saying?" and she answered, "It doesn't matter, dear"; and he prompted her: "About Buffy's dogs," and then she said, "Oh, yes—well nothing important, only Martha Mary's funniness," and she smiled.

He persisted, with that inner drawing-together that warned him it *might* be important, "Funniness about what—the dogs, or Buffy?"

"Well, both, I suppose. When we heard them crying so, you know, Martha Mary got quite worried, and she said she did hope nothing happened to them while they were over here because Miss Oliver did set such store by her dogs, and did I remember how she almost killed Mrs. Kavanaugh over that puppy? Of course I told her she was being ridiculous, and that Buffy—"

"But what an absolutely foul, stupid thing to go around saying!" he cried.

Unfortunately, just at that moment Martha Mary came in. He gave her a furious look, and was silent; but the moment she went out he began: "That's sheer malice, mother, because there wasn't anything even resembling a fight! Buffy simply—"

"I know, dear, I know. It's nothing to get excited about. I only mentioned it because—"

"But it is something to get excited about! At a time like this, to have her going around saying Buffy 'almost killed' Rose—it's an absolute lie!"

At that moment, quite without warning, he felt a bewilderment that stopped his words. Why? What was it? He looked at his mother; but if he had said something wrong she did not seem to have remarked it. Quite badly rattled, he nevertheless made himself go on.

"What happened was that Buffy simply went down and took the puppy back—that was all there was to it," he finished—a lame finish, he knew. What on earth was wrong with him?

"I know, dear, but then when the puppy did die after all, you remember there was so much talk—"

"But that wasn't Buffy! She never said a word to anybody about it! It was simply that idiotic Kavanaugh woman's conscience driving her all over the place to explain that it wasn't her fault, that she'd given the puppy the best of care, and it wouldn't have died if Buffy had left it with her, and so on. All of which was the sheerest bilge, and everybody knew it! She did neglect it, and she did go away and leave it shut up alone several times, and everybody knew that too—Buffy never said a word, she didn't have to! It was Mrs. Kavanaugh who did all the talking!"

It was perfectly clear: he couldn't imagine what had been wrong with him before, for a moment. And he said, to complete his recovery: "I suppose Buffy did feel terribly unhappy about the puppy, but she never complained to anyone. It was entirely Mrs. Kavanaugh—she started the talk, and she kept it up!"

His mother looked so gentle, so overwhelmed, beyond the waning candles, that he felt some regret for his vehemence.

"I do hope you'll explain all this to old mush-brain, before she poisons the neighborhood," he added, in joking apology.

"Yes, dear, I will. But please don't call her that, she'll hear you one day."

Only when they were going into the music room, to play for a little while until the mosquitoes went away and they could go out on the lawn, did his mother tell him about the telephone call. Then all she said was, "Oh—Buffy wants you to bring the dogs home, Waldon."

He could only stare at her.

"She didn't say when—I suppose morning would be all right, wouldn't it?"

"Buffy called me up?"

"Yes, dear. She just asked if you would please bring the dogs home."

"But when?" he said, beginning to flush. "What—why didn't you tell me? When—what did she say?"

She just looked at him patiently, to make clear that she had already answered this; and then the next thing he knew he was walking out into the hall—walking fast, away from her. When he went through the kitchen door he gave its frame a sudden wild blow that hurt his hand, but made him feel better. Martha Mary gave him one of her silent looks, and he glared back at her, and slammed the screen as hard as he could.

CHAPTER SIX

It was almost dark in the clearing, especially under the trees where the dogs were tied, and he had quite a time getting them off the communal rope and on to their respective leashes. He could tell one female by her being the listless one, but the other two dogs were just dachshunds, period, so far as he was concerned, and he certainly wasn't going to go feeling around to find out which ones got hitched together. What possible difference could it make anyway?

The main thing was to get going, as fast as he could. His fingers were clumsy with desperate will to recapture all that time—how long had it been?—since Buffy had called him. It couldn't have been so awfully long ago—she hadn't been home very long. Or had she?

Driving over, very fast, he made up his mind to ask her, in some casual way, what time she had called. As though he had forgotten to ask his mother. Unless, of course, he saw no one but Miss Min. Sometimes that happened. He was glad he had thought of that possibility in advance, and began planning reasons why he would have to speak to Buffy herself. Although surely, surely she would want to thank him herself for caring for her dogs—after all, none of them had known it would be only for the day.

The gate was open again, thank heaven, and as he came bucketing up the drive he saw two figures sitting in the old-fashioned face-to-face lawn swing, mildly swinging. So he needn't have worried. Buffy and her grandfather, swinging and talking in the deep dusk—he had seen them do that before; and it was a communion—of love; of age and youth—that touched him deeply. He drew to a gentle halt, and got out.

Buffy had seen him too, and was coming towards him. She was wearing shorts, as she did nearly all summer, and with her lovely long legs swinging freely, her wide shoulders so beautifully held, she did indeed have the air of a Diana. She called out something to him; but her words, and any answer he might have made, were drowned by a terrible answering racket from the dogs in the body of the pickup. He turned and unfastened the door and they shot out instantly—sprawling, recovering and racing towards her. At least, two of them did—one, crying pitifully, was still hesitating over the jump to the ground.

He was going to help it when Buffy came up and bent over, saying: "Why, Cookie, what's the matter with you? A little jump like that!" and she picked it up and held it, which made the other two frantic. Then she did turn and speak to him, smiling, but nobody could have heard a word of it.

The other person in the swing came up now, and Waldon saw with some surprise that it was not Dr. Oliver but Krieg. It seemed rather odd; but Waldon put out his hand and spoke politely (inaudibly, in the circumstances) and Krieg smiled his pleasant smile. It was rather interesting that his name should be Gavin—actually, the first Gavin Waldon had met; and he wondered if perhaps Krieg had been born in the British Isles. It was something they might discuss, later, when it became possible to be heard.

Buffy sat down on the grass then, to entertain and quiet all her dogs, and that left Krieg and himself *vis-à-vis* with nothing particular to say to each other. That was all right, except that Krieg's first remark was: "We'd just about given you up."

"Oh, really, why? Buffy knows I'm no dognapper."

It was a silly reply; but after all how did one answer so strange an opening? *We* had just about, indeed. Waldon said to the top of Buffy's head, rather crossly, "I forgot their food."

"It doesn't matter, I've lots."

She looked up at him then. In the poor light her face seemed ghostly, even sad; and he was sorry for his crossness.

She asked, "What's wrong with Cookie? She seems so strange."

"Strange how?" he said. He got down beside her, putting his hand on the little dog's head as she lay back in Buffy's lap. "Maybe that's the one that didn't eat it's dinner. Why don't you try feeding it?"

"She didn't eat? But she's terribly greedy! Did she have any kind of an accident?"

"Good heavens, no! What kind of an accident could she have, in my clearing? It's quiet as the grave."

"You weren't—running machines, or something?" she said, hesitant.

"Now, really, Buffy!" He took his hand away and got up, saying to Krieg to mask his annoyance: "Coutts, the mad scientist, no less."

Buffy got up and started back towards the swing, still carrying her dog. Krieg and he came after her.

"I thought you'd be back in New York by now," said Waldon, as they went along.

"Well, not quite yet. I can't say I'm sorry, it's very pleasant out here."

"Yes, much cooler. You're staying here, with the Olivers?"

"No, Mrs. Friend's putting me up."

"Oh," said Waldon. "Well, that must be pleasant."

A perfectly ridiculous exchange. And the worst of it was, he was already thinking of Krieg as Gavin, just because the name interested him so. He wasn't at all ready to start calling him Gavin … if he ever would be. Then it occurred to him that Krieg's staying on probably meant that Dr. Oliver was going to sue; and in the interest of this thought he sat down beside Buffy in the swing, without thinking twice about it. This became doubly awkward because Gavin—Krieg—didn't sit down at all. He was kneeling in the grass having some sort of mild roughhouse with one of the dogs—which he would soon regret, because they never wanted to stop.

"What's this one's name?" he asked.

"That's MacTavish," said Buffy; and, monomaniac, she turned back to Waldon. "Cookie's been bred, you see, and last time it wasn't successful. She seemed so well this time, I can't understand it."

"Well, I must say you're making me feel like a murderer, Buffy," he said. "For goodness' sake let me take her over to the vet, and be done with it."

"Actually, I was wondering if Dr. Silver would be there," she said. "I'm sorry—I'm not blaming you, Waldon. But she is so strange! Perhaps it's just because I went away."

"This one seems fine," said Krieg, still fending it off. It came back each time in wilder leaps, as Waldon saw with morose satisfaction.

"Well, go in and call," he said. "Here—I'll hold her. And if he's there, I'll take her over. I won't be able to sleep, thinking of you sitting here mooning over her all night and blaming me. Go in and call him."

"I'm not blaming you," she said again. "You would have noticed if anything had happened ... wouldn't you?"

"Oh, God," he said; and they were both silent.

Now the other dog had joined the game on the grass—which was getting out of hand, in Waldon's opinion. Buffy did nothing to check it. Neither did she go in and call the vet. The truth was that she could be terribly irritating at times, in a sort of passive, stubborn way. He supposed it was the reverse side, the accompanying flaw, of her gentle, childlike character, which seemed so heart-melting when he was away from her. Rather like his mother, whom he loved best when he wasn't home.

Also, Buffy brought out in him an amazing tendency to nag, which he resented, whether she seemed to or not. He realized it was up to him to control his tendency, since Buffy would never do anything about it but walk away. After all, since his was the more mature character, it was up to him to accept responsibility for their joint behavior when they were together, and he did accept it—was, in fact, on the point of turning to her with some new, pleasanter topic, when Krieg went out of his mind.

He suddenly went down quite flat on the lawn and began going over in side rolls, and then rolling back, covered with leaping dogs. And laughing, in what could be described as a series of giggles. It was a pretty embarrassing performance, among comparative strangers, and apparently Krieg realized this—he got up almost at once and began talking to the dogs in a sterner voice, saying: "All right, that's enough. No more. Down, now"—a perfect waste of time, of course.

"Come, get in the swing," said Buffy finally. "They won't follow you, because the floor pinches their feet."

He was obliged to do this, brushing at his suit and obviously trying to find something to say about his behavior. What he finally produced was: "I haven't had a dog since I lived at home"; which Waldon considered so perfect that he just let it lie there, in the evening air.

Then Buffy, after due consideration, replied: "Do you live someplace where you could have a puppy?"

"Well, in an apartment," he said. "That's not much of a deal for a dog, a New York apartment."

"I think it's all right for small ones," she said. "If you had someone to look after it during the day."

"No, I'm afraid I haven't. I share with another fellow, and we're both gone all day."

"Oh, well then you couldn't," she said. And at last, revealing the intricate workings of her beloved mind, she confessed: "I was thinking of giving you one of Cookie's puppies, if you wanted one."

"Gosh, I wish I could," he said. "I really do."

It was the kind of conversation that made Waldon feel as if his feet were being tickled—a sort of unbearable pleasure, which he bore in quiet as long as possible. Now he inquired, very quietly, "What kind of a dog did you have, when you lived at home?"

Krieg was seriously getting ready to answer this when Buffy, or the dog she held, or perhaps both of them together, made a sharp sound of distress. Then Buffy was looking up with quite a desperate expression— looking across the swing, at Krieg.

"I just *touched* her," she said. "I don't even know where! Oh—"

The dog cried again, and both Buffy and Krieg got up, teetering on the moving floor of the swing. Waldon tried to hold the seat for her and got his finger pinched, and while he was immobilized by this Buffy and Krieg got down and started walking away towards the house.

Buffy was saying, "He lives right next door to the hospital, and he doesn't mind my coming there if it's an emergency, but they do go out sometimes—I don't—"

They were going so rapidly that Waldon didn't catch up until they had reached the house. Then he had to get in front of Buffy to stop her.

"Look," he said, "just *give* me the dog, please, and I'll—"

Then she recoiled. That wasn't, of course, the exact word; but it was the one that came, afterwards, back and back into his mind, when he thought he was rid of it.

Drew back, drew back, he said over to himself, on the drive home. I simply startled her, and she drew back. And then Krieg opened the screen and she went in and I just left, I had enough and I left, if she's going to act that way let her do it herself. Krieg can take her over, if he's such a big dog-man. The whole thing is perfect nonsense, and she drew back. I only said ... and then she re—she drew back, she drew back, and Krieg opened the screen and I just left. She drew back.

This kind of intent thinking went on for quite a while, he couldn't stop it—like some dreary machine he had to watch until it ran down. It did run down, by the time he got home; and that was when he began to realize how miserable he was.

CHAPTER SEVEN

It was absolutely ridiculous to be so miserable about nothing.

He didn't even realize what was wrong until he found that he had come back to his private road and was bumping slowly along that, into his clearing. Even then, watching the ruts, he half-assumed there was some reason for his coming here—that he had left something undone around the workshop and come back to set it right before going on to the house.

Only when he had turned off his motor and lights and got down into what was, now, absolute dark—when he had to stand there, silent in so much surrounding silence, could he begin to assess the weight of misery he had brought with him.

There simply wasn't the least reason for it. He was always having this sort of up-in-the-air encounter with Buffy, and it never made any difference afterwards, neither of them thought of mentioning it again. As for Krieg, whom he had no intention of calling Gavin at any time, ever, he didn't in the least care what Krieg thought—if he did think.

Then what was the matter with him? It was frightening to be so miserable for no reason. Was he overtired? Or on the contrary, did he need to pitch in and do something tremendously physical before he went to bed?

He had a brief vision of attaching the hose and just flooding out that filthy garage, leaving it open to dry out before morning. Should he? But then he would need to move out a lot of stuff first—power mowers and spare parts and things that had got piled up in there. Or would a good drenching do them any harm?

He made one tentative movement towards the garage and was instantly assailed by such a *vertigo* of misery—as though movement stirred up what had begun to settle—that he stood still again, quite frightened.

What in *hell* was it?

I didn't know the damned thing was pregnant, he thought. My God, no. Sitting there under the tree holding a sackful of puppy embryos—he wouldn't have done it on a bet. And what difference did it make anyway? What earthly difference did it make?

Well, I can't stand here all night, he thought—a little crust of impatience forming over the abyss within him. Perhaps he ought to take off all his clothes and have a good sluicing under the hose, like that other time. Run naked up to the house, dodging through trees, and scoot up the back stairs! That had been exciting, in a strange, shameful way. He didn't really think it was something he wanted to do twice, though. And for no reason.

Because what reason could there be? It was Buffy who ran at night, but not naked. His mother had dreamed that. There wasn't any reason at all to take off his clothes, and risk losing his Guatemala belt again.

He was getting quite confused, and saw that the point had come where he would have to take a strong hold on himself. If he couldn't walk towards the garage then he would simply have to go the other way, towards the house. He tried that, and it seemed all right. By the time he got halfway he was breathing quite normally again, and inclined to be scornful of the whole thing.

All right, it had been a bad moment; but there was no reason for it at all. And he hoped Dr. Silver was sitting through a double feature somewhere. Twice. Then they'd have a good long chance for fascinating exchanges. Do you like dogs? Yes, I do. Well, how do you spell dog? Honestly.

He began looking ahead to see what houselights were on—none in the kitchen, of course, Martha Mary was gone long ago. And none upstairs, except Josephine's, away up. At the same time he became aware of hearing the piano, very faint. The music room was at the other side of the house. He came on, listening, and discovered that his mother was playing Brahms. Pretty thoughtfully, too. *That* wasn't anything he wanted to walk into.

He stopped in a movement that was almost a recoil. Then, recognizing this, he said aloud: "No, no—I recoil"; but it didn't seem amusing out loud. Not all by himself.

What he wanted, damn it, was some civilized company! But whose? Actually, if it hadn't been for all that hoo-ha, it might have been rather nice to go and get drunk with old Kurt. Sometimes if he showed up late with a fifth of good Scotch Kurt behaved quite pleasantly—at least until they were both so drunk it didn't matter. Probably the poor devil never saw decent liquor unless someone gave it to him. But if he went out tonight, it might look like an apology, and after all Kurt was the one who ought to apologize.

No; not Kurt.

He didn't particularly want to go to a town bar in his Bermudas—he had done it once, and the combination of his shorts and his moustaches had been a little too conspicuous for the town wits. A perfectly wild idea came into his head of driving down to New York, and for a moment he felt quite excited about it. But where would he sleep? He probably wouldn't be in any condition to drive back again, and he didn't know any hotel he could just stumble into—nor did he like to take a chance on digging up some friend from the old days, who would be still there, and still a friend. That ghastly club was out of the question, of course, as was the apartment, with his father there alone. No, he had better not go.

Standing there at the edge of the woodlot, gnawing a little at his moustaches, Waldon began to consider his chances of getting into the house and changing and getting out again, uncaught. The trouble was that, alone and waiting for him, his mother would be all ears. Unless she was really wrapped up in old Brahms, and not just killing time.

He came on, listening more exactly. Why the devil couldn't she have been playing Liszt, or something? Maunder, maunder, maunder—the stuff sounded like the old boy wrote it at night trying not to wake people up. And then forgetting—BOOM BOOM BOOM, till somebody banged on the floor, and then back to maunder maunder maunder.

Well, he would have to risk it. He moved resolutely forward; and as if in reward for his decisiveness it occurred to him he had a perfectly good excuse. He was taking Buffy in to the vet, and needed long pants. What could be simpler? Of course that would open the whole question of why they had to go to the vet and had he done something to the precious dogs; but a little tickle of rage at the back of his mind told him he would simply lose his temper at that point, and that would be that.

Nobody interfered with him at all. He walked right in, through the dark kitchen, up the back stairs and into his room. Turned on the light, chose, changed; light off, down the stairs, and out again. And the pickup down in the clearing. What could be better?

Goodbye, mother, goodbye, Brahms, goodnight, ladies, we're going to leave you now! "Civilized company" was probably a big fat euphemism for what he was going to find in any Beecham bar, but who cared? He didn't. There were always a lot of fellows from the road construction outfit hanging around Dorfie's, for instance, ready to argue about anything you could name. And so was he, by God, so was he.

The Volkswagen sped along beautifully, eating up the night road into town.

CHAPTER EIGHT

His mother came in and woke him up the next morning.

He was startled enough by this—she didn't even have a cup of coffee, for excuse—that he got right up on his elbows and stared at her.

Without a word she put the newspapers she was carrying down on his bed. He saw that they were the New York tabloids, which she never read, and had a nightmare sense of being still asleep, caught in some senseless dream.

Somebody had to say something, so he mumbled at her: "Where did you get those things?"

"Martha Mary got them. I asked her to stop by Marty's on her way this morning and pick up those holders for your father, and she saw these. Of course she brought them right to me."

Why of course? He couldn't begin to think, let alone read, but he understood now that it was about Buffy. Probably pretty bad.

He sat up, touching his head with tentative fingers, and his mother sat down beside him.

"Waldon, this is getting out of hand. I think I ought to tell your father about it."

"Good God," he said. "Whatever for?"

"Because I think he ought to use his influence. The Olivers are one of the most respected families here, and this oughtn't to be allowed—*whatever* has happened."

This was his mother at her worst—with the civic mold of Mrs. A. W. Coutts trembling all over her, like jello. He looked at her resentfully, and then pushed at her with his imprisoned legs.

"I wish you'd let me get *up* first," he said. "What time is it?"

She got up, but didn't yield much otherwise.

"I'm thinking seriously of calling him up," she said.

"Well, it's your funeral. Besides, what's the use? He'll be coming up tonight, won't he?"

"There might be something he could do down in New York," she replied.

He couldn't even decide whether this was an idiotic remark or not, until he could pull himself together, so he just went past her into the bathroom and shut the door. When he came out, tidy but not much happier, the papers were gone. That meant she was going to sit on them until he came and read them in her presence, so they could talk.

Well, he didn't really care. He wasn't in awfully much of a hurry to see what they said. He could guess. And after all, what more could he do? At the moment, he would just as soon leave the mopping up to Mr. Canine Krieg—as Mel Friend had apparently decided to do, too.

He came down, yawning, and found the papers left on the breakfast table for him—so she must have had a change of heart. His was the only place set, which meant it must be late, because his mother usually waited until nine-thirty or so for him. He touched the bell, and Martha Mary came in and told him it was quarter to eleven.

He said, "Damn"; and then: "I wonder if I had any appointments this morning...."

That was rhetorical, but she answered it.

"Yes, you did, Mr. Waldon—you were going to put in those little trees for Mrs. Duncan and she called up about it. But I told her you probably wouldn't get there this morning and did she want you to come this afternoon, but she said no, she wouldn't be there."

"Well, that was pretty officious of you, Martha Mary," he answered coldly; but she only said, "Thank you, Mr. Waldon," and asked him what he wanted to eat. Hopeless.

The papers lay there in front of him while he was drinking his coffee. He gave them a straightening push to see the headlines, but didn't open them yet. One paper had just two big words: DEB SLAYER? but the other crowded in more detail. COMPOSER'S KIN HELD IN CONN BLUDGEON DEATH, it said, down in one corner like an afterthought. Deb Slayer had a picture of Buffy, and this was what he studied longest.

It must have been an old picture, because she was wearing a suit—a tweedy suit—and a hat, of all things. She never wore hats, her short curly hair was like a cap in itself, and he looked at the hat for some time. On the whole, he thought it wasn't a success. The picture was cut off at one of her hands, held stiffly out for no apparent reason, and he finally figured out that this was a snap from some dog show, and she had been holding the dogs on a leash. She looked very tall, which she was, and awkward and plain, which she was not. The longer he looked, the more touching he found this private view of Buffy at one of the most serious moments of her life revived now and thrust on every loutish notice for remark. Deb Slayer, indeed! He wondered if perhaps his father couldn't do something about that—have somebody fired, or something. But the trouble with getting his father involved was that he never did what you wanted but only what he thought was proper, and it always turned out to be endlessly dreary and complicated. No; better keep papa out.

Where was his mother, anyway?

Getting up from the table, he considered asking—then reconsidered, and went out by the music room doors. Round the back, he got right to the garage before he remembered he had left the pickup down in the clearing—something he always did when he came in late, to break his mother of the habit of listening for him to drive in. Well; did he want it badly enough to walk down? Where should he go when he had it? It was too late to pick up the little ginkgoes and go on out to Duncan's, but he could—probably should—keep yesterday's missed appointment with old Peabody; that was just a grape arbor.

Or should he fix the Fosses' power mower and take it over? That would put him in a strong position to give them hell about tattling on Buffy. He ought to take the headlines along and show them; maybe he would.

He strolled into his clearing, and saw that the garage doors were open and that streams of water were pouring out of them! What on earth—had he left something turned on? He hurried over and peered in, and there was old sourpuss McKinnon, hosing the place out. He really did look sour, too. But what had he done with all the stuff in there? There was no use getting into discussion and hearing all about Safe bind, safe find, is what *I* always say, Mr. Waldon; so he ducked back and went in the door to his workshop.

His mother was there. Standing there. She was doubled over slightly, as if she were holding something but she wasn't holding anything. She was looking at him and her face was so awful he couldn't look away. The worst of it was she didn't even seem to see him. She was looking right at him, and she didn't see him.

He wanted to turn around and go right back out—that was all he wanted. But he couldn't move.

Then she gave a little gasp, and her eyes closed, and she sagged down against his worktable. That released him. He hurried over and caught her—thrust a chair where she would sit, and sat her in it. She swayed limp over his supporting arm, not making a sound. But when she raised her head her eyes held consciousness—she saw him now.

Wary, frightened still, he made himself ask: "What's the matter?"

She shook her head, still clinging to his arm.

"What is it, mother? Have you got a pain?"

After quite a long time she nodded, once.

"Well—what should I do? Shall I go get Martha Mary?"

But she didn't want him to leave her—her strong hand tightened on his arm, quite painfully. It gave him odd reassurance, and he prepared to stand patiently there by her, as long as she wanted him to. It had been a terrible fright—one of the worst she ever gave him. She had looked, really, as if she were going to die. As if it were death coming in the door to her, instead of himself, her son.

"Poor mama," he said presently; and with his free hand, he began to stroke her hair. "Poor little mama. I'm so sorry, sweetheart...."

He shouldn't have said it. She began, then, quite terribly to cry. Whatever it was, it wasn't over yet. She was trembling, too—harder and harder, in a very tense, violent way, so that her trembling shook him. Then the hand on his arm began pulling him down, forcing him down, so that at last he just had to get down on his knees, where their faces were on a level. Then she began looking into his face—looking, and looking—her eyes streaming tears all the time. She let go of his arm and took his face in both hands, and pulled it against her own head; and began saying over, like a moan, "My baby ... my baby ... my little boy...."

He remained passive, but he was becoming less overwhelmed, more alert all the time. He understood by now that her suffering was not physical; and in a grave and sudden intuition he knew what had happened, and what she had found.

At least, he thought he knew. If he could only have turned his head a little to see the closet, he thought he would be able to tell. But she was holding him so tightly he could not move, and one of her rings was pressing deeply upon his ear.

He said at last, very low, "Mama, you're hurting me"; and her hands slackened and slid away, fell into her lap. He moved his head back a little, looking at her doubtfully, and her whole face seemed to crumple under his gaze.

"Oh, baby, baby," she whispered. "*My God, my God—what shall we do?*"

It wasn't really a question to him, but he tried to answer it. He said, after a moment, "You shouldn't have come down here, mother."

She only shook her head—it went on shaking, like a kind of palsy, and she stared past him as if she didn't feel it. He risked turning a little then—enough; he got a clear glimpse of the closet door but it was closed and nothing lay on the floor in front of it. He wanted—*needed*, so much, to go and open the door and look inside, he knew he would know if things had been disturbed, but he couldn't do it. He couldn't do it while she was there.

He got back to his feet, her fearful eyes following him up, and said to her, urgent: "You ought to go, mother. You ought to go back to the house and lie down. Don't you want to do that?"

She wasn't understanding him at all. He had become like a sort of *object* to her, that she had to keep her eyes and hands upon; and he really did not know what to do.

Then he thought of McKinnon, next door hosing (the hard water-spatter had been going on all the time) and it was a great relief to remember him.

"Listen, wait here, darling," he said. "I'll get McKinnon, we'll help you back to the house."

But she cried out "No—no!" in such terror that real terror woke in him too, freezing him, as if he had just proposed something that would absolutely destroy them. It was a long minute before he could unfreeze again, and begin to get hold of himself, but even then he didn't know what to do.

It was appalling; he began to think it would never end, when all at once she reached out her hand to him, and he took it, and she pulled herself up. He put his arm around her and she stood against him, trembling, but more lightly.

She said in a low voice, "Take me back to the house"; and he answered, eagerly, "That's what I *want* to do, mother, but are you sure you can—don't you want someone to help?"

"No. No one. Take me."

A little nervous, he began to walk her forward then, towards the door; and except for a little stumble in the beginning she came along quite well, it was going to be all right. He held the door with one hand and kept the other under her arm, and she stepped out by herself and stood waiting for him.

He guided her carefully around the rivers that McKinnon was making all over the ground, and then into the wide woods path leading up to the house. She kept his arm, and went slowly, but she was hardly leaning upon him at all. Mostly she just kept that very tight grip upon him, as if her failure were more of vision than of strength.

It was quite a long path, going at this pace, and as they went along it together, in silence, he began to receive the curious impression that she was more recovered than she wanted him to know. More thoughtful, now, than stunned—although she was still awfully pale. He knew her so well ... so terribly, terribly well; and yet, what good did it do? He no more knew how to speak to her, or what to say—or what she meant to do—than if he had known nothing. It seemed as if they would never reach the house.

When they came to the edge of the back lawn she stopped and said to him, "Waldon—go back, and tell McKinnon to go away from there."

"But I can't do that, mother—it would look so funny!"

"No. Tell him to finish the garage, and go away. To do nothing more. He's not to put things back."

"Well, no—I want to do that myself," he agreed. He thought about it a minute more—he was really quite nervous by now—and she allowed him to think. Then he said, "All right. I'll tell him just to finish hosing, and then leave the rest to me. But what will you do? Are you going on in?"

"I'll wait here for you. Go quickly," she said.

But somehow he could not run while she was watching him. He trotted, self-conscious, until he knew he was out of sight, and then burst into long, relief-giving strides, running hard.

McKinnon was outside, looping up his hose, when Waldon burst out of the trees at him, and he looked startled and not very pleased, but he didn't speak. Waldon couldn't speak; so with a vague gesture he went inside his workshop and shut the door. His breath came in gasps, when he let it go—not just from that little run, but from some longer strain only now relieved.

Gasping, not caring that he did, he went directly to the closet and opened it and rummaged around on the floor in back, to bring it out piece by piece: the jacket, the pants, the shirt, even the tie. He no longer tried to tell whether they had been disturbed and then thrust back there, because it no longer seemed to matter; he just wanted to *see* them, to be sure that they were there. The suit was all she had missed last week, and he had told her he had taken it in to the cleaners himself—which was strange enough. But he *couldn't* take it to any cleaner. And there was nothing he could have burned the things in except the house trash-burner, and he was afraid to do that. What if these synthetics didn't really burn up, or else smelled to high heaven? And there would have been hundreds of buttons to pick out of the ash.... He had even thought, one day, of taking everything in to the launderette in town and stuffing it in a washing machine—but it seemed such a nervous, public kind of thing to do; and besides he knew that blood was hard to get out. Martha Mary always made a great fuss about getting out even a small stain.

He *had* tried, he had—it wasn't that he had stuffed them away in there and forgotten them! It was just that he didn't know what to *do*— he still didn't; and tears of vexation came into his eyes, nervous tears, only to think about it again.

Right at that moment, the door from the garage opened. He whirled around. McKinnon was coming in.

"Don't come in!" said Waldon sharply.

McKinnon stopped, but he didn't go out again.

"I'll just put those things back now," he said.

"*I'll* put them back!"

"I was told," said McKinnon, not moving.

"And *I'm* telling you to leave them where they are!" Waldon almost screamed at him. Then he got his voice down. "Some of those things are—quite valuable, you don't seem to realize—I don't want them knocked around—"

"They'll get less harm from careful moving than from standing about forever the way they do," McKinnon said stolidly. He went out and shut the door.

With shaking hands, Waldon gathered everything up again and wadded it as small as he could, and then got down on his knees and poked the wad away back. He put all sorts of things on the floor in front of the bundle—it didn't matter what, just things to discourage any random looking. Not that there would be any—his mother was the only person who would go poking into every corner like that—and even *she* wasn't supposed to have come in here! He had only meant for them to clean the garage, she ought to have understood that, but no—she couldn't bear for him to have anything that was all his own. Sooner or later, she always found some excuse, and got herself into it.

Well, all right, then. She had got herself into this, too; and now she was standing out there in an absolute state of trauma and it was all going to be his fault, his responsibility, since she wouldn't let anyone else come near them.

He took a last look around and then went out and shut the door. Sullenly, not hurrying any more, he went back up the path to his mother.

CHAPTER NINE

She was standing there as if she hadn't moved a bit while he was gone. When she heard him coming she raised her head ... and she really *did* look awfully queer. Really pretty awful. His thoughts wavered, losing most of their truculence. He came up in silence, and offered his arm again.

But as they started creeping over the lawn together, he said in a last rise of rebellion: "McKinnon's simply impossible. I wish you'd let him go."

"They'll all have to go," she replied. "So will we."

He gave her a startled glance, that she did not seem to notice, and then deliberately didn't answer. He steered her around to the music room door and in there, and at that point would have dropped his arm if she hadn't been holding to it so tightly.

"I want to go up to my room," she said.

They went on, up the stairs together. The house was quiet, for a blessing, and neither Martha Mary nor Josephine jumped out at them. Inside his mother's room he shut the door, with a great sense of relief, and then helped her to lie down on her bed. She raised one arm and pressed it over her eyes; so he went around and pulled all the blinds for her; but she didn't take her arm away even then.

"Sit down here," she murmured, laying her other hand on the bed beside her to show where she wanted him. He sat down there, taking up the hand and stroking it. She didn't say anything more but just breathed—very slowly, as if she were concentrating on it.

"Can't I get you something, mother?" he asked, after a while. Her head moved in a slow negative. She didn't speak.

The silence went on for quite a while. He began to feel restless, and moved slightly; but the moment he did her limp hand tightened upon his.

He didn't at all want to talk about it—about anything, with her, just then; but that breathing silence was becoming more than he could bear. And he hated shut-up rooms—sickrooms.

So he began, reluctantly, to speak.

"Mother—you know I wouldn't have had this happen to you for the world, but you—"

"Hush," she murmured, pressing upon his hand. "Not now. Not yet."

"But, mother, I *can't* stay here all day—people are waiting for me, I've got appoint—"

She took her arm away then and her eyes stared up at him, so wide open and wild-looking that he … he recoiled….

In a sharp movement of panic, he drew back. Got his hand free, and stood up.

"Waldon, Waldon, stay here—"

Her voice sounded terribly loud—and so hoarse and strange, after all that stillness, that she really did seem like a stranger—some mad stranger, whom he backed away from as rapidly as he could.

She flung herself forward on the bed after him.

"You mustn't go out! You mustn't go out! *Don't open the door!*"

In an instant, panic obedience, he stopped with his back against it; but his hand behind him was groping for the knob. If he didn't get out of there in another minute, he was absolutely going to go all to pieces.

Perhaps she realized this—although she didn't look as if she could realize *anything*—because she stopped getting off the bed and began holding out her arms to him instead; and she said in a much quieter voice (though still very strange): "Darling—darling, come back, mother only wants to help you ... *but you mustn't go out!*"

Her voice rose again, and his panic with it; but he still—frantically—tried to explain to her.

"But I have to go, I absolutely have to—can't you see that, mother? We *can't* stay all shut up here like this, it's absolutely insane—people will think we've gone mad! *I have to go out!*"

She was bracing herself to rise all the time he was speaking; she got on to her feet; and in that same instant he had the door open and was out in the hall.

He didn't run. He walked, very quickly, to the front stairs and went down them one at a time, but fast. She didn't call one word after him. At least she was still able, like himself, to remember the servants.

He got outside, and went round the other side of the house—making a wide circle even so. But he was recovered enough by now to be aware that he was doing it.

When she got like that, there was nothing to do *but* leave her. It might seem brutal, but it was the best, the only thing to do. Alone, she would go to work and pull herself together; but if he did what she wanted and stayed right there with her, she would work them both up into a perfect orgy of nerves and tears, and he *hated* it. He really hated it; not just afterwards, but even while it was going on, even when he was behaving as badly as she.

No, when she got like that he knew by now he just had to take over the responsibility for both of them, and walk out. Nine times out of ten, by the time he got back she was perfectly all right, and whatever it was had all blown over and never needed to be mentioned again. Or if there was something that still had to be said, at least he had had time to think about how to say it, without giving her any opening to make a scene. And to give his mother credit where she deserved it, she really would try to follow his lead—listening quite humbly, sometimes, and saying "Yes, dear," or "I know, dear," in a perfectly normal voice. She understood as well as he that those scenes shouldn't happen.

And he didn't blame her for them, he hadn't for years. She was a woman of terribly strong feelings—like his own; only being a woman, she had never learned to control them. If she had had any decent way to release them, she would have been all right. *More* than all right—magnificent. But what had happened? Her music, that whole passionate life of gift and response, had been turned into a parlor accomplishment for people like the Fosses; to play with another musician she had to *hire* him; and to play before anybody decent she had to hire a hall—and hire it as Mrs. A. W. Coutts, which prejudiced every critic against her. As for *Mr.* A. W. Coutts, Waldon had never been able to imagine anything taking place between his father and mother that he—or any child—could not have witnessed. And he remembered them when they were younger, too.

If it hadn't been for himself—he admitted this—his mother might have burst away into some (probably disastrous) love affair. But she was the kind of woman who belonged absolutely to any child she bore; and once he, Waldon, was there, her fate was sealed. She was Mrs. A. W. Coutts for ever and ever, then, with no possibility of escape.

No, she was a tragic woman, he never tried to evade that truth about her. Nor the equal truth of his own debt to her, for all she had given, and still gave, to him alone. On the other hand, he had long since reached the years when it was up to *him* to judge how he could best help her; and if the way he decided upon seemed sort of rough at the time, well, he was ready to take the responsibility for that.

He felt a lot calmer, by the time he had finished thinking it out. It was all stuff he knew by heart, of course, but still it helped to go back over the ground in a real emergency and make sure he really knew what he was doing.

He really did.

Meanwhile, he was a little surprised to find himself turning into the Peabody driveway—not that he didn't mean to go there, but he hadn't any recollection of going down to the clearing and getting his pickup, which he must have done.

Old Peabody, a retired Beecham bakery owner, was out poking around in his vegetable plot when Waldon drove in—which was all right, the vegetable plot was his own affair, he could make any mess he liked in it. He stared at the pickup, and then at Waldon emerging from it, as if he had never seen either one of them before; and then as Waldon approached, answered Waldon's lifted hand slowly.

"Oh, it's you, Waldon," he said. "Couldn't think what kind of a truck that was—I know most of them, that come round here."

"That's a Volkswagen, Mr. Peabody," said Waldon kindly. "German make—and the best value you can get in this country for the money."

"Is that right," said Mr. Peabody. "Well, they always were good workers—and I s'pose they need the money now, eh? Still I always used them light Chevvies for the bakery, and in all the years—"

"Yes, they have their points too," said Waldon. He didn't feel like dithering around anymore; what he wanted was to pitch in and *do* something. "Well, how about getting that grape arbor started?"

"Oh, that," he said. "'Fraid you can't do that today, Waldon. Cedar poles didn't come."

"Didn't come! Good heavens, why not? You mean you haven't even heard from them yet?"

"Well, I expect they'll be along pretty soon now," said Mr. Peabody. "And like you said yourself, there's no hurry anymore."

"Well, you want them to weather, don't you? Besides, it's the point of the thing—I mean, when they're supposed to deliver something, they ought to deliver it. That's no way to do business."

"Well, I expect they'll come along pretty soon," Mr. Peabody repeated. "Tell you what, I'll give you a phone call when they come. How's that?"

"Well, you know I'm pretty busy this time of year, Mr. Peabody. Of course, I'll do what I can, but I did happen to have some free time today—"

"Thought it was s'posed to be yesterday," said old Peabody, like a sly thrust; and Waldon looked at him coldly.

"It wouldn't have made much difference, would it? However, since I am here, why don't I take an inch or so off that grass for you? It's rather long."

"Oh, I plan to do that myself, Waldon—thank you. Got myself a new power mower, and I'm kind of looking forward to having some fun with it."

"Have you," said Waldon. Another time, he would have enjoyed seeing it, and would have taken time to instruct the old man in its use so he wouldn't wreck it the first time out. But he had really had enough of old P. for the moment, so he only said: "Well, let me know if you have any trouble with it"; and turned to go.

Well. He could just *wait* for his old grape arbor now.

What next?

He was speeding back towards the house, and slowed when he realized it. It wasn't time for that, *at all*. Still, while he was so close, why shouldn't he have a look at the Fosses' power mower? He had lost his desire to go over and yammer at them about Buffy—that seemed *awfully* long ago—but he could just tinker the thing up and then go cut off their grass with it. Another week and they'd have a real meadow there. It was just the sort of thing he felt like doing, too—not fixing the mower so much as just pushing it up and down, up and down, through good long grass. But it probably wouldn't take too long to fix.

A NIGHT RUN

The empty, damp-smelling garage reminded him of all the shifting and sorting he had in prospect—sometime. For the moment he just rooted out the Fosses' mower and began to look it over. It was quite a new machine, and no one had used it but himself, which had made him feel rather obligated to fix it—although he had suspected for some time before it quit that the thing was a lemon. And a lemon, of course, was the very devil to put right. It was always some imperceptible kind of flaw that you could check over a dozen times and never notice.

He spent a good half-hour checking away, feeling less and less patient—and really terribly tired of hanging around there in the clearing, all by himself. At last he gave up and shoved the thing in the pickup as it was. He put his own, much better, mower in too, and drove off to the Fosses'. It turned out that Mr. Foss was upstairs taking a nap—from the look of Mrs. Foss, she wasn't too wide-awake herself—and she was afraid the mower would wake him up; but Waldon soon put an end to that.

"If this grass gets much longer it's going to ruin any cutter," he said sternly. "Besides, it's a mess! Aren't you sick of looking at it?"

Well, she was, of course—but couldn't he come back a little later? Or come in and have some iced tea before he started?

"Look, I've just *squeezed* you in, as it is," he said patiently. "You know how things are around here in the summer! For goodness' sake, let me get you off my conscience while I can!"

He finally agreed to begin as far away from the house as he could, and heard a lot more about Mr. Foss's rheumatism that kept him awake all night, and then he got rid of her and went off to do what he wanted, at last.

From then on, the day should have begun to put itself together. For a while, he thought it was going to—his own mower was working beautifully, in spite of McKinnon, who would never leave it alone, and there was just enough alternate sun and shade on the Fosses' grounds to let him work up a good sweat without getting completely pooped. The thing was, he decided at length, that he himself just wasn't coordinating well. He didn't feel the easy swing and balance of muscle that he liked, where muscle and machine seemed to weld into one purpose, one power. Instead he began to feel like someone trying to dance with a perfectly impossible partner, the kind that baulked you at every step. And yet it wasn't the mower, of course, it was himself.

What on earth was the matter with him? And would it help if he stopped for a while? To tell the truth, what he would have liked by now would have been simply to stop; but he didn't like to do it after letting the grass go so long, and having to tell old Fossie about his lemon, and so on.

He went over to the house to get a drink of water, and that turned into iced tea, and then Mrs. Foss discovered he hadn't had any lunch and insisted on cutting some cold ham for him; and it ended up pretty restfully after all.

"I've got to the point where I have to come near the house now," he said, explaining his willingness to stay, "and I just hate to do it."

"Well, you're a sweet boy, Waldon," Mrs. Foss replied, "but it's all right. Mr. Foss found some wax stoppers and put them in his ears, so he can't hear you."

"How perfectly ghastly," said Waldon. "I'm always afraid they'll melt and trickle into my brainpan."

"Oh, they couldn't do that, dear," she was beginning; but then she saw he was smiling, and she smiled too. They talked for a while—Waldon told her about Edie, and the rumors she was spreading about Buffy Oliver, and she blushed a little but said only that Edie really was a handful sometimes. He asked her if she had seen the horrifying headlines about Buffy in the New York papers that morning, and described them. She turned pale then, but said steadily No, they didn't see the New York papers, but she thought the *Beecham News* had put the story quite fairly—after all, as distressing as it was, Buffy had been there, and she should have spoken up about it.

He glanced out of the window while she was going on like this—the drawing room windows, which overlooked the millhouse and its grounds; they seemed deserted and overgrown already. It was such a nice little place. He had always liked it; he hated to see it looking that way; and he said suddenly:

"I hope somebody nice will live there now."

"Why, so do we, of course, Waldon—but poor Rose was, was always a pleasant neighbor to us. We didn't see a great deal of her, it's true, but she seemed nice enough."

"She wasn't. She was a horrible woman," said Waldon; and it made a pause that neither of them quite knew how to handle.

Out on the lawn again, struggling with the damned machine, he was sorry he had startled her that way. He hadn't meant to. It was all part of this dreary, endless day in which nothing went right.

He didn't even consider not finishing the Fosses' grounds anymore. No, he would do it all, right down to the last obstinate grass blade. The day was spoiled, and would spoil whatever else he might attempt in it, so he might as well do this. Besides, he hadn't the spirit or desire to think up anything else to do. All he really wanted, when he came face to face with it, was not to go home.

So he spent the whole, long afternoon where he was. When the lawn was done he took a long time meticulously hand-clipping; and when that was done he turned up the earth in all the borders; and after that he would have started working on their mangy old shrubbery, but Mrs. Foss came out and stopped him. They were afraid it was getting so late that his mother would worry. But they were extremely grateful for all he had done, and Mr. Foss heard about his lemon without a murmur, so it wasn't all wasted.

He still didn't want to go home.

He didn't even want to go to the clearing. That was spoiled, too.

It was a little after six. But because it was Friday, they would be dining late anyway—his father came out on the 6:28. Should he go and meet him?

This chore, which he had rebelled against, and freed himself from years ago, now struck him as quite a possible thing to do. It would make a nice surprise for the old boy ... and then he would have someone to go home with him.

However badly things fell apart between his mother and himself, they had always managed to pull themselves together and put up a united front when his father came home. If he came home *with* his father, it would be even better.

He decided to do it, and put the Volkswagen towards town.

CHAPTER TEN

As usual, his father muffed the whole thing.

He was surprised enough, when Waldon caught him on the way to the taxis and made him look up (he always walked along as if he were counting the boards in the platform); but what he said was: "Junie? Where are you going?"

"I'm not going anywhere, I came to meet you," said Waldon proudly.

"Why?" said his father. "What's the matter, son?"

"For goodness' sake, nothing's the matter—I just came to *meet* you. Do you mind?"

"Oh," he said. "No, not at all. Very nice. Appreciate it."

But he didn't like it a bit when they got to the Volkswagen.

"Why didn't you bring the car?" he said, not moving to get in.

"Because I was working, that's why—I didn't have time to go home and clean up and change cars! Get *in*, father—it really isn't a sidecar, you know."

His father got—or rather, crept in; but he didn't like it. And he took an instant grip on the door handle, from which Waldon almost had to pry him loose.

"Relax, relax," Waldon told him. "I guarantee to get you home alive."

He didn't relax—Waldon didn't expect him to—but he did get up enough confidence to begin peering sidewise at his son after a while.

"Your mother send you, Junie?" he asked presently.

"Heavens, no. I haven't seen her for hours."

"She's all right, I suppose?"

"Well, you know mother," said Waldon, putting an end to *that*.

After a while his father tried again.

"Something special going on tonight?" he suggested.

"Nothing I've heard about. Certainly not another musicale, thank goodness."

"Oh, come now," his father said. "I thought that went off very well. And it's a pleasure for your mother."

"I think it's more of a torture, myself," Waldon replied; but that was deep water, and his father wasn't going to get into it. He gave up talking, and sat there holding on to the window the rest of the way.

The Hunts' car was in the driveway when Waldon turned up—Marcie must really have been struck to the soul by the "pansy" crack of Edith's, which was silly of her, because in the first place it didn't bother Waldon and in the second place he wouldn't have dreamed of repeating it to his mother. Or were the Hunts coming to dinner? His mother always had someone to dinner on Fridays and Saturdays, in order to avoid one of those silent, munching threesomes. But they hardly ever had the Hunts when Edith was there.

Marcie came out of the door as they came up to it; and she was alone. Martha Mary was on the other side of the screen, holding forth with some prolonged gabble, to which Marcie was saying "Yes, that's very true. Yes." She turned to greet them with relief.

"How nice to see you, I'm so glad we didn't just miss! But I won't come in again, thank you—I know you must be anxious about Helene, and I've left Daddy alone, too. Can I call you tomorrow and see how she is? I do hope it isn't going to be one of those viruses."

"What's the matter with Helene?" said Waldon's father—old flatfoot. But Waldon backed him up quickly.

"Yes, good heavens—what's going on? She was all right this morning, Marcie."

He was aware of Martha Mary's gaze from within, and added sharply, to her: "Oughtn't you to be upstairs with mother, Martha Mary?"

"She's been waiting for you, Mr. Waldon," she replied. He really could have struck her at that moment.

"Go tell her we're both coming right away," he said shortly, and made raised eyes to Marcie, which she received in sympathetic amusement.

"What's the matter with Helene?" said his father again.

"Why, Martha Mary says she has quite a high fever—and all of a sudden, too—as Waldon says, she was all right this morning. I hope it isn't that thing the Packards have—has she seen them recently?"

"I don't know," said his father. "What have they got?"

"Oh, she hasn't been anywhere near them for months," said Waldon quickly. "Don't worry, sweetie—she'll be calling you up herself tomorrow, you'll see. Can't you really come in and have one little drink with us?"

But Marcie wouldn't; and Waldon and his father came together into the empty hall, the totally quiet house. There was a moment in which they just seemed to be standing there, like visitors, waiting for direction. Then his father put his hat and briefcase on the hall table and looked at himself in the glass above it. Then, in the glass, he looked at Waldon.

"Go see her, Junie," he said. "You heard what Martha Mary said."

"You come too," said Waldon.

"I'll be along in a minute." And to avoid any more discussion, he went into the powder room and shut the door.

Waldon went up the stairs. His mother, except at the piano, was the quietest of women; but the house seemed absolutely dead without her moving about in it. Yet it wasn't so much the quietness as a sense of motion suspended, everywhere. No one was coming to look for him, to meet him—that was it. If he went into his room, no one would follow. It was he, now, who must go where she was; she wouldn't come to him.

He went along the hall.

Her door was open, and Martha Mary stood just inside. She moved back to let him pass, but he didn't at once go in. No sound at all came from the bed. He saw the covers had been turned back, and that she was lying there in her nightdress, and the nightstand was already covered with a cloth like a sick-table. He took all this in—it was familiar, it defined and quieted what he must feel; then he drew a long breath, and turned to Martha Mary.

She whispered, "Go over to her, dearie—she'll know it's you, and it'll help her."

"Is she asleep?" he whispered back. But he was already moving forward on tiptoe, peering to know for himself.

She was still terribly pale. Her eyes were closed, her lips slightly parted; her skin seemed to lie lax over a new thinness, and it shone. Her forehead and cheeks shone wet.

"The fever's gone down," murmured Martha Mary behind him—close, but he did not mind her there. "Take her hand," she urged him.

He took his mother's hand, which was entirely passive; and after a moment he began gently to stroke it. She really *was* ill, poor love. Out cold, too.

"The doctor gave her something to sleep, that's why she's sleeping like that," Martha Mary whispered, close to his ear. Her breath was warm on him, like a cow's, and he began not to like having her so close.

"Why don't you go down and cook," he whispered back, "and I'll stay with her a while."

She went creaking out of the room (she really did creak; it wasn't the floor), and Waldon sat cautiously on the slipper chair drawn up beside his mother's bed. He continued to hold her hand, and to watch her.

She was profoundly interesting to him, lying there like that. He did not know exactly what it was that he felt as he watched her—a kind of fear, perhaps, only not really unpleasant—was awe the word? He thought it might be; and the definition, accepted by his mind, increased the solemn pleasure that he felt.

She was totally unaware of him. That was the fascinating part of it. There he was, sitting so close to her—holding her hand, even—and she was totally unaware of him! He might have been trying for years to come upon her undetected, so exciting was it to find he had succeeded.

Yet, actually, it was an idea that had never entered his mind. How should it? She had always before felt his first approach—even at night, even from the deepest sleep, she would wake before he could reach her bed no matter how quietly he came, and would be looking at him when he leaned to look at her.

But she knew nothing of him now. Not a quiver, in the hand he held and stroked. He bent her fingers back a little, experimentally, and then quickly released them again; but she gave no sign.

It really was rather frightening. He couldn't decide whether he wanted it to go on or not; and as though suggesting the choice to her, without committing himself, he said in a very low voice: "Poor mama ... poor little mama, she's so tired...."

She made a moaning sound, and he stopped. He stopped stroking her hand, too, and sat very still. She moaned again, louder, and this time he put her hand back on the bed and left it alone.

It was too late. The moans went on coming out of her, and they didn't sound like his mother *at all*. They didn't even sound like a person, but like some kind of *thing* shut up inside her and dying there. And as if she could feel it, and it were hurting her, she began to make queer, senseless movements with the hand he had put down. Then she turned her head on the pillow in one violent movement—*flop*.

That was too much. He got up and went quickly out of the room, and shut the door behind him.

He went to the head of the back stairs; but he could hear Martha Mary quite plainly, rushing around and snapping at Josephine, and he thought he had better not interrupt her. In any case, he found he didn't *want* anybody else to hear those sounds his mother was making.

Perhaps she had stopped?

He went back and stood by her door, and he couldn't hear anything. Very carefully, he turned the knob and made a little opening to listen through, and after a while he could hear her again. But they were really quite faint sounds now, and much farther apart, and probably the best thing was just to leave her alone and let her go back to sleep.

He shut her door again with the same care, and then went into his own room to clean up for dinner. But he couldn't help feeling some resentment against Martha Mary for pushing him into a thing like that. What was the use of doping his poor mother up, if old mush-brain kept pushing people in on her? She ought to be left in peace, poor darling, that was all.

He couldn't decide what to wear, either, because he didn't know if anyone might be coming. It didn't seem very likely; but then his mother hadn't been in any state to call people up and put them off, and it was far too much initiative to expect from their *cordon bleu*.

However, when he came down (in jacket and trousers, just to be on the safe side) his father was alone in the living room, watching the news on television and sipping sherry. He was really quite a presentable looking old parent, when he didn't talk, and Waldon decided to have some sherry too, and brought it over beside him.

His father gave him an inquiring look as he sat down, and Waldon said: "Dead to the world. Not a bit of use going up now"; and his father nodded and went back to watching. He had one of his twenty-five-cent private-eye books open across his knee, to read during the ads (and probably during dinner, since they were alone) and he was using one of Marty's new holders as if he enjoyed it; and altogether he looked quite a comfortable old party—Waldon felt a real surge of affection for him.

He wasn't in the least prepared, then, to have his father turn a cold look on him the minute the news was over, and say sternly: "Now, Junie—what have you been doing to upset your mother this time?"

For a moment he felt really lost—simply ten years old again.

"What do you mean?" he said, even stammering a little.

His father didn't answer, and they had a most uncomfortable pause. Josephine came in and said dinner was ready, and his father got up and went out of the room. Presently Waldon followed him. He was beginning to get angry, and he wanted to wait until he really was.

"What *do* you mean?" he said again, the moment he got into the dining room. "I think that's a pretty disagreeable thing to say, father! She's *sick*, why don't you go up and look at her? You don't even bother to find out—you just assume it's my fault!"

His father still didn't answer. He was eating jellied consommé. Waldon started to pick up his spoon—he wasn't especially hungry, but he hadn't anything against food—until all at once a little bubble of Mrs. Foss's ham came up his throat. It was identifiably ham; but it tasted like sick, too. He put his spoon down again, and gave his father an angry look—but he was a little worried. Was he going to *be* sick?

While he was sitting there waiting to find out, his father started in again.

"Junie," he said, "I think it's time you came back down to the city. I've let you have a good try at this landscaping idea of yours, but frankly, son, I think you're just playing at it. You're too old to play. You're a grown man, now, Ju—Waldon," he said. "You're nearly thirty years old. Don't you realize that?"

Waldon couldn't answer. He didn't dare open his mouth.

His father looked at him for a minute.

"I don't mean the bank," he said then. "I agree that wasn't a success, and I'm not blaming you. And I agree with your mother that we should take your—uh—individual characteristics into account, in whatever we decide. But I do feel that—"

Waldon suddenly rose, with his napkin over his mouth. He said behind it: "Excuse me—I'm going to be sick—"

Even then, he wasn't absolutely sure, he just wanted to get upstairs *in case*. By the time he got to his room, though, he was sure—and he was sick. Really sick. He threw up *twice*, and then gagged for quite a while after that, and could hardly get back to fall upon his bed.

Nothing was worse than being sick. He lay there panting, because Martha Mary said that was a good way to stop being sick—just open your mouth and pant; but he felt too weak even for that. Besides, you were supposed to do it before, not after. He stopped panting, and then he just lay there.

Nobody came.

His mother, of course, wouldn't; she wouldn't even know, poor mama. But surely Martha Mary would notice his absence and ask about it, Josephine would say something to her—but Josephine was too timid to speak to his father, and it would be just like his father not to say a word either. It was perfectly possible nobody would come for hours—all night; and he did so terribly want somebody to come....

By and by he got up, shakily, and went in to get a little water. He didn't dare drink much, for fear of losing it again, even though he was so thirsty. You were supposed to drink something with sugar in it, too, to replace something you lost, but he didn't have any sugar.

He couldn't face going downstairs again.

Completely, totally miserable, he crept back and lay down on his bed. Nobody was going to come; he might as well accept it.

Then the door opened and Martha Mary came in.

He was so grateful to see her he couldn't say a word. She came across and looked down at him, and then she put her hand on his forehead.

"Well, the two of you at once, that's fine," she said. "You've been throwing up, haven't you? I can smell it."

"Yes," he whispered. "Twice."

"It's that twenty-four-hour virus, that's what it is," said Martha Mary. "It'll go through this house like wildfire, we'll all have it. There's no help for it now."

He said with faint interest, "Did mother throw up too?"

"No, it probably took her the other way," she said. "As it does me. Well, you're going to be a mighty sick boy for the next twenty-four hours, dearie, and there's nothing we can do about that, except make you comfy as we can. Let's get you cleaned up first and into your bed."

He helped as much as he could, and did whatever she told him. She was very strong and quick, but nice to him—the truth was that she loved them to be sick, but it was only because she made such a good nurse. He didn't even mind when she took his pants off.

When she had him all clean and tucked up, she went down and got some ginger ale for him, and the little glass sipper so he could sip without any trouble; and then she cleaned up the bathroom herself and left the shaving light on for a nightlight without even being asked.

"Well, now, sleep's your medicine, boy," she said, trying his forehead again, very kindly. "That's not much of a fever, you may have a light case of it, and we'll hope so. But sleep, now."

"I don't want those pills mother had," he murmured.

"And I wouldn't give you the stuff," she agreed. "I was against it for her. Nature'll give you your sleep, and the best kind."

"Leave the door open," he said; and when she was almost out of the room he added: "Tell my father what we have, Martha Mary."

She said she would.

CHAPTER ELEVEN

His mother woke him up in the middle of the night.

It must have been the movement of the bedsprings that woke him, because when he opened his eyes she was sitting there with her hands in her lap, not touching him at all.

He could see her quite plainly in the light coming from the bathroom; and his first feeling was one of great comfort that she had come, even before he remembered he had been sick.

Then he remembered *she* had been sick, too—and he sat up in bed a little, to try and see her better.

"What's the matter, mother?" he said. "Are you all right?"

She replied, "Yes, darling," in her own voice; and he said: "I'm glad. It was scary to see you like that."

"I'm sorry, dear," she said.

"I don't think you ought to take those knockout pills," he said; but she didn't answer that.

Did she know he had been sick? If she did not, he thought he wouldn't tell her just then; it was nice to have her just sitting there quietly for a while. He sat up some more and pulled his pillows up behind him; she leaned to help.

"Are you sure you're supposed to be out of bed?" he asked, while they were doing this. She had a strange smell about her—when she leaned over him that way he could just catch it, but not enough to decide what it was. He said, "You smell funny—is it medicine? I don't mean bad funny," he said quickly. "Just funny."

"I've burned those things, Waldon," she replied.

It was so completely unexpected that he didn't have any one reaction at all—just a flutter of possible ones, that reminded him of his tummy. He said weakly, "What do you mean?"

"I took them down and burned them in the barbecue pit," she said. "They're all gone. We'll never think of them again."

It was incredible. He still didn't know what he felt, or what he ought to say. She didn't seem to expect him to say anything.

Then he said suddenly, "It's gasoline. You put gasoline on them!"

"Yes."

"Did they—did they all burn up?"

"Yes. They're gone."

He had never thought of the barbecue pit. They never used it anymore. It was so far from the house he hadn't even noticed it in years.

He remembered about the buttons, then.

"What did you do with the buttons?" he asked, curious; and she answered at once: "I cut them all off. I put them in my button box."

He really felt quite shy of her, sitting there so calmly with her strong artist's hands folded in her lap, and this tremendous achievement behind her. Why hadn't he thought of the barbecue pit himself?

A faint—a very faint—querulousness came into his mind; and he could not help saying: "You must have looked awfully funny going all the way down there in your dressing gown, mother—you should have put your clothes on."

"I did, dear. I've been back for quite a while—I didn't mean to disturb you, but I couldn't get to sleep, I only wanted to see how you were."

Her voice trembled when she said this; and he was about to reach out and take her hand when, quite suddenly, she seized his.

"Oh, Waldon, Waldon—why did you go there? *Why did you do it? Why?*"

He tried to draw back, to draw away, but she only held him more tightly.

"You *knew* what kind of woman she was—you told me yourself the things people said about her, and they were true—you knew they were true! And you went there to her house—you went to her house alone, at night—you *meant* to do wrong, *you meant to do wrong!*"

"I didn't!" he cried. "No! I—"

"Yes! You went to her house because you *knew* she would make advances to you—and you let her, you let her! You would never have done what you did to her if you hadn't let her do those filthy, disgusting things to you first! Do you think I don't know? Do you think I don't know how a woman like that behaves with a boy *if he lets her?* And you let her, Waldon—*you let—*"

"Shut up!" he gasped; and wrenched his hand away, he flung his arms up against his ears. "Shut up! SHUT UP OR I'LL TELL! I'll tell them, I'll tell—"

She caught his wrist, pulled his arm down.

"And then to lie to me! All these days of lies, of lies! Did you think I didn't *know* you were lying to me? Do you think I don't feel it here—here—when you look at me and lie, Waldon? *Why did you lie to me about that woman?*"

All of a sudden, it seemed to him that his mind broke. He could not bear that hoarse, insistent voice any longer; and it would never stop. He fell forward, and lay upon his face.

After a long time, his head was turned, and he had air.

Then the voice began again, above him.

"Did you go in her bed with her?"

"No ... no," he sighed. "On the couch...."

"Was it the first time, Waldon?"

"Oh, yes—oh yes—it was horrible, don't talk about it...."

"*Why did you go there?*"

"I took—I fixed—her iron—"

She was thinking, there above him. He *felt* her thinking, as he could hear her breathing; and it seemed to him that the thought, and the breath, were his own, that she had taken from him; and he had none left.

"Was it—the iron?" she asked then.

"Yes. Please, please...."

"Where is it?"

"I put it—in the millpond—"

"What time did you go there? What time was it, Waldon?"

"I don't know, I don't know. You were playing ..."

"What was I playing when you left?" she insisted. "Think, Waldon! Was I playing alone, or with the violinist?"

He could do no more. The voice would have to go on, all night, forever—washing over him like lethal waters, and he had no more words, no more sounds, to check it.

He managed faintly to murmur: "No more ... no more ..."; and mercifully—miraculously—she heard him and was still.

The silence grew long, became a part of his stupor. Then the bed moved beneath him and his eyes fluttered open—but she was only getting up, going away.

She went out of the room without another word, and shut the door behind her. He heard the tiny click of the latch, and then nothing more.

She was gone.

His cocoon-like stupor began to disintegrate. Trickles of uneasiness came in, as if to replace her; and with them came the feeble, most unwelcome return of his own functions, that she had seized and held suspended above him there. He breathed, and heard his own breathing, and a chaos began in his mind that could turn into thinking, lonely thinking, that he would never be able to stop.

And yet he did not want her to come back.

It was the most desolate moment of his life.

The time when he had been sick, and alone, and nobody had come, had been paradisiacal compared to this—because then, he had *wanted* someone to come. Anyone. But in this wasteland of solitude and despair—with panic ahead, he could already feel it rising—he did not dare admit one soul. Not even her. *Especially not her.*

He lay absolutely rigid, clutching the bedclothes, with his face as nearly buried as he could manage, and still breathe. For he had to breathe now—he couldn't stop it.

A sound came into his room, into his head; and he was so overwrought that he almost leapt from the bed. But with enormous control, a tighter grip upon his blanket, he lay still. It came again; a birdcall. The first morning birdcall.

Incredulous, he began a tiny, inching movement of his face—freeing it so that he might peer, ever so slowly, towards the window. Light was there. Light was beginning out there, beyond his window! It was going to be day, the night was over.

Everything let go. His fingers, his held breath, the *oceans* of held-back tears that were making his eyes burn with dryness—all let go at once, and he lay lax and weeping and wholly yielded up to his release.

He woke very late the second time. Without any need to see his clock, he lay acknowledging the established warmth and murmurous sound of a day well along with itself. He could even identify the day as a weekend one, because of the constant, muted swish of traffic passing along their road. How pleasant it was to hear—how wonderfully alive!

He lay quiescent, and listened.

Then he began to distinguish house sounds, too, very faint though they were. And voices—outdoor voices. Someone was talking out on the lawn.

Reluctantly—too soon—he identified the voices. His mother and father were talking, out there. More than talking, they were *discussing*. He couldn't possibly mistake the rhythm of monologue and pause, of alternate, controlled voices, that meant discussion. And discussion meant him.

Now he got up—got up fast, lest in some hiatus of stillness one intelligible word of that discussion should float up to him while he lay there, helpless, to receive it. He didn't even want to know what they were saying, until he could get down and take his own part. Or be ready to take it, if he had to. Sometimes it was just a matter of making sure—listening out of sight to be sure that it was the same old treadmill of what-shall-we-do-about-Junie, leave-Waldon-alone. He never interfered with that. But this morning he had no confidence in any familiar routine. He didn't want to leave his defense to his mother, this time.

Hastily, awkwardly dressing—he got all the way into jeans and shirt before deciding to reject them and start over—he couldn't decide just why he felt this way. It wasn't that he mistrusted her, God knew. Perhaps it was just nervousness left from that awful scene last night, making him feel that if people were going to talk about him, he wanted to be there. He finally got himself put together, not very satisfactorily, and came on tiptoe out into the hall. There wasn't any reason for behaving this way up here, as he quickly realized—he certainly didn't have to sneak past Josephine! But it was a real effort to come downstairs openly.

One place was still laid in the breakfast room, but he didn't feel his usual pleasant need to go right in. On the other hand, now that he had rushed down here, he didn't want to go into the music room and listen to what they were saying, either.

This was so strange, after all his haste, that he stood a moment in real doubt—suspected some breakdown in his communications with himself. But there was no doubt of it—*whatever* they were discussing, he didn't want to hear a single word of it.

All right. He had to accept it, that was what he felt. And the moment he did accept it and turn away, relief appeared and grew within him at his escape.

Because he actually did feel as if he were escaping. Not just from discussion, or even from knowledge of that discussion, but from the house itself and everybody in it. From his mother, most of all.

Now he knew what was the matter; and it was so simple—alas, so familiar—that he couldn't understand why he had taken so long to discover it. It meant he didn't have a very happy day ahead, because he didn't enjoy these times when he stayed away from home, whatever she thought. But an unpleasant necessity that you understood was at least better than not knowing what in the world was wrong! That was worse than anything.

He was chagrined to remember that the pickup was in the garage—*blocked* in the garage, as usual, by Mrs. Mush-brain's old Plymouth. It would take years to maneuver himself out, and he had visions of simply everybody running out to stop him—Martha Mary waving a thermometer, probably, and his mother dragging along on his father's arm, pitifully calling. Oh, if only the pickup were quieter—as quiet as the car, for instance.

But why shouldn't he take the car? The key was always hanging in the garage, in case McKinnon had to drive his mother somewhere; and if his father had planned on going over to the club, his mother had surely quashed that plan. She sounded as if she were good for hours.

He took the car. As quiet as the Lincoln was, it lacked the pickup's maneuverability. He was sweating by the time he got it out, and there was still a lot of backing and filling to get headed down the drive, and all at once he just thought. The hell with it, and started off down the path to his own clearing.

The Lincoln really took it quite well. It had more of a rolling movement than the pickup, all those springs gave you the feeling of being gently tossed in a big blanket, but it certainly went along beautifully. And it was rather fun to drive, he ought to take it out more, for a change. When he got to the clearing he had an irresistible impulse to get out and go and have a look at that barbecue pit—an *unhealthy* impulse, as he recognized, but he yielded to it.

The bottom field wasn't so badly overgrown as he had thought—apparently McKinnon had been down here scything fairly recently—and he had an uncomfortable memory of how clearly he had been able to see Buffy here from the house. Still, that was only from his bathroom window, and nobody would be in his bathroom now unless it were Josephine, who didn't matter.

Or did she? She was such a rabbit one couldn't imagine her as having any thoughts, much less acting on them; but still.... He went more slowly, resisting a desire to look towards the house. If he were going to do it, he ought to do it quickly and naturally, as if he just wanted to check up on the barbecue pit for perfectly natural reasons ... whatever they might be. He walked more briskly, swinging his arms—paused, as if noticing the barbecue pit for the first time, and begun walking around it in a considering way, like an estimator.

She had really done a marvelous job. He could tell, because he *knew*, that rather a quantity of stuff had been burned here recently. But she hadn't even left much residue. What had she done with it? Or did that synthetic stuff just sort of disintegrate? He put a casual hand on the stone, and it felt warm, but that could be the sun.

No, actually, it was incredible how well she had done—and at night, too, and no doubt still feeling muzzy from that sleeping stuff. Had she made herself coffee—left any traces in the kitchen that Martha Mary would find? *Left any kind of traces?* What about that gasoline?

He pulled himself up, and turned to go back to the car. Of course she hadn't left traces. She had done a marvelous job; he just had to accept, and believe, in that total idea. And he did accept it.

He only wished he could feel more grateful to her.

The appalling truth was, that he didn't feel grateful at all. Maybe things were tidier, now that she had got into them, but that tidiness had cost him such wear and tear he couldn't be a bit glad of it. *Why couldn't she keep out of his business?* He had been perfectly all right without her. And now here he was, a nervous wreck.

If she was going to know, he would just as soon everybody did. He really meant it.

In this state of listless gloom, he let the big car, the stream of weekend traffic, bear him over to Max's. Kurt never came there on a weekend—he hated the crowds—and their coffee was pretty good.

Sure enough, the roadhouse was jammed, and all the tables were taken, but he found a place to stand at the bar. All the family were there, rushing around, and he mildly enjoyed watching them; but he waited until he could catch Max's eye.

As rushed as he was, Max came right over, and brought him his coffee at once. Waldon saw that he wanted to say something, and smiled at him.

"I hope you're not sore about the other day, Mr. Coutts," Max said then—since he clearly wasn't. "I didn't want you to do something you'd be sorry for afterwards."

"You were absolutely right, Max," he said kindly, "as you generally are."

"Mr. Schroeder was awfully sorry about the way he acted, after you left," said Max.

It was a lie—they both knew it; but that Max should take the trouble to tell it affected Waldon deeply. He felt tears come into his eyes, and he looked down, unable to speak.

When Max had gone, Waldon drank his coffee in a gulp, put down a quarter, and left. Out in the car again, he sat idle, trying to think where he could go. There was a whole long day ahead that he had to fill up. How should he fill it?

He couldn't, in his present state, begin to cope with anybody the least bit difficult; and yet if he went to someone kind—like Marcie, or Miss Min—he would just go all to pieces.

What on *earth* should he do?

The movies would be open, of course, since it was Saturday; but that was absolute rock-bottom—a local Saturday afternoon movie, with spitballs hitting him in the ear, and the sound track practically drowned out.

It was rock-bottom, yes; but it was all he could think of. He belonged there—he was *at* rock-bottom.

Slowly, acknowledging this—was he even very faintly comforted by the acknowledgement?— Waldon turned the big car and drove it towards the town.

CHAPTER TWELVE

It was such a terrible movie that it made him feel a little better. No matter what life was like, it was better than that; and he was relieved to get back on the sunny, commonplace street, into the casual, undramatic crowds. Over the way stood the dear old Beecham Free Library, moldering away in its eighteen-nineties red brick, and here was the cheerful, awful Sweet Shoppe, full of adolescent horrors shooting straws all over the floor. Should he go in too, and have a Beecham Bomb, with seven kinds of ice-cream and contrasting syrups?

The idea pleased him; but at the door his stomach moved in clear dissent, and he turned away. What he probably needed was food—plain food.

There was a Home Cooking place on one of the back streets where he sometimes went—not, God forbid, for the dreary evidence of her home life, but for the woman herself, a nice comfy old soul. He walked around there now, picking up a newspaper on the way (*not* from Marty) and found a booth to himself—the place was never crowded. The old soul came out and started to talk to him, but he didn't want that yet, and explained that he was starving. She was upset about that—it seemed the dinner menu wasn't quite ready, and the luncheon one was finished—but she finally agreed to make him some ham and eggs and went away to do it.

He began to glance idly through the paper. It was thin, because of Saturday, and really nothing in it he cared about. Not a word, of course, about Buffy. He wondered what the tabloids had said, that day he had neglected to read inside. Well, he would never know now—those papers had undoubtedly gone home with Martha Mary, to be hashed over there. Probably the grisly stories cut out, and saved in some rat's-nest drawer. How awful people could be, really—even the most harmless-seeming ones.

And for some reason, Josephine came into his mind. Why? Did he really care if she had seen him poking around the barbecue pit? Or was it just the sudden feeling that he didn't like sharing his home, his intimate life, with such a nonentity that you forgot about her—while she, with nothing else to think about, was probably making a rat's-nest hoard of her own about you....

He was getting morbid.

The ham and eggs came, quite decently cooked, and he ate them with increasing confidence. Not a murmur out of the old tum, so that was under control again, and stoking up like this made a tremendous difference. Come to think of it, he hadn't eaten since about this time yesterday, and that was only a snack, Mrs. Foss's ham.

He had some coffee—just awful, undoubtedly from lunch—and then strolled out into the heat again. Tummy absolutely fine, coffee and all. He went back to get the car—except that he forgot he had the car, and wasted a few minutes wondering where on earth he had put the pickup—and then, mildly amused, drove out of town again.

Where was he going now?

The question had lost its urgency, its desolation. He was still far, far from ready to go back home, but he did feel like a little company. Not much, and nobody difficult, though.

Presently, up ahead, he saw the Olivers' slate-blue roof among elm leaves; and it looked so attractive and familiar that he turned in the gate. No sooner did he get into the driveway than he realized he had made a mistake—there was quite a group sitting out on the lawn, including Buffy—but he was caught and had to keep on coming.

The worst of it was that he couldn't pretend it was an appointment—not in these clothes, and this blasted hearse of a car. No, it was definitely a call; he would just have to make it a short one, and bull it through.

They didn't yet know who he was, and Miss Min was coming towards the parking space with a polite, anxious look that would do for anyone, when he got out. Immediately her expression changed; and she said, with what sounded like relief mixed with some exasperation: "Oh, it's you, Waldon. I hope you're bringing back my basket!"

"What basket?" he said; and she answered impatiently, "Now you haven't lost it, have you? The one I gave you to carry the dogs' food in, of course! I know it didn't look like much, but it's a particular favorite of mine, I got it in France, and I couldn't bear to think it was thrown out!"

"Of course it's not thrown out," he said, soothing. "I know exactly where it is, and I can go get it for you this minute. Do you want me to?"

Of course she didn't; if he would just promise to bring it next time he came ... And of course, he would. Then they got to the end of that. Miss Min began to peer at him.

"What *did* you want, dear?" she asked, all ready to be anxious again.

"Good heavens, I don't want anything, Miss Min—I just stopped by to see how you all were. Is that so dreadful?"

"No, no, dear—it's very sweet of you, we're all quite well.... You seem so different," she added, clearly puzzling about it.

He was taken aback by that, until he realized what it was—which she would never do, or not until it was too late.

"It's the car," he told her gently. "I've got the family hearse, that's all."

She made her own connection, saying quickly, "Oh, yes, of course—and how is your father? I don't suppose we'll get to see him this weekend, either?"

"Well, actually, that was one of the things I stopped by about," he said, in an animated voice. By now he had identified the group on the lawn: Buffy and her grandfather, of course, and the Friends—and Krieg! So he was still here. Waldon hadn't any desire to be one of *that* group; but on the other hand, he didn't intend to be shunted off in full view of it. So he began, easily, to improvise. "It's been such ages since you've been over, mother's feeling quite sad about it, and we wondered if you wouldn't come to us next weekend—name your own time, of course, but we rather hoped you might make it Sunday dinner."

"Well, it's lovely of your mother to ask us," Miss Min began; she looked doubtful, even a little harassed, and he wasn't surprised when she went on: "Can't I call her tomorrow, Waldon? I'll have a chance to speak to the Doctor tonight, and then I'll call her first thing in the morning—will that be all right?"

"Darling, it's not a *secret*," he said gaily. "Come along, and let's pop the question now—actually, I think it would be rather nice if the Friends could come too, don't you? We've never had them, and we really should—but I don't want to intrude if you're talking *business*," he said, growing grave.

That shook her, as he had intended it to do.

"Oh, no, no—certainly not, what a strange idea!" she cried, quite lost, and began trundling him forward at once by one sleeve, to show that there was nothing up *theirs*.

Buffy looked over and waved, as they came; the Doctor looked over and didn't. Mel and Anita just watched, looking potentially anything—pleasant, not pleasant; Krieg, he couldn't bring himself to see. But in spite of quite a desperate unwillingness to be there at all—to go one step closer to that waiting, unwelcoming group—he managed to keep his head and find a manner that would do for them all: not too effervescent, because of Dr. Oliver, yet certainly not hangdog—though that was rather the way he felt.

Miss Min, to add to it, began calling out to explain him to the Doctor before anyone could decently speak.

"It's Waldon, dear, he just stopped by very kindly to see how we all are—"

"—and to bring you a little message, if I may," he rather bravely called out with her. Then they were there, and he could add more quietly "I'm so terribly sorry to be interrupting, I didn't know there was anything going on...."

"Nonsense, nonsense," said the Doctor brusquely. "Sit down, boy. Min—aren't there any more chairs? Buffy—"

"No, no, *please*," Waldon begged. "Honestly, I can't stay —only stopped by to say my piece, and then I've got to be off, I'm so sorry. It's only that mother wondered if you couldn't come to dinner next Sunday—you and Anita too, Mel, if you can—it would be such a pleasure—"

It was appalling; he had never felt—never *been*—so gauche in his whole life; and yet he did manage to keep smiling and glancing brightly from one to another of them (except Krieg). Nobody answered at once—nobody knew who ought to answer, of course—and he tried to repair this by saying to Dr. Oliver: "We do hope you can come, sir."

"Well, well, that's up to Min, of course, I don't see why not—very nice indeed of your mother—" Even the Doctor seemed at a loss, or rather as if someone were unexpectedly pressing a plate of fish upon him.

Miss Min began: "I told Waldon I'd call Helene tomorrow, dear—" and he mumbled, "Yes, very good idea. Very nice indeed"; and then Waldon turned his bright look upon Anita.

"You really must come, you know—you and Mel. It'll be a first-time, do you realize that? and we don't have exciting first-times nearly often enough, you mustn't disappoint us!"

Well, that was better—Anita seemed to think so too, for she smiled at him, and said they'd love to come, but she was afraid it couldn't be next weekend. They were having houseguests, she said, her eye going past him ... to Krieg? She hoped they could come another time.

"Well, you must," said Waldon, with a feeling as though he were bringing up all his guns in the hopes that one would work, "because it's just nonsense that you and father should be down there in the city all week and not even *know* each other—it's quite embarrassing for him, Mel!"

"Oh, we've met, Waldon," Mel replied.

Waldon perceived, in the same instant, that neither of the Friends believed him. They knew quite well—as he did himself—that his mother would never have arranged such a dinner party in the circumstances. As though she were trying to *horn in* on their council of war, by moving it to her house! Why hadn't he thought, before he spoke?

Well, he thought, rather desperately stooping to pat a dog (it turned on its back, and became very female), they would just think he had come to invite the Olivers and lost his head when he found them there; that was bad enough, but not fatal.

"Well, we'll just have to keep after you, then," he said, in a pleasant voice; and they said they hoped he would; and that finished it—not too badly. (Except that he *must* remember to tell his mother that the Olivers were probably coming.)

"Is this the one that was sick, Buffy?" he asked, looking at her for the first time. Her expression was sad; she was terribly sensitive, and probably suffering with him—he smiled, to show her it was all right now.

"No, that's Griselda," she replied. "They do look almost alike."

From her embarrassment, and a quick look round which showed him only one other dog, he gathered what was wrong—and spoke of it at once.

"Good heavens, don't tell me she's still at the vet's!"

"Oh, she's all right, I just spoke to Dr. Silver," said Buffy quickly. "He said I can bring her home very soon."

"But no puppies," said the voice of Krieg.

This was absolutely intolerable; and in a rush of release, Waldon allowed his anger and indignation to show in one long glance at that speaker. Then he rose, and said deliberately to Buffy: "Can I speak to you, just for a minute?"

"Go along, Buffy, go along," said her grandfather at once, as if they were two children to be shooed away together. Then in tardy amend to Waldon, he added: "Very nice to see you. Give your parents our thanks, Waldon."

"And tell your dear mother I'll call her in the morning," Miss Min added, winding it all up.

He said goodbye to Mel and Anita, and hurried away to catch up to Buffy, who was walking slowly towards the car. He was rather dreading coming up with her, to tell the truth; but he needn't have been. She said only, "Why are you driving your father's car? Is the Volkswagen broken?"

"No, it's all right."

He walked along beside her in silence, until they reached the car. Then, in a low voice, he began rapidly to speak.

"I know this isn't my affair, Buffy, and I'm not trying to—I'm not *asking* you anything," he said, to her already downcast face. "But if there is any more trouble for you about this—about Mrs. Kavanaugh, I want you to know that I'll tell them I was there. And you weren't. I'll tell them that."

She raised her eyes then. His heart gave one tremendous leap, and then fell quiet. He met her look directly.

Then she turned away again, and said in a listless voice, "Oh, Waldon—please don't. I wish you wouldn't do this."

He stammered, "What—do you mean?" and saw her turn away still farther.

"Please don't keep on telling people those things, Waldon. Alibis ... Nobody believes it, and it just makes more confusion. I had to say it wasn't true, about your seeing me in your field, that night—and they didn't know whether to believe me or not, and then they wonder what else not to believe. Can't you see that?"

Her sad, low voice said that she did not expect him to see it—didn't hope to be able to deflect him, was quite resigned to more embarrassment and confusion which he would cause her. And mesmerized by this view of himself, he could only sigh:

"I did—I did see you—"

"Yes, I suppose you did. But not that night, Waldon."

"No," he said, admitting it. "Not that night. Not that night."

He put his hands up suddenly, covering his face. "Oh, God, Buffy.... Oh, my God...."

"It's all right," her voice said quickly. "It's really all right—I'm sure they do believe me, now. But if you started saying something *else*—"

He didn't feel as if he would ever be able to speak again. He took his hands down, and without looking at her got into the car. He was aware of her, continuing to stand there—waiting, while he turned the Lincoln and sent it down the drive, swaying against the leaves on one side and then the other. He wanted to get out of there—get away, end it, forget it. It was hopeless.

Later, on the road, he deliberately tried to imagine her going back to the group, telling them that he admitted he had lied, that he was only what they all supposed him to be—a meddling fool. But he couldn't achieve even this much comfort. He couldn't imagine anything; he couldn't think. He only *knew*. Knew that he was still imprisoned beyond hope in his terrible silence—imprisoned as his mother was imprisoned, and *with her*. No one else could come in with them, and he could not get out.

He was imprisoned within her knowledge, and she within his deed. There wasn't any escape for either of them.

He drove home. There was no place else to go.

No one was on the lawn, although the chairs were still there—his mother's chaise, with its thick blue mattress, and his father's rattan chair drawn up beside it. He drove past, turning his head away, and put the Lincoln back in the garage. Hung up the key, so McKinnon could find it. Then he went round the house and in the front door.

His father was alone in the living room. Waldon came in and stood looking at him until he looked up. He put down the paper he had been reading, and said, carefully, "Well, Ju—Waldon. Just back?"

He was being careful; so his mother had won. No more talk of his going back to the city, no more reminders about how old he was, no more—no more what? What was it that she had won for him—from him? *What had she won away from them both this time?*

"What's the matter, Junie?" his father said then.

"What did mother tell you about me, father?"

His father didn't answer that in words, but his expression answered for him, at once. It said: I am not going to begin this all over again.

"I suggest you go up and see your mother," he replied coldly. "She's been waiting for you rather a long time."

"I don't want her to tell me, I want you to tell me," Waldon said. After a minute, to show he would not be ignored, he sat down.

"Was it about—about the musicale?" he suggested. His father looked cautious, potentially irritable. He was beginning to feel trapped.

"Well, what about the musicale?" he said at last. "I was there. So were you. It seemed to me to go off very well."

"No, I wasn't. I wasn't there all the time. I didn't stay, I left."

"Then I think you behaved extremely rudely to your mother," his father replied. But he couldn't hide what he was thinking: so *this* was what it was all about. This was all it was.

He added, lest Waldon perceive this (as he did): "You could hardly have thought of anything that would wound her more, could you?"

"I can't bear them, father. To see her so excited, and to know what a terrible letdown she'll have afterwards … because they don't matter. She knows they don't matter."

"That's hardly for you to judge," his father said.

There was a silence between them, in which his father picked up the paper again. But he was not reading, he was only hiding. The pulse in Waldon's throat beat as if the skin would burst.

He said, "I went to see a woman"; and the paper went down.

Then it wavered; his father couldn't decide whether to have heard or not.

Waldon waited. His father had to speak, before he could speak again.

His father said: "Junie … are you sure you want to tell me this?"

I killed her, said Waldon's mind at once. She made me—I can't tell you—She made me—

A blinding pain struck through his head and vanished. Then nausea rose in him like a gag. He never moved. He never would, until he had told. Until his father spoke to him, and he could tell.

In slow and carefully chosen words, his father began to speak.

"Son, I don't know what you think I know about this—what your mother has told me—even what she could have told me—" He paused, and then began over. "Sometimes, when something is lying heavily on our conscience, we feel that the whole world must know—must be waiting for us to tell what we have done. And it's right for us to feel this way, Junie—it's a sign to us that our conscience is alive, and on duty—trying to protect us even when it's too late. In one particular instance, too late," his father corrected himself. "But it's only children who have the right to yield to this impulse, son. A child needs to tell what he has done, because he needs to be *told* what he has done. Do you understand what I'm trying to say?"

He looked at Waldon a moment. Then he cleared his throat, and said, very low: "But when we are men and women, we know. We know what we have done, when we do wrong. Nothing we can say to others, or that they can say to us, can change that knowledge—we mustn't hope that it can. All we can do is to find the strength within ourselves to face what we know, to understand what we have done that makes us so unhappy, so that we will never be capable of doing it again. That is how a man's strength grows, Junie," he said, "by this great, great effort. That we must make," he said. "That we must learn to make.... Do you see what I mean, son?"

Yes, father, said Waldon's empty mind.

There was nothing left in his mind at all. It was like a great room full of leaves that a sudden wind had blown through—and light, now, streaming in upon all its bareness, blinding light ...

"... Too much light," he said faintly, and felt himself sliding from the chair.

In the darkness that came then, he could still receive sound. Sounds washed around him, confused and fluctuant, and he made no effort to sort them out. He made no effort at all, although effort was being urged upon him.... great, great effort.

He lay supine in darkness for a long time; until he heard Martha Mary say with far off clarity: "... shouldn't have left his bed at all today...."

He looked up and there she was—very red. It was she who tugged at him.

"Martha Mary ..." he sighed. "Tell my father ..."

"I'm here, boy, I'm here. We're trying to help you, but you must help us! Try to raise yourself, Junie!"

He saw his father too, then—very high, very far up in the air. His thin grey hair had come unstuck and was hanging forward in little strands over his forehead.... How terrible, how terrible, he ought not to look....

He closed his eyes as his father began to descend. Now he felt upon his arms their separate urging—his father's trembling, hard and painful grip that did not raise him, and the easy power of Martha Mary bringing him up upon himself, his body falling forward upon his legs.

They righted him, pulling again, and he came up upon his knees—swayed there, looked dumbly upwards, and was sick. The vomit rushed from his mouth with its own impatience, he was only the vehicle, the passage, and he did not care.

His father's grip left him and he swayed sideways, dangling from Martha Mary's hands. He moaned, "Let me down, let me down," and his father's nervous voice struck upon the air: "Good God, woman, put him down—let him lie down, stay there—I'll go call the doctor."

She did not obey. When they were alone she knelt and pulled his arm around her neck and rose under him, a great panting thing that pulled him stumbling forward, out of the room, across the hall. They began to go up the stairs like two drunkards—two shameless drunkards upon an endless stair, and he was crying weakly, letting his body sag, not caring if they both fell backwards, down and down.

Halfway, when she let him pause, his head fell back and he saw that his mother stood above them at the head of the stairs. Her face was still, intent with sorrow and compassion; and he managed to say her name.

She answered him only with his. Staring up at her, he felt himself at the disastrous end of some long mistake. All his wild fleeing away from her had been without reason, without any possible purpose. Gentle, sad, without reproach, she had been waiting here for him all the time.

CHAPTER THIRTEEN

The next day Waldon made no attempt to leave the house. His mother told Martha Mary to put out his silk Chinese pajamas in the morning, which was a nice thought, and gave him mild pleasure. It was exactly the sort of compromise his own enfeebled, fretful mind had been searching for, between staying in ordinary pajamas and getting dressed, neither of which appealed to him. He sent his thanks back to her, via Martha Mary. She was staying in her room, too.

Her door was shut when he went by it, on a brief visit downstairs to get the Sunday papers while his father was at church. There was no problem about whether he should look in and say "Good morning," because he wasn't *legally* up at all—just slipping down for the papers, and then straight back to bed. He did, unfortunately, run into Josephine in the living room, and he didn't like to ask her not to mention to Martha Mary that she had seen him—he couldn't in fact, think of anything at all to say to her, and went away depressed and irritated by the encounter. She was such a *slavey* mentality, it was hard to believe a girl like that could still exist.

But nothing, today, affected him much, or long. The Chinese pajamas had been a mild pleasure, Josephine a mild annoyance; neither stayed with him. Nothing did—except, luckily, the very excellent breakfast Martha Mary had sent up; and even with that, he had the feeling he could have gone without just as well. He felt detached—very relaxed, *let go*. Exactly, of course, the way he ought to feel.

Back in his room, he was faintly interested to find he didn't want to do much reading in the papers after all. He glanced through the Book and Magazine sections, which were conveniently small, but let the unwieldier Theatre and Arts slide to the floor after one wide-arm attempt to open it. After a moment he pushed the rest of the paper after it, and slid down on his pillows.

The shielded light of his windows, and the still leaves beyond the screen, held his gaze in a gentle fascination. He felt he could lie there for hours absorbing the fact of leaves and light, and glimpsed blue sky beyond. The background of small, constant country sounds coming in through that open space kept his mind lulled—no silence ever quite occurred to startle it into attention.

He didn't actually mind when Martha Mary came in, however, which she did a couple of times to see if he wanted anything. (More probable, to make sure he was staying in bed.) Well, he was very definitely staying in bed, with no impulse to do otherwise; and he didn't begrudge her the satisfaction of noting his sprawled body and half-closed eyes. She did take satisfaction from it, too—would go out and shut the door as if he were a nicely risen cake she had just peeped at.

Then he would hear her go next door (she was incapable of real quietness, even on that carpeted floor; actually, she was probably somewhat muscle-bound) into his mother's room. No voices reached him from there, since his mother's windows were around a corner from his own, but he could imagine Martha Mary's report, delivered with a lot of pillow-pats. "Resting beautifully, dearie ... lying there like a little lamb," and so on. For some reason, he couldn't quite go on to imagine his mother's reception of this news. He couldn't quite imagine *her*, today. Was she flat and pale and shiny-faced again, like that disturbing sleeper? He didn't think so, really, but the notion crept into his thoughts of her whenever they arose, and he tried to keep them at a minimum.

It wasn't too hard.

By and by he drifted into sleeping, and that must have lasted a long time. When his eyes opened again—long after his mind, to actual impression—the sunlight was off the leaves entirely. He would have had to sit up in his bed to see sunlight now, lying long and beneficent across the lawn; it must be nearly six o'clock. What a really heavenly day it had been ... and the best was, that he had no fear of paying with a restless night for his long drowsing. No, he felt the capacity for more sleep within him still, a bottomless source.

Was he hungry? He decided that he might be persuaded to be, if Martha Mary brought him something really nice. He had a not-impossible hope that she had roast beef down there, which she could slice very thin and then warm in some gravy for him. (His mother and father liked their beef much too red, which meant he never could have any cold.) And then some pickly sort of thing with it ... mustard pickles? Or little gherkins?

Where on earth *was* Martha Mary? He began, restless, to turn in his bed, which had gotten quite messy, too. At last he went so far as to get up and go to the bathroom—a flushing sound through the pipes was quite likely to bring someone. But no one came.

Then he realized that the household would be, at this time on a Sunday evening, centered around his father—feeding him, getting him ready to go to the station. He might just as well go back to bed and wait till he heard McKinnon take the car out—which he could, if he listened carefully.

But he didn't want to go back to bed and wait. He really was hungry, and the bed was a wreck, and his feet slid twice on the exasperating papers all over the floor. There certainly wasn't much incentive to stay obediently resting in bed if it ended up in his being left to *rot* there.

Why didn't his father go? Both his watch and his clock had run down, and he had nothing but lawn shadows to tell time by—and according to them, his father should already be gone. *Or was he going?*

Waldon, fretting by his windows, paused. It was a most unwelcome idea ... but could it be true? Would he think he ought to stay over, because both of them were sick? Waldon didn't really think so—this was the kind of weekend his father was inclined to shorten, rather than lengthen; but that presidential mind was totally unfathomable. If he thought it was right to stay, he would stay.

Sullen, Waldon leaned his forehead against the screen and stared down. He could imagine his father sitting down there, dug in for the evening. Fed; clamping one cigarette after another into Marty's ridiculous holders; happily tuning in on a long series of Sunday evening programs. Their comfort and stay, Waldon thought bitterly. Their moral support downstairs.

His door opened, and he gave a startled glance round. It was his mother.

"Oh!" he said; and then, foolishly, "I thought you were father...."

"No, daddy's gone," she said. She came into the room a little way, uttering this nursery formula, which belonged to those years of Sunday evenings when she would come up to a little boy waiting, wakeful and impatient, in his bed. Her tone was indifferent, so she had not used the phrase deliberately; still, he withheld any response of pleasure (even from himself) and stayed where he was.

She was dressed in some sort of house gown thing, and her hair and expression were both tidy; and while she seemed pale still, in the fading light, it was a matte paleness. Well; she was all right again, then; but he still withheld himself. What did she have to *say*, now that "daddy was gone"?

What she finally said was: "This room looks simply dreadful. Hasn't anybody been looking after you?"

"No," he said.

"Well, you can't stay here," she said, herself turning away. "You'd better put on a robe and come downstairs a while. Martha Mary can bring you something to eat on the couch."

And without even selecting the robe for him, much less helping him put it on, she went away.

Partly reassured, but withdrawn still, Waldon chose for himself—a deliberate *mesalliance* of terrycloth and Chinese silk. Then he went sulkily downstairs.

His mother wasn't there. She must have simply gone back into her room. There were no lights on anywhere; and when he came out to the kitchen, he found that clean and deserted. Martha Mary had gone. And Josephine, of course, had Sunday afternoons off.

It was perfectly extraordinary.

He walked back slowly, through the orderly, shadowed downstairs. How queer it was, this silence and neglect of himself, through which he was free to move anywhere. Queerest of all was the fact that his mother must have known Martha Mary had gone ... what was she thinking of?

He paused by the piano, in the music room, and frowning, put his recorder into its case. Then he opened one of the doors—locked, for some reason—and went out on the lawn. There, legs apart, he stood looking up and round in the tranquil evening air.

Indoors, a telephone rang. It was answered at once ... his mother's extension. Frowning again, he went back into the house.

In Martha Mary's immaculate large kitchen, he opened the icebox and began a leisurely inventory of what she kept there. He was not allowed to rummage in this icebox; neither was his mother, although Martha Mary showed her its contents every morning. But Martha Mary had cancelled her rights by going off and leaving him unprovided for, and he made no pretense of not looking—shifted dishes, removed their covers. She seemed to be obsessed by aluminum foil.

There was nothing there he wanted—certainly not that raw-looking roast, still faintly warm (surely warm meat ought not to be put into a refrigerator) nor the already congealing gravy. His interest in Martha Mary's kitchen didn't run to heating things up in pans. Leaving the icebox door open for the mild light it shed, he began looking in other places—cupboards, and even drawers. It was just random looking, by now. But at last he did acquire some peanut butter, and chili sauce, and bread, and made himself several sandwiches. When these were done it occurred to him that what he would really like would be hardboiled eggs—lots of them. So he found a large pot, filled it with water, and carefully arranged six eggs down at the bottom. Then he put it over a brisk flame—a lovely light in the deeply shadowed room—and took his sandwiches and some milk into the front of the house.

He couldn't remember when he had last had the place to himself this way—and just at this peaceful hour of the day, too. In the strange pleasure of it, he couldn't settle, but kept wandering, sandwich in hand, from room to room, noting how the light in each would fade between visits—but even the east rooms not in absolute dark. Then he began to perceive, on surfaces hitherto obscure, a new gleaming—from the moon. He went outside again and found this moon gibbous—waxing, surely, at this time of the month.

So she had had moonlight last night. That was how she had managed so well.

The unwanted thought dismayed him … as if his mother herself had joined him. His tranquility spoilt, he went inside again. But indoors, he found the long, tenuous evening had turned to profounder night; and he would have to turn on lights or go upstairs.

He could not bring himself to turn on lights. What would he do, when they were on? Stumbling a little, his mood lost, he retreated upstairs again.

Light edged his mother's bedroom door. He hesitated—and then looked in—putting in just his head, and that not far. She was sitting up in bed reading—he could recognize it from here—that Ouspensky-Gurdjieff thing; and that meant she would be out of reach for quite a while.

He said, with undisguised sadness, "Good night, mother"; and she replied "Good night, darling," and peered vaguely up, as if she could not see him very well, as perhaps she could not. He shut her in again and went to his own room.

It was a shock, just at first, to find this the way he had left it—newspapers, wrung sheets, beaten pillows. After a minute, he set about straightening things as well as he could—putting the papers in a pile, tugging at the covers, shaking up the pillows. Then, when he had done his best, he climbed back into bed, too weary even to change into real pajamas.

But he had hardly got stretched out when his door opened, and his mother stood there looking in at him. He could see, with instantly widened eyes, her outline—but not her expression. She said nothing.

"What is it, mother?" he made himself ask.

She said then, "You left eggs cooking, Waldon."

It seemed to him the strangest thing she had ever said to him. Until he realized how long she was standing there, it did not even occur to him to reply.

Then he said, "I'm sorry ..." and she accepted that in silence, and went away, leaving him wide awake. What did she mean by this? What did she mean by *any* of it—sending him downstairs when she must have known Martha Mary had gone—letting him scratch for himself without even an inquiry as to how he was making out—*and then coming down to see what he had done*. What was the matter with her? It would really be the end if she just turned peculiar and stayed that way—if he had to become a kind of Marcie Hunt, dragging a shameful old parent around with him the rest of his days.

He began to shiver, and pulled his blanket up, but that didn't help. Morning, and daylight, seemed a long way away.

CHAPTER FOURTEEN

In the morning, his mother told him about her plans for them.

She was out on the lawn, on her chaise, by the time he came down—he caught a glimpse of her out of the window, but she was reading away and didn't see him.

Monday was Martha Mary's day to stay home and work madly in her own house (which made Tuesday a day to keep out of her way), so that meant he hadn't much to look forward to at breakfast. Josephine could fry eggs, rather greasily, and work the toaster, and that was about all. They no longer pretended to discuss what he would have. He just banged the bell and buried himself in the *New York Times*, and presently the greasy eggs and cold toast arrived. Her coffee was so unspeakable that he kept a jar of powdered coffee for Monday mornings; she would bring it in on the tray without the slightest shame. He couldn't even trust her to mix it.

This morning she also brought him a message—delivered at once, in her breathless, say-it-before-I-forget-it voice.

"Your mother wants to see you before you go, Mr. Waldon."

"All right," he said, gloomy. "Surely there's some jam, isn't there?"

She fled to see, without a word. Then he thought of all the eggs he had made—no matter how cold and hard, preferable to these before him—and when Josephine came he sent her to get them. She was gone so long he went after her, and found her with the icebox practically dismantled, and no eggs.

She got up at once to let him see for himself, but he couldn't find them either. Weren't eggs of any kind always kept in a refrigerator? He roamed the pantry a little, under Josephine's mute regard, and then became convinced—suddenly and absolutely—that his mother had put them in the garbage. This idea enraged him so that he left the kitchen without a word and went directly through the house to the music room doors. There, just inside, and in a voice as toneless as Josephine's, he said:

"Mother, where are my eggs?"

If he had hoped to startle her, as she had startled him last night, he failed. She seemed barely to receive the words—put down her book (it was still Ouspensky) and looked at him for some time without answering.

Then she said, "Oh. I threw them away. I couldn't think what you meant," she added.

"I was going to eat them today."

"No; they were scorched," she said, already raising her book again. "At least, the pan was, and I thought they would taste of it."

"What absolute nonsense," he said, and turned away.

By now Josephine's offering was not fit to look at, let alone eat. He made his coffee, and then—like a man with a sore tooth which he cannot leave alone—took it out on the lawn to drink.

This time his mother did not put the book down until he came up beside her. Even then she left it open on her lap. He sat down, very carefully so as not to spill, and she said absently:

"Did you find them, dear?"

He didn't answer that at all.

She made a little more effort, then—at least, to excuse herself.

"These teachings are such a comfort to me, Waldon," she said. "I wish I hadn't given up my classes. If we had only stayed in New York in the winter...."

"It was your own idea to live here the year round," he replied.

"I know, I know. I thought you would be happier. I thought we both would be."

"Well, I haven't complained, have I?" he said.

"Waldon, don't shut me out," she said then—a remark to which there was no possible answer. Besides, what had *she* done, all last evening?

She closed her book and laid it on the grass, as if to make clear she wished to give him all her attention now. He waited.

"I had a long talk with your father yesterday," she said then. "He feels as I do—that we've reached a point where we need to make a change, for all our sakes."

"Oh, mother—why do you use such meaningless expressions?" he burst out. "Father doesn't need any change—he couldn't make one if his life depended on it! And I haven't the least desire to get shunted back to New York. What you mean is that you and father have decided it's time to shift everything round again, willy nilly, and so I'm to abandon my business, my friends, my whole life here that I haven't any desire to leave—"

"Waldon, Waldon!"

Her voice was so urgent and fearful that he paused—paused in speaking, at least, though his angry thoughts tumbled round still without expression.

"Waldon, I don't understand you," she said at last, in a breathless voice.

"And quite frankly, I don't understand you, mother."

"But you know we can't stay here now!"

He turned his head away in silence. Her hand came groping along his arm, making the cup he held tremble on its saucer. He stooped and put it down, thus evading her touch; she did not attempt to renew it.

"Waldon—dear, you do understand that, don't you?"

"No, mother, I don't," he answered then, and turned back to face her. "I don't understand this decision any more than the others you and father have been making for me, all my life! That I'm supposed to accept, and agree to, and even pretend I was a party to making! I'm getting a little old for these games, mother," he said, his own voice trembling now, "and I think it's time we all understood what's going on when we have these 'agreements'! If you want to force me out of every kind of life I manage to make for myself, then all right—you have that power. But let's stop pretending it's what *I* want, because it isn't! You and father aren't even faintly interested in what I want, and I think it's time we faced that too—we simply live in a perpetual deadlock between father's idea of how I should live and your idea of how I should live, and any feeble little beginnings I manage to make in between are just swept away every time, swept away!" he said, beginning to cry. He bit his lip, and turned away from her; and behind him she didn't make a sound.

By blinking hard and controlling his breathing, he managed to pull himself together—enough, at least, so that he could have got up and gone away. It was what he ought to do. Otherwise, they would just drift into the same old scene, tearing each other to pieces for no reason, getting nowhere. But this time, he didn't *want* to put an end to it—he didn't yet know why, he only knew that at his first motion to rise a disinclination—tangible as his mother's hand would have been—held him where he was.

Well, all right. He wanted to have it out, then. He *would* have it out.

He turned round, and looked directly at his mother.

She was just lying there, looking back at him. It was the sort of "poor-mama" look that was supposed to stop him in his tracks—pale, big-eyed, dry-lipped. Actually, it *did* always affect him, more or less ... and this time rather more, because of his own overwrought state. So there was a long moment when neither of them spoke.

Then, with great effort, she whispered at him: "I thought we might go to Italy...."

That gave him real pause. Made him so thoughtful he looked down, at his own fingers slowly interlacing.

To Italy....

Yet how like them, how *like them*—to offer Italy now! Now, when he had got all over the idea, lost touch with the people who had been going and urging him to come with them, lost the whole excitement and purpose of that lively group on Fire Island who had known exactly where they would go, what they would do, how they would live and work and *expand* in the Italian sunlight!

How long ago was it? The summer he had his MG—three, four years ago. He had even forgotten most of their names.

He raised his head, looking at her again.

"Both of us?" he said.

"Yes. I would be the reason," she said simply.

"I don't know what you mean."

"Yes, dear. Because of what Dr. Stone said, about my needing to travel and have change. And a milder winter."

"I thought that was ages ago."

"He still thinks so. But it was just that I didn't like to uproot you, when you seemed to be liking it so much here."

"But you don't mind uprooting me now," he said.

She didn't reply.

He sighed. "Well, I don't want to go anymore," he said. "I'm sorry, but I don't. If you had let me go when I wanted, the way I wanted—"

"But you know why we couldn't do that, dear—you know those weren't very responsible young men, that they didn't hesitate to sponge on you even here at home—they even broke your little car, don't you remember? We couldn't have let you go and be entirely at their mercy, so awfully far away—"

"That was your opinion of them, not mine! You might have done me the courtesy of allowing me to act on my own opinion," he said, suddenly heated. "After all, I was the one who was going with them, not you! And that accident might have happened to anyone—and Roy offered to pay, but then he wouldn't have had the money to go to Italy, and it would have been like punishing *him* because *I* couldn't go! They didn't 'sponge' on me—they never even thought of having or not having money. You and father were the ones who thought of that—and judged them by it!"

"Oh, darling—please don't quarrel! We mustn't, we *mustn't!*"

"If it's quarrelling to object to deliberate misstatement of fact about my friends—" he began; when she suddenly flung her hands over her face, and began to cry.

Well, let her. Let her. She had made him cry often enough—and her mercy to him then, her too-late mercy, was crueler than any face he would ever show to her.

He picked up his cup and went in to get more hot water. His hands were shaking so he made messes of coffee powder and sugar all over the cloth; and when he at last turned back and saw her standing in the doorway, a cry escaped him, and he nearly dropped the cup.

She said hurriedly, "It's all right, dear—it's all right! I was just afraid you would go away—cross with me. Please come back, we'll talk quietly—please, dear."

"I *was* coming back," he said crossly. "Good heavens, mother."

He stalked past her and out on the lawn again, the tepid liquid slopping all the way. Well, he would just pour it back in the cup, it couldn't be fouler than it probably was now. While he was engaged in this depressing transfer she arrived behind him, post haste. He began talking at once, to set their tone as a rational, quiet one, with no more emotion in it.

"Actually, mother, that whole subject is a painful one for me still, you see, and I don't like to bring it up at all—even the idea of Italy is still terribly sad for me. I know you didn't realize it, but it's true, and I think it's better just to admit it at once instead of trying to pretend, and bottle it up inside."

"Oh, don't do that, Waldon. Don't do that. You must tell me things."

"Well, I *do*," he said. "At least, I *try* to."

He took a trial sip of his brew; it was so awful he could hardly believe it, and put the cup down at once. His mother, although watching him anxiously, didn't offer to do anything about it; and he said with restraint: "I simply loathe Monday mornings around here. Is there any reason why Martha Mary couldn't just come and get us started, and then go back and do whatever it is she does all day?"

"Waldon," said his mother. She wasn't even hearing him. He abandoned the whole idea of coffee and sat down again.

"Well, what is it?"

"Don't be angry with me, darling."

"Mother, I'm not. I just said, What is it?"

She said after a moment, "I was just wondering ... if there were any place else you'd like to go? Perhaps just—to travel for a while? Around the world, perhaps?"

"No, I wouldn't," he said as patiently as he could. What was he to do with her, sitting there stuffed to the ears with Ouspensky and reeling out these fantasies for them both? "Mother, listen," he said. "Try to look at it this way. Can you imagine sitting there and trying to sell these ideas to father?"

"But I've already—"

"No, no—I mean *for* him. I mean asking *him* if he'd like to drop everything and go away indefinitely. Do you see?" She didn't, actually, look as if she saw anything at all. Her expression was one of total confusion, and it touched him. He went on very gently: "Even if he wanted to, he couldn't—you can see that, mother. Can't you? He just couldn't—and neither can I. Don't you realize a lot of people around here have made some pretty expensive commitments, just on my say-so, and that they're depending on me to carry out my plans for them? I ought to be over picking up the Duncans' gingko trees right now, for instance—they can't live forever in that burlap, you know. And old Peabody's got tons of cedar poles coming for a grape arbor I've talked him into building, and Miss Min has got a big special order in that it's too late to cancel, and—oh, just so many things, I don't want to bore you with them. But they're my responsibility, mother. I can't just walk away and leave them flat, can I?"

He waited, deliberate and kind, until she could take this in; it was awfully hard to tell what she was making of it.

And all she finally said was: "But—what is it you want to *do?*"

"But what I'm telling you, dear. To follow out my plans, go on building up my business. Really get *after* my place and finish it up—that road's a disgrace, even the pickup can hardly get over it, and the air conditioner alone is going to take about three days—and I can't work there in this weather until I do fix it. I'm sort of like Alice," he said, smiling. "I have to run as fast as I can just to stay in the same place. And then to keep losing a day here, a day there—it's just murder, I can't afford it. Let alone gallivanting off round the world!"

She had quite suddenly shut her eyes—either on some glimpse of understanding, or the abandoned hope of it. He waited to see which.

"Then you just want to stay here … go on here...."

"Yes, of course."

She opened her eyes again and fixed them on him.

"But I'm afraid for you here...."

"Mother, you're afraid for me everywhere," he said, and rose, without at once moving away. "You always have been, you know."

"Yes," she said. "Yes...."

"Well, then," he said (but good naturedly), "it's about time you stopped—don't you think so?" He leaned and kissed her forehead; her hands came up, and then went down without touching him as he drew away. "Also, I'd stop reading for a while if I were you," he said. "That's pretty heavy stuff to keep sucking in all the time."

On this note, a little more serious than he had intended, he began to walk away. She didn't call out behind him, although he was perfectly ready to stop and turn if she did. Well, once more he had patched it up—avoided a scene. And that evening, because of Martha Mary, they would go out to dinner, and the very act of behaving naturally together in public would help them farther along the road to normalcy. But somehow, he didn't feel as *finished* with this particular crisis as he should.

CHAPTER FIFTEEN

The Olivers' old Packard was in the drive when he got home, after quite a good day. The little gingko trees had been all right after all—some intelligent person at the express office had been keeping the burlap wet—and he had got them into the ground where he wanted them before Mary Duncan even came home. Altogether, very satisfying.

A NIGHT RUN

But he wasn't altogether pleased about the Packard. It meant Buffy was here—the old people didn't drive, and one of her main functions was chauffeuring them around. He didn't *mind* Buffy being there; but some residue of unpleasantness still surrounded the idea of the Olivers for him. The meeting on the lawn, perhaps, with Mel and Anita? But he felt quite indifferent to this memory. Something else. Well; it didn't matter. He would just go in the back way, and up to shower and change, and by the time he came down they might be gone.

He didn't even reach the house. By the time he had put the pickup away in the garage, Buffy was already coming around the corner of the house to meet him. He raised a listless hand, not very welcoming, and stood still.

"I heard your Volkswagen," she said, coming up to him. (She always felt it necessary to explain this sort of thing.) "I wanted to talk to you alone."

"Well—right now?" he said, in discontent. "I'm terribly messy—I was just going up to change."

"I thought you might," she said, "and I was afraid Aunt Min would leave before you came back."

"Why is she here?" he asked.

"Because I can't come next Sunday. So Aunt Min brought me to call today."

"*Honestly*," he said, with momentary fellow-feeling. Then, sharper, he asked: "Why can't you come?"

"I'm going to the Friends'. Anita had already asked me."

"I see," he said—and he did. Krieg again, and Anita matchmaking—as all the wives incessantly did, around here. He added, coldly, "Well, you didn't have to rush out and tell me about it—it's not all that important, is it?"

"That wasn't what I wanted to tell you," she said. But she didn't go on to say what it was.

He stood looking at her for a minute, accepting the fact that impatience on his part would only hold him up longer. This was the obverse side of Buffy's quietness; sometimes she got absolutely speechless.

"Well, come on in," he said, and sighed. "I want to get something cold to drink anyway. Just into the kitchen," he said patiently, when she didn't move.

She followed him then—waited while he rooted out a couple of cold beers, and didn't refuse hers until it was opened and poured and held out to her. Who did she think the other one was for?

"Really, Buffy," he said, "sometimes I think you live in a dream."

She amazed him by slowly turning pink. Over this pinkness she gave him quite a straightforward look.

"I'm so sorry," he said then (falsely, though). "What a rude thing to say!"

"Sometimes you are rather rude," she answered. "I think you were rude to Mr. Krieg last Saturday."

"Yes, I meant to be," he said promptly. "He's an awful ass, isn't he?"

She said after a moment, "I thought I'd better tell them what you said, about being there, that night."

"Whatever are you talking about," he replied, and walked away from her, to stand at the screen door. But he was no sooner there than he swung round again. "What an absolutely rotten thing to do, Buffy!" he burst out.

He couldn't say a word more, just then. His heart had begun beating quite wildly, and it was affecting his breath. But he let his angry silence, directed full at her, speak for him. She seemed quite aware that she had behaved badly.

Nevertheless she tried to defend herself.

"You said you were going to tell the police yourself, Waldon, and I was afraid you might."

"You didn't think anything of the kind! I said *if* there was any more trouble for you, I was *willing* to do this—that was all, and you understood perfectly well what I meant!" And unable to stop himself, he cried out: "You just wanted to pay me back for that—disgusting dog! Admit it!"

She wouldn't say a word. She only looked at him a moment longer and then started to go away. He got easily before her at the door, blocking her way.

What did he mean to do, holding her there? For a moment an automatic apology trembled in his throat, quite meaningless; he didn't make it. Instead, in a rapid low voice, he said to her:

"I would do anything to help you—anything! But if you only take what I say and twist it and hand it to that wretched little lawyer to use like a club on my head, then I'll take it all back, I'll deny it! I do deny it!"

He waited, fierce, to force her to reply. But she seemed ready enough to speak.

"I didn't do that. It's a perfectly crazy idea. And I don't want you to help me, I never did."

"You don't even know what you want, or what you've done," he said, quieter. "You *do* live in a dream, Buffy—running around like that at night, and thinking nobody notices it! *Everybody* knows it, and everybody thinks it's just as queer as hell, and it's enough to drive anybody frantic that cares about you! And you do need my help, you know you need it—or you wouldn't have come here today and told me what you did!"

She gave a sudden little shiver, standing there, looking down. His terribly sharpened vision caught it at once, and he put his hand on her shoulder. She struck it down.

He would have liked then—not on impulse, not wildly, but quite deliberately—to have struck her back. Across her face, raised to his. She seemed attentive for this possible response, even expectant; it confused him when she said only: "Let me out, please"; and he waited until that confusion passed.

Then, quietly, he asked, "Then why did you come?"

"It doesn't matter, it was a mistake. Let me out."

"It wasn't a mistake, you had a reason. What was it?"

She looked at him a moment. Then she said: "I came to tell you they half believe it's true."

"That I was there? Did Krieg say that?"

"It wasn't anything anyone said."

"But that's perfectly mad," he said, gentle. "You've misunderstood—how could they think—? You know for yourself that I couldn't have been there. That was the night of my mother's musicale, your aunt was here, she knows. I drove her home myself."

She suddenly wet her lips, as if she meant to reply. But she made no reply.

"Don't you remember?" he persisted. "Your grandfather wasn't well, so you didn't come. Do you remember now?"

"Yes," she said. "Let me go by, Waldon."

He hated to let her go. It seemed to him they had only begun, that they could have gone on and talked for hours ... but she looked as if she were going to make a break for it, if he didn't move aside. So, reluctant, he pushed the door for her and stood back against it. With the vista of other rooms before her, she waited a moment longer, still looking at him.

He smiled, and said: "Don't get too mixed up with these New York people, Buffy. They're not for us. You know that."

She went past him then; and he let the door return to place behind her.

He went back to finish his beer, thoughtfully, at the sink. His anger with her was entirely gone—it never lasted, no matter how exasperating she became—but a deeper, truer rage lay beneath, waiting to be examined. He knew what it was, and whom it was for—but he didn't want to examine it just now. He was too tired ... too disappointed, to think well.

Yes, disappointed was the word, he realized, slowly going up the back stairs with the other glass of beer. The eternal, constant disappointment that every meeting with Buffy left in him. Sometimes he even felt that it was all hopeless—that young as she was, the really *unnatural* life she led at home had already spoiled her for any good relationship. And yet her strangeness was her charm, that was the devil of it. He might as well face the fact, and continue to do the best he could with it, as he had done for so many years. Strange, dear Buffy ... he didn't really want to change her, except in her attitude to himself.

He heard the old Packard leaving, as he was languidly undressing for his shower; and that seemed strange too—he had been thinking of her as gone for such a long time, and she had just been downstairs. He smiled a little, dreamily, wandering over to his closet. Then, in a sharp leap of concealment, he got inside the door—his mother was coming into the room.

She said "Oh!" and went out again, leaving a slight opening through which they might speak. But he really didn't have anything to say to her—except useless remonstrance. She didn't immediately speak either. He went into his bathroom and shut the door.

There, even under the soothing streams of the shower, he could not recapture his gentle mood. His annoyance at being surprised (*haunted* was almost the word; constantly haunted) stirred up the anger with Krieg he had been trying to suppress, and he found he was ready to think about it after all. Of course the fellow wanted to get back at him—he might have expected that. Having stepped out of line, and been quietly but definitely rebuked, Krieg now had a smarting ego to appease. And the revenge he had chosen revealed a mind at once shrewd, naive and unscrupulous. Or perhaps a native naiveté upon which had been imposed the lawyerly training to sharp practice, sudden and unexpected attack. Yes; he thought that was it. This sending over of Buffy (poor little Buffy) with that threat-veiled-as-a-warning was like an echo of Mel Friend himself. A weak and distorted echo, Waldon, thought viciously. There was even something *unbalanced* about it.

Why—*why* hadn't he given Buffy some warning? Some real warning, not just that little cautionary phrase as they parted? Of course he hadn't had time then to think it through; and then the combination of Krieg's message arriving *through* Buffy—as if it were her own—had confused him, too. Well, it was clear now that she was getting into pretty undesirable company—thanks to her grandfather. Waldon had felt from the first that the choice of Mel Friend was not a happy one. It had been just a sort of *hunch* at the time, but a sound one—now it was a considered opinion. The Olivers were all unworldly; and Mel and anyone he trained would be worldly in the most distasteful sense of the word. There was certainly trouble ahead there—and not just for Buffy, who after all never got too much involved in anything. No; old Dr. Oliver and Miss Min were the ones who had better look out. Before they knew where they were, Mel and his cohorts would have them committed to all kinds of publicity and expense—not to satisfy the old man's quite justly affronted feelings, but to feed Mel's need to splash around in the tabloids as sensationally as possible.

Why hadn't he seen all this sooner? And now that he saw it, what was he to do? He wished Miss Min wasn't gone, and that he still might have had the chance for a quiet word with her, here, in his own house, without interruption.

Except that his mother was here too.

Remembering this—and the reminder came in visionary form, an actual image of his mother listening, trembling, while he tried to talk quietly to Miss Min—he had a momentary sense of being absolutely surrounded. Really, it was too much—to try and cope with the daily problems of his life, a man's life, and at the same time carry this load of nervous sensibility around, which his mother imposed upon him!

If she would only *go away*, and let him straighten things out for himself!

Just then the bathroom door opened slightly and her hand appeared, depositing a clean pair of shorts upon the bathroom stool. He just stood still. If he had moved then, he would have picked up those shorts and ripped them into shreds. And thrown the shreds back out at her.

That was the state she was getting him into.

He took his time, calming himself down by the slow following of his complete bathroom routine. He would even have trimmed his moustaches, if the scissors hadn't been out on his dresser.

Yet when he came out at last, she wasn't there. Some sixth sense had warned her, and she had gone away—left his clothes carefully laid out on the bed, and gone away. He stood looking at what she had chosen for him to wear—and then rejected every bit of it. Went to the closet, the chest, and made his own much more positive selections. If she didn't want to appear in a restaurant with him in his Bermudas, too bad, she could stay home. And boil eggs.

Dressed, and in a little better temper, he came down and found her waiting in the living room. She had on a new little cape stole of some intricate knitted stuff, and he bent to examine it; it was quite pretty. That, perhaps, gave her courage to say: "Let's go to Silvermine, dear. I just feel like looking at the swans."

"Oh, good heavens, that's much too far," he objected, straightening up. "I don't feel like driving all that way. I've had quite a day, you know."

"But think how nice it would be, sitting outdoors over the millpond...." Her voice died in her throat, and she gave him one agonized look and was still. This was the kind of thing she was going to begin doing in front of people. He knew it. So did she.

He stood looking at her, and making up his mind. Then, decided, he said quite gently: "All right, come on. I'll take you."

He drove the big car evenly along the winding, blacktop roads, through the leafy summer evening. The radio was on, to WQXR, and he was aware of her relaxing there beside him, letting down, losing that terrible tenseness of hers. He couldn't talk to her while she was that tense; nobody could.

By the time they got to Silvermine, he decided he could risk opening a little casual conversation with her. There weren't very many people there—no one at all near their little corner table on the porch, where his mother could watch the upside-down evening world of leaves and sky in reflective water. She was doing just that; and he waited to let her speak first, which she presently did.

"How strange that the water-world seems clearer and brighter than the real one," she murmured, staring out. "Do you see that it does, Waldon? Or is it just my eyes?"

"No, dear, that's the way it is," he said comfortingly. "Something to do with refraction of light, I suppose."

"I suppose...."

"I put in Mary Duncan's little gingko trees for her today," he went on. "They're really quite charming, I hope it might start a little fad. But what a difficult sort of woman she is."

Instantly, anxiously, her face came round to his.

"Oh, darling, you mustn't fuss with Mary! I know she's quite a decided person, but she's so active in the neighborhood, you know—her opinion carries quite a lot of weight."

"Not with me, I'm afraid," he said, smiling. "And don't worry, I haven't any desire to 'fuss' with her. But I can't understand why she troubles to hire an expert opinion if she doesn't want to take it. It would be so much simpler and cheaper just to get a man in to dig holes."

He was still smiling—she, anxious still. It made a momentary deadlock, which she suddenly broke.

"Waldon, there's just one small thing I want so much to say to you— I hope you won't be angry."

This meant he would. Only she hoped he wouldn't show it. All right; he wouldn't. With the last trace of his smile, he said: "What is it, then?"

"If you could just ..." She looked nervously round; they were entirely private. "If only you could bring yourself to say 'Rose' instead of 'Mrs. Kavanaugh,' dear. I mean, if you have to speak of it—at all—"

His smile had frozen, and she saw that. Saw it, and couldn't stop—went floundering on.

"It's so terribly noticeable, darling—I mean, with you, because you always do use first names, you know. I was wondering myself, last week—I thought perhaps it was a way you had found to—to shut something unpleasant from your mind—"

She was shaking all over. Exactly like old Mr. Hunt. He felt no anger at all—just a terrible gravity, and the knowledge that he couldn't put off speaking to her any longer. It had to be now.

He leaned towards her, fixing his eyes upon her face. "Mother. Be quiet, dear—it's all right, I'm not angry."

"Oh, Waldon—"

"Don't cry," he said, a little sharper. She had looked as if she might. He allowed a pause, in which she showed him she could control herself, before he went on.

"Mother, I'm terribly worried about you. Terribly. And not just this past week. You shouldn't have hidden away what Dr. Stone told you— he was right, mother, you do absolutely need to get away. I've felt myself, for a long time, that you were getting much too close to, well, to a real nervous breakdown, mother. I don't mean to sound brutal, darling, but it's just a thing that people have to face—and when we do face it, it's not so terrible after all. I think it's just a kind of lethargy, a dread of moving, that keeps you from doing anything to help yourself. Isn't there something about that in Ouspensky?"

"Inertia," she murmured. "The momentum of inertia. Yes...."

"Well, there you are," he said. "All you need is to overcome that inertia, and the biggest part's done. I'll help you, you know that."

"But—I thought you didn't want to travel ..." she said, watching him in bewilderment. She still didn't get it. He drew a long breath, decided against any more smiling.

"It's not that I don't want to, it's simply that I can't. But that doesn't mean that *you* can't, mother. And frankly, I think a complete change would have to mean a change from me, too, whether you like the idea or not. Don't you see? You're so much in the habit of thinking we must do everything together—that you're *responsible* for me, the way you *had* to be for so many years—but that's over, darling, can't you see that?" Now he let himself smile again. "What you need is the chance to look around and *realize* that it's over—that you're a complete, wonderful person who can do things all by herself. Or not entirely by yourself, of course," he added quickly. "Somebody awfully nice could go with you—someone like Marcie Hunt, perhaps? It's really time that Edith took on her share of the old man."

"You want me to go away—without you, Waldon?"

He hesitated; it sounded pretty bald, like that. But this wasn't the time to draw back.

"Yes," he said. "That's exactly what I think you should do. Just—"

"*No.*"

It was so desperate a sound—a real cry; one of the water birds below them might have made it—that it imposed a following silence on them both. This time, it was he who looked round. A waitress was coming towards them.

His mother sat perfectly immobile while she was there. Waldon thought it better to leave her that way, and pretended to be examining the evening in his turn.

As soon as the girl had gone, he began quietly: "We can't talk about this emotionally, mother. Here, or anywhere."

She received this in continued silence, looking down.

"I know it's a hard idea for you to accept. And I know you feel you're refusing it because of me. Because of what's best for me." In spite of himself, his patient tone was getting a little edgy. "But don't you think *I* ought to have some say about what I think is best for me? And for you too, for that matter? You just can't *see* the way you're getting, mother—I mean, you couldn't be expected to, of course. Nobody can be that objective about himself. But frankly, darling, it's just terribly hard on somebody who—who has his own problems, and who's trying to—"

"It's no use, Waldon," she broke in—very low, still without looking up. "I can't leave you now. *I can't leave you now.*"

While he was still in pause—really not knowing how to go on after that, or even if he *could*—she suddenly rose and said: "I want to go home."

Then she began blindly walking away through the other tables.

For a moment he just sat where he was. Then—since somebody had to—he pulled himself together and went after her. He met their waitress on the way and stopped to explain—feeling like a poor actor, though God knew it was true—that his mother was ill, and they were leaving. He thrust a five-dollar bill into her hand, which she received blankly, and hurried through the rooms, down the stairs, out the door. His mother was just standing there, by the side of the road. She didn't look towards him or speak. He went over and got the car and drove back beside her, leaning to open her door.

Through that door, as though on some marvelous apparition, she stood and stared in at him. He had to get out at last and come round, and put her in; and that was awkward too. He could only thank heaven it was Monday, and no one was around to see how she was behaving. But he wouldn't risk another show like this with her—he couldn't. Clearly, this was their last public appearance together ... indefinitely.

CHAPTER SIXTEEN

Waldon got out of the house early the next day and stayed away. Not that his mother was being importunate, or even *visible*. So far as he knew she was still in her room, to which she had gone as soon as he got her back from Silvermine. But it was getting so that he couldn't take the house itself, with those *emanations* of quivering nerves coming through all the walls at him.

She knew that he was sensitive, like herself—it had always been a great point with her that he should be. So what did she imagine him to be feeling when she behaved this way, hour after hour, day after day? The most charitable viewpoint he could take was that, for the present, she simply wasn't capable of thinking of anything—that it just hadn't yet occurred to her what an absolute purgatory it must be for him, to live with somebody in this condition—and at such a time!

Quite frankly, the only way he could cope with it was to get away, try not to think about her. If it hadn't been for all his commitments—and the need to make fresh ones, of course, or else just abandon the whole idea of his business—he would have gone away himself. He had really reached that point. It wouldn't have been an easy thing to do, because he was past the age when you just rocketed around with puppylike enthusiasm, exploring anything. No; it would have been a real wrench to leave this little world he knew so well, and where he was accepted and known, and go away; but business and all, he might very well have done it—*except that he didn't dare to leave her*. It made him tremble to think what she might do if he suddenly walked out. She was perfectly capable, in one of her frenzies, of putting the police to trace him.

It was a real trap; he didn't know what to do about it, except get out of the house, keep away from her, try to occupy his mind on other things. But it was so *hard*. He couldn't get up any of his usual *zest* for what he was doing—could hardly keep his mind on it at all. This morning, for instance—after following old Mrs. Fairchild (and a lot of bothersome grandchildren) all over her grounds for *hours*, he had to face the fact that he was being just as indecisive as she. He didn't get one idea—except maybe to cut back the lilac bushes a bit.

It was frightening. His whole *persona* was at stake ... and he didn't know how to save it.

He went to Max for lunch, making sure first by peeping in the windows that Kurt wasn't there, because he wasn't in any shape for disturbed personalities today, however rewarding. Max wasn't there either, and his rather intimidating old father gave Waldon beer instead of iced coffee. That finished him; he had to go back and sleep for a while after that.

Not, of course, in the house. In his stupefied condition he did drive in the front way, but he had sense enough left to keep on going, back to the clearing. It seemed an awfully long time since he had been there, and that mess old McKinnon had left made the place seem quite strange, at first—he didn't have any real sense of coming home at all. He had, in fact, one of those moments of displacement, in which he felt like someone coming to see where Waldon Coutts *had been*, instead of himself coming back to his own.

That made him so miserable he couldn't even get to sleep. He could hardly stand, until he lay down; then as soon as he lay down it was all he could do to keep from getting up again. He actually had to *make* himself lie still, and try to think sleepy thoughts.

While he was concentrating on this, he heard someone out in the clearing. Very definitely someone—quiet, but shod—no stray animal stepped on sticks like that. He lay perfectly still. Then came another very quiet sound that he couldn't place at all, then more silence.

Waldon got up and silently crossed the floor. Through the open window he saw Krieg looking at his pickup. Looking inside it, he seemed to be, through the window—although at that very moment he turned his head and saw Waldon looking at him.

His expression didn't change at all, as a discovered person's usually does—which deprived Waldon of the necessary impetus to challenge him. He did manage to ask, "What are you doing?"—but it came out rather weak. Then he felt obliged to go just outside the door. Krieg was coming slowly towards him.

"Looking for you. Your housekeeper said she thought you were down here."

Waldon couldn't help asking, "You didn't see my mother?"

"No, I didn't ask to. Miss Oliver said she wasn't very well."

"Wasn't—? Oh," said Waldon. "Yesterday, you mean. She's perfectly all right now."

Krieg said he was glad to hear it, and there was another pause. Waldon couldn't keep his glance from wandering to the pickup; and Krieg followed it.

"Very interesting car," he said. "I've never seen one up close before."

"Oh," said Waldon, again. He began to feel quite desperate about himself; and added, in a voice much too loud and sudden: "What do you want?"

"Well, to talk to you," said Krieg. "I seem to have struck a snag with Bu—Miss Oliver, and I thought perhaps you could help me clear it up."

"How do you mean?" said Waldon. He added, "I can't ask you in, there's no place to sit."

"Quite all right. You wouldn't like to go down the road and have a beer? My car's in your drive."

"No," said Waldon, cautious. "No, I don't believe I'd have time for that. I've just stopped by here to pick up some things, you know." He had only one clear instinct about this meeting—that it should be kept as short and unsettled as possible, with both of them standing there at the door. There wasn't much Krieg could do then except stick his hands in his pockets and begin a modified roaming—which he did. He even scuffed a bit, with one shoe.

"Look, Waldon, not to beat about the bush," he said, "I'm beginning to feel that you and Buffy have some sort of private knowledge about that night, which you're juggling round for reasons I don't get—and if that's true, it's a damned dangerous game. If there's any juggling necessary, for God's sake let me do it. Whatever this is, I'm sure you're making far more out of it than you need to. Than you should, if you want to see Buffy in the clear. And that's what you do want, I gather."

"Miss Oliver *is* 'in the clear,'" said Waldon fiercely. "I haven't heard anyone *else* suggest she isn't!"

Krieg stopped being casual then, and glanced at him.

"Oh, come on, now," he said. "What's this all about? I'll be damned if I'm not beginning to think it was she who saw you, instead of the other way round. Is that it?"

"No," said Waldon. "I don't have to talk to you about it. You'd better get out of here."

"No, you don't have to talk to me about it," said Krieg, ignoring the last part. "Although you were pretty anxious to talk about it the day I came, you remember. What's the point of all this? Why do you keep saying you've seen Buffy here and there, when she keeps saying you haven't? First you saw her in the field, and now you didn't see her in the field but down by the millhouse, at a time when *she* says she wasn't there. Why?"

"I said I *didn't* see her there," said Waldon quickly. "My God, can't you get anything straight?"

"Oh, you didn't see her," Krieg repeated, without surprise. "I see—meaning you were there and she wasn't, is that it? Were you there, Waldon? Buffy thinks you were."

"That's a lie," he said. "Buffy never said that. It's not true, she knows it isn't true." Then he got a sudden, firm hold of himself. "I'm not going to discuss it with you any more, Krieg," he said. "You've distorted everything that's been said to you, everything—and so far as I'm concerned nothing more is going to be said. I only wish I could keep you away from Miss Oliver, too."

"Well, I rather wish I could keep you away from her, just now, Waldon," Krieg replied—and started strolling after him, towards the house. Waldon stopped dead, turned.

"My name is Coutts," he said. "Krieg."

"Yes, I know. A. W., Jr. Let's go on, shall we? My car's up there."

But Waldon, head high, would not move.

"You're completely out of bounds, and you know it," he said. "You're going to be in serious trouble, if you keep this up."

"Oh, I don't think so. I'm not really much concerned with your personal problems, Coutts," he said. "All I want is a clear channel with my client—but if that starts muddying up, then I have to find out why. You can see that, can't you—Coutts?"

"You'll never have a 'clear channel' with Buffy! You couldn't begin to understand her, in a hundred years!"

This time, Krieg looked down. He said after a moment, "Well, in some ways, I suppose that's true.... But in the matter we're discussing," he said, "she's quite transparently honest, Waldon. Loyal—but quite transparent. I think you were there."

He went past Waldon, and up the path. Waldon let him go. The minute he was out of sight Waldon ran quietly until his slow, striding figure was once more in view—and kept it so, across the lawn and towards his car. Krieg made no attempt to go into the house.

Once this was certain, Waldon stayed where he was. He was still among the trees and continued to stand there, chewing at his moustaches. Then, quickly, he started round the house. He passed the music room doors and went clear round to the front, as if to see his home as Krieg had seen it when he first came. He went up and opened the screen door, looking in on the wide, cool, handsome hall ... and saw, to his horror, his mother standing just inside the living room entrance. She looked like a seedy Lady Macbeth.

He rushed silently up to her.

"My God, what are you doing down here, like this?" he breathed. "Don't you know someone was just—"

"Oh, who?" she cried as quickly, clutching at him. "Waldon, who was it? Who was that man?"

Her rising hysteria clamped down on his own.

"No one," he said, after a moment. "Come on. I'll take you back up."

"Waldon, Waldon, you don't tell me things, you don't—"

"Come *on*," he said, between his teeth, and began half-dragging her across the hall. For some reason he felt convinced Krieg's departure was a sham—that he was going to double back quickly and catch them in this complete disorder before Waldon could get his mother out of sight. The hall, the staircase, seemed interminable; and she was weeping steadily, and he himself was sweating like a pig, out of sheer nervousness.

But nobody appeared except Martha Mary, at the back of the downstairs hall; and he answered her like something at *bay*, absolutely snarling, so she didn't come after them, at least.

She just stood there.

"Well, there's no reason to talk to me like that, Mr. Waldon," she said. Her eyes looked very watchful; he made himself answer more quietly.

"Martha Mary, I'm doing my best to get her quiet and back in bed, *please* don't add to the confusion!"

She said nothing, but watched them out of sight. God knew what she said about them to other people.

In his mother's room, as soon as he had got her on the bed, he went back and shut the door. She was still sobbing, in a dry, tail end kind of way, and had her arm across the upper half of her face. Even now, she hated to be seen when she was so messy. He certainly wasn't trying to look.

He sat down on the slipper chair and looked at his own hands for a while, until he felt that she was aware of him there. Then he said: "All right, mother—you win. We'll both go."

She took her arm away slowly, so that she could see him.

"What do you mean?" she whispered at last.

"I mean that it's impossible to go on like this, with you acting this way. I've got to get you out of here."

She didn't say anything, but her look—like that of a dog who understood perfectly well what the people were saying—began to rasp horribly on his nerves. He got up, and went round to the back of the slipper chair, gripping it hard.

"Well, why is that so awful " he burst out. "You were making it sound like quite a jolly jaunt, when you were the one that wanted to drag me away! All right, it's the same deal—what's so dreadful about it now? Sunny Italy!" he said wildly. "Or sunny Indo-China, or sunny Timbuctoo—I don't care! Where do you want to go?"

She received this in the same dumb manner, all imprisoned behind those eyes. He saw he was going to have to collect himself—take over for both of them, as usual.

He *did* collect himself, with a tremendous effort. And came back, and sat down on the bed beside her. Took one of her hands.

"Look, I'm sorry," he said. "It's just nerves. I'm all right now. How about you?"

She said something in a whisper, that he couldn't hear. He bent down.

"What?"

"It's too late...."

"What's too late?" he said, straightening. He frowned—made himself stop frowning. "What do you mean, mother?"

"Too late ... to go ... anywhere...."

"Oh, nonsense," he replied; and got up.

He walked a little, watching his own feet. It helped him to talk.

"You're just feeling pretty sunk now, that's all. All right, maybe we'd better not talk about it anymore—but I am quite serious, mother," he said, pausing to look at her again. "You do have to get away for a while—and if you won't go without me, then I'll have to drop everything and go with you, that's all."

She wasn't getting a word of it; it was a complete waste of time.

"Look," he said, coming back. "You're out on your feet—that's what's the matter with you! I don't think you're sleeping at all at night—are you? Aren't you taking that stuff anymore?"

She shook her head, faintly. He began to look round her room.

"Well, where is it?" he said. "I'm going to give you some right now—a good kayo, that's what you need. Then you'll be fresh as a daisy tomorrow, and we'll get on with it. Where are those pills?"

She sighed, and closed her eyes, turning her head away. Suddenly he thought: Oh, the hell with it; and he went out and ran down the back stairs. Martha Mary was just standing at the sink, staring out of the window—as if she were waiting to be summoned. She turned and gave him a gloomy look.

He said briskly, "All right—we're under control and ready to go to sleep. Where's that stuff of hers, Martha Mary?"

"She's not supposed to take those drops just any time, Mr. Waldon."

"Well, she's going to take some now," he said sharply. "How long do you think she can go on with no sleep at all? Or do you care?"

She started to walk away, without a word. He thought for once he had gotten under that rhinoceros hide of hers (not the most convenient time to have done it, though); but she only went into the servants' bathroom, and then came back with a little dropper-topped bottle.

"Good heavens," he said, "do you actually keep it down here?"

"I'm supposed to measure those drops, Mr. Waldon. Dr. Stone said I was."

He said after a moment, "Martha Mary, are you trying to be completely insufferable? I am fully as capable of counting drops out of a dropper as you are. In case you don't know about these things, it's only the patient that isn't supposed to administer his own dose—and that is simply because a drowsy patient might forget and do it twice. Is that clear? Dr. Stone was not implying that nobody in this house but you is capable of dropping drops, in case that was your understanding."

Steady-eyed, without a word of apology, she handed him the bottle.

"Well, that's better. Now—how much, and how much water, please?"

"Milk," she said. "Four drops."

"Four? All right. And in milk? Well, give me some milk, then."

She stood like a rock—then moved as he did, making them collide. The milk looked rather enticing, and he went and got a glass for himself, holding it out just as she was recapping the bottle. She filled it in silence.

"Now a tray, please," he said, since he didn't have three hands. Anyway, why couldn't she remember to bring things on trays? But his irritation was going down, now that he had this material for his mother's repose—and how simple it was! Really, women were incredible, the way they mismanaged. He went back upstairs almost cheerful.

His mother lay exactly as he had left her, wide eyes and all. Probably she lay that way all night long, too, without an idea of helping herself—and certainly no help from Martha Mary. He felt a surge of indignation on his mother's behalf—and real pity, too, as he set the tray down.

"All right, darling, here it comes. Blessed nirvana. And sunny Italy, too."

Intent on unstoppering the bottle, he heard her make a little sound; but when he looked towards her she was silent.

"What?"

"No, no...."

"Mother, how can you *be* so silly? You don't get good *marks* for suffering, darling—and you're not going to. Now watch."

It was clear stuff, a little greenish. He saw with fascination the four perfect drops fall into the milk. And sighed.

"Lovely, lovely!" he said; and then: "Shall I have some too?"

Her eyes left it up to him. Just briefly, he really felt quite tempted! But probably he had better not; it must be awfully strong.

He sat her up a little, and put the glass into her hand. She looked into it, and then began to drink.

"Does it taste?" he asked, watching her. She shook her head. "Well, that's good. I wonder what it is? It must be pure opium, don't you think? Probably worth a fortune on the black market."

She was being rather slow. He replaced his supporting arm with pillows, and sat down to drink his own milk with her. All of a sudden, she gave him a faint smile; he smiled back. It was turning out rather a good moment, in its tiny way—like a drop distilled from all their past good moments together, to put into this desolate present.

When she gave him her glass and lay back again he watched with interest, but probably it didn't work so fast.

"Do you feel it yet?" he asked.

She looked at him—then gave one small nod, and closed her eyes. It was really quite thrilling.

He was tiptoeing away when—quite flustered—he remembered the bottle and turned back to get it. A fine thing if he left *that* there! Though she had no more milk—surely that would remind her.

He went next door and put the bottle firmly in his own cabinet. After all, when they were in Italy there would be no one but himself to look after his mother—and it was time Martha Mary understood she was taking too much into her own hands; this would be a silent first rebuke. Or if she said anything, not so silent. He rather hoped she would.

CHAPTER SEVENTEEN

Later that afternoon Waldon drove down to New York. He had suddenly realized—without any panic, just a sense of immediate recognition—that he had better change the tires on the pickup. The millhouse had a tar-surface driveway (ugly thing), and that night had been too cool to soften its surface; but he was not absolutely sure he had not backed off it here and there in turning. The ground had been dry, but might have taken some impression.

Of course it wouldn't be too serious if his tire tracks were there. He had never denied an occasional dropping by to see la Kavanaugh, although he did remember telling someone he hadn't seen her for ages—which was true. But for all he knew, they might be able to tell exactly *when* specific markings had been made. It didn't seem likely;

but there was no harm in being prudent about it.

He didn't know why this simple errand should depress him so. Ordinarily he enjoyed a little run down to the city; and he had approved—for a while—the cool and unemotional way he had reacted to the idea of the tires. But by the time he reached the Connecticut state line he felt quite blue.

Why? Did he feel himself to be yielding in some way to pressure from Krieg? Because Krieg's examination of the pickup had served as a reminder to himself? He didn't really think so. It was more obscure than that. In some way the trip was bringing the whole business—of that night; of *her*—up into his thoughts again, and in a *different* way— as if through an unsympathetic vision.

The police angle, he supposed. God knew that must be dreary! He had never understood the passion some people (his own father!) felt, for ploughing through case after case of police investigation, just to see some poor devil cornered at last. Now that he thought of it it was quite a sinister side of his father. Did it actually gratify him to read these things? And how?

Well, this was unprofitable thinking—he didn't intend to go on with it. The trouble was that he didn't have any other kind of thinking to put in its place. And just for an instant, tooling along on the Parkway, he remembered with envy his mother at home, as he had last seen her. *She* wasn't having thought-troubles any more.

He had had to go into her room to get some money—it was too late to make the bank, and he didn't want to wait till morning—and he hadn't much liked the idea of seeing her again. His automatic association with those drops was one of agonized and sweating impotence—a consciousness knocked out in spite of itself, and struggling to return. But when he finally made himself go in, she wasn't like that at all. She was just sleeping. Beautifully, naturally sleeping—and the thing had been working in her for a full hour. So that other time must have been some emergency dosage—six or even eight drops, maybe. If that were true, as few as ten might be fatal. And Dr. Stone had left this powerful stuff in the hands of old mush-brain!

Four, he thought. I must remember, four. Four. Just then he came to the East Side underpass, and swerved over to take it. Long Island was full of communities, he might as well go there. It didn't really matter— any place where he wasn't known. They were hardly going to take down the license number of someone who merely bought four new tires. Four. Four.

But it might have been even smarter to have driven the *car*, and taken the pickup tires off at home. Why hadn't he thought of that? The car was so much more anonymous, everyone noticed his pickup. Should he turn round and go back?

He slowed ... and then shot ahead again. The hell with them. He was being as "smart" right now as he intended to be, and furthermore that was what was making him feel so low, he knew it now. He was having to descend to their level, and be "smart." To deny everything simple, natural and honest in himself ... and become, for these hours, like a bad character in one of his father's bad books. A smart guy.

Right then, he almost turned back for good. Refused this corruption of himself. Let them play it their way, he would continue to play it his.

But what if he *had* left tire marks?

It was so hard to know what to do. Out of depression, lack of resistance, he just kept on going, finally. But he knew what he thought about his errand, now. He hated it.

When he finally found a tire store, some place in Great Neck or Little Neck, he couldn't even summon up interest in playing his part. What he had planned was to get four new *tubeless* tires, and to make a lot of uncomplimentary remarks about the old-fashioned kind he had got with the pickup, and how he was having nothing but grief with them. But now he didn't care enough to take the trouble.

He just said, listless, "I want new tires on there. All round. How long will it take?"

When he finally got an answer, instead of a barrage of stupid questions, he turned around and walked out. Half an hour to kill.

He killed it. When he came back the new tires weren't on—they hadn't even begun. Feeling pretty close to murderous, he went in and found the man he had talked to—just stood and glared at him, until he stopped talking to someone else and came over.

He looked wary, spoke a little too easily.

"Well, where'd you go off to?" he said, getting in first. "I can't get those tires on till you tell me which ones, can I?"

"I said all of them," said Waldon, between his teeth.

"Sure, sure—but what do you *want?* Now like I told you, I got these specials on this week, but frankly, Jack, that's not as good a tire as what you got on there. Now if you want—"

"I want the specials," said Waldon. "If you can get them all changed in fifteen minutes. Otherwise I'll find another tire store."

"Kind of in a rush, aren't you?" said the man. He stood there with a little, covert smile on his face—a real monument to smartness. Figuring it out.

"Well?" said Waldon. He took out his wallet, and three twenties out of that, and stood holding them.

"It's your money, Jack," said the man; and he turned to the pickup. He said nothing more to Waldon, but whistled between his teeth as he worked. Waldon watched and said nothing to him, until the first wheel came off.

Then he said, "What about my tires—the ones that are on there? What are you going to do with them?"

"Well, on them specials I can't do much, Jack. Just the regular, like I told you—we don't handle used tires here."

"But they're practically new!" said Waldon sharply.

"Practically ain't new, Jack. That's the only way I can look at it, if you want them specials. You can save yourself money and get a better tire, like I told you, if—"

"Never mind," said Waldon. He turned and walked out on to the street. How miserable, how degrading. Why had he done this—and when would it ever end? If the pickup weren't dismantled, he felt he would have got in it this minute and driven away, away—over that hissing moron, if necessary. He had to wait. He had to wait. There was nothing to do now but wait.

By the time the waiting was over, he had lost all interest in how long it lasted. He supposed, from the whistling idiot's sly look, that it had been a lot longer than fifteen minutes; but he didn't care. Let him have his little triumph of smartness—and the practically new tires he was extorting as well. Waldon didn't care. He didn't care about anything anymore, except getting out of there.

Through a beginning evening, tranquil and cool, Waldon drove back home. It was the time of day he liked best, ordinarily, but nothing reached him now. As if some invisible thick atmosphere kept pressing round him, and he had to keep dispelling it by straightening, taking a deep breath like a sigh. And then it would gather again....

He came home without relief—it was just the place he had been coming to, because there was nowhere else to go. He put the pickup in the garage; Martha Mary's Plymouth was gone, thank God, but for some reason she had locked the back door. He went round to the music room, then the front; everything locked! Why? He sorted through his keys, not even sure he carried one to the house; but it was there, and he presently let himself into an unlighted, silent hall.

In that hall, for some time, he stood and listened. Then quietly, two at a time, he mounted the stairs and went to his mother's door. That opened into dusk; but he could make out her form—he thought—lying on the bed.

He said very quietly, "Mother—?"

Her wakeful, equally quiet voice answered his. "Yes, dear."

He came in, still doubtful.

"Don't you want some light?"

"I don't think so. Not yet."

She had on a different sort of thing than when he had left her asleep. Otherwise she was lying there just the same. There was a dish and spoon, empty, on her table, like something left from a supper tray. Everything looked to be all right; but he remained uneasy.

"You oughtn't to be here alone this way," he said at last.

"Josephine's upstairs," she answered, indifferent.

"Do you know what Martha Mary did? She went round and locked up the whole place before she left!"

"I told her to."

"Oh," he said. "But—how funny, mother."

She didn't reply.

"People will think we've already gone," he added, to turn it into a joke. It didn't turn.

"Well," he said then, "if you don't want me for anything, I'll go down and see what I can find to eat."

"All right, dear," she replied. Total uninterest.

Perhaps she was still rather doped from the drops. If so, he didn't much care for this stage. It wasn't very pleasant to share a house with someone being a zombie.

This time his solitary evening downstairs went terribly slowly—and this in spite of rather better luck in the icebox, some cold chicken, and cold asparagus, which he adored. And half a pie. Really quite nice, if he only had some decent coffee.

He made himself a drink instead, and wandered in to watch television for a while. That was like a drug. He supposed it really wouldn't do to give her another dose until quite late—so it wouldn't accumulate, or whatever the stuff did. But definitely one to sleep on, he thought. This once, anyway—because she had so much catching up to do. And he didn't think he could bear another night of knowing that she lay there, beyond the wall, just *staring*.

When he went upstairs at last, there was light under her door; and he thought, like a confirmation, Ouspensky. He would certainly put a stop to *that*. Without even looking in he went directly to his own bathroom to get the drops.

They weren't there.

He wheeled and ran down the back stairs. If she had locked the servants' bathroom, he would break in the door. Smash it. And when she came in the morning, she wouldn't set foot inside this house. Ever again.

The bathroom was unlocked. The drops weren't there, either.

Now his rage fell into a flat calm. He stood quite quietly, gnawing the tips of his moustache. She had taken the drops home with her, then. He accepted this as a fact, and considered it.

Well. This was the end of Martha Mary.

He had no intention of saying anything to his mother. In some way, she was linked in his mind with Martha Mary now—to be excluded from any knowledge of his cold anger until it was time to act.

At what point he had begun to include his mother with Martha Mary, in this exclusion of the offenders, he did not know. She was just there; and he felt that she belonged there. Was it because of the locked doors, and her indifferent voice saying:

"*I told her to.*"

He stood still upon the stairs to recall her voice, her look—to judge her by them. But his effort was clouded by the memory of a whole history of disappearances, surging back upon him now. All because of her. From the shotgun some friend of his father's had sent him when he was twelve—so quietly, indefinitely "put away"—right up to the racing Porsche his father had been going to buy him—and then, mysteriously, would not. As if he, Waldon, were some dangerous mechanism that had constantly to be de-activated!

He went on, passing her door with a cold and steady attention. Now the light was out. He did not for a moment believe that she was asleep. No, she was lying there waiting for him to come back, to complain. Or not to complain, but just to accept another in the long series of decisions against him.

He neither accepted it nor dreamed of complaining. What he did mean to do was his own affair; and she would presently know how he meant to handle it.

CHAPTER EIGHTEEN

Waldon was eating his breakfast the next morning (alone), when a car came up the drive. He waited, frowning, for the door chimes to rout Martha Mary out of her lair (Josephine was still upstairs). Then, changing his mind, he got up and went to see who it was himself.

It was a good thing he had. Two men were coming up the walk, and one of them was Frank Coby from the Beecham Police Department. He couldn't put a name to the other one, though he'd seen him around. Luckily, they weren't in uniform.

He tried to push the screen open for them, found it was locked, and spent an exasperating moment releasing the catch.

"Well, Frank," he said then, "come in. We're not really in a state of siege, although Martha Mary seems to think so."

"Thanks, Waldon," he replied, stepping just inside. "Lot of people taken to locking their doors now, she's not the only one. You know Joe Kovacs?"

"Well, not by name," said Waldon, offering his hand. "You're not local, are you, Joe?"

"Sure," he said, grinning. "Down Route 22, below Brewster—my folks been there for years."

"Well, come in and have some coffee," said Waldon, leading the way. "I'm just on my second cup."

He didn't ring for Martha Mary, but put his head through the door and said curtly: "Some more coffee and two cups, Martha Mary. And don't bother my mother about this, please!"

He tried to look her in the eye as he said this, but it was a waste of time.

Frank and the Kovacs fellow were just standing there, looking around, when he turned back.

He said impatiently, "Sit down, sit down!" and sat down himself, replacing his napkin. They sat in slow, careful movements, as if the chairs might break. One of them cleared his throat, but they didn't say anything.

"Well, what's going on?" said Waldon. "Have I run over somebody's cow?"

They both grinned; and Frank said: "I expect you'd know if you had, even in that Folk-Wagon of yours." He pronounced the "l" carefully; Waldon let it go.

"Then what's up?" he said. "You want some toast? There's plenty here."

He put more jam on his own, at the same time listening to hear if Martha Mary were going upstairs. The trouble was that you couldn't hear the back stairs from here. He gave a sudden, admonitory bang on the bell, in case she were thinking of it.

"No, nothing, thanks," said Frank hastily. "The thing is, Waldon," he said, plunging in, "somebody's sent in word that you might have something to tell us, about the night Mrs. Kavanaugh died. Now just a minute," he said, raising his hand. "I know it's hard for you folks—you're all neighbors, you don't like to speak up about each other. We run into that already, we *expect* to run into it—"

"I know all about those miserable Fosses," said Waldon coldly. "You don't have to cover up for them."

"I'm not covering up for anybody," said Frank, reddening, "and I hope you're not either, Waldon. Because there isn't any need to—we're not out to get anybody, and that's the truth. But we sure as hell are out to get every little piece of information anybody's got, about what was going on round the millhouse that night. Or even what wasn't going on. For instance, anybody that went by and saw *nothing* has got something to tell us, providing he'd know what time it was. Or if he noticed windows were light or dark, or shades up or down—something like that. You'd be surprised how a lot of pieces of information like that help—and how hard we got to dig just to get them. Now, if you'd been by there, say, some time before midnight—maybe just slowed up, or glanced in—"

Waldon put down his toast.

He said wearily, "Frank, believe me, I know all about this little 'tip' of yours—a lot more than you do—and it makes me sore as hell to see them *using* you like this! Certainly we're a country town," he said, growing heated, "but we happen to have a lot of big names around here—my father, for one—and that's what they're counting on, can't you see that? Every time they make the New York tabloids in connection with some big names, that's one more piece of free advertising—and free advertising is what counts with them, Frank—not us. Not you, or me, or the Olivers, or Beecham itself. Why, you don't suppose Dr. Oliver could pay enough *in money* to make this case worth their while, do you? Of course he couldn't! But he's a *name*, my father's a *name*—"

"Now, wait a minute, Waldon," said Frank. He was already standing up—Kovacs, slower, was struggling up too. Waldon stared up at them both.

"I've got nothing against you, Frank," he said, "although I do think that was a pretty spiteful impulse on somebody's part, to take Miss Oliver down to *jail* that way—and Dr. Oliver was certainly justified in protesting. But I told him at the time I thought he'd picked the wrong person to handle his protest, and now I think even *he* must—"

"Listen, Waldon," said Frank. He began to sit down again—and Kovacs to sag obediently at the knees—when both of them straightened again. Waldon, following their eyes, saw his mother in the doorway.

She wasn't looking at him. She was dressed, her hair brushed. Except for that awful pallor, she might almost pass for normal. He noted these things quickly while he got to his feet.

"Good morning, mother," he said—just a shade too loudly.

She glanced at him then, and smiled a little. "Good morning, dear...."

"This is Frank Coby, from town. And Joe Kovacs, they've just stopped by to see me."

"Of course.... Please do sit down...."

Murmuring, she went round to her own place, so that they might sit again; but they continued standing there—and in came Martha Mary (to no summons) with the coffee.

They wouldn't, of course, take any then. Because they had to be getting along, they had just stopped by.... To cut all this short, Waldon got up and went out to the front hall with them.

"Listen, Frank," he said, as soon as he judged they were out of earshot. "Your people know exactly what time I was near there—when I brought the Fosses home. So far as I know I didn't even glance at the millhouse—and if you want my opinion, neither did the Fosses. Then *or* later. They were out on their feet the last time I saw them."

"This is before midnight that I'm talking about," said Frank doggedly. "Long before."

"I was right here, any number of people can tell you so—and if my word isn't good enough for you, then go check up on tire marks or something, good God, I don't care what you do! Just don't let those people get you to playing their game, Frank, because—"

"I'm not playing any game," said Frank shortly. "All right, Joe." They both went out of the front door; and Waldon, pausing there in thought, distinctly heard one of them say *"Brother ...!"*

He didn't care; his thought wasn't for them. When he felt sufficiently impassive, he hurried back to the breakfast room. His mother gave him a timid glance—then prolonged it, when he went on with his toast without a word.

Finally she couldn't leave well enough alone.

"I hope I didn't interrupt anything, dear," she said faintly.

He just looked at her—a brief look. She was eating yogurt, not a very pleasant thing to do at the breakfast table.

When she was sufficiently unnerved by his silence to hear him with her whole attention, he leaned towards her and said quietly: "I want you to tell me one thing, mother. *How much have you told Martha Mary?"*

Instantly she got about three shades paler.

"Nothing—nothing!" she whispered; and she looked so horrified that he was (at least momentarily) assured that this was true.

She couldn't leave that alone, either.

"Waldon ... what do you mean? Why did you ask me that?"

He wasn't going to answer. Then he decided he would.

"She is behaving very queerly. It occurred to me that it might be *on your orders,"* he said, looking at her hard.

"Queerly ... how?"

This time he didn't answer. She put her spoon down and sat staring at nothing. At last, in the same whisper, she confessed: "I don't dare get rid of her, Waldon...."

"You'll have to get rid of them all when we go, won't you?" he observed, in a normal voice. "Father will hardly want to keep the place running just for his occasional benefit."

She continued to stare in silence. But when he rose to leave the table, she moved with him—ahead of him.

"Come outside with me a minute," she murmured.

"Mother, I don't know why you believe no one can hear what you say out on the lawn. You and father are—"

"Just a minute," she said, not hearing him. He sighed and followed her.

She didn't even stretch out on the chaise—just perched on its edge with her hands gripping each other in her lap, and began at once:

"Waldon, we *don't dare* leave here now—don't you see that?"

"No," he said. "I don't." He didn't sit down at all.

"But you don't realize—"

"Mother, you're the one who doesn't realize," he interrupted her. "You don't have any idea of the state you've got yourself in. I don't even dare let people *see* you anymore—don't you know that? I'm not blaming you, mother. I'm just trying to deal with things as they are—as I've tried to do all along. When I said it wasn't necessary for us to go away, it was true then. But it isn't true anymore. You've got to go away from here for a while, and if you won't go alone, then I'll have to go with you. That's all there is to it."

She said suddenly, in a perfectly clear voice: "If we run away now, they'll know you did it."

He was so taken aback that he moved away from her—and then, in a rush of anger, continued moving. Without another glance back, he walked around the house and out of her sight.

Getting out the pickup, a really wild feeling of emergency took hold of him. She was absolutely falling to pieces, he had to face it. She was practically out of control right now. He oughtn't to leave her out there on the lawn, by herself, even for a minute!

And yet he had to, he had to.

He absolutely *threw* the pickup down the road, blaring at everything he saw—cars, pedestrians, even empty crossroads. The worst of it was, he could feel that he wasn't driving *well* this morning—yet he couldn't, he didn't dare, slow down.

In town, in Richards' Drugstore—an old, non-chain place they always patronized—he went directly back to the dispensary and poked his head in. Mr. Richards was there, as usual, pottering around in his white coat; he looked quite startled to see Waldon burst in on him that way. Well, all the better.

He didn't even bother to think it out, but just started off.

"Mr. Richards, we're in a mess," he said rapidly. "I need another bottle of that knockout stuff of mother's, right away—have you got some more?"

Mr. Richards parried feebly.

"Knockout stuff, Waldon? Your mother's—?"

"That prescription of Dr. Stone's," said Waldon impatiently. "You remember, that emergency stuff you had to send her. Well, this is another emergency, and the bottle's broken—can you make me up some more, right away?"

"Dear me, Waldon, that wasn't a renewable prescription, I'm afraid. You didn't think to stop by Dr. Stone's, and get—"

"I can't reach him! He's over at the hospital, and they won't even give him a message—and besides, what difference does it *make*, Mr. Richards? I don't want to renew it, I only want to replace it! It was a perfectly new bottle, she just got it!"

"Most unfortunate," said Mr. Richards. "Really most unfortunate, Waldon—that's rather a strictly controlled drug, you know—"

"Surely we aren't the first people who ever dropped a bottle," said Waldon, showing despair. Mr. Richards was touched. He wavered.

"I would really have to have some word from Dr. Stone, you know, Waldon. He would have to be—I would have to have a second prescription for it."

"Well, all right—he can send you one. Or I'll get it and bring it in. But you don't need it as soon as we need that bottle, Mr. Richards."

Mr. Richards turned away.

"Well, you mustn't forget, now. As I say, this is rather a strictly con—"

"Good heavens, how could I forget about *this?*" said Waldon simply.

When he came back with the bottle, in its neat twist of paper, Mr. Richards said he was very sorry to hear Waldon's mother was ill again, so soon.

"Yes, it's awfully discouraging—actually I'm just going to have to whisk her away somewhere, on a trip—Dr. Stone says it's the only thing.... Thank you so much, and I'll bring you the other prescription...."

He shot away, feeling quite breathless. Even in the pickup again, he couldn't quite discard his "act"—it had been too real! And then it was bothersome about that other prescription, he would have to get it, of course, and he didn't quite see how. Perhaps just stick to the dropped bottle story—after all, it was a thing that did happen. And Dr. Stone would hardly call up his mother to ask if it were true.

But he would mention it, the next time he saw her.

Waldon drove rapidly home, chewing at his moustaches. That was a habit that had suddenly overtaken him—he was catching himself at it constantly, these days, and it was such a loathsome thing to do! Well, when all these pressures were off him, he would stop it quickly enough—just as he had broken himself of the moustache-stroking habit. It was one of the minor things that would come right, when he had the major things under control.

She had gone indoors. That was the first thing he saw when he drove in, and it worried him. Ordinarily she lay out there for hours. What had made her go in? What had she wanted to do, the minute his back was turned?

He left the pickup in the drive and bounded indoors—but quietly. She wasn't downstairs. Martha Mary was alone in the kitchen—he could tell, by listening a moment at the door. In the upstairs hall, he could hear Josephine in his room; his mother's door was shut. He looked in, and there she was—wide-eyed on the bed again, staring at nothing.

He shut himself in, and came towards her as naturally as possible.

"What on earth are you doing back here? I thought you were all settled out on the lawn for a while."

"I was too tired...."

"Then you can't have slept last night. Did you? And you're not going to sleep now—I can tell to look at you. Mother," he said, grave, "how long do you think I can stand it, just having you lie here night and day this way?"

Her eyes filled with tears, and she turned her head away.

"I'm sorry, darling...."

"Sorry doesn't do anybody any good," he said firmly, and leaned over her, putting back her hair with gentle fingers. "What you need is more drops. And you're going to have them."

She looked up into his face then. But she didn't speak.

He gave her a final pat, and went out—down the back stairs. Martha Mary didn't speak when he came in. He went to the refrigerator, in a matching silence, took out milk; got glasses from the cupboard. Found a tray in the pantry.

At that point, she turned to him.

"What do you think you're doing, Mr. Waldon?"

"Why, my mother and I are going to have a glass of milk together, Martha Mary," he said evenly. "That is, if you don't mind?"

She was completely stymied. Milk was for drops. But he didn't have the drops. So why did he want the milk? He could just see her poor old brain churning around; it was worth every minute of the trip to town.

"And I suppose you don't," he added, slow.

It wouldn't have surprised him to see her make a dash for her bag and begin wildly rummaging in it—he felt sure for a moment that she would; but she disappointed him. She just gave him another long stare, and then said uncertainly:

"You be careful what you're doing now. Your mother's not up to it."

Up to what? He couldn't imagine; he didn't care. It had been a really delicious moment.

He came into his mother's room still faintly smiling, until her poor puzzled face took his enjoyment away.

"All right soon, darling," he said then. "Coming right up."

He had to go out again to unwrap the bottle, but that was all right—he would have had to get the other one from his bathroom. He came back presently holding up the little bottle for her to see; but he was hardly inside the room before she gave one cry—and was silent.

It unnerved him terribly. When he came over to her, she had turned her head away—and at such a queer angle!

"What is it?" he said, not pleased. "Have you got a pain?"

She didn't even answer.

All of a sudden he couldn't stand any more of this. He just opened up the bottle and saw there was stuff in the dropper and concentrated on getting four drops of it into her milk. By the time he had done that she had turned her head back again.

"Here you go," he said, leaning down to prop her up.

"*No*...."

"Oh, yes. Come on."

He got her up, and put the glass in her hand. She didn't look at it—just at him.

"Down the hatch," he said, a little impatient, and picked up his own glass.

She closed her eyes, whispering something. "Blessed nirvana"? He decided that was it; and in relief, in encouragement, he smiled at her.

"That's right, darling. And sunny Italy, too."

They drank together, as they had done before; but somehow it wasn't so relaxed and pleasant for him as the first time. He tried not to show it, but sat patiently until her milk was gone, long after he had finished his. And by then she had hold of his hand in that strong grip of hers. He fidgeted a little, but it only made her hand tighten.

"Don't leave me...."

"I won't. I mean, I'm not going anywhere today—just down to the workshop, to clean up that mess McKinnon left me. So I'll be back pretty early, and you'll have had a good sleep, and then we can have a nice long evening together...."

What on earth did she imagine he had said? He was just babbling along, to send her off pleasantly, and all of a sudden she was absolutely radiant! He couldn't even begin to respond to a look like that—as if the heavens had opened before her, and all the happy secrets of Ouspensky come tumbling out!

Her eyes closed, her hand fell away from his; she lay there white and sweating, with that blotto smile still on her lips.

Marvelous stuff.

CHAPTER NINETEEN

Dr. Stone's car was in the driveway when Waldon came back up the path that afternoon. He had had to come forward out of the trees to identify it, but as soon as he did, he turned round and went quietly back to the workshop.

After ten or fifteen restless minutes, he returned. The car was gone. It was a little after four o'clock.

He went in by the music room doors, after a little struggle with the locked screen, which made him curse Martha Mary all over again.

Then he met her in the hall. She was just coming downstairs. The trusted nurse.

"Martha Mary," he said; and she stopped.

"If you persist in locking me out of the house, we're going to end up with no locks left on the screens, you know. I just had to break the one in the music room."

"There's no call to do that, Mr. Waldon! There's always someone to let you in—all you have to do is ring."

"I haven't any intention of doing anything so absurd," he replied; and went past her up the stairs.

His mother's door was open and she was up, walking in a random sort of way about her room, until she saw him. She went and sat quickly on her bed, then, as if it were home base. God, she was getting queer.

And her sleep didn't seem to have done her much good.

"Wasn't that Dr. Stone that just left?" he asked, coming in.

"Yes."

"Why? I mean, why was he here?"

He didn't need to watch her—her voice always told him what he needed to know.

"Just to see how I am."

It was such a curious, flat voice that he had to look at her after all. It didn't do him any good.

"I know, but why should he do that? Did someone tell him you weren't well again?"

She said presently, "Perhaps Martha Mary called him. Sometimes she does."

Well, he knew that. It was possible. Still—why was she looking so funny?

He said bluntly, "Why are you looking so funny, mother? What did he say?"

"Do I look funny, darling?"

Actually she didn't, now that she was smiling a little. And discounting the fact that she *always* looked rather funny now.

"Well ... perhaps not." He wandered over and sat in the slipper chair, still vaguely discontented. "I suppose he woke you up," he added, in disapproval.

"Oh, no—I wasn't asleep." She leaned back on her pillows and said then, in a dreamy way, "I didn't really sleep at all—and yet it was as though I were asleep and awake at the same time. It was very strange—and rather wonderful."

He couldn't share her pleasure.

"You didn't sleep at *all?* But I don't see how that's possible, I put in four drops. And you drank it all, I remember you did."

He was increasingly disturbed, as though some last certainty were eluding him. Even the drops couldn't be counted on! He hadn't realized until then how much he was counting on them, to get a little peace.

"Oh, I'm sure it's all right, dear," his mother said—as if in answer to his thoughts. "I expect it acts differently at different times, that's all."

"Perhaps you're building up a tolerance," he said, still frowning.

She answered that quickly.

"Oh, no—this doesn't work that way. In fact, Dr. Stone—" She hesitated; and he looked up at her. She went on at once: "Dr. Stone reminded me again to be careful in using them."

"Well, you are careful. Why should he say that?" And then his dismay burst out in annoyance. "Honestly, I can't see the point in your having them at all, if they're going to be turned into a big bugaboo! They simply make you sleep—or they should. And God knows you need sleep. What's so awful about that?"

"Nothing, darling—it's all right. And I did have a beautiful rest, I felt so much better."

"You do?"

"Yes, really. I was just about to get dressed and come downstairs."

"Well, then," he said. "You see."

"You go along and clean up, and I'll be down as soon as you are."

"I'll take you to Silvermine, if you like," he offered—the impulse suddenly presenting itself. "You didn't get much of a look at your swans last time."

But she wasn't up to that. He hadn't really expected her to be.

She was downstairs before him, dressed in one of the pretty pastel chiffons he liked so much. She had made up her face, and put on some of her amethysts, and she seemed quite conversational. But she didn't want to have a Martini with him.

"Oh, nonsense," he said. "It's just another sort of relaxer. Don't tell me he's lowered the boom on poor old gin!"

"No, no—I just feel more like sherry tonight, for some reason," she replied.

He didn't believe her; but it wasn't worth fussing about.

Ordinarily, this restful hour—which began their long evenings together—would slide away unperceived, like a summer twilight, in sips of gin and low murmuring back and forth. They were so accustomed to each other, so at one, that each seemed to release the other's thoughts; they never lacked things to talk about. But tonight some privacy made a barrier between them; and they never got past it.

Waldon did not think the privacy came from him, and he very soon gave up struggling against it. Very soon after that, he began to wish his mother would—and like a suggestion, he got up and switched the television on.

"Let's see what the news is," he said; and at once, as if they might expect to hear that their country was at war, she fixed a strained look on the screen and became rigid.

What made this even sadder was the fact that they were too early for news, and he couldn't seem to find anything but children's programs, with blurry cartoons and chocolate drink ads. She gave these her passionate attention until he couldn't stand it anymore, and switched the thing off.

"Look," he said then. "Are you sure you don't want to run on down to Silvermine?"

She couldn't disguise her hesitation; and so persistent was the empathy between them that he knew, even now, how the suggestion filled her with fatigue and despair. Still, he didn't withdraw it—once they got started, she would see it was nothing: just a quiet drive, and a quiet dinner outdoors. And it would kill most of the evening that lay before them, until he could reasonably get out the drops again.

She said at last, "I think it's too late to disappoint Martha Mary, dear."

"Martha Mary is the least of my worries, darling," he replied, rather sharply. "Come on, now—where's that pretty little stole thing? I'll run up and get it for you."

She sat perfectly still. He turned away, to go up and look for himself; and with unbelievable quickness she caught him at the door. Still she didn't speak—she didn't look as if she *could*; and at that point he gave up.

"All right, then," he said drearily. "Let's face it, mother—you aren't even up to being downstairs. Let's get you back in bed, and Martha Mary can bring you a tray up there."

"Stay with me...."

He didn't reply: he couldn't trust himself to.

Up in her room, she still hung on to him like grim death; and he made no effort to dislodge her.

He just said, "I'd better go down and tell Martha Mary."

"Oh—yes," she said then. But it was another several seconds before her hands let go.

He went down the back stairs.

"Mother's going to have a tray after all," he said, passing through the kitchen. "I'll eat out."

The screen latch held beneath his hand. That, he broke quite savagely; and got out.

It was no good. He knew before he left the driveway that it was no good. Sometime, no matter how late, he would have to come back again. And nothing would have changed.

He thought—almost with disbelief—of the easy, happy escapes of other days. Then, he had only to get himself and his pickup away undetected, and the whole teary mess fell behind him. The world outside lay infinite with possibility, and he had only to choose.

That was because when he came back, he knew it would be over. Now it would never be over. This would neither change nor end.

Nevertheless, he kept on going. He had taken the car, because of Silvermine. Only he wasn't going to Silvermine. Unless he went by and got Buffy to come with him.

Buffy never went anywhere with him. But everything was different now, this might as well be different too. He might as well take Buffy to Silvermine too.

He turned in the Olivers' gate and went up their dusky drive. There were lights downstairs; no one on the lawn. The dogs were quiet. But he had them in mind, how they would be shut in the kitchen, and went strangely round to the front door. There was neither knocker nor bell; he rapped lightly on the screen, and heard the faraway dogs begin.

After a while Miss Min came hurrying into the hall. Peering; holding her napkin.

"Who is it?" she called; but he waited till she came near and saw him.

"I'd like to speak to Buffy, please," he said then.

"Oh!" she said. "It's you, Waldon. To Buffy? You want Buffy?"

"Yes, please."

"But what for, dear?"

This wasn't in the least unusual. He just repeated, "Let me speak to Buffy, please."

"Are you all right, Waldon?" she asked then, still peering.

"Yes."

"She's having her dinner, you know.... Well, just a minute—I'll tell her."

She trotted away, without unlatching the screen for him to come in. That wasn't unusual, either, and he didn't want to come in. He was content only to wait there, until Buffy came.

She came directly towards him and opened the door and stood just outside, her hand upon it. With haste, as if to some feared, expected meeting. It almost broke his heart, to see Buffy changed too. He couldn't speak to her.

"What's the matter?" she said. "What's happened?" She sounded doubtful, but not really so different after all. He found his voice.

"Krieg sent men up to see me today. From the police."

She thought about that. He could see her breathing. Then she said—still in her own voice, but low: "I didn't tell them anything."

"Don't believe them, Buffy."

"They didn't say anything to me."

Silence gathered round them then—quiet, evening silence, that he received like a beneficence. That he needed, in endless quantity.

She said, "What are you going to do?"

For a long time, he could not gather himself to reply. Then he said, listless: "I'm ... going to Silvermine. Come with me."

That effort of speech stirred in him the impulse to move, as well—to reach out and see, like a nostalgia, her habitual small movement of retreat. This time she didn't move at once. He had time to feel her warm, rigid wrist beneath his fingers before she slipped back inside the screen door. She stayed there, looking out at him, with such big eyes!

He said gently. "Don't be afraid, Buffy"; and she answered in a small, breathless rush of words: "I'm sorry—I'm sorry—I tried to like you, Waldon—"

She turned round and ran for the stairs. Ran up them, out of his sight.

Miss Min would hear that. She would be coming to see.

But he stood where he was a moment longer. Then, sighing, he crossed the quiet grass to the car. Even in the car, he did not at once drive away. It had been such a strange, *good* meeting—the only one he could remember that hadn't sent him away upset. He didn't really want to go away at all.

Then he saw Miss Min's head poking out of the door, looking towards him; and that was the reminder. So he started the motor and slid away, down the drive.

He still kept on going towards Silvermine—taking back roads, driving the big car slowly. It was almost dark before he realized he could hardly see where he was going, and turned on his lights. That was what people had been yelling at him about, he supposed.

He smiled, and turned the car towards home. This was far enough; it was time, now. He could go back.

The house was all locked up, but he expected that. Somebody had left a light on downstairs, and that troubled him for a moment—Martha Mary would never be so thoughtful, and Josephine didn't come into the front of the house in the evenings. He went through all the rooms, but his mother wasn't down here.

Then he went upstairs. There was light around her door. He went on past it and down the back stairs and got the two glasses full of milk. This time he brought them into his own room and set them on his dresser while he got the bottle out of his stud box, at the back of the drawer. He could see, a little, from the light left on in his bathroom. He squeezed the dropper once, to fill it, and then once to empty it, and then he put the bottle away again and took the glass next door.

But at her door, he remembered his own milk; he had to go back and get it, and for some reason this upset him terribly—his hands began to shake. He kept thinking, I'm doing this wrong; over and over, when he knew it wasn't true.

She was sitting up when he came in—came in edging carefully round the door so as not to spill. He said absently, full of this care, "It's time now"; but she didn't reply.

While he was setting her glass down—his eyes never leaving it, because that was *hers*—something heavy fell from the bed on to his foot. He glanced down quickly, but it was just Ouspensky.

Holding his own glass, he said again: "It's time now," and stood looking at her.

She didn't look any different—actually, he hardly saw her, except as a lighted form that he expected to be there. But all at once a conviction of mistake gripped him—so severe, that he nearly cried out.

What was it, what was it? He didn't know, he couldn't think. Standing there before her, he simply couldn't think. He picked up her glass again. Set down his own. The two separate, always. That was right. Then, muttering "Excuse me …" he went out of the room.

Back in his own room, holding her glass, he could stand quietly and try to think what it was. But he couldn't think. And he mustn't stay away too long, it would look so funny. So at last he got the bottle out again and put in another dropper full—it was all he could think of to do—and then he went back.

This time he got inside more confidently, so that must have been what it was, and he came up and gave her her glass right away. Right into her hand.

"Now it's time," he said, relieved.

He kept his eyes on the glass, and her hand that held it, but nothing happened. What was she waiting for? He didn't like to ask.

Although he didn't want to, he sat down and took up his own glass. There was something he ought to say, too. *She* said "Give me your hand"; and he gave it to her; but that wasn't it.

He didn't want his milk this time, but he drank it, and she drank hers. They were much quicker, this time. It was quicker, once you had made up your mind. He thought of saying that to her, and then didn't. But he was perfectly willing to stay there, keeping her hand. He just didn't want to talk.

All of a sudden she said, "God made you, my darling"—in such a terribly sad voice that he raised his head a little, as if to speak. But he couldn't find the answer.

Sunny Italy.

It came into his mind a long time later, what he ought to have said. Now that it didn't matter. But it had got into his mind now and stayed there—like a great, warm, buzzing bee; the warmth was what he wanted. But he didn't say anything.

Then she wrenched her hand away. All of a sudden, violently, so that he fell forward a little and had to brace himself on the bed. That swayed, swaying him, to some violent continued motion of hers. He watched her as well as he could, sideways—she was pushing at her pillow, as if she wanted to push it off the bed. Why? He got quite a clear glimpse of her then, and she did look awful—like that other time. But if it was going to be like that, he would have to go away.

She was making those noises, too.

He decided to get up, just as she got the little bottle out—knocked it out from beneath her pillow in one raging sweep, so that it spun across the sheet and fell from the bed. He leaned at once to pick it up ... or meant to. But in a heavy pause, he saw that there was no need, because it wasn't his bottle. It was hers.

She had had it. Right there, under her pillow. Was that the mistake?

He tried desperately to think what he should do, now that it was too late. Had she put more in her milk, when he had to go back to his room? But that was *his* milk. He knew he had left his milk there, and he had taken hers away.

Was that the mistake?

Quite desperate, he would even have asked her now—but it was too late. She was locked in that remembered moaning stillness again, and it was too late....

On the floor, on his knees, his hands went groping blind along the floor after the bottle. Because she had known it was his. She had meant to do it. His forehead against the mattress held up his head—he felt he could last like this a long time, until he found it. He had to find it, he didn't want to go with her. He didn't want to go. Or sunny Italy, because it wasn't warm, it was terribly cold—he had never been so numbly cold, and the mattress no longer kind pressed out his sight—an endless dark, from which he could no longer turn away; and his hands grew still.

THE END

www.ingramcontent.com/pod-product-compliance
Lightning Source LLC
LaVergne TN
LVHW010202070526
838199LV00062B/4458